Pr

"A fun tale —Midwest Book Review

"Charming, romantic. . . . This new series should be a real hit!" —Fresh Fiction

"McLane's trademark devilish dialogue is in fine form for this series." —*Publishers Weekly*

"This first of McLane's new Cricket Creek series is a delightful bouquet of romances set in a small town that needs saving." —*Romantic Times*

"No one does Southern love like LuAnn McLane!" —The Romance Dish

He's No Prince Charming

"This is a laugh-out-loud story and one you won't want to put down." —Fresh Fiction

"Had me smiling like a loon . . . a delightful read." —Book Binge

"Sensitive . . . sweet, sinful, and utterly satisfying!" —Romance Novel TV

Redneck Cinderella

"A pure delight. . . . [McLane is] the queen of Southern romantic comedy." —Manic Readers

"As satisfying as a frozen fruit pop on a hot, lazy summer day." —*San Francisco Book Review*

"A hysterical, sexy, highly entertaining read!" —Errant Dreams Reviews

continued . . .

A Little Less Talk and a Lot More Action

"[McLane] has a knack for rollicking Southern romances and her newest is no exception."

—*The Cincinnati Enquirer*

"[A] fun and flirty contemporary romance about grabbing that second chance." —Fresh Fiction

Trick My Truck but Don't Mess With My Heart

"Sweet . . . a real Southern fried treat." —*Booklist*

"[A] quick-paced, action-packed romantic romp . . . hilarious." —Romance Designs

Dancing Shoes and Honky-Tonk Blues

"Lighthearted comedy and steamy romance combine to make this a delightful tale of a small town that takes Hollywood by storm." —Romance Junkies

"A hoot a minute. . . . LuAnn McLane shows her talent for tongue-in-cheek prose and situations . . . a winning tale not to be missed." —Romance Reviews Today

"A fun story filled with plenty of laughter, tears, and all-out reading enjoyment." —Fallen Angel Reviews

"A fabulous story. . . . Get ready for a deliriously funny, passion-filled rumba in this book."

—The Romance Readers Connection

"A fun small-town drama starring a delightful, seemingly opposites lead couple and an eccentric but likable support cast." —The Best Reviews

Dark Roots and Cowboy Boots

"An endearing, sexy, romantic romp that sparkles with Southern charm!"
—Julia London

"This kudzu-covered love story is as hot as Texas Pete, and more fun than a county fair."
—Karin Gillespie, author of *Dollar Daze*

"A hoot! The pages fly in this sexy, hilarious romp."
—Romance Reviews Today

"Charmingly entertaining . . . a truly pleasurable read."
—*Romantic Times*

Wild Ride

"Sensual, touching . . . a thrilling, exhilarating sensual ride. I implore you to jump right in and hold on tight!"
—A Romance Review

"Scintillating romance set against the backdrop of a tropical island paradise takes readers to new heights in this captivating collection of erotic novellas. The three tales are steamy and fast-paced, combining descriptive romance with creative love stories."
—*Romantic Times* (4 stars)

Hot Summer Nights

"Bright, sexy, and very entertaining."
—*New York Times* bestselling author Lori Foster

"Spicy."
—A Romance Review

"Super-hot summer romance."
—BellaOnline

"Funny, sexy, steamy . . . will keep you glued to the pages."
—Fallen Angel Reviews

Also by LuAnn McLane

CONTEMPORARY ROMANCES

Catch of a Lifetime: A Cricket Creek Novel
Playing for Keeps: A Cricket Creek Novel
He's No Prince Charming
Redneck Cinderella
A Little Less Talk and a Lot More Action
Trick My Truck but Don't Mess with My Heart
Dancing Shoes and Honky-Tonk Blues
Dark Roots and Cowboy Boots

EROTIC ROMANCES

"Hot Whisper" in *Wicked Wonderland* anthology
Driven by Desire
Love, Lust, and Pixie Dust
Hot Summer Nights
Wild Ride
Taking Care of Business

Pitch Perfect

A CRICKET CREEK NOVEL

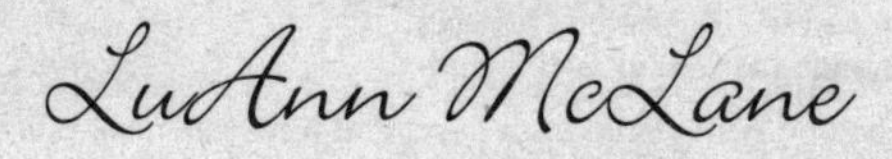

SIGNET ECLIPSE
Published by New American Library, a division of
Penguin Group (USA) Inc., 375 Hudson Street,
New York, New York 10014, USA
Penguin Group (Canada), 90 Eglinton Avenue East, Suite 700, Toronto,
Ontario M4P 2Y3, Canada (a division of Pearson Penguin Canada Inc.)
Penguin Books Ltd., 80 Strand, London WC2R 0RL, England
Penguin Ireland, 25 St. Stephen's Green, Dublin 2,
Ireland (a division of Penguin Books Ltd.)
Penguin Group (Australia), 250 Camberwell Road, Camberwell, Victoria 3124,
Australia (a division of Pearson Australia Group Pty. Ltd.)
Penguin Books India Pvt. Ltd., 11 Community Centre, Panchsheel Park,
New Delhi - 110 017, India
Penguin Group (NZ), 67 Apollo Drive, Rosedale, Auckland 0632,
New Zealand (a division of Pearson New Zealand Ltd.)
Penguin Books (South Africa) (Pty.) Ltd., 24 Sturdee Avenue,
Rosebank, Johannesburg 2196, South Africa

Penguin Books Ltd., Registered Offices:
80 Strand, London WC2R 0RL, England

First published by Signet Eclipse, an imprint of New American Library,
a division of Penguin Group (USA) Inc.

First Printing, September 2012
10 9 8 7 6 5 4 3 2 1

Printed in the United States of America

PUBLISHER'S NOTE
This is a work of fiction. Names, characters, places, and incidents either are the product of the author's imagination or are used fictitiously, and any resemblance to actual persons, living or dead, business establishments, events, or locales is entirely coincidental.

The publisher does not have any control over and does not assume any responsibility for author or third-party Web sites or their content.

This book is dedicated to my son, Ryan, and his lovely wife, Meghan. Through sacrifice and dedication you both exemplify the meaning of unconditional love.

Acknowledgments

I would like to give a shout-out to Guy Fieri of the Food Network. Watching your road show, *Diners, Drive-ins and Dives* gave me the inspiration for Wine and Diner. Seeing regular folks who are living life "on point" and "off the hook" is what Cricket Creek is all about. I'd like to think that Wine and Diner would be one of your Triple D Hot Spots!

Thanks again to the amazing editorial staff at New American Library. From the lovely covers to the detailed copyedits and everything in between, I couldn't ask for a better team. I also want to give a special thanks to my editor, Jesse Feldman. Because of you, I no longer fear revisions (well, not much) but welcome your insight and input. Working with you has been a joy.

As always, thanks to my agent, Jenny Bent. I wouldn't be able to navigate through the world of publishing without you in my corner!

I would like to extend a heartfelt thanks to my readers. Your e-mails and support mean the world to me. My wish is for my stories to bring you joy, laughter, and always a happy ending!

1

Destination Unknown

"OH NO, NOT NOW!" MIA SCOWLED AT THE RED CHECK-engine light and gripped the steering wheel tighter. "Come on, I filled you with premium gas, you old clunker. What more do you want from me?" she grumbled, but when the light flickered and then went out she managed a slight smile. "That's more like it." She patted the battered dashboard, making the miniature hula dancer swing her ample hips. "Okay, I take the old-clunker part back," Mia added in a soothing tone and then settled back against the worn seat.

Having been an only child raised by a long string of disinterested au pairs, Mia Monroe was no stranger to talking to herself or to inanimate objects. Since she had often been left alone to entertain herself, Mia's possessions became treasured friends and admittedly were probably one of the reasons that as an adult she had become a shopaholic. "Dad just doesn't understand." She sighed and glanced over at her shiny black Prada purse, which appeared ridiculously out of place perched on the worn cloth seat that must have been red at one time but had faded to a dusty rose. The lack of credit cards inside of her matching wallet made her shiver, even though the battered Camry's air conditioner had failed her just outside of Chicago. Soon she might actually break a sweat. "Shopping is my therapy," she explained with a defensive pout, but the words sounded a bit hollow and she frowned. "Nothing wrong with that, right?" she added without as much conviction.

Mia flipped her long platinum blond hair over her shoulder only to have the warm wind from the open window blow it right back across her face, momentarily blocking her view of the road. She swerved into the right lane, drawing the deep, angry honk of a massive truck.

"Sorry!" Mia winced as she jerked the car back into her own lane. The hula dancer's hips wiggled like crazy and Mia giggled in spite of her dire circumstances. She decided that when she purchased a new car the happy hula chickie was coming with her. Oh and she *would* purchase a brand-new car with her very own hard-earned money. "And I'll pull up that circular drive and park it right at my father's front door!" she announced to the hula dancer, who bobbed her head as if in disagreement. "Oh, don't go shaking that head of yours. I will do it if it's the last thing I ever do!" Of course Mia didn't have anything ironed out, like where she would live, or a really super job lined up or anything of that nature. *Minor details,* she thought with a lift of one shoulder, but then she frowned when she recalled her last conversation with her dad. "You'll be back by the end of the summer," Mia mocked in her father's deep tone of voice. *Labor Day,* he had added. *Something you've never had to do.*

"Ha!" Mia said and smacked the steering wheel hard enough to make her hand smart. "I have . . . skills! And just who does he think is going to plan his lavish parties at his house? Huh? Entertain his clients?" She flipped one hand in the air and swerved again. "And just who will find impossible-to-get Cubs and Bulls tickets to seal the deal?" She gave her hair another toss, only to have it fly back across her face. She gave it an impatient swipe, but several strands clung to her lip gloss. "I was his personal assistant and did it for free!" she grumbled. "He'll never be able to replace me. I have connections all over Chicago." She glanced at the hula dancer. "So what if I ran up a few credit cards? Bought a few things here and there and, well . . . everywhere? I'm helping the economy, right? It's my civic duty or whatever that's called." She waved her French-tipped fingers back and forth, and the sunshine glinted off her diamond tennis bracelet.

When the hula dancer stared back at her with accusing brown eyes, Mia sighed. "O-kaaaay, so I abused the credit cards a tiny bit. Traveled a little too much in the company jet." She lifted one slim shoulder. "But that jab about me never having a real job was uncalled for. And my fine-arts degree is not worthless! I worked hard for my father. He just didn't appreciate my efforts." She pressed her lips together in an effort not to cry. "I should have been on the official payroll!" she sputtered, but it wasn't that tired old argument about her working that had driven Mia away from her home and out into the cold, cruel world without credit cards or her baby blue Mercedes coupe. It was overhearing her father negotiating a ruthless business deal that had turned her blood cold. When Mia called him out on the hostile takeover of Hanover Candy, a family-owned, Chicago-based company, she had been furious. She had grown up with and gone to school with Hailey Hanover and couldn't imagine that her father would take advantage of tough times for the locally owned company, which made various flavors of hard candy sticks that Mia often got to sample before the general public. She had suggested and was responsible for tasty flavors like cotton candy and cherry cheesecake. How could he go after her friends?

When her father had calmly explained that deals like these paid for Mia's lavish lifestyle, she hotly declared that she no longer wanted his money and would fend for herself from this day forward!

There was only one problem. She didn't exactly have a plan in place when she stuffed her Louis Vuitton suitcase full of random clothes and stormed out of her father's estate. "Oh well, this will be an adventure!" she declared with much more moxie than she was actually feeling, and then suddenly felt a little light-headed. "Low blood sugar," she mumbled, refusing to believe it was nerves. She decided to find a nice restaurant to eat a little lunch, perhaps a Cobb salad, or then again a panini would do nicely.

"Okay," Mia said firmly but then sighed. So here she was in . . . Where was she again? Oh yeah, in *Kentucky*, driving down the interstate in an old Toyota Camry that she had bought off of Manny Perez, their gardener. When Mia had offered to purchase Manny's car, he had rattled off something in Spanish about gas and oil while shaking his head and making hand gestures, little of which Mia had understood. But Mia's polite insistence and a cool thousand bucks had sealed the deal. One of the many things she had learned from her father was that money talks, and when all else fails, use leverage. So she had flashed cash and a pretty-please smile at Manny and he had handed over the battered vehicle without further protest.

When Mia's stomach grumbled in grumpy protest, she looked at the passing signs for something to capture the interest of her taste buds. She wasn't very familiar with fast food, but Cracker Barrel sounded interesting. Mia had seen plenty of signs for the rustic restaurants along her aimless journey, and there was the added enticement of shopping right there in the establishment. "Someone sure was thinking!" she said and was about to pull off at the next exit when she noticed a billboard advertising the Cricket Creek Cougars baseball stadium located five miles down the road.

"Hmm . . . why does that sound familiar?" Mia tapped her cheek but then suddenly remembered that her father had attended opening day last summer. She also thought he might have some other business connection in Cricket Creek, but she couldn't put her finger on it. She didn't always pay close attention when her father rambled on about his business dealings, but she knew that he had also traveled to Cricket Creek quite a few times over the past few months. She did recall that he had mentioned that the head chef from Chicago Blue Bistro had moved there to run a restaurant and that the food was excellent.

"Ah . . . ha!" Mia smiled when she spotted a billboard for Wine and Diner. "I do believe that was the very cute and clever name." She nodded slowly and then mustered up another smile. "Well, Wine and Diner, here I come!" When her stomach rumbled in anticipation she pressed on the gas pedal, but her smile faded when the car gave a funny little lurch and the check-engine light flickered and then came back on. "Oh no you don't!" she pleaded, but this time the red light stubbornly remained lit. Luckily, the Cricket Creek exit was only a mile down the road.

Mia eased her chunky clog off the gas pedal and gingerly steered off the exit. She spotted a sign pointing to several restaurants and turned left toward town. "How quaint!" she said as the Camry chugged down Main Street. Colorful mid-May flowers spilled over the tops of large terra-cotta planters lining the sidewalk. An old-fashioned bakery named Grammar's caught her eye, along with several antique shops. When she spotted a vintage clothing store with a sale rack out front, her shopping addiction kicked into high gear, but she lifted her chin in steely determination and kept on driving.

When Mia stopped for a red light, she watched people meander down the sidewalk and wander in and out of the shops. The town had a warm, welcoming feel to it and the chatter of shoppers sounded cheerful. Mia was used to the hustle and bustle of Chicago, and while she loved the energy of a big city, this slower pace had an instant calming effect on her frazzled nerves. She inhaled deeply and the sweet scent of spring filled her head, making her sigh with pleasure.

Laughter brought Mia's attention to her open window and she smiled softly when she spotted children playing in the city park. Young mothers watched over the frolic and fun, bringing a pang of sadness to Mia's chest. When her father's first business had failed, Mia's mother left Mitch Monroe for a man with more wealth. Heartbroken, he had sued for full custody of Mia and had won, but his obsession with financial success kept him from spending much time with his two-year-old daughter, and thus had begun Mia's long string of au pairs. But just when she would become emotionally bonded to her caregiver, the au pair would move on, leaving Mia feeling sad and making it much safer to find happiness with material things rather than people.

As an adult and no stranger to therapy, Mia realized that her father's intense drive to succeed was a direct result of his wife's desertion, but that didn't change the fact that Mia had been a lonely little girl longing for her father's attention and her mother's acceptance.

Oh, Mia had visited her mother but had always felt like an outsider in her mother's new life. Over the years her visits had become few and far between, and sadly she believed that her mother had been mostly relieved.

A honking horn startled Mia out of her musing. "Oh, just hush!" she grumbled as she eased the car forward, but her mood lightened when she spotted Wine and Diner on the corner. The brick building with the cute red awning looked inviting, but it was the aroma of grilled food wafting through her open window that had her hurrying to locate a spot in the parking lot. "Well!" Mia had to circle twice before sliding into a vacant space, an indication that Wine and Diner was a popular place to eat. "Finally!"

After she turned the key, the engine coughed and sputtered as if in distress or perhaps relief. "Oh, please start when I get finished eating," Mia pleaded and gave the dash a quick pat. The door opened with a tired-sounding squeak and she gently closed it before hurrying toward the entrance of the restaurant.

When Mia entered Wine and Diner she wasn't surprised to find a line of patrons waiting to be seated. Her mouth watered in anticipation of a good hot meal when the aroma of food wafted her way, and she barely suppressed a sigh. Mia looked at the name tag on the hostess's black shirt. "Hello, Bella. How long of a wait?" she asked with a big smile but with a hint that she was in a hurry and might leave, even though it was far from the truth. Mia had learned from her father to always use a name and to try to remember it.

Bella nibbled on her bottom lip and peered down at her chart. "Mmm, about fifteen or twenty minutes?"

"Oh." Mia couldn't keep the disappointment out of her tone but then tried another tactic. "Wow, has anyone ever told you that you look like Eva Longoria?" It was true. She did. "Except, you know, younger."

"Actually, I get that a lot. So would you like to wait?" Bella politely persisted.

"Well, I'm just passing through and in a bit of a rush," Mia replied slowly but then leaned forward and shook her head. Somehow this homey atmosphere made her feel guilty for fibbing. "Actually, that's not true. It just smells divine and I'm famished."

"I totally understand. And trust me, you won't be disappointed." Bella glanced over her shoulder and then back at Mia. "Well, would you mind sitting at the back counter? There's a vacant stool there."

Mia looked at the open seat between a big, burly dude in overalls who sported a Santa-like beard and a younger guy in jeans and a baseball cap. While they appeared friendly enough, Mia had issues about sharing her personal space. She swallowed hard and was about to tell Bella that she would wait, but then she spotted a waitress carrying a tray laden with delicious-looking comfort food and nodded. "A stool at the counter would be perfect. Thank you so much."

"Super." Bella raised one dark eyebrow just slightly, making Mia wonder if the hostess knew her dilemma. "You may seat yourself. Enjoy your lunch," she added with a smile.

"Thank you!" Mia made her way to the rear of the dining room. She passed a lovely array of desserts beneath a revolving glass display counter but told herself not to indulge and kept on moving. Oh, but then her eyes were drawn to a room to the right that had a script sign that read WINE AND DIVINE. It was a gift shop!

Mia's footsteps slowed to a near stop when she spotted a rack of colorful woven scarves that looked baby soft, and her fingers twitched with the need to touch. She tried to avert her gaze, but when sunlight from the window glinted off a tray of jewelry, she was tugged that way as if pulled by a magnet. She actually rounded a table and craned her neck to see a shelf of lovely candles that she was sure smelled divine like the sign promised, but her stomach rumbled in protest. Her need for food was making her light-headed and was the only thing that kept her feet walking toward the round stool. Well, *that* and the little voice in the back of her head that reminded Mia that she was without credit cards and had very little cash left. She did still have her father's gas card tucked in her wallet, so at least putting fuel in the temperamental Toyota wasn't going to be a problem. Mia cringed as she thought that her next meal might have to be a shriveled-up hot dog twirling on one of those greasy silver grids in a convenience store so unlike the delicious Chicago-style dogs sold from street vendors.

Trying her best not to bump the bearded guy, who was totally taking up more than his share of the allotted space, Mia leaned a little to the right as she scooted onto the stool. She was almost successful, but her hobo-style purse slid from her shoulder and whacked the elbow of the younger guy just as he lifted his arm to take a drink from a tall glass.

"What the . . . ," he griped as he doused his burger. Water splashed down the front of his shirt and he hissed when ice cubes clinked against the counter and landed in a neat little heap between his legs.

"Sorry!" Mia squeaked and started snatching napkins

from the little metal holder. She tried to dab at his sopping shirt, but he made some sort of rude growling noise and jumped up from the stool. Without looking at her, he scooped the remaining pile of ice from the stool and dumped it back into his glass. "Sorry," Mia repeated in a lower voice, but all she got was his narrowed gaze. "It was an accident!" she repeated in a firmer tone and felt heat creep into her cheeks when she realized that they had become the center of attention.

"You could have been more careful." He plucked at his T-shirt, which was clinging to him like a second skin.

Mia tried not to stare at his nicely defined chest but failed. "I'll pay for your meal," Mia assured him politely and nodded to the waitress who hurried over to the scene. "Please bring him a fresh burger and fries."

"Not necessary," he said in the same clipped tone and sopped up the water pooled on the counter.

"But you haven't eaten your meal."

"No, I mean it's not necessary for you to pay for it."

"I insist!"

"Okay." He lifted one shoulder and sat back down just as Mia reached over to brush a remaining ice cube off the shiny red vinyl stool. His butt landed on her hand, making her yelp.

"Ouch!" Mia yanked hard just as he stood, making her give a hard elbow to the bearded guy to her left. He grunted and sent his grilled cheese sailing over his head and onto the floor just as a waitress hurried by. Her foot slipped on the soft sandwich, causing her tray to tilt. She yelped and jerked the tray upright but overcompensated, sending French fries flying and burgers flipping into the air.

Mia put a hand to her mouth as the rest of the scene unfolded as if in slow motion . . .

Two tall milk shakes wobbled back and forth as if swaying to the piped-in music and then tipped forward, sending cherries shooting into the air, followed by a waterfall of chocolate shake spilling to the floor. A busboy rushed forward but slid through the puddle of shake like he was on ice skates and crashed into a seated man, who went from squeezing ketchup onto his onion rings to spattering it into the face of his female companion. She screamed and leaned backward, allowing the red stream to squirt the face of the man directly behind her. He jerked sideways and knocked over all three beverages on his table and sent silverware clanking to the floor.

And then there was silence . . . well, except for the cheerful sound of the bluegrass music, which seemed to be mocking Mia. She swallowed hard while considering if she should make a mad dash for the front door. While calculating how fast she could actually dash in her chunky shoes she sneaked a peek at the waitress behind the counter, who was swiping at her eyes. Dear God, was she crying? When Mia swiveled her head, she noticed that the belly of the Santa look-alike was *shaking like a bowl full of jelly*, Mia thought with dark humor. Was he crying too?

Had she reduced an entire lunch crowd to tears?

"Well, if that just wasn't the funniest damn thing I've witnessed in a long-ass time," the bearded man said in a deep voice punctuated with bouts of low-pitched laughter. He slapped his thigh. "Don't that just beat all?" he asked, but Mia avoided his gaze and kept her head down.

"Don't I know it," the waitress agreed and swiped at what Mia realized were tears of laughter. A titter began at the table next to the counter and rolled into full-blown amusement until everyone in the joint was doubled over except, notably, Mr. Tall and Brooding standing next to her. He sat down with an angry plop, folded his arms across his wet chest, and sighed.

"Just what are you moaning about?" Mia demanded hotly.

"Oh, let's see. My ruined lunch." He glanced down and plucked at his chest. "My sopping shirt and cold crotch."

"Oh, stop," Mia sputtered and pointed to the menu. "Wine . . . and Diner. Without the *h*, so quit your *whining*."

He snorted at her sorry attempt at humor. "Really?"

"Really," she confirmed close to his ear, since everyone was still laughing and reliving the incident while the busboys mopped up the many messes. "I said I was sorry and that I'd pay for your lunch. I'm at a loss as to what more I can do."

"Well, Princess, you need to pay for everyone else's that you ruined while you're at it."

"Don't call me princess," she pleaded. It was her father's pet name for her, which had been cute when she was a child but had not been so sweet an endearment this past week.

"Really?" He took his baseball cap off and let his gaze travel down her pale blond hair, over her classy Ralph Lauren white linen shirt and black cuffed capri pants to her Jimmy Choo crushed patent leather clogs, finally coming to rest on her diamond tennis bracelet. She wasn't quite sure from his hooded expression if he liked what he saw or not.

"Really!" she repeated firmly and shot him a glare that she hoped would intimidate him, but he gave her a sardonic arch of one eyebrow. "I am very . . . um . . . *down-to-earth*," she said, even though she wasn't quite sure that she truly was all that . . . earthy.

"Gross," he growled, and for a horrifying second Mia thought he was referring to her appearance, but he picked up his sopping-wet bun and grimaced.

"Oh, it's not that bad," Mia grumbled and then motioned for the laughing waitress, who flipped a long braid over her shoulder and headed over to the counter. "Um, this little . . . situation might have inadvertently been my fault," she began but paused when the guy next to her had the nerve to sigh. Mia swiveled on her stool to face him. "Excuse me?"

"*Might* have been your fault?"

Mia fisted her hands on her hips. "You were the one who spilled your water everywhere!"

"Only because you knocked it out of my hand, Princess." He drew out the nickname and arched that exasperating eyebrow again.

Mia narrowed her gaze and refused to acknowledge how hazel his eyes were or his straight white teeth or the sexy dark stubble covering a strong, square jawline. And his leg, suddenly pressed against hers, did not cause the hot shiver that slid down her spine. It was . . . anger! "I was merely trying not to bump into the gentleman next to me."

"And smacked me with your suitcase instead."

"It was my purse!"

"Could have fooled me. What do you have in there anyway?" He rubbed his bumped arm while he glanced down at the shiny leather bag and his other eyebrow joined the arched one. "Bricks?"

Mia rolled her eyes at him. "Nothing much." Not much money anyway.

"Really . . ."

"Stop saying that!"

"What?"

"Really . . ." She mocked his deep voice. Out of the corner of her eye she noticed that the waitress was watching the exchange with amused interest. Mia was normally self-conscious about what people thought of her, but right now she was too steamed to care.

"Whatever, Princess. Oh wait, I can't say that either. Any other orders you want to give me while you're at it?"

"Yes, stop being so . . . *rude*!" Mia shot back and tried to add a glare, but her voice shook and her bottom lip had the audacity to tremble. She was used to people fawning over her instead of finding fault, and she suddenly feared that her father was right. Perhaps she didn't have the strength to make it on her own after all! When her eyes welled up, she turned away and hoped he didn't notice. "Would you please replace anyone's lunch that got ruined and put it on my tab?" she requested with a smile at the waitress.

"That won't be necessary, sugar." The waitress returned the smile and added a wink. "I'll take care of it."

"I don't want you to do that!" Mia was horrified that a waitress would have to pay for her screwup.

"It was an accident," she said soothingly and flashed the guy next to her a look of warning. "Now, Cam, I know that you're still fairly new around these parts, but we don't cry over spilled milk shakes around here." She turned back to Mia. "Now, what would you like for lunch? May I suggest the special, chicken-fried steak, mashed potatoes, and green beans? It's a house specialty."

"Oh, thank you so much." Mia tried not to wince at the amount of calories in the special and raised one shoulder. "I was thinking of a nice salad with dressing on the side," Mia replied, but then Cam, as the waitress had called him, sighed as if he was reading her I-know-your-type mind. Mia raised her chin. "But the chicken-fried-steak special sounds too scrumptious to pass up."

"Gravy?"

"Yes . . . extra!" she said but had to suppress a shudder. "And water with a very thin slice of lemon."

"Coming right up."

"You won't regret it," the Santa look-alike promised.

"I'm sure I won't," Mia answered loud enough for Cam to hear. "And I'm so sorry I caused your sandwich to sail across the room."

He shrugged his beefy shoulders. "Hey, don't worry about the ruined lunches or the mess. People are pretty good-natured around here, and the woman who waited on you is Myra Robinson, one of the owners."

"Oh, thank you for letting me know."

"No problem." He extended his hand. "I'm Pete Sully. I own Sully's Tavern just down the road. If you're staying here in Cricket Creek, stop in and I'll make you a perfect martini on the house."

"Why, thank you, Mr. Sully," she said, even though she doubted he could make a perfect martini. "I'm just passing through or I'd take you up on it."

"Call me Pete," he insisted in a gruff voice laced with southern charm that made Mia smile in spite of her embarrassing mishap. "And if you change your mind, little lady, let me know."

"About the martini?"

Pete grinned. "Naw . . . about just passing through."

"Oh, there's no chance of me staying," she said, but when the guy next to her chuckled she added, "This is a lovely town, but I'm a city girl."

Pete shook his head. "City dwellers staying in Cricket Creek seems to be a trend here lately," he warned her. "So what's your name, if I might ask?"

"Mia Mon . . . ," she began but then swallowed hard and thought fast, ". . . ee." While she wasn't exactly a full-blown celebrity, her name was often in the tabloids, and besides that, she really didn't want her father hot on her trail.

"Mia *Money*?"

"Yes," she answered firmly and ignored the quick intake of breath from the guy next to her. He pressed his leg against hers as if saying *Yeah, right.* "Mia Money," she repeated.

"Any relation to Eddie?" Pete asked with a grin.

"Eddie?"

"Eddie Money," Pete said and then sang, " 'Two tickets to paradise . . .' "

"Oh, the singer . . . I don't think so," she added with a shake of her head and then gratefully turned her attention to the plate of food that suddenly arrived. She wasn't a very good liar and hated being lied to but felt the need to protect her identity. "Oh . . . my." She looked down at the huge helping of . . . everything. A scoop of mashed potatoes was squished between the golden breaded steak and green beans seasoned with some serious chunks of ham. Thick white gravy flecked with pepper covered the golden-fried meat and formed a puddle in the center of the big helping of fluffy potatoes.

Dear God.

"Everything okay?" Myra asked with a hint of uncertainty and then placed a small blue plate of two big connected yeast rolls and two pats of butter down next to her tall glass of water. She noticed that the slice of lemon was paper-thin, as requested.

"Yes, everything looks . . . amazing," Mia replied as she slowly unrolled her silverware from the paper napkin.

"Well, good. Enjoy your lunch," Myra added with a smile. "Holler if you need anything, okay, sweetie?"

"Thank you." After inhaling a deep breath, Mia picked up her knife and fork, wondering just where to begin.

2

Delicious Surprise

"THANKS," CAMERON SAID WHEN HIS FRESH BURGER and fries were placed in front of him. He flicked a discreet glance at Mia and when he witnessed her stunned expression as she stared at her food he had to hide his grin by popping a hot, crispy fry into his mouth. He would be willing to bet that Ms. Money had never eaten something as decadent as chicken-fried steak smothered with white peppered gravy, and mashed potatoes probably never got past those pouty pink lips. She had low calorie/high maintenance written all over her gorgeous face.

Wait . . . that *face*. Didn't he know her from somewhere? "Would you please pass the ketchup?" Cam asked and took the opportunity to get a closer look at Mia Money when she handed the bottle to him. "Thanks," Cam said but got only a polite, distant nod before Mia turned her attention back to her heaping plate of food. For some reason he didn't like her curt dismissal but didn't really understand why it bothered him so much. After all, he had been sort of a jerk to her, so he couldn't really blame her. But hey, he just couldn't resist putting snooty chicks in their place. Cam had been a pool boy while working his way through school and had been treated like a second-class citizen too often not to have a chip on his shoulder where rich chicks were concerned. So why *was* she getting to him?

Maybe it was because attention from women was something he took for granted and Mia was clearly snubbing him. Cam took a bite of his juicy burger and wondered again why he cared, especially since she was merely passing through town. And yet, after swallowing his food he felt the need to slide another glance her way. He watched with amusement as she gingerly put a small bite of chicken-fried steak slathered with gravy into her mouth. Her eyes widened while she chewed, making Cam wonder if she was going to spit the steak right out.

Oh dear God, but then she closed her eyes and *moaned* with what sounded like sheer pleasure. Cam squeezed his burger so hard that mustard dripped onto his plate. He tried but couldn't keep from turning his head and looking at her. She was so engrossed in her meal that she didn't notice his stare, and she dipped her fork into her mashed potatoes. She seemed to savor the potatoes before eagerly tackling the green beans, making sure to spear a hunk of ham in the process. After swallowing, she smiled as she sliced her knife through the steak and then popped a more generous bite into her mouth. "Mmm . . ."

When Mia moaned again, Cam had to look away, and it ticked him off that the prissy little chick could get to him so easily. He really did not care for snooty women, and she had *snoot* written all over her. "Would you please just stop?"

Mia stopped in midchew and swiveled his way. After swallowing she asked, "Stop eating? We are in a restaurant, in case you didn't notice."

"No, just stop . . . moaning!"

"I wasn't moaning," she hotly denied and then looked around as if to see if anyone was watching, but the diners seemed to have returned their attention to their meals now that all of the earlier commotion was over. She leaned close and said in his ear, "But then again, perhaps you've never heard a woman moan before." Up came the snooty little nose, and with another lift of her chin she popped a green bean into her mouth.

Cam gave her a heavy-lidded look that he reserved for women he was trying to get into bed . . . not that he was trying to get *her* into bed or anything. He merely wanted to get the point across that he had no trouble in that particular area, and so he leaned in and whispered, "On the contrary."

"I meant in *pleasure*." She drew the word out and added a roll of her eyes but then blushed before she turned her attention back to her food.

"Oh, baby, me too." His low, sultry tone was rewarded when she swallowed hard and coughed. Was he actually getting to Miss Priss? He sure hoped so. "And an occasional scream."

She shook her fork at him and snorted. "As they're running out the door?"

"Not hardly," Cam boasted and then felt kind of silly, wondering why in the hell he was going this route.

"Are you always so full of yourself?"

"Are *you* always so full of food?" he asked and was rewarded with a slight grimace. She frowned down at her plate and he could see the calorie counter clicking away in her brain. She licked her bottom lip and then put her fork down before taking a drink of her water, as if trying to dilute the gravy swimming in her stomach. When she failed to start eating again, Cam suddenly felt like a horse's ass. "Hey, I was only kidding," he said more gently and nodded toward her plate. "Keep enjoying your lunch and I'll leave you alone."

"Do you promise?" she asked with such conviction that he wasn't sure whether he should be offended or should reassure her.

"Yes," Cam said, but she looked at him with uncertainty. Although it was obvious that she came from wealth, there was vulnerability in the set of her mouth and the depths of her eyes that brought out some protective emotion that Cam didn't even understand. He wasn't a dragon-slayer kind of guy. "Hey, I keep my promises," he told her with a slight shrug, but it was true. Admittedly, he could be a real jerk, but he always kept his word. Cam took another bite of his burger and wondered again why he felt the need to tell her that. Mia Money was just passing through his life, and it didn't matter squat what she thought of him. But while he tried to turn his focus back to his meal, Cam remained keenly aware of the woman sitting beside him.

He absently took a bite of his pickle spear and shifted his mind to baseball, the reason he had moved from Florida to this little Kentucky town in the first place. Noah Falcon, one of the owners of the Cricket Creek Cougars, was giving him a shot to get back into baseball after getting booted out of the Chicago Cubs farm system. Cam had proven his talent, but Noah Falcon had given him fair warning that he had to keep out of trouble or his days as a Cricket Creek Cougar were numbered. Ty McKenna, manager of the team, wanted no part of Cam's wild ways, but Noah insisted on giving him a chance with the stipulation that Cam keep his nose clean.

Granted, he had always been somewhat of a head case, but because of his talent Cam was used to getting away with it. But the major leagues weren't high school, where his wild ways had been brushed under the rug for the sake of a state championship. Nope, he found out the hard way that screwups wouldn't be tolerated. He chalked it up to the recent rash of publicity involving pro athletes getting into trouble, which had forced franchise owners to clamp down on bad behavior.

Cam dipped a fry into ketchup while he thought back to the series of events that had ended his minor-league career. During a closely contested game, his hotheaded reaction to a blatant intentional pitch at his head had him storming the mound and taking a swing at the pitcher. Both benches immediately emptied and there was a nasty brawl that was played endlessly on YouTube and reported on ESPN. Cam shifted in his seat at the memory. Hey, the damned pitcher had gone further than just a brushback. He had given him some serious chin music! What was he supposed to do? Stand there and take it? Most players would have done the same thing.

Cam sighed before taking a long swallow of his water. Okay . . . there was a bar fight that resulted in fifteen stitches in his hard head and landed him a night in jail. Oh, and a reckless-driving ticket. Cam ground his teeth at the thought. He hadn't been driving recklessly. He could damned well handle a car at over one hundred miles an hour. He was merely speeding and didn't need to have his license suspended!

Cam sighed once more. He was going to have to tread softly and keep a low profile. There was only one problem: No matter how hard he tried, trouble had a way of tracking him down. He popped another fry into his mouth and attempted to ignore the intoxicating scent of expensive perfume wafting his way, but when Mia's thigh brushed against his, he sighed again, drawing her unwanted attention. He wasn't sure why, but he had the distinct feeling that trouble was sitting right next to him, and so he tried to ignore her stare. It was a damned good thing she was just passing through town, because uppity or not, he wasn't sure he could keep his hands off of her.

"What's wrong?"

Cam was about to give her a flippant response, but the sincerity in her eyes stopped him cold. Since he couldn't tell her that her body brushing against his was driving him nuts, he simply shrugged. "Nothin'."

"That was a something-is-wrong sigh," she persisted, and although she didn't say it, she had I-know-the-feeling written all over her pretty face.

Cam nodded toward her mostly full plate. "Stop worrying about me and eat your lunch." He meant his tone to be dismissive, but he really did want her to go back to enjoying her meal. Then again maybe he just wanted to hear her moan once more.

Not good, Cam thought with an internal groan. Spoiled, rich women suckered him in and then spit him right back out. They always had a thing about his bad-boy image, and yet he was never good enough for mama and daddy. Of course, if he made it to the major leagues, they'd have no problem hanging his arm.

"Wait . . ." Her delicate blond eyebrows shot up. "You're upset because I'm not eating enough?" She angled her head. "That's so sweet," she added and gave him a maybe-I-was-wrong-about-you look.

"Sweet?" Cam chuckled. "Believe me, there's nothing sweet about me, Princess." He nodded toward her plate. "Eat your lunch," he added gruffly. The fact that she seemed genuinely concerned hit him in the gut. When was the last time anyone had cared? His deadbeat dad and his overworked mother never had. They both resented his very existence, but he sure bet that if he ever made it they would come running with their hands out. Lack of support and compassion from his parents was one of the things that had always driven Cam toward success. He wanted to show them he was worth something, dammit! Unfortunately, the huge chip on his shoulder also held him back. That was why he had to steer clear of anything that remotely resembled trouble, and it irritated him that Mia was getting to him. "It's really none of my concern if you eat or not."

Mia gave him a look beneath her lashes that suggested that she didn't quite believe him and then sliced through her steak. She raised her fork into the air, showing him an almost normal bite. "Happy now?" She popped it into her mouth and smiled while she chewed.

Cam tried not to be drawn in by her smile. He wasn't very successful but pretended otherwise. "Add a big bite of potatoes and I'll go back to leaving you alone."

"Good," she responded firmly, but her smile faltered, and damned if it didn't bother him! He needed to finish his burger and get the hell out of Wine and Diner. With that in mind Cam polished off his lunch in quick order and then motioned for Myra.

"Anything else I can get for you today?" Myra asked, and he swore she made a slight motion toward Mia. "Dessert maybe? I have some chocolate cake baked fresh this morning."

"Sounds amazing, but no, thanks," Cam replied. When Myra placed his bill in front of him, Mia reached over and snatched it up.

"Remember? I've got this," she said in the firm tone that suggested that she was used to getting her way.

Well, not today, Cam thought and shook his head.

"No, I insist," Mia said and would not release the small slip of paper to him.

"Okay, Princess, whatever you say." Cam finally relented when he realized that people were starting to watch the exchange with interest. He really did need to keep a low profile, and it sure wouldn't hurt her pocketbook to pay for his lunch, so he folded his arms over his chest, which was still a bit damp. "I won't argue."

When Mia leaned down for her massive purse, he noticed just how petite she was and reminded himself that he went for tall, leggy women, but when her pale blond hair slipped over her shoulder and onto his leg, he suddenly wished he was wearing shorts instead of jeans so he could feel the silky texture on his bare skin. When his pants suddenly became tighter, Cam shifted on the stool and got a little irritated at her for causing a sexual reaction. Women were another thing he needed to keep away from if he wanted to stay focused on baseball.

Cam was eager to leave and head on over to the stadium for some batting practice. Even though it wasn't mandatory, he wanted to show Coach McKenna that he was serious. Ty McKenna was known as Mr. Triple Threat during his pro baseball career because he could hurt a team with his bat, his arm, and his impossible diving catches. He appreciated hustle, and Cam was going to show it to him. With opening day right around the corner, he wanted to secure a starting position.

"Um . . . ," Mia said, drawing his attention.

"Yeah?" Cam looked over and noticed her fumbling through her purse.

"I seemed to have left my money in my car. I'll be right back," she promised and slipped from the stool.

"Okay," Cam replied but then glanced down at his watch and grimaced. He swiveled around to stop her, but she was already near the door and he didn't want to shout. Cam took off his cap and shoved his fingers through his hair. He really did need to get going. He had to change clothes before batting practice started, and time was running out. The little fiasco created by Miss Money had made lunch last longer than he had anticipated. With that in mind, he motioned for Myra. "I need to pay for my lunch."

"Thought that cute little minx was taking care of ya," Myra said with a wink.

"Well, I'm in a hurry to get to practice, so I'll take care of myself." Cam stood up and reached into his back pocket for his wallet, but while he was pulling out some money he remembered seeing a look of panic come over Mia's face and he suddenly wondered if she was short on cash. He frowned. Chicks like her usually put everything on a card anyway. Something felt odd and his instincts were rarely wrong. "Hey, I'll pay for hers too," Cam said and gestured to Mia's half-eaten meal.

"Sweet of ya," Myra said with a nod that sent her big hoop earrings swinging back and forth. She accepted the money with a smile.

"Keep the change."

"Thanks, sugar. Now, get your butt on over to practice. We want another winning season."

"Will do." Cam thought Myra was a pretty cool chick for someone who must be in her fifties. She wore hippie kind of clothes and said just about whatever she wanted. He liked down-to-earth, honest people like her. He also learned that this diner had belonged solely to Myra before she retired and handed the reins over to her niece Jessica, who was married to Ty McKenna. They had a little baby that Jessica often carried around in a pouch strapped to her chest while she worked. According to Coach McKenna, Jessica was a kick-ass chef at a popular restaurant in Chicago before coming home to take over the diner. She had an older daughter who worked at the diner on occasion but was some kind of writer, if he remembered right, and she was engaged to Jason, the friendly dude who was building a beer garden on the upper deck of the stadium.

Small towns, Cam thought as he walked out the door and into the sunshine. Everybody knew everybody and had some kind of connection, and if you listened closely enough you could learn just about everything about everybody. There was some backstabbing, but most of the gossip was on the friendly side. People were all smiles and waved to one another. He, on the other hand, had grown up in a trailer park and wasn't used to such warm fuzzies. Sure, some of his neighbors had been good people, but others . . . well, not so much. And the rich clients he had cleaned pools for were for the most part arrogant assholes, or at least he felt that way. Daughters and even some wives would come on to him, and yet he would always be the culprit, often getting fired for no reason other than jealous husbands or fearful fathers. Yeah, he admittedly had a prejudice where wealth was concerned, which brought his mind back to Mia. She didn't seem like she would dine and dash, but when Cam looked around the parking lot, he didn't spot a luxury vehicle, which she surely would be driving.

"Really?" Cam mumbled under his breath when he spotted her very blond head inside the driver's side of a beat-up old Toyota. With a frown he walked her way. "Hey," he said and leaned down toward the window. She yelped and put her hand over her mouth but then frowned.

"Did you have to sneak up on me?" she accused in a snooty tone that grated over his nerves.

"Sorry, but you were taking forever and I have to get to ball practice," he replied tersely before noticing the heap of change piled in her lap. So she was counting pennies to pay for lunch? Something wasn't adding up. Cam felt a stab of compassion, and his anger immediately cooled. All too often he had witnessed his mother scrounging for coins to pay for something as simple as a meal from the value menu at a fast-food restaurant.

"Oh," she said in a softer tone and then chewed on her bottom lip while she stared at the small heap of change. When she raised those big eyes to look up at him, Cam knew that she was short.

Cam remembered the same look in his mother's eyes and was glad he had paid for Mia's meal. He also knew pride, so he tried to choose his words carefully. "Look, don't be pissed, but I was in a hurry so I tossed down some cash. It took care of both of our tabs."

"Thank you." The arrogant tone was replaced with throaty emotion that she failed to mask.

Cam rested his hand on the roof of the car and leaned closer. "Are you okay?" he asked, and though he knew he shouldn't get involved, those big blue eyes were drawing him in. Although she nodded, she also swallowed hard, and as sure as he was standing there, Cam knew that Mia was in some sort of situation. Someone as gorgeous as her might be running from some rich bastard. It would explain the crappy car but expensive clothes and jewelry. He hoped she wasn't being stalked or threatened and on the run. *Not your problem,* his good sense whispered in his ear, and yet his mouth opened and said, "Are you sure there isn't something I can do to help?" He wanted to bite his damned tongue for asking, but the thought of anyone harming her felt like a kick to his gut. He remembered his mother being smacked around by more than one jerk, and it was a memory that haunted him still. Cam also recalled that when he tried to step in and defend his mother, she would often turn on him instead of the hand that hit her. Getting involved meant getting hurt, and yet he still couldn't stand to see his mother's pain. He felt that same kind of emotional tug-of-war right now. Cam swallowed a sigh. "Mia?"

3

Going with the Flow

MIA LOOKED DOWN AT THE PITIFUL PILE OF CHANGE IN her lap and had to suppress a shudder. She'd thought she had more cash on her, but after paying Manny for the car, she was broke. Flat broke. For the first time in her life Mia felt the anxiety of not having enough money to cover her bill! It was horrible but humbling and made her stomach feel queasy. How on earth did people live with this fear on a daily basis? She was so close to tears for so many reasons that she couldn't even muster up the courage to speak.

"Mia?" he persisted, his gentle but firm tone almost her undoing.

"Um . . ." She gazed up into Cam's hazel eyes, which seemed to change from green to blue with his mood. He appeared so sincere and oozed such masculine strength that it was difficult not to take him up on his offer, but she cleared her throat and gave her hair a flip. "Thanks for the offer, but no, I'm . . . um, fine. Just having a little, uh, cash-flow problem at the moment."

"Is there anything I can do to get you where you're headed?" he insisted.

Again it was so tempting to ask for some money just to get her going, but she was suddenly sick and tired of depending on others for her meal ticket, and so she raised her chin with determination and gave him a negative shake of her head. "Thanks for buying my lunch, but really, I'll be fine."

Cam frowned and looked as if he was going to protest but then glanced at his watch and pushed away from the car. "Okay, well, good-bye, then. Have a safe trip to wherever you're heading."

"Thanks," she said and gave him a weak smile. It was weird, but although she barely knew him, it felt odd to be saying good-bye. She felt a pull that she didn't quite understand but chalked it up to her need to lean on someone for help. Well, from here on out she was going to fend for herself!

"No problem," he said and after giving the roof of her car a pat he nodded and turned around. Once again Mia felt a sense of loss as she watched him walk away, while absently acknowledging that he had a really nice butt. After a moment she stuck the key in the ignition and said a prayer that the car would start. "Yes!" Mia said when the engine turned over, but she frowned at the stubborn check-engine light. She decided to look for a repair shop of some sort and see if the car was okay to drive, but her answer came in the form of dark smoke seeping from beneath the hood. "Smoke can't be good," she said to the hula dancer but then spotted a sign at the end of the block that read, FRED'S TIRES AND REPAIR. The car choked and sputtered, and by the time Mia made it to the corner, smoke was billowing out from under the hood. As soon as she pulled into the parking lot of the repair shop, she grabbed her purse, tugged the hula dancer from the dash, and hopped out of the car. If the car was about to go up in flames, there was no time to save her suitcase!

Mia ran toward the entrance and pushed the front door open. She frantically looked around before spotting a small worn sign taped to the counter that read, RING BELL FOR SERVICE. She pounded on the bell, making it ding over and over while she looked out the window at the smoking car. Finally, an ancient-looking little man clad in grease-stained work pants and a blue shirt that said FRED in scripted yellow meandered through the door, causally wiping his hands on an orange towel.

"All right already, you can quit your dingin'," Fred said in a good-natured tone. "How can I help ya, little lady?"

"Oh." Mia pulled her hand away but then gestured toward the window. "Fred, I think my car is going to blow!"

"Blow?"

"Explode!"

"Ya don't say." Fred peered out the window but didn't seem to be all that alarmed.

"And my suitcase is in there," she urgently added, hoping Fred might rescue her clothes for her. Although from the looks of him it would take both of them to heft it from the trunk of the smoking car.

"Did your car quit on ya?" he asked in that slow drawl. From talking to walking, everyone in Cricket Creek seemed to go in slow motion.

Mia gave him a jerky nod. "Yes, it just . . . died."

"Probably locked up your engine. Put any oil in it recently?" Fred asked, but when Mia merely blinked at him, he shook his nearly bald head. Tufts of hair stuck out above his ears, making him look like Yoda. "I'm guessing not."

"So, just what does the engine locking up mean?" she asked in a small voice.

"That you need a new one or this one rebuilt. Let's go take a look-see."

"But it could blow any minute!" She had a mental picture of the car bursting into flames like something out of an action film. She and Fred would go flying backward and both be knocked out cold! And she would surely scuff her shoes. The hula dancer's head bobbed back and forth as if saying, "Don't do it."

"Na . . . ," Fred scoffed as he walked around the counter and over to the door. He had an odd gait, as if his knees would no longer bend. "You coming?" When he held the door open for her, she reluctantly followed at what she considered a safe distance. Mia watched him lift open the hood with his rag wrapped around his hand, and she held her breath while waiting for his verdict.

"Well?" she asked, and when it was evident that there wasn't going to be an explosion, she inched forward and craned her neck to look at the engine.

Fred unscrewed a cap and pulled out a long stick. "Well . . . well," he mumbled and then clucked his tongue.

"Well, what?" Mia prompted, but she had a sinking sensation in her gut telling her that the news wasn't going to be good.

"Not a drop of oil in here, missy," he said, clucking his tongue again and then arching a bushy eyebrow at her. "Shoulda kept an eye on it."

"I just bought the car." Like with her father, Mia felt compelled to defend herself, but now some of Manny's disjointed gestures and scattered English made more sense. "So what does this mean, exactly?"

"Well, like I said . . . that engine needs to either be replaced or rebuilt."

"Can you do that?"

"Yep, I damn sure can."

Mia let out a sigh of relief, but then her eyes widened. "Um, how much?"

Fred nibbled on the inside of his lip, causing his mustache to twitch. "Depends on how cheap I can get an engine at the junkyard."

"The junkyard?" That sure didn't sound like somewhere you would want to get something as important as an engine.

"Where else can I get one? They damned sure don't grow on trees, you know."

Mia bristled a bit—his comment sounded like something her father might say to her. How was she supposed to know where you got car engines? "Can you give me an estimate?"

He scratched his bristly chin. "Three . . . four thousand."

"Dollars?" Mia gasped.

"No, candy bars." He chuckled but then sobered. "Sorry 'bout yer luck," he said in a kind tone.

Luck? Like money, Mia never really gave luck much consideration, but she found herself sighing. She had purses that cost that much and had never given it a second thought, but now it felt like millions. "But the car isn't worth that."

He shrugged one slim shoulder. "It will be with a new engine. Look, I can make some calls and give you a better idea later today. I'll search for a deal and treat ya right."

"Thank you," Mia said, not that it mattered. Mia shifted her purse higher on her shoulder while her mind raced. She didn't have any money or any credit cards except for the gas card. She felt tears well up and felt her chin wobble. Her father was right: At twenty-four years of age, she wasn't capable of taking care of herself for more than a day, much less all summer. She was going to have to tuck her tail between her legs and call home.

"Or I could buy it from ya for a few hundred dollars."

"But then I wouldn't have a car."

Fred shrugged. "You could put it toward a new one," he suggested but then looked at her with an odd expression. "You runnin' from somethin', girlie?"

"No! I'm . . . proving something," she said, as if that explained how she was standing there in clothes that were worth more than her car and no cash in her wallet.

"I'm guessing you're broke?"

"Temporarily."

"So that's a yes."

"Yes," she answered glumly. "Any suggestions?"

"Could you call somebody for help? To come and get ya or wire ya some money?"

"No," she answered firmly. She stiffened her spine. Calling her father was not an option. "Any other thoughts?"

Fred tilted his head to the side and rubbed his chin thoughtfully. "Is that bracelet real?"

"Yes."

"You could pawn it."

Mia frowned. "You mean take it to one of those places that give you money for your valuables?"

"Yep, there's one around the corner on Second Street."

Mia had seen these shops on television and perceived them to be scary and seedy. She looked down at the shiny bracelet her father had given her and touched it lightly. It wasn't the monetary value. Mia really had no concept of money . . . well, she hadn't until now. It was the fact that her father had given it to her for her twenty-first birthday. He had been away on a business trip for her actual birthday but had brought the bracelet back with him. Like always, Mia had associated his gifts with love and couldn't bear the thought of parting with it. There had to be another solution.

"Or you could always get a job. Hey, I'll store the car for free until you can save up enough for the repairs."

"That's very kind of you, Fred." A job sounded like fun and Mia perked up at the suggestion. "Any idea where I could work?"

"Well, what is it that you do?"

"Do?"

Fred frowned. "You know, for a livin'. What are your skills?"

"Well . . ." Mia considered that for a long moment. "I'm . . . good with people."

"Okay." Fred looked at her kind of funny but then nodded. "Well, that's a start, I suppose. Good thing is that they're hirin' all over the place here in Cricket Creek. The baseball stadium has brought this here town back to life, and a new season is about to begin. Why don't you grab a local newspaper, head on over to Wine and Diner, and look over the want ads? Maybe somethin' will jump out at ya. You got enough on ya to rent a room, I guess."

"Uh . . ."

"I recommend someplace in town where you can walk until I get your car fixed."

"Good point," Mia said. He seemed so concerned that it touched her heart. "But, Fred, you might want to come up with a price of just buying my car too?" She wiggled her fingers in the air. "You know, just to keep that option open."

"Sure, as long as you have a clear title."

"Oh . . . of course." Mia nodded and gave him a wave of her hand like she knew what he was talking about. In that moment she knew that having her father take care of everything while she flitted around the world was not in her best interests. Yes, she had seen and done things that most people only dreamed about, but she knew very little about, well . . . real life. And it was about time she learned to take care of herself.

If only she had a clue . . .

And yet she gave Fred a confident smile like she knew just what the hell she was doing. "Thank you, Fred. I'll get back with you," she said in a serious tone and then extended her hand for him to shake. She tried not to wince when she saw the grease on his hands and the crud beneath his fingernails. She had hand sanitizer in her purse, so she gave his hand a hard squeeze just like her father had taught her.

Mia hefted her purse up onto her shoulder and lifted her head high while she walked down the street until she found a metal box with the local paper. She put four precious quarters in the slot and with the *Cricket Creek Courier* tucked beneath her arm, she entered Wine and Diner like she was on a mission . . . which of course she was. Mia smiled at Bella, the cute hostess, who looked at her in surprise.

"Well, hello again," Bella said. "Decide to come back for dessert? I recommend the pecan pie made fresh this morning."

"No, just coffee." Luckily she had enough change for that small indulgence.

"Would you like a booth?" Now that the lunch rush was over, the restaurant was much more quiet and without a wait.

Mia thought for a second and then decided on a location where she could see what was going on since she had a lot to learn. "No, I'd prefer a seat at the counter again, if you don't mind. I promise to be careful," she added with a small smile.

"Sure." Bella raised her eyebrows as if in surprise but nodded. "Go right ahead. I'm sure there's a fresh pot of coffee brewing. I might take a break and have a cup myself. Lunch was nuts and I'm starting to hit a wall."

"I understand," Mia said in a soothing tone, even though she didn't. Unless you counted shopping, Mia had never experienced having to stand on her feet all day long. She noticed a gorgeous bracelet that Bella was wearing and pointed to it. "Oh, your bracelet is stunning."

"Thank you." Bella smiled and raised her wrist for further inspection. "My mother designs jewelry and she made this one. Some of her pieces are over in the gift shop, and I think there is one similar to this one if you're interested. She's opening a shop down on the riverfront called Designs by Diamante."

"Well, she certainly is talented," Mia commented.

"Yes, she is, and I'm thrilled that she's finally going to be able to pursue her dream." Bella turned the bracelet on her wrist to give Mia a better look.

"It's gorgeous. Good for her." Mia thought that it must be uplifting to have a dream . . . a goal. She hadn't given goals or dreams much thought until now, and it made her feel a little empty. Mia leaned closer and admired the detail and the soft pastel colors. "Is she hiring?" Mia asked in a hopeful tone. If there was one thing Mia knew, it was fashion, and she loved unique jewelry.

"Not for a few weeks." Bella gave her a questioning look. "I thought you were just passing through town."

Mia pursed her lips. "My car died and I'm a little . . .

strapped for cash at the moment." She held up the paper. "I'm going to have to find a job while Fred repairs it."

"We're hiring here at Wine and Diner for the summer rush," Bella offered.

"Really?" Mia felt hope blossom in her chest. Finding a job wasn't going to be so difficult after all.

"Do you have any experience in the restaurant industry?"

"In what capacity?" Mia asked slowly, since the answer was a big fat no. Her father had taught her respond to a question with another question if you didn't know the answer or wanted to skip past it. You could always learn more that way.

"Lots of positions are open." Bella straightened the stack of menus and then walked around to join Mia. "I'll grab that cup of coffee and introduce you to one of the owners. I think Jessica is taking a break with baby Ben, but Myra is around here somewhere."

"Thanks so much," Mia said and followed Bella over to a vacant stool. But even though the restaurant was nearly empty, she could hear the kitchen staff buzzing with activity and she imagined that dinner was going to be just as crowded as lunch.

"Regular or decaf?" Bella asked as she put a thick white mug on the counter.

"Regular, please." Mia inhaled the rich aroma while Bella poured the steaming brew into the sturdy mug. "I love the smell of coffee."

"Me too, and the stronger the better." She put a small saucer heaped with creamers in front of Mia and smiled. "I'll go and round up Myra."

"Thank you." Mia hoped the little incident that she had caused earlier wouldn't be held against her. After adding two tubs of cream, she took a bracing sip of the strong coffee. She cradled the warm mug in her hands and swiveled around on the stool while taking a look around. The restaurant retained the charm of an old-school diner, but she knew that the updated menu had an impressive wine list. To the left of the gift shop were French doors that led to what appeared to be a lounge and some rather upscale seating. Mia looked out the side windows and noticed an expansive outdoor patio and lovely gazebo that would make for comfortable dining alfresco or hosting parties or even weddings. She nodded with appreciation. This was a far cry from a greasy spoon. Someone certainly knew what they were doing.

"Well, hello there, sugar."

Mia swiveled around at the sound of the somewhat amused tone laced in the female southern drawl. "Hi," Mia said and felt a little heat creep into her cheeks.

"Come back to cause more havoc?" Myra asked with a good-natured grin.

"Actually, she's asked about a job," Bella said as she poured herself a mug of coffee and then loaded it up with cream and sugar.

Myra tilted her head to the side, causing her hoop earrings to dangle sideways. "Is that right?"

"Yes," Mia answered. "The engine quit on my car and it seems like the repair is going to be expensive. Bella said that you're hiring for the summer rush, so it would be perfect for me."

"We sure are in need of some kitchen help and a couple of waitresses for the day shift." She extended her hand across the counter. "I'm Myra Robinson, by the way. I own this restaurant with my niece Jessica."

"It's nice to meet you, Ms. Robinson. I'm Mia Mon . . . ee," she said, almost giving her real last name.

She shook Mia's hand. "Same here, but call me Myra. I'm supposed to be retired, but with the arrival of my great-nephew, Ben, Jessica had to cut back, so I came out of hibernation." She gave Mia a measuring look. "So . . . do you have any experience as a waitress?"

"No," Mia admitted slowly, "I was a . . . uh . . . party and event planner and recently got, uh, laid off." Raising her eyebrows, she sat up straighter. "But I am a quick learner and very good with people." Actually, she was good at giving orders rather than taking them, but she could surely do the flip side, right? How hard could it be? "And I know my way around a menu. I've dined in countless restaurants all over the world," she added fervently and then realized she was going too far, drawing a curious look from both Myra and Bella.

"You've never worked a day in your life, have you, sugar?"

"I have!" Mia bristled a bit, even though Myra's comment was said with gentle humor. She had arranged and hosted countless lavish parties for her father and had helped coordinate many a charity event, doing everything from getting donations to hiring the band. "I just haven't always gotten paid for my services," she added a bit defensively. "And I've fallen on some hard times. Lots of people have these days."

"True enough. We sure know all about that here in Cricket Creek," Myra agreed quietly and exchanged a glance with Bella. She reached beneath the counter and then placed some paperwork in front of Mia. "Fill this out and we'll get back to you."

Mia glanced down and spotted words like *social security number*, *previous address*, and *references* and felt her heart plummet. She looked right and left to make sure no one else was within listening distance. "Listen," she said softly, "I'm not in any trouble or anything, but I'm trying to keep my whereabouts on the down low, if you know what I mean."

Myra frowned. "Is someone stalking or trying to hurt you?"

Mia waved her hands in the air. "No, nothing like that. Let's just say I have something important . . . well, at least important to me . . . to prove. Can we slide past the formalities and just let me earn some money? Just until I can get my car repaired?" She gave Myra her best doe-eyed look, the one that always had her father eating out of her hand. "Please?" she asked, but at the thought of her father she felt her eyes well up with unshed tears.

She had always thought that Mitch Monroe was one of the most upstanding and ethical people that she knew and had always felt a sense of pride that she was the daughter of such a dignified, successful man. "I'm not opposed to good, honest work, and I think this restaurant is a charming stroke of genius combining home cooking with a modern flair."

Myra looked at her thoughtfully for a moment but didn't commit. "I don't want any trouble following you here. I have too many people in this town that I care about to put them in harm's way."

Mia took this as an indication that Myra was considering hiring her and had learned from her father that if you see an opening, you should pounce. "I'm not in any trouble. I swear." She crossed her heart and then felt sort of silly that she had used that childish gesture, but Myra smiled.

"You remind me of Madison, my great-niece."

"And that's a good thing, right?"

Myra inclined her head. "She's a handful, but yes."

Mia felt Myra wavering even more and smiled. "I also noticed that you have a sign advertising an apartment for rent upstairs." She slipped her diamond bracelet off her wrist and extended her hand toward Myra. "This is real and worth several thousand dollars. I don't have cash yet, but it can be a deposit on the rent."

"Oh, sweetie . . ." When Myra looked down at Mia's outstretched hand and then glanced over to Bella, Mia held her breath. Bella shrugged but didn't put forth any argument.

"Do you want me to go and get Jessica?" Bella offered.

"No, she went home to take a nap with baby Ben." Myra nibbled on the inside of her lip for a second and then nodded. "Okay, Mia, I'll hire you on a trial basis, keeping you off of the official payroll. You have free room and board and three meals a day. Keep your tips for spending money and saving toward your car repairs. Sound fair enough?"

"Excellent!" She was hired! Well, unofficially, but still . . . she didn't have to go running home to Daddy. Mia felt like jumping for joy.

"But," Myra warned while pointing a finger at her, "the moment I sniff any kind of trouble following you, I'll toss you out on your pretty little ear. Do you understand?"

"Yes." Mia nodded her head rapidly and shoved her hand forward. "Deal!"

After shaking her hand firmly, Myra smiled. "Okay, let's take you upstairs to your new home away from wherever . . ."

Mia smiled back and felt a surge of excitement. "Thanks so much. I won't let you down. I promise."

Myra gave her a level look. "Well, girlie, I don't know what you're into, but you have a firm handshake and looked me in the eye, and believe it or not that tells me a lot. I've always been a good judge of character, and I believe you. Now, let me show you around and we'll go to Fred's and get whatever you need out of your car. And you best get a good night's sleep, because there's nothing easy about the restaurant business. You're going to work your tail off. You ready for that?"

"I'm ready," Mia said with a brisk nod as she followed Myra over to the steps. Oddly enough, she wanted to call her father and let him know that she already had gainful employment and a roof over her head, but then a lump formed in her throat. Her father was the first person she always turned to, but instead she swallowed hard and inhaled a deep breath. She wondered if he was worried about her and felt another stab of guilt but then shrugged it off. After all, he was the catalyst for her leaving. *Let him worry,* she thought with a stubborn lift of her chin, but the lump in her throat remained.

4

Tough Love

"OH, BOY . . ." MITCH MONROE TILTED BACK IN HIS LEATHER chair and stared out the picture window overlooking his kidney-shaped pool. Sunshine glinted cheerfully off the water, but for the past two days nothing could bring a smile to his face, not even talking to lovely Nicolina Diamante, who had brought passion and fun back into a life that had been consumed with work. Mitch ran a hand down his face and sighed. Just hearing Nicolina's sultry voice had him longing to have her in his arms, but after nearly a year of planning, she had officially moved to Cricket Creek to open her jewelry store. Mitch had used his silent partnership in the Cricket Creek Cougars baseball complex as an excuse to visit the quaint river town, but it was really seeing Nicolina that had him heading to Kentucky so frequently. He also gave her some retail-related advice, though not only was she creatively talented but she had a sharp business sense as well. He enjoyed their lively conversations about the store opening, and he loved having her beside him in his bed. Mitch wanted their relationship to move forward even more quickly, but Nicolina remained a bit guarded. He knew she wasn't entirely comfortable with his wealth, and the distrust he sensed on her end bothered him. At the same time he found it refreshing that she wasn't after his money. In fact, she had refused his offer to front her capital for her store, preferring to get started on her own.

Nicolina was an amazing woman, and his feelings for her were starting to grow deeper the more he got to know her. He had hoped to visit Cricket Creek this coming weekend, but having Mia storm out of her home had his stomach tied in knots. He wasn't going to rest until he located his daughter.

"Oh, Mia, what have I done?" Mitch whispered, but he wasn't referring just to Mia's leaving. Hearing Nicolina talk about her close relationship with her own daughter, Bella, had made Mitch realize that he had worried way too much about making millions and hadn't spent nearly enough time enjoying Mia's company.

Mitch ran a hand down his face once more and sighed. He had spoiled Mia with material things in a misguided effort to make up for his absence. He had always thought there was tomorrow to spend time with Mia, but in the blink of an eye she had grown up and all of those tomorrows were long gone. Mitch knew he had failed her in more ways than one. He wanted her to be strong and independent and instead Mia was cultured and educated but lacking some important tools needed to live a full, rewarding life.

"And it's my own damned fault!" Mitch growled and smacked his fist into his open palm. He thought of Mia's big, sad eyes every time he had left for a business trip, missing birthdays and school events. He had justified leaving by telling himself he was making money for his daughter's future, when in truth for years he had been showing his selfish, cheating ex-wife what she had given up by leaving him after his first business had tanked. After that Mitch had been on a mission to make money and had missed Mia growing up in the process. He leaned his head back against the cool leather and wished he could recover some of the time he'd spent sitting in boardrooms, when he could have been traveling with Mia or at the very least sitting across the dinner table from her talking to her about her day. He knew his daughter had always adored him . . . and that made the lost years even worse. Now having her angry with him was almost too much for Mitch to bear.

Mitch looked out the window at the empty lounge chairs. Even though it wasn't quite summer, Mia had always loved to be near the water at the first sign of warm weather. Right now Mia would have probably been lying by the pool with a fashion magazine or hanging out with some of her equally wealthy friends discussing where they would jet off to next. If she saw him at the window, Mia would always lift her sunglasses, smile, and wave.

"Dammit!" Mitch gritted his teeth, grabbed a baseball-shaped stress ball off his cluttered desk, and started squeezing it. Mia was a sweet, loving girl, but he had spoiled her terribly, and when it came to real-life issues and problems, she was clueless. But having his daughter think that he had orchestrated a hostile takeover of Hanover was just about killing him.

Of course that wasn't the case at all. He and Charlie Hanover had grown up together, and what Mitch had really done was bail his old friend out so that the struggling candy company could expand and grab a larger share of the marketplace. Once Hanover Candy recovered, Mitch would allow Charlie to buy him out. Mitch fully intended to make money on the deal, but in the end all would be happy. When Mia had misunderstood his intentions, in a sudden burst of inspiration he had allowed her to think the worst in an effort to get her to wake up and realize that his business dealings could sometimes get tough. Mia had been taking her wealth for granted and he wanted her to do something with her life other than shop. If something happened to him, Mitch wanted to know that his daughter could make it on her own, but she failed to take life seriously. He had tried to reason with her before about this same issue without any luck. She had recently run up some hefty credit card bills, and it was about time that she got a big dose of reality and learned to work on her own.

Mitch squeezed the ball harder and tried not to worry. He had only been trying to get Mia's attention and pound home the point that wealth didn't come easy and sometimes carried a hefty price tag of its own. Granted, he should have cleared the air about his role in the Hanover Candy deal after teaching her a lesson, but he hadn't really expected Mia to immediately stomp out the door in a self-righteous huff. When he was about to hop in his car and roar down the road after her, though, it was Manny the gardener who had laid a gentle hand on his arm and stopped him. In his broken English, Manny had managed to tell Mitch to let her go. Mitch hadn't been convinced until Manny had let him know that the old oil-leaking Camry wouldn't make it too far down the road anyway. But here it was two days later without any word, and Mitch was worried sick.

Mitch did manage a slight smile when he remembered the stubborn set of her chin when he had told her she wouldn't last until Labor Day on her own. She might be spoiled, but like him, Mia could never refuse a challenge. She had done plenty of charity work and always raised more money than the previous chairperson. And she was amazing at throwing parties and events. She entertained his clients with poise, and in truth, if he didn't make amends with her, he was going to miss her in more ways than one. Mia was a lot smarter and much savvier than she gave herself credit for, and she could easily be on his payroll, but he knew that his employees would treat her with kid gloves and he wanted her to find success outside of his company before he would even consider having her work for him. He had tried to explain that to her, but Mia always thought he was simply trying to blow her off and not take her seriously.

"Ah, Mia," Mitch said with a sad shake of his head. He picked up his cell phone and thought about calling her but then refrained. If she were in any real trouble, she would call him, he reasoned, but then he shook his head. "Maybe not." She could be pretty darned stubborn, another trait she had no doubt gotten from him. When he thought of the possibility of her broken down on the side of the road, a cold shot of fear slid down his spine. He wouldn't get a good night's sleep until he knew that Mia was safe. But he also wanted her to experience being on her own and making her way, so instead of calling her he scrolled through his contacts until he came to longtime friend and private detective Dan Tanner. They had known each other since Mitch had hired Dan to find out if his suspicions were right about Clarisse cheating on him. Mitch had used Dan's services a few other times for business and was always satisfied with his work. Mitch clicked on Dan's name and a moment later Dan picked up.

"Hey, Mitch, what's up?"

"Well, I have a job for you."

"Shoot."

Mitch propped his feet up on his desk and explained what had transpired with Mia. "I haven't heard from her. Can you track her down and tail her for a while? Let me know she's safe without her seeing you?"

"You have any idea what direction she was headed?"

Mitch sighed. "None."

"Friends she might be staying with? A boyfriend?"

"She doesn't have a boyfriend, and if she were with friends I would most likely have heard about it. But like Manny said, the old car might not make it too far. She has no credit cards except for my gas card, and last time I checked she hadn't used it."

"But she has a smartphone, I hope?"

"Yeah, the latest and greatest thing out there on the market."

"Good. I should be able to track her phone and catch up to her. She knows me, so I'll send Tate Carpenter. He's a former cop and really good. We'll have a tail on Mia in no time."

Mitch closed his eyes and swallowed. "Thanks, Dan. I

won't be able to get a wink of sleep until I know she's safe."

"I'll get on it right now. Shoot me a recent picture and give me her cell phone number. As long as she has it turned on, we can track her down."

"Great!" Mitch said, and his mood lightened a little bit. He was worried, but he was also curious about what she was doing. Maybe Mia was going to surprise him, but then again she just might show up on his doorstep any minute. As much as he wanted to see her beautiful face and wrap his daughter in a big hug, Mitch also hoped that Mia would actually show him what she was made of . . .

5

No Soup for You

ALTHOUGH HE MANAGED TO HAVE A GOOD NIGHT'S SLEEP, Cam felt a little apprehensive as he walked down the hallway leading to Ty McKenna's office. He knew he hadn't done anything to land him in hot water, but years of being called to the principal's or coach's office to face the music came flooding back to him. Even though he came off as cocksure, in truth Cam's knees had always been knocking whenever he had gotten in trouble. He just never let it show. The potential for losing his position on this team scared Cam much more than he pretended, but then again he never let on about how he felt about a lot of things. It was so much easier to act like a badass who didn't give a rip than to show any kind of true emotion, especially fear.

Because he was always such a valuable player, Cam had often got off with a mere slap on the wrist or even scot-free, but those days were over. He was doing his damnedest to keep on the straight and narrow, and hopefully his past hadn't come back to rear its ugly head. Cam swallowed hard. The past had a mean way of doing that. He just hoped it wasn't now. "Oh, well, here goes nothin'," Cam whispered. After taking a deep breath, he put on a confident face before rapping on the door.

"Come on in."

Cam opened the door. "Hey, Coach, you wanted to see me?"

"Yeah." Ty rolled his head in a circle and then leaned back in his big leather chair. He appeared bone weary as he yawned. "Ah . . . sorry. Baby Ben has been keeping me up. He doesn't seem to know night from day."

"Sorry to hear it."

"Yeah, Jessica has been taking the lion's share of the work, but the little dude is messing with my beauty rest." He chuckled while massaging his temples. "It's amazing how just a few little pounds of person can turn your world upside down," he grumbled, but it was no secret that Ty adored his wife and doted on his infant son. "He better be a hell of a ballplayer, is all I can say."

"I'm betting he will be," Cam commented, but he wanted to bypass the small talk and get straight to the point. "So what can I do for ya, Coach?"

"Well, I was talking to Noah about the roster, and I know first base is your position, being a southpaw, but since you've got some speed we were thinking of having you as backup center fielder. It will make you more versatile, playing some outfield, and let us give Nate Porter some relief from behind the plate during the dog days of summer by putting him over at first base once in a while. Whadaya say about our plan? Thoughts? Suggestions?"

"Hey . . ." Cam shrugged but almost shivered at the cool shot of relief that slid down his spine. "You're the coach."

"But I want your thoughts. Are you comfortable in the outfield?"

"Yeah." Cam nodded slowly, actually liking the idea. "I played some center field in high school, and like you said, it will make me more valuable to get some experience in the outfield at this level. Plus, I want to do what's best for the team," he added, and he wasn't just blowing smoke up Ty's ass, even though it used to be his specialty.

Cam had been an expert at telling coaches—and women—what they wanted to hear.

Ty leaned back in his chair and laced his hands behind his head. "And?"

"And I sure like winning." True, he wanted to be back in the minor leagues playing for a shot at the big show, but in a short period of time he had come to like Ty McKenna, Noah Falcon, and some of his teammates. Playing baseball for the Cricket Creek Cougars wasn't going to be as bad as he had once thought.

"Good to hear it. Look, I know it's my call, but Noah and I really do have your best interests at heart." Ty gave him a tired grin. "Not to mention, the more guys we send up to the minors, the easier it will be to recruit. Everybody wins."

"You gotta like win-win situations."

"It could be that for us all," Ty said as he lowered his feet to the floor. "You know that Noah is from Cricket Creek, right? It's important for this team's continued success since it means revenue for the entire town. Local businesses, especially the shops, inns, and restaurants, will benefit from strong attendance at the ballpark."

"Last season must have gone well. There seems to be growth along Main Street."

"You're right." Ty nodded. "But the first year we were new and exciting. We need to keep filling the seats."

"And you do that by winning."

"Yeah, but sending you guys up is important too. It's exciting for the fans to see the success of the players they come out to watch. We had Logan Lannigan last season, and as far as I can see you're the most talented player we have this year. I want to see you get back where you should be, Cam."

"Thanks. That's my goal."

"You have the drive and the talent. Just keep your nose clean."

"I plan on it."

"It's pretty easy to do here. There's really not much in

the way of trouble. Sully's Tavern can get rowdy at night, but big-ass Pete keeps things under control. So you've got that going for ya."

"I'm so over bar fights."

Ty chuckled. "That's what I like to hear. Well, listen, batting practice is called off because of more damned work being done to the infield. We'll just have a short team meeting instead." He shook his head. "Owen Lawson, our groundskeeper, is a helluva guy but a perfectionist. He's Noah's soon-to-be father-in-law, so I just grin and bear it."

"Noah Falcon is engaged?" Cam remembered that he was a notorious playboy back in his day. He just couldn't picture it.

"Not officially, but it's gonna happen."

"Someone local?"

Ty nodded. "Olivia Lawson, the drama teacher at Cricket Creek High School. They met when they starred in a play together last year. Beautifully written by my stepdaughter, I might add."

Cam frowned. "A local schoolteacher? Dude, Noah used to have supermodels on his arm. What's up with that?"

"Love, my friend. It bites you when you least expect it. Not that Olivia isn't pretty and a sweetheart. Noah is damned lucky to have her."

"I didn't mean anything . . . I'm just sayin'."

"I know. You'll understand someday." He stood up and stretched. "You're getting another shot, kiddo. Don't blow it."

"I won't." If anybody else but Ty McKenna had called him *kiddo*, it would have gotten under his skin, but Triple Threat Ty was one of his childhood heroes, and even at this level Cam felt honored to be on his team. "Count on it."

"Like I said, you've got the skills. The rest is up to you. Okay, I'm gonna sneak home and take a well-deserved nap." Ty yawned. "See you bright and early tomorrow. Don't be late."

"I won't." Cam said and meant it. He had learned early on that being late for practice was a major mistake. Cam followed Ty out of the stadium and into the parking lot. He gave his coach a wave as he headed over to the high-rise condo complex where he and most of the Cougar roster and staff lived. Cam thought that the place was pretty damned sweet. It was a big surprise when he arrived, since he had envisioned much less in the way of accommodations. They also gave the players a big break on the rent as long as they took units on one of the bottom floors that didn't have a river view, and that was perfectly fine with him. For a guy who had grown up doing without, this was more than doable.

Cam opened the door and tossed his baseball cap onto the small dining-area table before heading to the fridge to grab a cold bottle of water. The condos were furnished with the basics for the baseball players, which was good since he wasn't much of a shopper or decorator. All he needed was a sofa, a television, and a bed. The rest was just gravy. Most everyone had roommates to share costs, but because Cam came on late in the preseason, he didn't have one. Cam really didn't mind, though. After a couple of stellar years at the University of Florida, Cam had received a three-hundred-thousand-dollar signing bonus as an early draft choice by the Chicago Cubs. Because of his dirt-poor upbringing, he had saved and invested most of it and could afford to live on his own. Still, he had panicked when he was let go after only three years of minor-league play. Athletes who got into trouble weren't being picked up for new contracts, and despite his ability, no one had been interested in him as a free agent because of the scuffles he had gotten into. Too much bad press had started a no-tolerance trend that cut Cam's career short. But he had the talent and the drive and wasn't about to squander a second chance at living his dream and proving his worth.

Since the weather had warmed up, Cam decided to shuck his jeans in favor of some cargo shorts, a T-shirt, and sandals. Next on the agenda was lunch. He really needed to take a trip to the grocery store for some supplies instead of constantly eating out, but the food at Wine and Diner was just too damned good, and reasonable compared to the city prices he was used to. With that in mind, he slid on his Oakleys, put on his Cougars cap, and headed out the door.

The bright sunshine felt good on Cam's face, and the pungent scent of river water made him want to find time to go fishing. The fish he'd caught as a kid had ended up as dinner, and while he had no desire to clean fish, he did still love to catch and release. Being on the water had a soothing and calming effect that he missed. Cam looked toward the nearby marina and made a mental note to check out the cost of boat rentals later in the day.

Since Wine and Diner was just a few blocks away, he opted to hoof it, but then again walking was nothing new to Cam. As a kid he either had to walk to practice or ride his bike with his battered baseball glove slipped through the handlebars. Cam shook his head at the memory. He damned well knew that if he ever made it big, he was going to help underprivileged kids get the equipment they needed in order to play.

Cam tugged open the door of Wine and Diner and smiled at Bella, the cute little hostess. She was his type of girl . . . gorgeous and kick-ass feisty, but he knew she was in a relationship with Logan Lannigan, who was playing in the minors and from what Cam heard was doing very well. Not that Cam would hit on beautiful Bella anyway. Chicks spelled trouble, and he was going to steer clear of women while he got his shit together. "Hi, Bella, got a booth open?"

"Hey, Cam. I sure do. You missed the lunch rush, so we're pretty wide open."

"Nice."

"Follow me," she said and grabbed a menu.

He tried not to ogle her sweet little tush, which was poured into tight black pants. She was short but put together in an awesome curvy package. Watching her move with sensual grace reminded him just how long it had been since he had been with a woman. *Don't think about it,* Cam warned his sorry-ass self and moved his gaze from her ass to . . . "No way!"

"This booth isn't okay?" Bella asked with a slight frown.

"No . . . it's fine," Cam replied, and he slid onto the leather bench seat and took the menu she offered, but his gaze immediately returned to Mia Money, who was waiting on tables! Well, she was attempting to wait on tables. Strands of her pale blond hair escaped her ponytail and she had a decidedly frazzled look. "You hired her?" Cam looked at Bella with raised eyebrows.

Bella flicked a glance in Mia's direction. "Yeah, she's a little bit flighty but seemed nice enough. Myra wanted to give her shot. Mia's car is in the shop and she doesn't have the cash to have it fixed."

Cam nodded slowly and watched Mia fumble through taking an order from a table of preppy-looking guys wearing designer polo shirts. From the looks of them, they were probably passing through Cricket Creek. "Has she even been trained?"

"Um . . ." Bella rolled her eyes. "Actually she's a fast learner, just like she promised. She already knows the menu inside out and can recommend what wine to go with it."

Cam raised his eyebrows. "At this time of day?"

"Apparently she thinks all meals need wine."

"But?" Cam prompted when Bella rolled her eyes again.

"She gets totally flustered and spills things." Bella leaned forward and said in a low tone, "I think she's much more used to giving orders than taking them."

"Then why'd you put her out on the floor?" Cam watched Mia struggle with a heavy tray of food. It tipped slightly to the side, causing everything to shift, but she quickly compensated and put it down with a clatter. He noticed that her hands shook, and he wanted to go over there and hug her . . . *Wait—hug her?* Cam was not a hugging kind of dude. He shook his head. "Yeah, she's clearly out of her element." But he thought of the beater car and her lack of funds and frowned. Nothing was making sense.

"One of the waitresses was sick, and Mia insisted that she could handle it." Bella flicked another glance in Mia's direction. "Myra decided to let her jump right in."

"How's she been holding up?" Cam asked and tried not to notice how cute she looked in the retro-style uniform. Damn, she was pretty in pink.

"Better than I expected."

"Meaning pretty bad."

"Yeah, I feel sorry for her. She's trying so hard but screws everything up. There have been a couple of YouTube moments."

"I can imagine." Yeah . . . he had quite an imagination where she was concerned.

"She should be over to take your order in a minute if she can ever get that table waited on. Those guys seem to be giving her a tough time."

"Why don't you help her out?"

Bella gave him a curious look but then shrugged. "I offered, but she insisted that she could do it alone. I finally gave up trying. She should do okay now that the big lunch rush is over."

Cam nodded and then remembered her pitiful pile of change. "Where is she staying?" He hated to think of her without someplace safe to live.

"Ohhh . . ." Bella arched an eyebrow. "Sounds like you're concerned, Cam."

"Just curious."

"Right . . ."

"Hey, my only concern right now is baseball," Cam insisted as he took the menu from her.

"Sure it is." Bella pointed to the ceiling. "She's living in the apartment upstairs. Well, I'd better get back to my post." She gave him a wink and then glanced in Mia's direction and shook her head when Mia dropped a handful of straws onto the floor. "See ya at Sully's tonight?"

"Maybe." Cam nodded absently and then concentrated on his menu, but after a few minutes he realized he wasn't reading selections but listening to the asshats bitching at Mia. He ground his teeth in an effort not to get involved. A moment later Mia rushed over to his table. Her eyes widened when she recognized him.

"Oh, hi," she said a bit breathlessly and pushed at a lock of her hair.

"So you're working here?" When she gave him a deadpan look, he grinned. "Okay, stupid question."

"May I get you something to drink?" Her tone was cool and professional but had a nervous edge that made him want to say something reassuring, but he didn't.

"Just water."

"Lemon?"

"No, thanks. I don't like fruit in my drinks."

"Okay, one water coming up." When Mia poised her pencil in front of her pad and licked her lips, a hot stab of longing slid directly south. Damn, the girl looked fine even when she was flustered. "Do you need a minute or are you ready to order?"

I'll have you, popped into Cam's brain and made him shift in his seat. "What's today's special?"

"Pot roast, mashed potatoes, and your choice of one side. You can add a salad for one dollar. One dollar! Can you believe it? Oh, and the glazed carrots are simply divine."

"Sounds good."

"Oh, and may I suggest a nice glass of merlot?"

Cam almost laughed, but she was so sincere that he couldn't make fun of her. "Uh, no, thanks. I think I'll stick with the unfruited water."

"Okay." She frowned. "So does that mean that you want the special?"

"I'm not sure. Bring me a tossed salad to start with. Thousand Island dressing."

"Excellent choice," she said, as if he was dining in a five-star restaurant.

"Thank you," Cam answered in a fake-serious tone. "It was a tough decision."

Mia pressed her lips together. "I can imagine. Jessica makes it from scratch. Well, she makes all of her dressings fresh. I watched her. It was fascinating." She drew out the word and did this little hand-flip thing that looked so out of place with her job that Cam almost chuckled. He had seen the same kind of irritating phony gestures from countless rich women, yet Mia seemed sincere, causing Cam to be . . . *charmed*?

Nah, couldn't be! He was merely amused. And yet . . .

"Oh, I've been telling everyone."

"Telling everyone what?"

"That just about everything here at Wine and Diner is made from scratch with no preservatives. Most of her vegetables are organically grown and many of them purchased locally when in season."

"Good to know." Cam had to hide his grin. Mia Money was cute enough to get big tips even if she sucked at serving.

"I'll be right back with your salad and beverage."

"Thanks." Cam watched her walk away with more interest than he wanted to have in a woman. Not only did he find her as sexy as hell, but he was intrigued as well. Her manicure, flawless skin, and glossy hair screamed *pampering*, and yet here she was waiting tables while her battered old car got repaired. And while she had that air of confidence that came with having wealth, she also had a nervous edge that had Cam wondering just what she was running from.

Cam looked back down at the menu and grinned at the bits and pieces of local folklore and Kentucky recipes peppered throughout the extensive selections. New versions of standard classic diner favorites gave the restaurant fresh appeal without losing the throwback charm. He usually just ordered a burger or the special, but he decided to branch out and try something different today. With that in mind he studied the extensive choices.

"Wow." Cam felt his heart lurch when he saw Stone Soup listed on the menu along with a sidebar explaining the timeless fable. His overworked mother had often been too tired to pay much attention to Cam, but once in a while she read a bedtime story to him before he went to sleep. A battered book of fables had been his favorite, and seeing Stone Soup sent an unexpected ache of sadness straight to his heart. His mother would sometimes end the story by ruffling his hair and placing a quick kiss on top of his head. That simple gesture was as close as he ever felt to being loved.

Cam sighed at the memory. Other than late at night, his mother was mostly absent, working no-end double shifts that paid very little but required lots of hours. Fatigue often made her testy, causing Cam to stay out of her way as often as he could. He had played lots of sandlot baseball, since his mother couldn't afford a real uniform on a Little League team, and yet he attributed his real love of the game to that experience versus squabbling parents and only-playing-to-win coaches.

"Here's your water and your salad."

Cam looked up in surprise. "Oh . . . thanks." He had been so engrossed in his thoughts that he'd failed to see Mia approach his table. She seemed a little flushed, and when she gave the rowdy group of guys a nervous glance, he frowned. "Are those dudes getting out of line?"

"They're just a bunch of arrogant . . ." She paused and got a thoughtful look on her face before rolling her eyes and adding, "Ass clowns!"

Cam arched one eyebrow. "Ass clowns?" Even though Cam found her assessment of the *ass clowns* amusing, he wasn't convinced that they weren't bothering her, but he firmly reminded himself not to get involved. Odd, but after first meeting Mia, Cam would have thought that these guys were the type she would have hung around with, and yet she seemed annoyed. "Really?" He observed her expression closely, but she scrunched up her cute little nose and nodded.

"Absolutely." Mia gave him a slight grin, but he thought it looked a little bit forced. "Have you decided on your entrée?"

"I think I'll have a bowl of Stone Soup."

"That's all? Soup and salad?"

"You might be able to convince me to have dessert."

"I recommend the apple crisp. Myra made some early this morning. The kitchen smelled so amazing that I was afraid that simply inhaling would put on weight."

Cam was about to tell her that she didn't have anything to worry about on that score, but one of the ass clowns was flagging her down.

"Hey, this Coke is diet," he complained and shoved the glass in her direction.

"I'm sorry, I thought you asked for diet."

"Well, you're wrong again. And this ketchup bottle is empty." He shoved it at her as well.

"I'll get you another one."

"Hurry up. We've got places to be."

"I will."

When Cam noticed a little quaver in her voice, he stabbed his fork into a cherry tomato with more force than needed.

"And you forgot the extra pickle on my burger."

"Okay."

"And how about some hot sauce, baby," one of them said in a smarmy tone that set Cam's teeth on edge.

"Coming right up," Mia said and turned on her heel.

"You'd better hurry or you'll get stiffed. But then again, maybe you'd like that."

Mia stopped in her tracks and whipped around so fast that Diet Coke sloshed over the rim of the glass. "That's enough!"

"Really?"

"Yes. This is my first day on the job, but I have had enough of you!" Color was high in her cheeks, but she stood her ground. Cam held his breath, hoping the ass-hats would shut up.

"Oh, baby, it's never enough. Come sit on my lap and find out." He put his hand suggestively on his crotch.

Well . . . damn! Cam felt anger thump against the inside of his chest and barely refrained from springing to his feet. "Hey, treat her with respect or leave."

"Fuck off, dude."

"I mean it," Cam warned in a calm tone, but his heart was pounding. He simply could not sit back and listen to them any longer, but the last thing he needed was a damned fight. He didn't want to get injured or land his ass in trouble! Plus, there were three of them and one of him . . . not that it had stopped him before. Cam held his breath and hoped they would shut the hell up.

"Cam, it's okay," Mia said in a worried tone. "I think they've been drinking," she added in a stage whisper.

"We have," the streaky blond one said. "And we're just getting started. My boat is docked at the marina. Wanna go out with us, babe? I'd love to see you in a bikini." He curved his palms suggestively and licked his top lip.

"That's it," Cam growled and pushed to his feet. He sure wished Myra or Bella would come forward to toss them out on their ears, but neither of them was around and the diner was mostly empty. *I'm on my own* ran through his head, but wasn't that the way it had been all his life?

"I thought I told you to fuck off," the streaky blonde sneered. "Unless you want your ass kicked."

"Get the hell out of here, pretty boy." Cam pointed to the door, and all three actually scooted back from the table. When they stood up, Cam felt a familiar rush of adrenaline. While they might have him in numbers, Cam was big and buff and had spent a lifetime learning how to be intimidating. He flexed biceps encircled with barbed-wire tattoos and sent them the patented scowl he used to rattle pitchers. He gave Mia a meaningful glance, hoping she would go find Myra or some big burly line cook, but she stood there wide-eyed and rooted to the spot, clutching the Diet Coke in one hand and the empty ketchup bottle in the other. He wasn't about to actually ask her to go for help, and so he planted his feet and got ready.

"Let's bounce," the tall one said as he tossed a couple of twenties on the table. When his pretty-boy posse nodded in agreement, Cam felt his tense muscles relax a fraction. It appeared that he was going to avoid a fight after all. Wow . . . that would be a first!

6

Bloom Where You Are Planted

GO FOR HELP SLAMMED INTO MIA'S BRAIN, BUT HER FEET felt glued to the floor, and although her lips moved, her vocal cords failed to respond. Hopefully they would just . . . leave. Mia had never been exposed to anything like this before, and she suddenly had empathy for the women in the service business who had to put up with this kind of sexist crap. No one deserved to be treated like this! She narrowed her eyes at them, and the heat of anger began to thaw out the cold, hard ball of fear lodged in her throat.

To think that just a few days ago she had been lounging poolside chatting with her friends about going to Paris for the weekend to shop for clothes. Now all she longed for were some sensible shoes meant for standing all day long. Mia suddenly thought about all of the people who bent over backward each and every day to make her life cushy and felt a sharp stab of guilt. Until today she couldn't remember the last time she had broken a sweat.

Mia held her breath while watching the little drama unfold. Surely those guys weren't going to mess with Cam. It suddenly occurred to her that she knew the type all too well—all mouth and money—and it made her feel a little queasy. Were these the types of people that she hung out with? The thought made her clutch the ketchup so hard that the bottle deflated, causing the top to shoot off with a loud pop. That noise drew Cam's attention, giving the streaky-haired jerk the opportunity to lunge forward and take a swing at Cam's face. Mia saw it coming and with a little squeal she tossed the Diet Coke in his tanned face . . .

Oh, make that his tanned, stunned face.

"You little bitch!" He yelped and, blinking furiously, started swinging wildly, connecting with nothing but air. Cam dodged his flailing fists, but when his friends suddenly jumped into the fray, it was another story. One of them caught Cam with an uppercut to the chin, and the tall one clipped his shoulder, making Cam stumble backward and bump into a table. Meanwhile, Coke in the Face recovered and connected with Cam's midsection.

Mia saw red and with a little squeal threw the ketchup bottle at Coke in the Face. It connected with his head with a not surprising hollow thump, sending him into anger overload. He actually swung at *her* . . . big mistake, because this turned Cam into a fighting machine. He swatted the three of them away like pesky flies, but drunken idiots that they were, they kept leaping back into the fray, bumping into each other in their efforts to throttle Cam. Mia watched wide-eyed at Cam's ability to keep them at bay without really getting winded. Oh, but then she spotted the tall one grab a big sugar dispenser and heft it over his head. When he lunged at Cam, Mia let out a scream of warning and jumped onto his back.

"You . . . you jerk. Put that down!" She started swatting at the sugar dispenser from behind, but he held it just out of her reach. He swirled in a circle in an effort to shake her, but Pilates had made her legs strong. "Put that down!" She hung on and started batting at his head.

"Get off me, you crazy little bitch!"

"Don't call me that!" With sudden inspiration she grabbed his ears and yanked hard and was rewarded with an oath. He tried his best to dislodge her, but she hung on to his ears until he was pleading with her to stop. "Really, who's the little bitch now?" Mia challenged, even though she had never uttered such a thing in her entire life. "Huh?" It felt empowering to fend for herself, and so she tugged harder, hoping he'd look like Dopey after she was done with him. "Say it!" she demanded.

"Ouch! Say what?" He bucked and spun like a big old bull, but Mia held on tightly.

"Say that you're . . . whoa . . . sorry!"

"What in the world is goin' on in here?" Myra shouted above the pandemonium.

Mia's attention was diverted by Myra's angry hands-on-hips stance, and Mia unfortunately loosened her grip just as he shook her sideways. "Oh nooooo!" Mia went flying through the air in what could have been a pretty cool twirling dance move, except there was no one to catch her. Somehow the protect-yourself-from-dying part of her brain sounded the red alert and she had the sense to tuck and roll to the ground. She landed with a resounding smack on her backside and spun in a circle three total times before coming to a slow-motion stop at the rubber soles of Myra Robinson.

Coke in the Face, Tall Guy, and the other dude took the opportunity to bolt out the door. "Hey, get back here!" Mia shouted, but they ran like the hounds of hell were after them.

"Mia?" Myra asked in a low and not at all happy tone. "Answer my question!"

Mia swallowed hard and slowly raised her gaze to her employer of one single day. "They started it," she replied in a small voice. "Those guys were being really mean."

"Mean . . ." Myra gave her a stern stare.

"Yes." Her answer sounded lame and childish even though it was the truth. "Weren't they?" She looked over to Cam for help.

"Yeah," he agreed. When he reached down and offered his hand, she grasped it firmly. After he tugged her to her feet, she noticed with a frown that his bottom lip was swollen and bleeding.

"Oh my gosh! Cam!" Mia grabbed some napkins and handed them to him. "Are you okay?"

"I'll live." He gingerly dabbed at his lip.

"Those jerks!" she said darkly before turning around to face the music.

"Are you gonna quit your pussyfootin' around and tell me just what exactly happened here, Mia?" Myra wanted to know. The hands on the hips remained, as did the arched eyebrow.

Mia opened her mouth, but before she could explain her innocence . . . well, not her innocence exactly but the reason she had been hanging on to the back of a customer attempting to stretch his ears, the front door swung open. To Mia's dismay a police officer the size of a refrigerator came lumbering into the restaurant. And he wasn't smiling.

Oh boy . . . She flicked Cam a glance, and he didn't look happy either.

"Hey there, Bo Mason." Myra greeted him with a tight smile. Mia wondered if that was a good or bad sign.

"Myra, there was really no need to call the police." Mia felt her heartbeat accelerate and she gave the rotund policeman a once-over. Handcuffs dangled from his belt and he had a mean-looking gun poking out of the holster. "I can explain." Mia swallowed hard and imagined a cold, damp cell with dinner on a metal tray and a stinky toilet exposed to the view of the rest of the scary inmates. She glanced at the door, thinking she should run like the wind. Her shoes, however, were not made for waitressing, or running from the law, and so she dismissed that idea almost immediately. At least for now.

Plus, being a fugitive from the law after two days away from home? Oh boy, her father would have a field day with that one. She turned her questioning gaze back to Myra.

"I didn't call anyone." Myra raised her palms in the air. "Bo, what brings you here?"

Please say you're coming in for a late lunch! Mia pressed her lips together and wondered if she should offer him a menu to distract him.

"Got a frantic phone call that some customers were being assaulted by a blond waitress named Mia." He paused and gave Mia's temporary name tag a pointed look and then turned his attention to Cam. "And a big dude with a bad attitude." Bo hitched his pants up and blew out a big sigh. "Just so you know, I am the town sheriff, not the po-leeece," he announced with an air of importance. "I am an elected official and have the best interests of this town right here." He patted his chest. "So now, just what do ya'll have to say for yerselves, I wanna know?"

"They started it!" Mia sputtered. She looked at Cam and hoped he would step in and take over, but he gave her a discreet negative shake of his head and so she took the hint and shut her mouth.

"Started what, now?" Bo whipped out a pad and pencil. He licked the tip and stood there with one bushy eyebrow cocked and his pencil poised and ready. Mia hadn't had any actual run-ins with the law unless you counted a parking ticket, but she thought back to television crime shows and knew she had the right to remain silent, and so she did. "You gonna answer me, girlie?" Bo boomed and gave her a thunderous stare that made a shiver slide down her spine.

"They were . . . were harassing me!"

"Harassing you?" Bo scribbled something on his pad and then looked at her expectantly.

"Yes!"

"How so?"

"They were asking me for . . . stuff!"

"Well, you are a waitress, aren't you?"

"Yes, but . . ."

"Then it's your job, right?"

"Yes, but . . ."

"And did you throw a soft drink in the customer's face?"

"Yes, but . . ."

"And a ketchup bottle directly at his head?"

Mia swallowed. This wasn't going well.

"Mia?" Myra angled her head in question.

Mia glanced at Cam for help.

"They were giving her a very hard time," Cam spoke up, but there was a tired tone to his voice, almost like he had given up trying to defend himself.

"Giving her a hard time by asking her for . . . stuff?" Sheriff Bo's sarcastic tone got under Mia's skin. "Like what stuff?"

"Hot sauce!" Mia replied and wanted to elaborate, but her face felt as if it were on fire.

"So . . . ?" Sheriff Bo prompted.

Mia leaned forward. "In a smarmy, suggestive way, and then said I would be . . . be . . . *stiffed*!"

The other bushy eyebrow rose and he said, "As in no tip for poor service?"

Myra gave her a sympathetic look, not unlike many looks she had gotten from people who thought she was nothing more than a pretty face without a brain. "Honey, you do know what that means, right?"

"Yes, but—"

"And then you got really angry and tossed the Coke in his face?" The sheriff asked.

"If you let me answer, I'll explain!"

"Don't you give me any sass, girlie."

"I know my rights!" Mia said, even though she had no clue.

"Really now?" The sheriff started scribbling on his pad, making her nervous.

"Yes!" Mia pressed her lips together and wondered if this was when she was supposed to say that she would like to call her lawyer. But whom would she call and what would she use for money? Contacting her father popped into her mind. He would get her out of this sticky situation in nothing flat. Money had a way of doing that. But then she thought of those arrogant jerks, who were likely roaring away on their big boat, laughing their butts off while knowing exactly what was happening. An *innocent* little waitress was getting grilled by the law, and an *innocent* bystander was taking the heat for their bad behavior! It wasn't right!

"Mia?" Myra demanded in a stern tone.

Mia looked to Cam once more for help. He had been man enough to stand up for her, so why was he backing off now?

He glanced away as if gathering his thoughts and then said, "They were rude and obnoxious."

"And just who are you anyway?" the sheriff wanted to know.

"Cameron Patrick. I play for the Cricket Creek Cougars."

"And you think your celebrity status gives you license to rough up customers?"

"He was the one roughed up!" Mia pointed to Cam's swollen lip. She looked at Myra, who had seemed like such a cool lady, and hoped for some support. "Myra, he was defending me!"

"Were there any witnesses?" Myra asked in a more gentle tone. "Bella maybe?"

Mia shook her head sadly. "I don't think so. The lunch rush was over. Whoever was here had all left, and I think Bella took a break."

"Probably ran them out," the sheriff commented. "Myra, just how much do you know about this here girl?"

Mia's eyes widened at her employer.

"Mia, I warned you that you would be fired if you caused any commotion."

"I know, but . . ."

"You should have come to me if those boys were harassing you."

"I was trying to handle things myself instead of running to you for help. And then it all happened so fast. Are you really going to fire me?" Mia swallowed back tears. Fired after one day? She was such a loser! "Myra, they were really being terrible to me!"

"Did they touch you?" the pesky sheriff asked.

"No, but—"

"Physically threaten you?"

"Not at first, but—"

"Oh, then after you threw the ketchup bottle and jumped on someone's back?"

"He was going to assault Cam!"

"With what?" the sheriff asked. "Did he have a weapon?"

"A sugar dispenser!"

"So he was going to sweeten your boyfriend to death?" The sheriff stopped writing and snickered at his lame joke.

"Bo, that was uncalled for," Myra warned.

"Aw, come on, Myra. Don't ya see what was goin' on here? Those boys were flirtin' with his little girlfriend here and he got all fired up." He pointed his pencil at Cam.

"You weren't here and that's not what happened," Cam responded tightly.

"Boy, don't you go giving me any lip." Bo planted his big-booted feet and lifted his double chin. "I won't stand for it."

"What you should be standing for is her." Cam pointed at Mia. "She was being harassed by those assholes. I did what any man would have done."

"Started a fight?"

"I told them to treat her with respect. You're standing here giving us a hard time when the real culprits are laughing their asses off."

"Boy, I'm warning you . . ."

"Warning me not to tell the truth? Is that against the law?"

"Don't go telling me how to do my job." He hitched his pants up even higher and poked a finger into Cam's chest.

Cam narrowed his eyes at the stubby finger. "Somebody should."

"You're treading into dangerous territory," the sheriff warned.

Cam damn well knew it, but the condescending tone and the jabbing finger sent him back to a dark place where he was treated with disdain and disrespect each and every day. He somehow remained silent, even though he was seething on the inside.

"That's right, *boy*, just keep that piehole of yours shut," he sneered, and to his credit, Cam did, but then the sheriff had to go and shove him with that damned finger once again, harder this time.

"Keep your hands off me."

"You trying to tell me how to do my job again?" Bo narrowed his eyes.

"Bo!" Myra pleaded. "I've got this under control. You don't have to go any further."

"Just keeping the peace, Myra." Bo looked back at Cam. "And making my point," he added and gave Cam one last hard jab of warning . . .

And Cam shoved back.

"That was a mistake, boy." He unhooked the handcuffs. "I'm taking you in."

"What?" Mia sputtered. "Are you insane?"

"Girlie, one more word outta you, and I'm hauling you in too."

"Bo, this isn't necessary," Myra protested more firmly, but the sheriff ignored her and slapped the cuffs onto Cam's wrists. When Cam winced, Mia wanted to jump on the sheriff's back and pull his ears too.

"These baseball players think they can do whatever they please, starting with Noah Falcon. He isn't all he's cracked up to be, and this town treats him like a king. I was a much better ballplayer back in high school than he'd ever dreamed of being. He just got lucky."

"Right . . ." Myra rolled her eyes, but Bo failed to notice.

"Damned straight. Don't know what Olivia Lawson sees in him neither."

"Yeah, when she could have had you," Myra said in a deadpan tone that would have had Mia grinning, but seeing Cam wearing handcuffs took the joy out of Myra's sarcasm. "Come on, Bo, let Cam go."

Bo pursed his lips. "No can do. Gotta send a message to Mr. Noah Falcon and his bad-news baseball players." He puffed out his chest. "Gotta do what I was elected to do," he boasted and shoved Cam toward the front door.

"Stop! You can't do this to him!" Mia protested and got a glare in return.

"Myra, get this here girl under control or she's coming in with me too."

"Mia, it's okay," Cam assured her, but there was a sad look in his eyes that tugged at her heart. And this was her fault!

"Keep going," the sheriff said and gave Cam a hard shove out the door.

Mia whirled around and raised her hands into the air. "Myra, what are we going to do? Cam was telling the truth! You believe me, don't you?"

"*We* aren't going to do anything. You got yourself into this mess, missy. You'll just have to go down there and bail his cute ass out of jail."

"But . . . but I'm broke!"

Myra sighed. "Look, I'll give you an advance against . . . well, hell, I'm not paying you wages."

"Loan me the money and I'll pay you back."

"Oh, like I haven't heard that one before." Myra closed her eyes and inhaled a deep breath. "Okay . . ."

"Thank you!" Mia did a little jig. "Oh, and I guess this means you haven't fired me?"

"Not yet. But you're on thin ice."

"You won't regret it."

"Heard that one a million times too . . . ," she said but

then grinned. "Mia Money, do you always cause this much commotion?"

"Pretty much . . . but it's never on purpose!"

"Well, at least you're honest." Myra flipped her braid over her shoulder. "Come on, let's get you some cash to bail your ballplayer out of jail. I don't blame ya. He sure has a nice butt."

"He's not *my* baseball player." Although she had noticed Cam's very nice butt.

Myra paused in her tracks and gave Mia a grin. "Yeah, well, the summer has just begun and I have a feeling the two of you are gonna heat things up around here."

"Myra, I'm waiting for my car to get fixed. I'm not settling down in Cricket Creek."

"Oh yeah, I've heard that one too. Now, believe me, I think that you should bloom where you are planted, but this place grows on a person."

"I can see why." Mia laughed as she followed Myra down the narrow hallway. She hadn't felt this alive and energized in a long time. Perhaps she was . . . blooming.

7

Something to Talk About

NICOLINA DIAMANTE SCOOTED THE WIDE STRAP OF HER laptop satchel higher onto her shoulder and watched a big, beefy sheriff exit Wine and Diner while shoving a handsome young handcuffed man toward a squad car parked at the corner. Handcuffs on a patron from Wine and Diner? A cold shot of fear for her daughter slid down Nicolina's spine, and she hurried toward the entrance, anxious to know what had transpired. But when she reached for the handle of the front door, curiosity had her glancing over her shoulder. She frowned when the sheriff roughly pushed the young man toward the backseat hard enough for him to clip his shoulder on the side of the car.

When the kid grunted and fell onto the seat, the sheriff chuckled. "Sure hope you didn't bruise your throwing arm, hotshot," he sneered before slamming the door.

Nicolina had no idea what the kid had done, but she despised mistreatment of anybody and she felt the hair on the back of her neck stand up. When she narrowed her gaze at the sheriff, he must have felt the heat of her disapproval boring into his back because he turned around to catch her glaring at him. The smarmy grin he gave her made her stomach churn, but she'd lived in the city long enough to know not to show fear or intimidation. With a lift of her chin, she gave him a level look in return. The man had the nerve to tip his cap at her before giving her a rude once-over that made Nicolina fume, but before she shouted something she would regret—and she had been known to do so—Nicolina turned and yanked the door open just as a lovely young woman hurried out the door.

Nicolina frowned. Although she was still fairly new to Cricket Creek, she thought she knew all of the waitresses at Wine and Diner, but the blonde didn't ring a bell. Then Nicolina paused and nibbled on her bottom lip. It was just a passing glance, but something about the girl felt familiar and tugged at her memory. When nothing surfaced, she sighed. It seemed that the older she got, the less she remembered. "Damned menopause," she mumbled as she walked across the restaurant.

Because there was always a lull in the late afternoon, Nicolina usually slipped into a booth for an extended coffee break with Bella before the evening rush, but today she hurried up to the counter and waved Myra over. "Hey, what's going on? I just saw a young man being hauled away by the police, and none too gently, I might add. Was somebody arrested in here today?"

Myra rolled her eyes and nodded slowly. "Yep, sure was."

"Oh my God, were you robbed? Where's Bella?" Nicolina's legs suddenly felt like noodles and she had to sit down on a stool. She put her laptop on the counter and shot Myra a look of concern.

"Don't worry." Myra reached over and patted Nicolina's hand. "Bella was in the back playing with baby Ben while Jessica made dinner rolls, but I think your daughter's talking on the phone with Logan right about now. Do you want me to round her up?"

Relief washed over her. "No, I was just concerned that something bad had gone down," Nicolina confessed while Myra poured her a steaming cup of her usual blend of half decaf and half regular coffee. After adding a splash of cream, she looked at Myra questioningly. "So what did happen?" she asked, but before Myra could answer, Bella came bounding into the dining room.

"Oh my God!" Bella shouted. "I missed it! Did Cam really get arrested? Did Mia actually jump on some dude's back? Hi, Mom! Oh damn, I was talking to Logan and missed all the good stuff."

"None of it was good," Myra pointed out.

"Are you kidding? This is the most excitement we've had here since . . . well, since Mia arrived and caused the food riot. People are still talking!"

"Food riot?" Nicolina asked. "I'm the one who missed everything. Why is that?"

"Because you come in here during the dead hours, Mom. You have to get out of that store of yours more often. I know you're busy getting the inventory ready to open, but still, how much jewelry can you design?"

"Lots!" Nicolina felt her cheeks grow warm. What her daughter didn't know was that it was visits from Mitch Monroe that were taking up most of her spare time. Not that she minded. The man was an amazing lover. "Now tell me about this food riot," she said, trying to change the subject.

"There wasn't a food riot. Merely a little . . . accident." Myra poured two more cups of coffee and leaned her hip against the counter.

Nicolina took a sip of her coffee. "Caused by that blonde . . . Wait, what did you say her name was?"

"Mia," Myra answered.

"No . . . really?" Oh boy, was she right? Mia was Mitch's daughter's name. But what would Mia be doing in Cricket Creek waiting tables? "What is her last name?"

"Money," Bella replied. "Why, do you know her, Mom?"

Nicolina almost said, *Maybe*, but then hesitated. "I'm not sure." She had to talk to Mitch first. He wanted his silent partnership in the Cricket Creek baseball team to remain private for business reasons, and although Nicolina had started seeing Mitch while still living in Chicago, they had decided to keep their budding relationship to themselves. Well, *she* had decided to keep it on the down low, even though Nicolina rarely kept anything from Bella and felt a little guilty doing so now.

"Mom?" Bella gave her a questioning frown. "Are you okay?"

"Oh . . ." Nicolina tapped her fingernail against the thick white mug and wondered what to do. "Yes, I just have a lot on my mind, and then when I saw that sheriff shoving that boy into the squad car, my heart just about stopped."

"Okay," Bella replied but gave her a look that said that she wasn't quite buying it. "That sheriff is such a jerk. He wants special treatment whenever he comes in here, and it totally ticks me off," she said and then looked at Myra. "I'm sorry, but I treat everyone the same way. That's what I did at Chicago Blue, and I do the very same thing here at Wine and Diner. I don't care if you are a cop or a movie star."

"And you should be that way," Myra assured her with a nod that made her hoop earrings swing back and forth. "Bo has had a stick up his ass where Noah Falcon is concerned since high school. Noah was a star and Bo rode the bench. He talks trash about Noah as much as he possibly can. Put up a big fight when the WELCOME TO CRICKET CREEK, HOME OF NOAH FALCON sign was erected. And when Ty McKenna moved here from Chicago, Bo became even worse. He hates being upstaged by anyone, especially athletes." She shook her head. "He loves to pull over Cricket Creek baseball players. Has it in for the whole doggone team."

"Well, that's just plain silly," Nicolina commented. "The baseball complex brought this town back to life, didn't it?"

"Damn sure did." Myra slapped her thigh. "And the strip mall where your shop is going in down by the river is going to bring us even more business. The high-rise condos are finally filling up. Yes, times are changing—and for the better." Myra smiled. "For the first time in a long while we have people moving here rather than moving away." She gave Nicolina a wink. "We especially love Chicago transplants."

"Mom, speaking of Chicago, have you seen Mitch lately?"

"Oh, here and there," Nicolina answered vaguely.

"So he's come to see you here in Cricket Creek? How come I didn't know?"

Nicolina raised one shoulder. "He's come here for business reasons, Bella. You know he is a partner in the strip mall and has been giving me *business* advice."

"Are you talking about that silver fox who has been in here a few times?" Myra fanned her face. "Woo-wee . . . that man is fine. Isn't he some sorta big shot in Chicago?"

"I . . . yes," Nicolina answered and then stared down at her mug.

"Oh . . ." Myra's eyes widened. "You two got something going on?"

"He's giving me business advice on running Designs by Diamante." It was true. Mitch had been invaluable to her and had patiently answered hundreds of questions both big and small. But Nicolina had also kept her heart guarded since moving to Cricket Creek to open her jewelry store. In truth, she had thought that her relationship with Mitch would end when she relocated, but she had forgotten that his ability to fly into town on his company jet made the distance between them shrink.

"Where have you two been hiding?" Myra prompted.

"Yeah, Mom." Bella narrowed her eyes and waited.

"Bella, you've been busy as hostess here and traveling all over creation to see Logan play ball. Not to mention all of the online publicity you've been doing for the shop." She sliced a hand through the air. "And we haven't been hiding. We've been *working*. Mitch has other interests here besides me," she added but then clamped her mouth shut once more before she revealed too much.

"Right . . . ," Myra said with a slow nod.

"I'm just way too busy for a relationship anyway."

"If you say so," Bella replied but gave her mother a level look that indicated she wasn't really buying it.

"That being said, Mitch has been very helpful. As a friend, that is," Nicolina insisted. "You know, Bella, a business acquaintance."

Bella rolled her eyes. "You do realize that you're protesting way too much. How often has he been here?"

Nicolina shrugged. "It varies." At first it had been once a week, but the visits had become more frequent . . . and more passionate. She hoped her voice had an airy tone, but when an image of Mitch popped into her head, she felt heat in her cheeks once more.

"Meaning more than you're willing to admit?" Bella asked.

Bella had been furious when Nicolina had divulged last summer that she felt out of her league with Mitch Monroe. It was still true, but she had underlying reasons that neither Mitch nor Bella understood. Mitch had made his growing feelings for her apparent, but Nicolina wasn't ready to let down her guard. Nicolina knew why she wasn't ready and averted her gaze from her daughter's sudden scrutiny. Mitchell Monroe was charming, funny, and kind and turned her to putty in his hands with a simple kiss . . . but, well, call her crazy, but she dearly wished he was just a regular guy instead of a multimillionaire.

She cleared her throat and decided to turn the subject back to the arrest. "So tell me what happened here earlier. Who was that boy and why was he arrested? And was Mia involved?"

"Nicolina, is there something I should know about Mia? You mentioned that you thought you might know her. Do you?" Myra asked.

"Oh . . ." Nicolina wasn't sure if it was really Mia Monroe, and so she merely shrugged. "I was probably mistaken. I'm guessing she isn't from around here."

"Her car broke down and she was in a tight spot, so I hired her. But I don't want any trouble here and I damned well let her know that," Myra persisted.

"Her car broke down? What kind was it?"

Myra lifted one shoulder and glanced at Bella for help.

"Old . . . a Toyota, I think."

"Oh." Nicolina took a thoughtful sip of coffee. Mitch's daughter driving an old beat-up car? Not on your life. He talked about Mia as much as she talked about Bella, and it was apparent that he was protective of his daughter. Mitch wouldn't allow her to drive an unreliable vehicle. And Nicolina knew that Mia still lived at home. The first person she would have called if she'd gotten in some sort of trouble would have been her father. "Oh . . . I just caught a fleeting glance of her. I must have been mistaken." She hoped that she was right. If Mia Monroe was waitressing at Wine and Diner and driving a beat-up car, something wasn't right. As soon as she left the diner she was going to call Mitch and find out if there was anything strange going on with his daughter. "So tell me what went down with the arrest," Nicolina said. If the girl really was Mia Monroe, she wanted to have as much information for Mitch as possible.

"Yeah," Bella said and sat down on a stool next to Nicolina. "I want the details too! Man alive, Mia sure has stirred things up here the past couple of days. I wonder what she will do next?"

8

Spring Fever

NOT HAVING A CAR REALLY SUCKED, MIA THOUGHT AS SHE hoofed it down Main Street to the police station. Myra had given her directions, and unlike in Chicago, just about everything in Cricket Creek was within reasonable walking distance. Still, she was in a hurry and a car would have been nice right about now . . . and of course flagging a passing cab wasn't an option. Adding to her discomfort, the sky had clouded over, leaving a definite nip in the late spring air. By the time she arrived at her destination, Mia was shivering and her tired feet ached.

"Okay," Mia whispered as she paused for a second to catch her breath and get her bearings, "now where do I go?" The courthouse was a stately old brick building with a white domed roof in the center, reminding Mia of the courthouse in the movie *To Kill a Mockingbird*. Mia was a big fan of classic movies and she suddenly felt as if she were stepping into the past. A giant oak tree sprouting tender green leaves graced the side yard, and a row of deep red petunias lined the sidewalk. Two large planters chock-full of flowers perched on both sides of the front porch, and a rustic grapevine wreath decorated the front door. Even in her rush, the homespun beauty wasn't lost on Mia.

Myra had instructed Mia to go in the double doors in a building to the left, where the police station was located. As Mia had imagined, it was small but it was a police station nonetheless, and entering made her feel a bit nervous. Still, she took a deep breath and pushed the heavy door open. After glancing around, she walked up to the desk with an air of what she hoped was confidence, even though she didn't have a clue as to how to spring someone from the slammer.

An older woman with a perky salt-and-pepper pageboy cut smiled at Mia, putting her a little bit at ease. "May I help you?"

Mia glanced at the nameplate on the desk. "Nancy, I'm here to bail someone out," Mia explained.

"Name?"

"Mia Mon . . . Money."

"Mia Money?" she asked uncertainly.

"Yes," Mia replied firmly. "Mia Money . . . no relation to Eddie."

Nancy frowned. "When was Mia Money arrested?"

"What? Oh . . . no, that's *my* name."

Nancy chuckled. "Well, Miss Money no relation to Eddie, who are you here to bail out?"

"Oh, um . . . Cam . . . Cameron . . ." What was his last name?

"Cam Cameron?"

"Cameron is his first name."

"Last name?" she asked with a hint of amusement.

Mia felt heat creep into her cheeks but then used her father's method of slyly sliding right past something he didn't know. "He was brought in just a little while ago."

Nancy slipped on her reading glasses and clicked away on her keyboard. "Cameron Patrick?"

"Yes." Mia took a chance and nodded. After all, how many Camerons could have been arrested in Cricket Creek?

Nancy slipped her glasses off and let them dangle from a gold chain around her neck. "Bail has just been posted at two hundred and fifty dollars. We only take cash or a money order."

"Not a problem." Mia slipped her purse from her shoulder and reached inside for the cash that Myra had loaned to her.

After taking the money, Nancy said, "It will take a little while for the paperwork. As soon as I finish I'll call back to the holding cell to release Cameron."

"Thanks," Mia said and tried not to wince at the term *holding cell.* She had a mental vision of someplace damp, dirty, and full of spiders. She barely suppressed a shudder. Cam was in jail because he'd come to her defense, and it made her feel terribly guilty. "Would you mind letting him out soon? We have, uh, dinner reservations."

"Reservations, huh?"

Mia nodded firmly. "And they were so very hard to get," Mia added, hoping that she didn't have to come up with a restaurant name. The only place other than Wine and Diner she knew of was Sully's, and reservations at a bar and grill probably weren't necessary.

Nancy arched an eyebrow and looked as if she were suppressing a grin. "I just bet reservations were hard to get here in Cricket Creek. Special occasion?"

Mia swallowed hard. She hated lying. "Um, our anniversary." She now understood how one fabrication quickly led to another.

"Aw, well, now, sugar, I'll do my best. You can have a seat over there." Nancy pointed to a wooden bench against the far wall. "Hopefully it won't take too long to spring your boyfriend."

"Thank you." Mia nodded but then leaned in a little closer. "Cam's actually innocent of any real wrongdoing, you know," Mia said but kept her serious tone low in case the big, mean sheriff was anywhere nearby.

"I'm sure," Nancy whispered back, but Mia didn't think she was taking her seriously. Unfortunately she got that a lot.

After glancing left and right, Mia added, "No, really,

Cam was actually a hero. He came to my rescue like a true gentleman." She placed one hand to her chest. "Well, you know, except for the little . . . scuffle."

"That was very sweet of your man to get into trouble on your behalf," Nancy said with a bit of a wistful sigh and glanced down at a romance novel on her desk. "Everyone deserves a hero. Somebody to stick up for them. Care. Kiss . . . wake up to in the morning. Okay, I'd better stop."

"I know what you're saying," Mia agreed automatically, but she then realized it was true. She hoped that gaining Nancy's sympathy would speed up the process.

"Is he your husband or boyfriend?"

Mia noticed the lack of a wedding ring on Nancy's left hand and felt a pang of sadness. "We're not married . . . you know, yet. We're celebrating . . . uh, the day we met."

"Oh, how adorable! Yeah, well, if he's a keeper, y'all better hang on tight. All the good ones are already taken or, you know . . ." She extended her hand forward and tilted it back and forth.

Mia frowned for a second, but then it dawned on her what Nancy was getting at. "You mean gay?"

"Uh-huh." Nancy nodded slowly and sighed as if from personal experience. "I do mean gay." She sighed again. "Some gentlemen prefer blondes and some gentlemen prefer . . . other gentlemen."

"So true," Mia said with a serious nod, but then Nancy laughed.

"Oh, you were kidding!" Mia was often the last one to get the joke.

Nancy shook her head. "No, honey, I sure do wish, but I can laugh about it now. He was a trucker of all things . . . Who knew?"

"Well, I'm sure your soul mate is still out there," Mia assured her with a bit of a wary smile. She wasn't used to people being so forward with personal information, but small-town folks seemed to be much more forthcoming, going right past chitchat to the good stuff.

Nancy chuckled. "Well, at my age they're dropping like flies." Again Mia wasn't sure if she should laugh, but when Nancy chuckled, Mia joined her. "Honey, all I can say is that if this Cameron Patrick is hero material, you're one lucky girl."

"I'll remember that," Mia said and mulled Nancy's comment over after sitting down on the wooden bench. She clutched her purse on her lap and tried to relax even though she felt out of her element. But after glancing around, Mia almost managed to laugh out loud. Out of her element? That was an understatement if there ever was one, and she started mentally ticking off the reasons why. Okay, she was in a police station bailing out an almost total stranger with borrowed money. Just a little while ago she had tossed a Diet Coke in a man's face and then jumped onto another man's back and attempted to snap his ears from his head. Oh, and let's see, she had left her father's estate in a battered old car and was now living in a small town under an assumed name while weaving a tale that just kept on growing. And to top it all off, all she had in her wallet was a few dollars from tips, and she already owed money.

Panic started to well up in her throat, and her fingers itched to call her father to end this nonsense and put her on the next flight back home to Chicago. By this weekend she could be in Monte Carlo or Cabo San Lucas. Mia sighed. Maybe if she closed her eyes and clicked her heels she would end up snuggled in her own cushy bed. It was worth a try! She brushed away a lock of hair and noticed that her fingers were trembling. Oh boy . . .

But Mia suddenly sat up straighter. That pitiful pile of tips in her purse was money she had earned. And . . . she had been hired not because she was Mitch Monroe's daughter but based on her very own merit. Okay, she had pretty much begged, and, well, she had really sucked at her job, *but* Mia was prepared to go back and try again if Myra allowed her. Instead of standing on the sidelines letting everything be done for her, Mia had jumped into the fray—literally—and it felt pretty damned good. Well, except for her aching feet! She glanced down at her perfectly stylish but utterly painful shoes. Her first purchase with her paycheck was going to be sensible footwear, she thought with a wry grin. But when she rolled the word *sensible* over in her brain, Mia actually snorted. From her extravagant lifestyle to her designer shoes, absolutely nothing in Mia's life remotely resembled being sensible. When another snort drew Nancy's attention, Mia wiggled her finger beneath her nose pretended she had sneezed.

"God bless you, sugar."

"Thanks," Mia replied but then sneezed for real, drawing a frown from Nancy.

"You're not dressed warm enough for this unseasonal weather. Somebody sure musta pissed off Mother Nature."

"I know." She wondered if there was a jacket in the hodgepodge of clothing stuffed in her suitcase. Probably not . . .

"Well, that will never do." Nancy scooted her chair back from the desk and stood up. "I'll go search in the lost-and-found box for a sweater."

Mia waved a hand in Nancy's direction. She was cold but not exactly thrilled about wearing discarded clothing from a jail. "Oh, I'll be f-f-f- . . . aaah-choo!"

"Sure you will."

"No real— Aaah-choo!"

"I'll be right back," Nancy insisted and then hurried down the narrow hallway before disappearing into a room.

Mia shook her head but smiled softly. Here she was a complete stranger and Nancy was concerned for her welfare. Fred had promised to fix her car as cheaply as possible and keep it stored until she could pay, and without a penny down. Myra had hired her out of the goodness of her heart and Cameron had come to her rescue twice. Mia already knew more people in Cricket Creek than she knew in her gated community back in Chicago.

Wow . . .

Mia released her death grip on the leather strap of her purse and a reassuring sense of calm washed over her. "Not only *can* I do this, but I will pay back everyone who put their trust in me, especially Myra," she whispered with a quiet sense of determination. She *wanted* to do this . . . and not to prove anything to her father but to prove something to herself.

A couple of minutes later, Nancy reappeared with a cute little blue hoodie that had the Cricket Creek Cougars emblem in the upper corner. "Here ya go. See if this fits. Probably a little bit big, but it should chase away the chill. Noah Falcon brought over some promotional stuff the other day that I had forgotten about."

"Oh, I couldn't take some free stuff meant for your employees," Mia protested, even though the soft cotton felt warm and wonderful.

Nancy rolled her eyes. "Sheriff Mason isn't too fond of Noah, and he shoved it all into a back room in a big old huff, so don't worry about it."

"Well, in that case, thanks," Mia said and shoved her arms into the sleeves. It was a little bit big but warmed her cold arms. "So the sheriff doesn't care for Noah Falcon?" Even though Mia knew the answer, she wanted the scoop.

"Crazy." Nancy pursed her lips. "That Cougar complex has revitalized this tired little town. Business has picked up everywhere, and the new shopping strip down by the stadium is going to be a nice addition to the area. Shops and a couple of restaurants, and there is talk of a future hotel and convention center that will bring in business all year round."

"Silly man," Mia said as she zipped up the hoodie.

"Old rivalry that goes all the way back to high school, but yeah, *silly man* is putting it mildly. I know I'm grateful to Noah Falcon and Ty McKenna for bringing life back to our community. If it hadn't happened soon, Cricket Creek would have become a ghost town. Family-owned businesses would have gone under and let the franchises swoop in and take over."

"That would have been a shame! This place oozes charm."

"I'd like to think so," Nancy agreed. "Plus, the baseball games are fun. I'm looking forward to the new season."

"Oh . . ." Mia suddenly thought of her father's involvement with the Cougars and wondered how much he actually had to do with the entire development. If she had to guess, she'd guess it would be a lot. "I can imagine."

Nancy tilted her head. "I thought your boyfriend was on the team. Surely you'll be at the games."

"Oh, for sure," Mia said firmly. "I was, you know, speaking in general terms. I'm just glad to hear that it's a success and bringing in more growth."

"Yes, this town has been brought back to life in more ways than one," Nancy added before turning her attention back to her computer.

Although Mia realized that she knew only a small portion of her father's business dealings, this was the positive type of thing she always associated with him. Although Mitch Monroe commanded a presence much like Donald Trump, he had a much more easygoing demeanor. Mia certainly never suspected him of doing anything as harsh as taking over the company of a valued friend, and she was still reeling from their last conversation. Mia shook her head slowly. While she knew that her father made piles of money, he gave back in a big way, and Mia had organized many charity events for him. Mitch Monroe was shrewd, yes . . . but ruthless? It didn't add up, but then again she had overheard his phone conversation and he hadn't denied a single accusation. But oh God . . . she missed him! The desire to whip out her phone and tell him about her adventure in Cricket Creek was so strong that she barely refrained. She chewed on the inside of her lip. Maybe just a little bitty text message? Oh, and this situation was so tweet-worthy! Her friends would be in hysterics, Mia thought with a grin, and she reached inside her purse for her cell phone.

Wait a minute. Mia knew that her friends would think this was one big joke, and that realization brought her up short. How often had she witnessed snobbish, rude behavior from her very own friends, much like the table of asshats that Cameron had ended up fighting . . . oh right, and she had fought as well. They'd deserved to get their butts kicked!

"No!" she said so loudly that Nancy glanced over the top of her reading glasses.

"Sugar, I'm sorry it's taking so long. You didn't hear it from me, but Sheriff Mason drags his feet when he wants to, I'm afraid."

Mia widened her eyes. "You mean he's letting Cameron rot in a jail cell on purpose?"

"Well, I don't think your young man is to the rotting stage just yet, but yes." Nancy held up her romance novel; it had a hunky guy on the cover that made Mia think of Cameron. "I don't have books on my desk because we're overflowing with crooks around here."

"Can I visit him?" Mia had a vision of taking him a picnic basket of food with a secret weapon wrapped in a ham sandwich. "Take him some supper?" She glanced at the vending machine. "At least a candy bar, or maybe a Coke?"

Nancy chuckled. "Now, aren't you just as cute as a button. Where are you from anyways? It sure isn't from around these parts."

"Oh . . . uh . . ." Mia hesitated but then said, "Here and there. The Midwest."

"Thought so." Nancy nodded. "Y'all got that kinda funny accent."

"Really? You're telling me *I* have an accent?" Mia pointed her thumb toward her chest. "You're the one with the southern drawl, Nancy."

"Southern? Honey, slow and easy isn't just an accent

or drawl. It's a way of life. I'm sure we move at a more leisurely pace than you're accustomed to."

"Yes," Mia admitted, "but that's not such a bad thing."

When Nancy glanced back down, Mia said, "Oh, I don't mean to keep you from your job." Especially if it was paperwork to get Cameron out, Mia thought with a slight grimace.

"What? Oh, sweetie, I was on Facebook."

"Really?" Nancy didn't look like the Facebook type, but then again, what did she know? Apparently not much.

"I finished up all of my paperwork a while ago. I'm actually itching to finish reading my book. The hero and heroine are about to do the horizontal tango, if ya know what I'm sayin'."

Mia frowned for a second but then giggled. "I do."

"Yeah, I'm afraid it's as close to sex as I'm gonna get."

Mia couldn't believe she was having this conversation with a total stranger, but then again she was finding that small-town folks seemed to speak their mind and then some. "You don't know that."

Nancy leaned forward on her elbows. "Oh, honey, I'm sorry to say it, but that ship has sailed."

"Hey, don't give up! Your prince might still come."

"Well, I've kissed enough frogs in my day, that's for damn sure," Nancy said just as the door opened.

Mia's heart pounded with the anticipation of seeing Cameron, but a tall, gray-haired man in dusty work clothes entered the room. He had a neatly trimmed beard, slightly shaggy hair, a kind smile, and very blue eyes that zoned in on Nancy. "What's this I'm hearin' 'bout you kissin' frogs?"

"Oh, I'm just goin' on," Nancy said with a wave of her hand, but Mia noted with interest that she appeared a little flushed. She tucked her hair behind her ears and gave him her full attention. "Has it stopped rainin' yet?"

"Yeah, just misty and damp. Not my favorite kinda weather."

Nancy frowned. "Well, now, Tucker, you shoulda come in outta the rain. You'll catch your death!"

He shrugged. "Aw, sun's tryin' to break through. Let me tell ya, I've worked in much worse conditions. I've been trimmin' the hedges and I wanted to get it done before dinner. Needed something cold to wet my whistle, though. I'm damned near parched," Tucker replied, and for the first time he seemed to notice Mia, who was sitting there quietly taking in the exchange. "Howdy there." He gave her a polite nod.

"Tucker, meet sweet little Mia," Nancy said. "She's a new waitress down at Wine and Diner."

"Nice to meet you, Tucker."

He smiled, making his light blue eyes crinkle at the corners. "Same here. I'm part of the old-timers' breakfast club down at the diner. Reckon I'll be seein' ya around."

"I hope so," Mia said softly and felt a bit of heat in her cheeks. If she didn't get fired. "Are you the groundskeeper?" Mia asked, wanting to change the subject.

"That among other things," Tucker answered as he slipped a dollar into the slot on the soft drink machine. It spit it out and he laughed and slipped it back in. "Danged machine never wants to take my money. I can fix just about anything, but I enjoy being outdoors."

"Well, the courthouse looks amazing," Mia replied. "It's nice that they didn't tear it down and put up a modern building. And the grounds are meticulous."

"Thanks." Tucker smiled and then popped the top of a root beer. "There've been some fights over it at town hall since the old courthouse is a bit hard to maintain, but some things are worth keeping. Well, speaking of that, I'd better get back to work. Nice to meet ya," he said and, after taking a swallow of his drink, turned to Nancy. "You comin' to breakfast this Saturday mornin'?"

Mia noticed that his tone seemed carefully casual, but those intense blue eyes held such hope that Mia almost sighed. She wished someone would look at her with such longing.

"I believe I will," Nancy answered just as evenly.

"Good to hear." Tucker took a long swallow of root beer. "Well, I guess I'd better get back out there and rake up the clipped branches."

"All right, then," Nancy said but then held up one finger. "Oh, hold on, I *almost* forgot that I saved you a few of my oatmeal raisin cookies. Baked a batch last night." She lifted one shoulder. "Was bored and needed something to keep my hands busy."

Yeah, right, Mia thought.

"Thank you much, Nancy. They're my favorite, and nobody makes 'em better than you," he said as he took the cookies from her. "I'll return this," he promised and held up the plastic container.

"Aw, no need."

"Are you kiddin'?" Tucker grinned. "I want to ensure a refill."

"All right, then."

"Thanks, I'll be dipping these in some cold milk later tonight. Hope to see ya Saturday," he said and then turned to Mia. "Nice to meet ya, Miss Mia."

"Same here."

Tucker gave her a little salute and then headed out the door.

"Well, now," Mia cooed with an arch of one eyebrow. "Is *he* one of the frogs?"

"Naw, we're just friends," Nancy scoffed, but Mia detected a bit of a blush.

"Well, he sure is handsome. Is he single?"

"Well, now I, uh, suppose so."

"Meaning *yes*."

"Uh-huh." Nancy fidgeted around with random items on her desk. "He's been divorced for a long time. Stupid woman ran off with another man."

"So what are you waiting for?" Mia raised her hands skyward. "Christmas?"

Nancy stopped fidgeting and laughed. "Girlie, I declare, you might not be from Cricket Creek, but I'm thinking you just might belong here after all."

"I'm just in a sort of holding pattern while my car gets fixed."

"Really now? Don't be so sure. We've had a steady influx of city folk recently. You just might be next."

"Don't get me wrong, Cricket Creek is a cute little town, but I don't have any plans to move here permanently," she replied, but at that very moment Cameron was ushered into the room. As soon as she laid eyes on him, her heart started beating faster and her stomach did a little fluttery butterfly thing, making her feel a bit lightheaded. When their eyes locked and held, she felt warm all over, almost like she had a fever. What was up with that? Maybe she was coming down with something . . .

"Oh boy." Nancy took one look at Cameron and let out a low whistle. She winked at Mia. "Oh, sugar, I'd surely change my plans if I were you. Hot damn."

9

The Calm Before the Storm

"THANKS FOR BAILING ME OUT," CAMERON SAID AFTER they stepped outside.

"It was the least I could do. I should be the one thanking you for coming to my defense."

"No need." Soft rays of sunshine were breaking through the clouds, but it did little to lighten Cam's mood. He had missed a team meeting and this little incident could get him ousted from the team. "Those guys had it coming to them," he added darkly.

"No need to thank you? Are you kidding?" Mia put a hand on his forearm, causing Cam to pause at the top step. "You don't even know me and yet you've come to my rescue twice now."

"Don't go mistaking me for a hero," Cam warned once more while trying not to be affected by the light touch of her cool hand on his bare skin. He almost succeeded, but her soft smile just about did him in. "I don't deserve it."

"Well, that's debatable." The soft smile remained. "But lucky for you I'm not in the mood to argue. Now, what I do know is that you deserve for me to buy you dinner. But my, uh, funds are somewhat limited." She scrunched up her cute, perky nose. "Okay, make that very limited. The best I can do is coffee or perhaps a beer at Sully's."

"You really don't owe me anything, Mia," he said firmly.

"Oh . . . okay." When her face fell, he tried not to feel guilty.

"Besides," he said in a gentler tone, "I have to head over to the stadium and explain to Ty McKenna why I missed a team meeting. Hopefully, he won't get wind of my arrest."

Mia's eyes rounded. "Could you really be in big trouble?"

"Maybe," Cam replied, trying to sound casual.

"Like in getting booted off the team?" She squeezed his arm and swallowed hard.

"It's . . . possible."

"Well, then, I'm going with you."

"No, you're not."

"Oh, yes, I am!" Mia's tone suggested that she often got her way without any argument, making Cam think once more that she came from wealth. But her pink uniform and the blue hoodie reminded him that she was a struggling waitress at the local diner and drove a beater car. "Come on, let's go." She started down the steps.

Cam hesitated. He was used to fighting his own battles.

At the bottom of the steps, Mia turned around and fisted her hands on her slim hips. She looked up at him with challenge in her eyes. "What are you waiting for? You don't have to face the music alone." Her chin came up. "Cameron, I've got your back."

Hearing his name in her reassuring tone coupled with the pleading look in her pretty eyes was his undoing. When had anyone come to his defense? For that matter, when had anyone given a rat's ass about him, period? Other than how well he could play baseball? *Never* slammed into his brain and sank down to his gut. But while he had to admit that it felt damned good to have someone actually care, a flash of fear snaked down his spine. Letting down his guard made him feel vulnerable, and he liked to feel bulletproof. In Cam's experience, depending upon someone else was setting himself up for a fall. How many times had he stood by the curb waiting for a ride home from baseball practice that never arrived, while other moms and dads picked their kids up in minivans? Cam had learned to ride his bike, fix his own dinner . . . and depend upon no one. "Thanks, but seriously, I'll work it out."

"What? I'm your witness." Mia raised her hands from her hips and reached toward the sky. "Come on, let's go do this thing. I can help. Really."

Cam would have refused again, but something in her eyes told him that maybe she had never been taken seriously. "Okay," he relented and slowly descended the steps.

"Good." She followed in those ridiculous shoes that didn't fit the mold of a down-and-out waitress. "If you lost your spot on the team because of me, I wouldn't be able to sleep at night. I won't let that happen," she stated, but the slight waver in her voice gave him pause. Cam suddenly had a sneaking suspicion that while he had always fended for himself, Mia had always depended upon others. But she seemed determined to prove *something*, and truth be known, he was in some deep shit and she just might be his only salvation.

"We'll have to walk," he warned her with a glance at her shoes. "My car is back at Wine and Diner and we need to go in the opposite direction. Ty and Noah might not be there much longer and I need to get this cleared up. But we'd better get going because there's a chance of a storm later."

"I'm getting used to walking," she acknowledged with a slight grin. "It's better for my calves than being driven around all the time," she said when he reached the bottom of the steps.

"Driven around?" Has she just let something slip?

"I meant driving," Mia quickly amended. "Silly me . . . ," she added with such conviction that it didn't ring true. He wanted to ask more, but she started walking before Cam could get more out of her. She was hiding something. He was sure of it.

When they arrived at the baseball complex, Cam's heart thudded even though the walk was relatively short. Even if he tried to keep the incident from Noah and Ty, this was a small town and news traveled fast. He might as well come clean. Cam took a deep breath and paused at the front door. He was usually an expert at keeping his emotions hidden, but some of his internal worry must have shown on his face because Mia put a gentle hand on his arm and smiled. Cam hated that his fear was apparent and narrowed his eyes. "What?" he asked a bit harshly. Being an ass had been his smoke screen all his life, and Cam usually took some satisfaction when it worked, but when her smile faltered it was like a swift kick to his gut.

"I just wanted to tell you that everything will be okay," she said softly. When she gently squeezed his arm, it was all he could do not to shake her off, but he didn't want her to know how her concern was affecting him.

"Yeah, well, they need me on the team." Cam shrugged as if it didn't matter all that much, when of course he was shaking in his shoes, but Mia's sincere, unwavering gaze actually helped to calm his nerves just a bit. Even though he wasn't at all convinced that everything *was* going to be okay, her attempt to reassure him felt . . . nice. As a kid he had often longed for a hug or even a slight indication that someone cared. Once in a while he got a rather clumsy bedtime pat on the head or a smile from his mother, and when he did, Cam soaked it up like a dry sponge soaked up water. But the rare show of affection always left him wanting more, so he had learned to harden his heart and expect nothing. The fact that Mia had managed to find a chink in his armor made him feel exposed, and so he frowned and pulled his arm away from her gentle touch.

"Hey, you did the right thing," Mia insisted. "You stepped in when others would have looked away. No one can fault you for that."

"You'd be surprised." Cam chuckled without humor. Some of the fights he had managed to get himself into were actually because he was coming to the aid of someone or trying to break up a fight, but he always managed to catch the blame.

Mia's eyes widened again. "So you think you're in some *really* deep trouble?"

Once again he hated to see her in distress. "Look, when you've got something somebody wants or needs, they always manage to look the other way where rules are concerned," he said, even though he didn't really think that about Noah Falcon. And Triple Threat Ty McKenna was a hard-nosed coach. Cam inhaled another deep breath. He was probably screwed, but he didn't want her to know it. "Come on, let's go. It will be fine." He hoped.

"I'm sure it will be." Mia smiled but appeared worried.

"Let's go." Cam pushed the front door open and held it for Mia to enter just as it started to sprinkle. A loud clap of thunder had her hurrying to get inside. "We need to go to the offices on the fifth floor," he said as he walked over to the elevator. "Hopefully, Noah will still be here."

"It would be nice if you could get this straightened out pronto." Mia nodded and pressed the red button.

"You got that right," he said and once again tried not to be curious. Really . . . who said *pronto*? Her language was often more formal than he was used to, and at times she seemed to be quoting someone older.

On the way up she seemed to be deep in thought as she stared up at the blinking numbers. He hid a smile while wondering if she was practicing a speech to Noah in her head. Cam took the opportunity to study her profile. She really was pretty and looked so cute in the blue hoodie that he suddenly wondered if he was completely off base about her being rich. Not that he tended to pigeonhole people, but he was good at assessing a situation. With Mia, though, he continued to be at a loss. It made him feel a bit off-kilter, but not in a totally bad way.

In baseball Cam had gotten the opportunity to meet people from all walks of life and from all over the globe. While he didn't like to stereotype, especially since he had often been on the receiving end, in his experience women of wealth were self-absorbed and wouldn't be likely to go out of their way to come to his defense. He had never been worth the time or effort. He just couldn't figure Mia out.

Oh, but one thing he did know was that Mia had a full, lush mouth made for kissing, and damn if he didn't want to push her up against the wall, taste her lips, and feel her body next to his. He inhaled deeply, trying to chase that erotic image from his brain, but her light floral fragrance filled his head and didn't help matters. Crazy that his mind would head in that direction given his current circumstances, but it sure as hell did, and damn, it would not budge.

When Mia turned and looked at him, something of what he had been thinking must have shown on his face, because her eyes widened slightly and her cheeks turned a light shade of pink. Again, this type of reaction wasn't typical of a rich, confident woman. He had to be wrong. Or maybe he just wanted to be wrong since he had sworn off getting tangled up with self-absorbed, self-serving women a long time ago.

"I was wondering . . . ," Mia began, but before she could finish her sentence the lights flickered and the elevator jerked in staccato movements, throwing Cam off balance. He stumbled sideways and twisted to avoid bumping into Mia, but he ended up pushing her up against the wall. He flattened his palms against the cool surface on either side of his shoulders while the elevator continued to shake in tandem with the lights. "What's happening?" she asked breathlessly and fisted her hands in his shirt.

"Get down in the middle of the floor," Cam ordered, and when she immediately obeyed he covered her body with his. If the elevator was going to crash he wanted to shield her from as much harm as he possibly could. She clung to him and he could feel her body tremble.

"Cam, I'm scared!"

"It's okay. I've got you," he said in her ear. The thought of any harm coming to her clenched at his gut, and he curled his body around hers while the lights continued to blink. The floor vibrated and the elevator lurched again, and then everything went dark. Cam held his breath, thinking that they really might plunge to the basement, but the vibration ceased and everything went completely still.

"What do you think is wrong?" Mia whispered.

"My guess is that the thunderstorm that had threatened all day long finally hit hard and the electricity went off."

"Oh." Her hands remained fisted in his shirt, and Cam liked it. He also liked the feel of her curves pressed intimately against him. "Shouldn't there be a backup generator or something?" She continued to whisper, making him grin.

"Well, if there is one, it's not working." God, she smelled amazing. He barely refrained from nuzzling her neck. He should move and put some distance between them, but his aroused body would not even think of budging.

"So we're stuck?" Her soft breath caressed his cheek, and it was all he could do not to kiss her.

"Yes," he finally managed to articulate. "It seems that way."

"How long do you think we'll be stuck in here?"

"For a while, I hope." Oh crap, he hadn't meant to say that out loud.

"What? Why?" Her breathless whisper tickled his cheek again and sent a hot flash of desire south. Cam tried to cool his ardor and swallowed hard. "Cam?" she persisted and then shifted beneath him.

Dear God . . .

"So I can do this," he finally replied and then lowered his head and covered her mouth with his. Cam didn't know what reaction to expect, but having come from humble beginnings he knew not to hesitate when an opportunity presented itself. Having a beautiful woman pinned beneath him in the dark was one of those times when it was better to react than to think. Besides, after this sucky day, what did he have to lose? If she gave him a quick knee to the balls, then so be it . . .

But she didn't.

With a soft moan Mia opened her mouth beneath his and kissed him back like there was no tomorrow. Which, given the situation, maybe there wouldn't be, he thought with dark humor. So . . . why fight it? At least that's how he justified his actions, and with that thought in mind he deepened the kiss, savoring her sweet, soft lips. When he trailed the tip of his tongue over her full bottom lip, she let go of his shirt and threaded her fingers through his hair, slanting her mouth as if asking for more, and Cam gladly gave it. Their breath mingled, tongues tangled, and he didn't want the kiss to end. He rocked against her and devoured every inch of her sweet, warm mouth until a trickle of sweat down his back reminded him of the dire straits they'd found themselves in. In the back of his befuddled brain he knew he should try to call for help. He kissed her for another long, delicious moment before he reluctantly pulled his lips from hers.

"What are you doing?" The touch of disappointment in her tone had Cam smiling in the dark.

"We should probably call for help," he replied and almost groaned in disappointment when she released her fingers from his hair. After rolling away, he shoved his hand into his pocket for his cell phone.

"Oh, you're right," she said, but she scooted closer to him in the pitch-black darkness.

When Cam's cell came to life, he looked at the glowing screen and shook his head. "No bars in the elevator. I was afraid of that."

"There should be an emergency call button that goes to a twenty-four-hour service," Mia said.

"Right, I'll try it." Cam turned his cell phone to illuminate the wall and then reached up and pushed the button. "Hello?" he shouted into the speaker, but he got only crackling static in return. "So much for that."

"What do we do now?" she asked while shrugging out of her hoodie.

"Well, what you're doing is a start."

"I'm hot!" she explained.

"I won't argue with that," he said and turned the cell phone in her direction to illuminate her face. When she giggled, he thought once more how cute she was and leaned forward to give her another lingering kiss. Perhaps it was being trapped in the elevator or the leftover emotion of the wild and crazy day, but Cam couldn't remember when he had been this attracted to a woman. No, it wasn't just attraction. He was drawn to her in ways he couldn't even explain. And while he knew he should back off for a whole slew of reasons, at this very moment he simply couldn't. Besides, it kept his mind off the fact that they were trapped in an elevator for unknown reasons, after hours, with no way out. And for the moment he didn't have to think about being tossed off the team for getting thrown in jail.

"Wow . . . ," Mia said when her giggles ended.

Cam kept his phone illuminated and directed at her face. "What?"

"Who knew that there was such a charmer beneath all of that broody bad-boy sulkiness?"

"Nobody."

"Excuse me?" When Mia tilted her head in question, Cam refrained from telling her that he was anything but a charmer and that she was bringing out attributes in him that no one ever had squeezed out of him before. "Explain yourself."

"Nobody, Mia. Like I said, I'm not a hero or a charmer by any stretch of the imagination."

"Once again, I beg to differ."

"Well, maybe I'm just rising to the occasion."

She arched one golden blond eyebrow. "Is that a double entendre?"

"Not at all," Cam answered with a deep chuckle and then leaned back against the elevator wall. "It's a fact."

"Really?" she asked, but even in the low light of the cell phone he could tell that she was blushing.

"Want to find out?" He kept his tone teasing, but he sure hoped that she said yes.

"I think I—," Mia began, but she was cut off when the lights flickered and then came back on. The elevator groaned and then began to move upward while they blinked at each other. "Thank God!"

"Yeah." Cam nodded his agreement, even though he was thoroughly disappointed that he didn't hear her answer. While he didn't want to be stuck here all night, a little while longer would have been just fine with him. A few seconds later the elevator reached the fifth floor, but just as the doors began to inch open, the lights went out again.

"Oh no!" Mia exclaimed and clung to Cam. "What do you think is going on?"

"Well . . ." Cam leaned forward and tried to pry the doors open without success. He peeked through the small opening. The light was dim but he could see over to a window, and a flash of lightning confirmed his suspicion that a thunderstorm was the culprit. "I'm pretty sure this is a power outage from a storm." He stepped back for her to see.

"Oh . . . yeah, I see lightning flashing all over the place. It must be some really strong wind." She stepped back. "But at least I feel better about the door being open a little bit."

"Are you claustrophobic?"

"Apparently." Her reply was light with humor, but Cam also heard a thread of fear in her tone. "And I'm not exactly a big fan of storms. My bedroom had big windows and I know it's silly but I used to think that the trees tapping against the glass sounded like someone—or worse, some beady-eyed monster—trying to get in my room. I would huddle beneath the covers and only peek out with my eyes."

"That's not silly," Cam said. He remembered all too well having the same fear, but he'd never let on how scared he was. He knew all too well how precious sleep was to his mother and never dared going to her bedroom for comfort. "Didn't you run to your parents' bedroom?"

She hesitated, and he could feel her stiffen. "My parents divorced when I was very young. My mother moved on with her new life and new family. I lived with my dad and, well . . . he was gone a lot."

Cam could feel her pain, and a flash of anger had him asking, "Mia, who raised you?"

She paused again. "Babysitters," she finally answered. "And I don't mean Mary Poppins," she added with a short laugh.

"Well, that had to suck."

Cam felt her shrug. "He was a busy man. He did the best he could under the circumstances."

"I hear a *but* in there," Cam couldn't help but say to her.

Mia sighed. "But he was too worried about showing my mother what a loss it was for her to have run away with another man and—" She paused and swallowed hard.

"And neglected you?"

"Oh, *neglect* is a harsh word. No, not neglect. He just . . . I don't know. Cam, I don't know if I can even explain it."

"Well, at this point all we have is time."

"You have a point," Mia said but then fell silent for a

moment. "I know that my father loves me. I just don't feel as if he . . . values me as a person. Well, at least a productive person. Does that make sense?"

Cam had to clear the emotion from his throat before he could answer. "Yeah, you feel like you're more trouble than you're worth."

"I didn't really feel like that so much. It's more like I sometimes felt . . . invisible?"

"Yeah, I get that," he answered quietly. "In my case I wish I could have been invisible. I had a tired single mom and a deadbeat dad. They both resented my existence."

"Oh, Cam, I'm sorry."

"Don't be." Cam chuckled softly. "It only made me determined to be a success. Sounds like you are going through much of the same thing. I guess we had somewhat similar childhoods."

She paused for a second, as if she was going to elaborate, but then sighed. "Well, I've decided that I don't have anything to prove to anyone except to myself."

"Now you're talking."

"Yeah, no more pity parties."

"Agreed. I fell into that category for a while, and it almost cost me my career."

"Oh God . . . I hope I didn't ruin things for you again! I am so sorry!"

"Hey, I made the choice to intervene. Don't blame yourself for this. And it was my previous behavior that got me into this mess to begin with. Seems as if I like to learn things the hard way."

"Still . . . ," she began, but he put a fingertip to her lips.

"Hey, sounds like you've got your own problems to deal with. I'll find a way out of this. I always seem to land on my feet." Her concern touched him. "But thanks." God how he wanted to kiss her. "Listen, it really could be a while before the power comes back on."

"So what do we do? Any bright ideas?" she asked but then gave a slight laugh. "No pun intended."

Cam chuckled at her humor, thinking that despite

speech and mannerisms that at times seemed more mature than she appeared, there was an odd innocence about her that made him think that she had seen more than most people and yet had been sheltered from the real world. While there was no doubt that he was physically attracted to Mia, he was both interested and intrigued, and that was something he had rarely felt about a woman.

"Well . . ." Cam hesitated for a second and tried to think with a clear head, but when her soft, alluring scent wafted his way, he gave in to temptation. "Yeah, I have a few ideas." He wasn't sure how bright it was, but Cam pulled her into his arms and then pressed her up against the wall. "Maybe you need something to take your mind off of your phobia," he said just before he bent his head and kissed her.

With the doors open a few inches, they could hear the sound of the rain and perhaps hail pelting against the windows. Lightning flashed and thunder rolled, but Cam barely noticed. When she tugged his shirt from his waistband and smoothed her hands up his back, her touch excited and yet soothed him, causing his worries to melt away. The storm would end and his troubles would come roaring back, but all he could think about right now was the sweet, sexy woman in his arms. Tomorrow would come soon enough, but for now he was all about savoring the moment.

Cam realized that he had wanted to kiss her from the moment she had sat down next to him at Wine and Diner. What he didn't know was how it was going to make him feel. Damn, she got to him on a physical level, but having her in his arms brought out tenderness that he had never experienced before. She made him hard with need, but he wanted to protect her from all harm.

What the hell was up with that? It was as if she had cast some sort of spell on him. Damn, he should pull back and end this before they went too far, but his body would not obey his brain. Cam kept kissing her and kissing her, and when she threaded her fingers through his hair, he groaned with the sweet pleasure of it all. Perhaps it was the storm that raged outside or the inner turmoil stemming from the trouble he was in, but Cam was hit with a solid smack of emotion the likes of which he had never experienced before.

Without breaking contact with her mouth, he reached up and started to unfasten her uniform. The buttons were round and fat and the slight tremble in his fingers made him fumble. When Cam groaned in frustration, Mia hesitated a mere fraction, but then she reached up to help him.

"Thank you," he said in her ear. He was met with a low, sexy chuckle that slid over his skin like a warm caress. He nuzzled her neck and inhaled her alluring scent, which made him think of a sultry summer night, earthy and sweet, with the promise of a cool breeze. When she sighed and arched her back, he wished he could see her better in the dim light that flickered with each flash of lightning. Time felt suspended, and he wouldn't have been surprised if he suddenly woke up in his bed, drenched with sweat.

Oh, but in his wildest dreams Cam couldn't have conjured up a mouth so sweet or skin so soft. And while baseball had always been his life, his salvation, his reason to put his feet on the floor in the morning, for the first time in his life Cameron Patrick wondered if there was something more.

Cam's heart thudded at the unexpected thought, but before he could even digest the meaning, a steady beam of light filtered through the opening between the doors.

"Hey, this is Owen Lawson, the groundskeeper. Is anybody in there?"

Cam reluctantly pulled his lips from hers. "Yeah, Mia Money from down at Wine and Diner and Cameron Patrick."

"Well, I'll be damned. Hey, little Mia, I've heard about

you. Seems like you've found yourself in a fix again, haven't you, child?"

"It appears so."

"Well, don't fret. I'll get ya outta here lickety-split."

"Thank you."

"Hey there, Cameron. Aren't you the first baseman that can smack the jacket off of the danged baseball? I watched ya in batting practice. The Cougars are lucky to have ya. Watcha doin' in here this late anyways?"

"I was going to talk to Ty or Noah."

"Oh well, it'll have to wait. Everybody's gone except me. I was headin' for my truck when the storm hit, so I hightailed it back into the building. Then I thought I'd better check around."

"Good thing, because we're trapped in here." Cam stepped away from Mia, who began to fumble for her buttons.

"Well, hellfire," Owen said. "I had a feelin' I should come up here and scope things out. We're having a helluva storm out there, don't ya know. Hail danged near as big as golf balls. Ain't seen nothin' like it in years."

"Can you get us out?" Cam asked and then flicked a glance at Mia, who was smoothing back her hair.

"I'll do my best. Y'all hang tight."

"We're not going anywhere," Cam said and was rewarded with a chuckle.

"I'll just go and get me some tools."

"Oh my God . . . ," Mia whispered as she continued to adjust her hair and clothes. Cam swore her blush glowed like a damned matchstick in the darkness. "I can't believe this is happening."

Cam was used to women wanting him in the heat of the moment and then regretting it later. Damn, would that ever change? He had a hard time swallowing his disappointment, but he was an expert at not letting it show. "Don't worry. I don't kiss and tell," he said tightly.

"That thought never entered my mind," she answered

in a small voice that was like a rubber-band snap to his heart. "You came to my rescue twice, Cam. I know you're not going to spread any rumors that would harm my reputation." He couldn't see her frown, but he could feel it. "I can tell you have more integrity than that."

"Thank you." He acknowledged her compliment without remembering that he was supposed to be a bad-ass and keep her at arm's length. Well, he thought with an inner grin, he had already blown that all to hell anyway. Mia had a way of throwing him off guard. Other than on the baseball field, no one had ever put any real trust or value in him before. He was much more used to getting reamed out than praised. In a short period of time Mia had made him feel more self-worth than he had experienced in a long time . . . meaning, well, *a lifetime*, and he didn't even have to hit a ball or make a diving catch to get it. He liked the feeling. He liked it a lot. He liked *her* a lot.

"No thanks necessary," she replied and then put a light hand on his arm. This time Cam didn't shake her off, and he really wished that they weren't about to be rescued. "What are you thinking? I can almost hear the wheels turning."

"Honestly?"

"Well, yeah, honesty is preferable," she replied with a hint of humor.

Cam hesitated and then sighed. Maybe it was the cloak of darkness or maybe because she somehow put him at ease, but he suddenly decided to come clean. "I grew up cleaning pools for rich assholes. And I totally fit the stereotype of the pool boy being hit on by lonely wives and spoiled daughters. I fell for a couple of the daughters, who ate me up and then spit me out. Believe me when I say that I've sworn off of them forever."

"I don't blame you." She rubbed her hand up his arm. "I'm sorry that you were treated that way. I hate it when wealth and power are used to hurt or take advantage of others," she said hotly.

"When I met you, I seriously thought you were one of them. I can usually spot one a mile away. Obviously, I was dead wrong." He waited for her response, hoping that she would shed some light on her background.

"Oh, believe me. I totally understand. More than you know."

"So you've had the same experience?"

"In a roundabout way," she answered slowly, but then she fell silent once more. Cam wanted her to elaborate, but Owen returned and let them know that a tech was on the way and they would be rescued very soon.

"Well, that's a relief," Cam said, even though he wished he had more time with her.

"Yeah, it sure is," she answered, but he suddenly felt some uneasiness in her demeanor that he couldn't explain.

Cam could almost feel her withdrawal, and she actually stepped away. Disappointment washed over him, but he decided it was for the best. He had bigger things to worry about, but when thunder boomed and lightning flashed through the small opening, she gasped. Unable not to, Cam reached over and took her hand. "Hey, it's going to be okay. We'll be out of here soon."

"I know." She didn't move closer but didn't pull away either. "I just need to learn to stand on my own two feet and not be so scared. I'm so tired of being a wimp!"

"Really?" Cam gave her hand a squeeze. "Um, just a little while ago you were attempting to yank the ears off of a dude while hanging on to his back. That's pretty out of character for a wimp, if you ask me."

"I was scared! I just reacted."

"Being scared but stepping up anyway is called being brave, Mia."

"Sounds like you've been there."

"A time or two, I guess." Until her comment, Cam wouldn't have considered himself to be brave. But how many times had he longed for a hand to hold and had to just gut it out? *Countless* whispered in his head. In the moment he gave a much deserved pat on the back to the lost little boy inside him who had pedaled to baseball practice in the rain, huddled in his bed in fear, and sucked up pain so he could play ball. He swallowed the hot wave of emotion that suddenly clogged his throat. That brave kid inside of him deserved to play major-league baseball! He just hoped he wouldn't be kicked off the team, blowing his very last chance.

10

Show and Tell

TO THE WORLD, NICOLINA DIAMANTE PRESENTED HERself as a confident, self-assured woman, but in reality she was a big bundle of insecurities. Thunderstorms were a perfect example. The pelting rain and howling wind scared her out of her wits. She liked to be in control, and storms made her feel small and powerless. But when she was raising Bella back in Chicago, booming thunder would always bring little Bella bolting into her mama's bed to huddle beneath the covers. Nicolina would soothe and comfort her sweet child, never letting her own trembling fear show.

After an initial round of severe storms, rain now politely pelted the roof of her loft apartment. Tree branches tapped against the windows as if asking permission to come inside, away from the nasty weather. But within just a few minutes frequent lightning flashed like strobe lights, followed by the distant crackle of thunder. Ah, but while the weather intensified on this particular night, Nicolina snuggled in a warm cocoon beneath the soft down comforter on her big brass bed. She felt safe and secure wrapped in the strong arms of Mitchell Monroe. They had already made sweet, passionate love for more than an hour, and she was finally drifting off to sleep when a sudden sharp clap that sounded like a gunshot made her twitch.

"Sweetheart, it's okay." Mitch drew her even closer while murmuring more words of reassurance.

"I was simply startled." To this day Nicolina hated to show any sign of weakness. Humble beginnings coupled with being a single mother in a big city caused Nicolina to keep her chin up and her backbone stiff, knowing firsthand that the weak were often preyed upon. She taught Bella to show some grit because getting ahead was the survival of the fittest.

"It's perfectly okay to be afraid," Mitch gently assured her.

"Really now?" Nicolina had never met a more self-assured, confident man. "What could you possibly be afraid of, Mitch?" Her tone was teasing, but when she felt him go still, Nicolina frowned while she waited for his response.

"You'd be surprised."

"Try me," she offered softly and then waited silently when he hesitated still. They had gotten to know each other so well and shared so much, but Nicolina sensed that there was a piece of him that he kept locked away. She longed to draw him out and peel back that layer, but another boom of thunder made her tremble, and he pulled her flush against his warm body.

"Oh, I fully intend to try you, Nicolina. Every sweet inch of you."

"Please do," she answered, drawing a low chuckle from him. He let her know early on that he preferred her earthy sensuality to coy pretense. Although she had issues with her curvy body, she made no bones about enjoying sex. But she didn't push for an answer to her earlier question, knowing it was better to wait until he was ready to expose his fears. Surely he had them . . . everybody did.

"I know it sounds clichéd, but I can never get enough of you." Firm, capable hands cupped her breasts, and when he nuzzled her neck with his warm, moist mouth, a hot shiver of desire made her body tingle. Her toes curled into the soft sheet and she purred deep in her throat. "Nicolina, I think about you all day long."

"God . . . ," she breathed when he caressed the smooth underside of her breast. She moved upward, wanting him nearer to her nipples, but he teased her with his thumb, getting closer and closer but not quite there. When another roll of thunder sounded as if it was right next to her window, Nicolina sucked in a breath. But her fear only heightened her arousal, and she arched her back, giving Mitch better access to her body. When he gently rolled her sensitive nipple between his thumb and finger, she moaned and pressed her back against his chest while moving her hips erotically against his erection.

"Ah . . . Nicolina, I can't believe you have me wanting you all over again. You make me feel like a teenager," Mitch said in her ear, and when he slipped his hand between her thighs she sucked in another breath. His finger found her folds, and although the storm raged all around them, all she could think about was his touch. "Your skin is like warm velvet. Baby, you drive me wild."

Nicolina laughed. "Calling me *baby* makes me feel young . . . at least at heart."

"Baby . . . my sweet baby!" He laughed with her and then kissed her shoulder while he stroked her gently. His caress was light but firm against flesh that was tender from their previous lovemaking. It was a sweet, aching desire, lacking urgency, but it went deeper and was even more satisfying as a slow simmer rather than a flash of heat. When he stroked her harder, she sucked in an audible gasp and he chuckled. "Too much for you?"

"Never!" she boasted.

"Good!" He laughed harder, and it made Nicolina smile from her heart.

Laughter was something else they shared, and it was wonderful. Love and laughter, Nicolina decided, were two things that belonged together and that not all couples shared. Wait . . .

Couples? Were they an official couple? Of course they were. She had been seeing him exclusively since last summer.

The thought made her ecstatic and yet fearful. "Oh!" Her breath caught when he found her sweet spot, and all thoughts of fear vanished. Mitch was an amazing, giving lover, and for the first time in her life Nicolina felt . . . *cherished*. Yet her damned insecurity continued to rear its ugly head. Mitch was a rich, powerful man and to top it off was incredibly handsome. Silver hair and tanned skin set off arresting blue eyes. He kept his body lean and toned and could have any woman he wanted. Would he tire of her? Want someone younger? Thinner? Taller?

"God, you're beautiful," Mitch said as if reading her mind. He seemed to do more and more of that lately.

"You're kind to say so."

"Nicolina!" He pushed her onto her back and gently took her chin in his hand. "I'm not being *kind*."

"I am—," she began, but he dipped his head and smothered her protest with a lingering kiss that had her melting into the mattress. When he finally pulled back, he braced himself on one elbow.

"You are a beautiful woman. Don't ever doubt it, okay?"

Nicolina pressed her lips together.

"Please?" He trailed his fingertip over the firm set of her mouth. "Believe me."

Nicolina swallowed hard. "But you could have any woman you wanted." She looked away after her soft admission. It wasn't like her to vocalize such a thing, but she was falling for him and she supposed she craved validation.

Mitch rolled his eyes toward the ceiling. "That's doubtful, my dear, but even so, Nicolina . . . I want *you* and only *you*," he insisted as he gently tugged her chin to face him. "And you aren't just any woman. You are the only woman."

Her heart pounded, but she remained silent.

"Hey, in this relationship, *you* are the one holding back. Believe me, I should be the one with doubts," he added, and something flickered in his eyes before he hid it with a slight smile. "Not only are you beautiful, but sensual . . . graceful. But what we have goes deeper than looks or even attraction. Nicolina, at our age we deserve the whole package. You're smart, creative, and best of all you make me laugh! Tell me, what more could a man want?"

Nicolina licked her bottom lip and lowered her gaze.

"Seriously?" He gently shook her chin until she gazed up at him. "Nicolina?"

"I'm sorry, Mitch. You must think I'm fishing for compliments. How embarrassing."

He gave her a full megawatt smile that made her weak in the knees. "You will never need to fish for compliments with me. I'll just say it. I don't care how old you are, Nicolina. You are one gorgeous, sexy woman. You have elegance about you . . . a certain grace that transcends age and is timeless. Rich or poor, young or old . . . any man would be lucky to have you!"

She had to smile and put a hand to his cheek. "You aren't just any man."

"I hope I'm your man," he said in a teasing tone, but she could see in his eyes that he was serious. How could such a successful, handsome man have any doubts?

She tilted her head. "Of course you are."

"Then I am a very lucky man."

Nicolina sighed. "Thank you. Again, I don't want to sound so *needy*. I despise needy women!"

He only smiled, making his eyes crinkle at the corners. "As long as it's me you need, it's perfectly fine. I know I *need* and *want* you. I use my involvement in the baseball complex as an excuse to come to Cricket Creek. Noah and Ty are fine at this point without me, and this strip mall is almost finished. Nicolina, the reason I come here so often is to be with you. I hope you know that."

Nicolina laughed. "You are so good for me." Yes, she took pains with her appearance, and deep down she knew that even at her age she turned heads, but in a world that worshipped youth and pencil-thin figures? Well, she was short and had curves to spare. Her crowning glory was her thick, rich, dark brown hair with a hint of auburn added at the salon. There was no denying her Italian roots. She talked with her hands, and despite her hidden worries, she was a little spitfire and had passed those traits on to Bella. She could get fired up in nothing flat, but Mitch didn't seem to mind. In fact, he seemed to enjoy their animated conversation as much as the passion in the bedroom. She hid her smile . . . well, perhaps almost as much as the passion. Nicolina had waited all of her life for a man like him . . . why did he have to be so damned rich? His wealth unnerved and intimidated her. And she supposed he was so wonderful that she was afraid to let herself believe it could all work out. Stupid, she knew, but still . . .

"Ah . . . I can see doubt in those lovely eyes of yours." Mitch trailed a fingertip down her cheek and then gave her a slow smile. "Sometimes, it's better to show how you feel rather than to tell," he said and then dipped his head and captured her mouth with his once more. He kissed her thoroughly, deeply, and with such passion that Nicolina found herself arching her back and offering herself to him all over again. She wrapped her arms and legs around him, and even while the storm raged outside, for the first time in her life Nicolina felt safe and secure. She both loved and hated the feeling. It was like jumping out of an airplane with a parachute. In theory, Nicolina knew it was safe, but the fear of a crash landing was what kept her from jumping. So she buried her face in the crook of his neck so he couldn't see the raw emotion that she just couldn't hide and instead lost herself in the moment. He made love to her with slow, easy strokes, taking his sweet time until she tilted her hips upward, letting him know that she was close to climax.

"Oh . . . Mitch!"

"Baby, you feel amazing . . . so hot, so ready." He moved faster and drove deeper, harder. Waves of pleasure washed over her, and she clung to his broad shoulders while he came with her. Then, as always, he kissed her tenderly and pulled her close. She rested her head against his chest and loved the rapid beat of his heart beneath her cheek.

Nicolina knew that in his business dealings he could be hard-nosed and determined. Other than the love he had spoken of for his daughter, this softer side of Mitch Monroe belonged solely to her, and in truth she treasured being held in his arms even more than the passion. Not that the passion wasn't . . . amazing. She'd never known it could be like this.

Of course another burning question was, How long could they sustain a long-distance relationship? Nicolina was finally getting to realize her dream of opening her own business, so moving back to Chicago wasn't an option, especially since Bella had moved here, if not permanently, at least until Logan moved up to the major leagues. She inhaled a deep breath and let it out slowly. If truth be told, it was getting more and more difficult every time Mitch left, but could a man of his stature give up the big-city lifestyle to live in a small town? She was guessing not.

Nicolina frowned. Perhaps she should end this before she got in even deeper, before words of love were spoken. She was only setting herself up for a long, painful fall, and damn, it would be so hard to pick herself up and get on with life. It had taken her years to get over the betrayal of Bella's father, and she shuddered at the thought of having to do it again.

"Cold?" he asked in that deep, sexy voice of his.

Unable to trust her voice, Nicolina gave him a negative shake of her head. She closed her eyes tightly and willed tears not to flow. She should end this! It would be better in the long run. But her heart constricted at the thought of never seeing him again, never feeling his touch.

Dear God, what am I going to do?

She should share her concerns with him, but she knew she would sound needy and whiny again and she just couldn't bring herself to do so. Besides, her throat had tightened with unshed tears, so talking would sound more like a croak. *Not cool,* as Bella would say.

Mitch could always pinpoint the instant when Nicolina pulled back, and he felt it now . . . even while basking in the warm glow of their lovemaking. He turned to his side and slid her even closer, spooning her against him, and although she responded with a soft sigh as she snuggled back against his chest, he could feel the slight tension in her body. He kissed the top of her head and then moved his hand gently up and down her arm. No words were spoken, but he was silently letting her know that he could be a patient man when needed.

Mitch knew what he wanted, and in business he went after his goal full speed ahead. But with Nicolina, he wouldn't push. Mitch fully understood her reluctance to give in to the feelings that were growing stronger each time he came to visit. She had admitted that she had loved with all her heart and had been betrayed much in the same way that he had with his ex-wife Clarisse. Of course, they had discussed that they would both do it all over again because even though the pain had torn them up, it had also resulted in having daughters they both treasured.

Mia . . . the worry of her whereabouts was about to drive him crazy. Tate Carpenter was on her tail, but Mitch's phone had gone dead during his airplane flight, and he had put it out of his mind since falling into bed with Nicolina. Losing himself in her loving arms was such a blessing. He only hoped he could break down her barriers and convince her to trust in him once and for all.

Mitch thought he should probably check his messages now, but he was reluctant to leave Nicolina's side just yet. Something was really bothering her, and as much as he promised himself not to push, he didn't know if he should hold his feelings for her back much longer. Surely, if she knew how much he cared, she would open up and trust him with her worries. He wanted to be there for her in all ways possible. He wanted to tell her that he loved her. Those three little words had been on the tip of his tongue so many times lately, but he never felt the confidence to say them. Rejection from her wasn't something he could handle, especially right now, and so he managed to hold back . . . but just barely. Mitch was a man who had made millions by being firm and decisive. This fear . . . this damned walking on eggshells was killing him.

Sure, they had complications. Mitch was damned afraid of putting his heart on the line again even after all these years, but he also knew when a risk was well worth taking. And yes, he lived in Chicago and traveled extensively. But he had seen the damage his absence had done to Mia. The older he got, the more he realized that there were things in life that were much more important than money and power.

Mitch ran a hand down his face. Why wait? One thing he knew for sure was that losing Nicolina wasn't an option. A sigh escaped him, drawing her attention.

Nicolina rolled to her back and faced him. "What's wrong?"

Mitch gave her a crooked smile and slid a fingertip over her bottom lip. Ah . . . she knew his moods as well as he knew hers. He hesitated, since those three little words were once again tripping over his tongue, but then replied, "I'm worried about my daughter, Mia."

"Do you want to talk about it?"

"Yes." He explained the painful last time he had spoken to her and how she had mistaken his bailing out Hanover Candy for a hostile takeover.

"How could she think such a thing?" Nicolina asked with such sympathy in her tone that it went straight to his heart.

God, it's good to have someone care. "I guess it's the way the one-sided conversation sounded to her."

"But why would you let her believe the worst?"

He raised one shoulder. "I was trying to make a point. While I wanted to challenge Mia to go out on her own and learn to fend for herself, I sure didn't think she would take off like she did. And I guess her belief that I could be a coldhearted bastard hurt. I let my emotions get the worst of me."

She placed a hand on his cheek. "Hey, it happens. I've had some knock-down-drag-outs with Bella." She wrinkled up her nose. "And I can be a tad . . . overbearing. I'm working on that."

"Ah, I love Mia so much, but I fear I haven't been such a good father."

"Don't be so hard on yourself, Mitch. Listen, anyone who thinks they are a perfect parent is kidding themselves."

"I know." He sighed. "But when Clarisse left me, I was eaten up with anger and let my pride get in the way of my good sense. I should have spent more time with my daughter and less time making pointless money."

"You love her, and that makes up for lots of mistakes and regrets. We can't change the past. Concentrate on the future."

"I just wish I knew where she was," he said, but he frowned when Nicolina's eyes widened and she put her hand over her mouth.

"Oh my goodness!"

"Nicolina, sweetheart, what is it?"

"I think I know where your daughter is, Mitch!"

"What?" He came up to a sitting position. "Where?"

"You're not going to believe it, but right here in Cricket Creek. I think she's a waitress over at Wine and Diner."

Mitch shook his head. “You’ve got to be mistaken. Mia . . . a waitress?”

“I only saw her in passing as I entered Wine and Diner, but when I asked, Bella said she was new and her name was Mia. I thought it might be her, but when I found out she was driving an old beat-up car I dismissed the notion.”

Mitch chuckled. “It’s an old Toyota that belonged to my gardener.”

“Well, then, it makes perfect sense.” Nicolina raised her hands. “She was a lovely blonde. Mitch, she has to be your daughter!”

As if on cue, Mitch heard his phone ring over where it was plugged into the charger. “Excuse me, I should get this.”

“Absolutely.”

After a quick kiss on her lips, he pushed up from the bed, hurried over to the dresser, and picked up his cell phone. After glancing at the screen, he looked over at Nicolina. “It’s Tate Carpenter, the detective I hired to tail Mia. We’re about to find out if you’re right.”

When Tate quickly confirmed Nicolina’s suspicion, he gave her a nod. She responded with a thumbs-up. “Stay on her tail, Tate, but don’t let her know it. I’ll keep out of sight here in Cricket Creek until you get here, and then I’ll sneak out of town.” After hanging up, he sat down on the edge of the bed. “Keep this knowledge to yourself, okay? Don’t even let Bella know who Mia really is.”

She reached over and put her hand over his. “My lips are sealed.”

Mitch grinned as relief washed over him. “Wow, my little girl is hanging in there. She already has a job and hasn’t come running home like I said she would.”

“She likes a challenge.” Nicolina chuckled. “I think she’s more like you than you think.”

“I do believe that you’re right.” He nodded and then smiled slowly. “This is going to be interesting.”

11

True Grit

MIA WOKE UP EVEN BEFORE THE ALARM, AND AFTER A quick cup of coffee from the Wine and Diner kitchen she jumped into the shower. While the warm water pelted her back, she shaved her legs and then squirted some shampoo into the palm of her hand. As she massaged her scalp, she rehearsed the speech she was going to give Noah Falcon. There was no way on God's green earth that she was going to let Cam get tossed off the team because of coming to her sorry-ass rescue! She had to grin when she suddenly realized that she was beginning to think and sound like she lived in Cricket Creek. This little town was already growing on her, and she didn't want to let any of its residents down!

Mia stomped her foot for good measure, sending a splash against the tiled stall and slipping in shampoo suds in the process. "Whoa!" she yelped and caught herself just before falling. Soap got in her eyes, but she turned her face up to the spray and laughed in spite of the sting. In the past few days she had felt just about every emotion, ranging from fear to anger to desire. And while not all of those feelings were what you could call fun, except, well, the desire part, Mia felt more alive and energized than she ever knew possible. While she had only been in Cricket Creek for a few days, her life back in Chicago somehow seemed . . . distant. She actually felt more connected *here*. *Weird,* she thought, while thinking that if she were back home right now, she would most likely still be sleeping in with no real plans for the day other than . . . what?

"Fluff," Mia said as she reached up to turn off the faucet. She thought about the fact that her days had been filled with shopping, hair and nail appointments, facials, and doing lunch with women who merely picked at their food. They would glare at her pretty much normal appetite, making her feel guilty to the point of putting down her fork. She shook her head. That blue-plate special at Wine and Diner had been pure bliss but would have been met with gasps from her friends. She also acknowledged that she should have had some backbone and should have bucked the socialite system. But she hadn't.

"Pure fluff and no grit." It felt great to get up with a sense of purpose this morning, something her life had been sorely lacking.

As Mia squeezed the excess water from her hair, she frowned at the realization that she hadn't heard anything from people whom she considered close friends. At least she *thought* they were friends, but she supposed she had thought wrong. In the days she had been out of the social loop, not one so-called *friend* had bothered to inquire where she was or what she was doing. Then again, perhaps no one had called because no one even realized that she was gone! "Am I really that meaningless?

"Evidently." Mia sighed as she pushed back the plastic curtain and stepped out of the shower. Some of that was her fault. While she shopped and traveled with the best of them, nightlife had never been her thing. Pulling all-nighters at clubs coupled with the rest of that scenario simply didn't appeal to Mia. Part of the reason was that her father had frowned upon it, and the other part was that Mia didn't see the point of partying until the break of dawn. On top of that, she had seen the results, and rehab wasn't something she had ever wanted to have to do. She supposed it was also because she'd never wanted to disappoint her father.

Mia sighed again as she leaned over and toweled dry. In truth, if she really thought about it, she had never really felt as if she fit in anywhere. Perhaps that seed of insecurity had been planted in her brain as a child when she had tried to visit her mother and her new family. College had been the closest she had come to a normal existence, but after graduation she had been at loose ends, just floundering around. And romance? Oh, she had dated here and there, but no one had ever set her world on fire. Until her elevator interlude with Cam, she had never felt the mindless passion that made you want to rip your clothes off and make wild, passionate love. Just the thought of his mouth pressed to hers made her feel warm all over. Until now she had thought that the weak-in-the-knees feelings written about in books were simply pure fantasy.

"Well, I was wrong," Mia admitted as she lifted her head to view herself in the steam-filled mirror. Her hazy reflection represented how she had been living her life . . . fuzzy and disoriented. The only time she had felt any sense of worth was when she was putting together parties for her father's business clients or serving on a committee for a charity event. She was, in fact, excellent at event planning, but really, what good would those skills serve in the real world? "Okay, I'll put that thought process into motion later." At the moment someone needed her, and she wasn't about to let him down.

With that in mind, Mia wiped a squeaky clear circle in the mirror and shoved her getting-ready routine into high gear. She had learned from her father the importance of arriving early and always being prepared. Luckily, Myra had been willing to have her come in late to work, so all her ducks were in a row. Well, at least so far. Mia made a mental note to buy something nice to repay just some of the kindness Myra had bestowed upon her. Oh, wait, she was broke. Funny, but in the past Mia had tossed money around like confetti or bought gifts as payment for just about everything. Well, those days were over. Mia sighed but then brightened when a sudden thought occurred to her. She would just have to do something sweet for Myra instead, like work extra hours or something. "Well, there!" she said and she smiled at her reflection.

She planned on getting to the baseball complex before ten o'clock, which was when Cam had mentioned he was going to arrive to, well, finally face the music. He had insisted that she didn't have to plead his case and she had finally given in . . . Well, at least she had pretended to back down and let him "fight his own battle," as he had put it. What he didn't know was that she planned to lay the groundwork of forgiveness before he even arrived at the stadium.

Mia blinked at her face in the mirror and said a silent prayer that she was making the right decision and not doing more damage than good. She also hoped that Cam wouldn't be pissed. "I'm doing the right thing," she said, but she didn't sound too convincing. She frowned. "I am!" Mia repeated with firm resolve and then started applying makeup with a quick, light hand. With time of the essence, she went with a simple hairstyle by holding her hair back with a gold clip at the base of her neck. "There," she said with a nod and then hurried into the bedroom. She slipped on the cream-colored linen suit that she had randomly but thankfully packed and then located the most sensible shoes she could find, since of course she would once again be hoofing it over to the stadium. Luckily, the storm had brought a cool front with it and the walk wouldn't leave her wilted when she arrived. Other than sitting poolside or working out in her Zumba class, Mia wasn't used to breaking a sweat, but she had a feeling that was about to become a thing of the past. After this meeting she would have to rush back home and change into her uniform. Waiting tables wasn't for sissies.

After spraying on a bit of perfume, Mia grabbed her purse and was out the door. As she walked through town toward the river, she marveled at how many people waved and gave her friendly smiles. Shops were beginning to open, and when she passed Grammar's Bakery, a customer opened the door, bringing the yeasty scent of bread baking mingled with freshly brewed coffee Mia's way. Her stomach rumbled in dire protest, and although another strong cup of coffee would have hit the spot, she was on a mission and kept on walking. It was harder, however, to pass Violet's Vintage Clothing, especially when a sale rack was being wheeled out to the sidewalk. She paused and touched a gauzy blouse that was calling her name. "Twelve dollars?"

"And fifty percent off today only," announced a friendly clerk. Her snow-white curls covered her head like a frothy cap and she had a wide smile enhanced with very red lipstick. Mia guessed her to be in her seventies, but there was vibrancy about the woman that reminded Mia of Betty White—with a southern accent. "The color would complement your lovely blond hair. It's a bit big, but a wide belt would fix that and would work very nicely with your slim figure."

"And skinny jeans," Mia agreed with the enthusiasm of a seasoned shopper. "Oh, and some ballerina flats!"

"Perfect! I have a rack of belts inside the shop if you want to come in." She extended her hand. "I'm Violet, by the way."

"I'm Mia."

She angled her white-capped head. "Very pretty name. It suits you."

"Thank you, Violet. I just adore your shop!" Mia peeked inside at the racks of clothes and accessories and gave a sigh of longing. "Oh, Violet, I'm in a rush, but I can assure you I will come back and browse!" Of course, browsing was all she could do until she got paid.

"Oh, wonderful. It would be such fun to dress such a beauty! Hurry back, Mia."

"Oh, you'll see me again," Mia promised and then forced her legs to keep on moving. She firmly reminded herself that she was not only broke but owed money, so shopping shouldn't even be on her radar. Yet further down the street, Hats Galore captured her attention. To her credit, although she slowed her pace, she continued to walk. Then the Book Nook pulled her like a magnet, and she craned her neck and sighed when she spotted shelves crammed with paperbacks. Even as a child Mia had read voraciously. She supposed it was yet another way she had filled her time and escaped into another world while her father traveled. She made a mental note to browse there too as soon as she got the chance.

At the end of the block, a florist shop called Flower Power was so cute that Mia had to grin. She always made sure that her father's house was filled with freshly cut bouquets, most of them from the Monroes' own gardens, lovingly cared for by Manny. At that thought she felt a sudden flash of homesickness, but she pushed it aside. When she could afford it, she was going to pop into Flower Power and buy a beautiful bouquet of roses for her apartment.

Over the years, Mia had spent countless hours in high-end department stores up and down the Magnificent Mile in Chicago, armed with credit cards. In fact, she had shopped in exclusive designer shops all over the globe, and yet she always preferred small boutiques much like the ones on Main Street in Cricket Creek. She was unsure why, but then it hit her. It wasn't just the quaintness of the shops or the unique merchandise.

It was the people.

There was a certain sense of caring here that went beyond trying to sell her something. Here, in this small town, it started with Fred offering to hold her car until she could save the money to get it fixed, and then continued with the chance that Myra had taken on her, including offering her a place to stay. In a cold world where Mia had often felt valued only because of her name and her wealth, Cricket Creek represented a warm welcome and unconditional acceptance.

Like Wine and Diner, much of Main Street looked freshly renovated, and she hoped that the revitalized town was going to make it. It was no secret that family-owned businesses were at risk in a global economy that was ruled by franchises. Mia realized that these people were not only trying to make a living but attempting to save a way of life that was becoming rare. She had witnessed firsthand how hard they worked and hoped with all her heart that the comeback remained a success.

As she approached the baseball stadium, she noticed a newly constructed strip mall that somehow retained the quaintness of the rest of the town. The brick storefronts reminded her of brownstones in Chicago, and when Mia suddenly wondered how much of this her father had a hand in, she stopped in her tracks and put a hand to her chest.

"Wow," she breathed when it occurred to her that although she had spent his money freely, Mia knew very little about what Mitch Monroe actually did for a living. While she acknowledged that some of that burden fell on her father, Mia had to swallow a hot lump that lodged in her throat. When had she ever taken interest in what he did? Asked questions? She had thrown so many parties and organized events for his clients without even knowing much about them either. And while she had soaked up a lot of business savvy simply by osmosis, how much more could she have learned? Taking an actual interest would have gone a long way, she was certain.

"God, just how shallow am I?" she whispered, but she knew the answer. "About as deep as a puddle," she muttered. "Wow . . ." She looked out over the wide expanse of the river and inhaled a deep breath to keep from melting into an actual puddle of tears. Although she needed to head into the baseball stadium and track down Noah Falcon, Mia suddenly felt the need to sit down for a moment on the wooden bench overlooking the water.

Mia swallowed and gathered her scattered thoughts. Okay, she knew she wasn't bitchy like many of the people in her circle of friends. Mia could be moody but didn't consider herself to be mean. At least she hoped she didn't come off that way! And she wasn't wild and didn't live life in the fast lane like she had witnessed over and over. She sniffed hard and at least gave herself that much. But she was . . . what? For a moment Mia stared out over the river and thought about it. How would she describe herself?

She was always polite to the hired help, and she tipped well. She was *nice*! Oh, and honest. Except for the whole Mia Money charade, Mia tried to be truthful. She hated liars and cheaters. She had seen firsthand what they had done to her father. So what was it? What was she lacking that had created that big gaping hole in her life? Mia couldn't even put a finger on it at first, and then she had an Oprah *aha* moment that had her sitting up straighter before slumping back down.

"I get it!" She was unappreciative . . . of, well, *everything*—from the gourmet food she consumed to the luxury car she drove to the world she had traveled. In truth, that even extended to her friends. If one wasn't available, she had a long list of others that she could plug in without even caring which one. An exception was her friend Cat Carson, but she was so busy with her music career that Mia rarely saw her anymore. "It makes sad sense," she whispered. She had so much that it all meant so very little. "Incredible." Mia inhaled a deep breath of river-scented air and shook her head. "I really get it now." What her life had been lacking was . . . *meaning*. "Well, doesn't that just suck," she said dully. Then she thought about it for a few more minutes.

The merchants she had passed on the way here were hard at work opening shops that were obviously still struggling to keep the doors open. Wide smiles and friendly waves were in abundance, though, despite the shaky economy. But by looking around Mia knew that this went deeper than just selling products. This was about preserving not only a town, but a way of life that was pure Americana and yet becoming scarcer as the years passed. She could tell that it meant much more to them than simply making a buck. It was about pride of ownership and preserving a family business or farm for future generations. Just like Hanover Candy, Mia thought with a sad pang that went straight to her gut and twisted. How could her father do such a thing, especially to a longtime friend? While Mia fully acknowledged the sad realization that her life was lacking substance, she had always believed in her father's integrity.

She sat there for a moment and relived that last conversation with her father that had led to her bouncing out of town in Manny's car. Something didn't make sense. Mia nibbled on the inside of her cheek, deep in thought, until the loud honk of a barge heading down the river startled her out of her trance. She blinked in the bright sunlight and wanted to sit and contemplate the missing piece of the puzzle until the answer came to her, but she really needed to get into Noah Falcon's office before Cam arrived. With that in mind, she picked up her purse and stood up.

Once inside the elevator, Mia felt her cheeks heat up at the steamy memory of the hot kisses shared with Cam. Riding in an elevator would never be the same. She firmly told herself not to make too much of it since it was one of those trapped-together situations where one thing led to another and all that. Besides, she was going to be living in Cricket Creek for only a short time, so why start something she couldn't finish? There was only one problem with that decision: She had never had a man make her melt the way Cameron Patrick was able to. The romantic in her wondered how on earth she was going to be able to walk away from that feeling without exploring where it could lead.

Mia sighed. "First things first," she muttered. A second later the elevator arrived on the fifth floor, and although Mia hoped she appeared confident in her expensive suit, in reality her knees were a little bit wobbly. Still, she marched right up to the receptionist and requested to see Noah Falcon.

"Is he expecting you?" She was a tiny wisp of a thing but had a tone that suggested she didn't mess around. Mia looked at the nameplate on the desk, which read MAGGIE, and smiled.

"No," Mia admitted, "but, Maggie, it is a matter of extreme urgency."

"Well"—Maggie's pointed little chin came up—"if your urgent matter doesn't pertain to opening day, then it will have to wait."

"It does." Mia tried not to cringe at her obvious lie.

"In what capacity?" Maggie challenged, clearly not believing Mia, and yet there was hope in her tone that indicated to Mia that the Cougars had some sort of situation on their hands.

"Well . . ." Mia swallowed, and her heart knocked against her ribs. She had her foot in the door but didn't know quite how to open it wider. She just totally sucked at lying! "Um . . ."

The secretary sighed and gave Mia a pointed look. "Mr. Falcon is swamped, so you'll have to come back when you have an appointment." She turned her back and started typing.

Mia swallowed hard. She wasn't used to being dismissed like this, and it rattled her, but just when she was about to give up, she heard a male voice coming from an open office door. Her ears perked up and she gleaned enough information to know that whoever was performing the opening-day concert had just canceled. She perked up. This was right up her alley! "Um, excuse me?"

Maggie swiveled around and gave Mia a bland look.

"Actually, I'm here to discuss opening-day entertainment," she announced and immediately started going through the Rolodex in her brain that contained famous people she knew. Luckily, there were quite a few.

"Why didn't you say so?" Relief washed over Maggie's face. "Oh, good. What was your name again?"

"Mia Money."

"Money?" Maggie asked and scrolled down a list that Mia obviously wasn't on.

"Like money in the bank," she added. She was beginning to like her facetious last name.

"Hmm, can't find you."

"I was added last minute. You know, to save the day. Opening day," she added in a firm tone full of meaning.

"Well, in that case, head on back." The fact that she wasn't on any list suddenly didn't matter. Maggie pushed the intercom and announced the arrival of Mia Money to Noah Falcon and then pointed. "First door on the left."

"Thank you," Mia said in a clipped businesslike manner and then headed down the short hallway. When she entered the spacious office, Noah Falcon looked up at her with a handsome but frowning face. "Good morning," she said breezily. She wondered if she should go into her rehearsed speech about Cameron Patrick or gain some leverage first.

"Morning." Noah gave her a slight smile, but his brows remained drawn together. There were dark circles beneath his eyes, suggesting lack of sleep.

"So you're lacking opening-day entertainment?"

"Yes," he said hesitantly, but he angled his head as if trying to place her. Mia didn't think they had ever met, but he could have seen pictures of her with her father. "I don't mean to sound rude, but do I know you? Ty McKenna, the head coach, has a baby who never sleeps, and I've been helping him along with doing a million other things to get ready for opening day," he added with a sigh, and then gestured toward a chair in front of his massive desk. "So forgive me in advance."

Mia took a thankful seat and then gave him a bright smile. "No, we've never met, but I think I have a solution to your lack of an opening-day concert."

"How did you know about that?"

"It's my job to know things," she said and was somehow able to keep a straight face. "You're in luck."

"I sure hope so." Noah scrubbed a hand down his face and thankfully didn't ask who she was or whom she worked for. She could only lie badly so fast. "I wanted to start off the season with a sellout crowd, so I booked a big-name country concert before the game, but they had to bail due to a schedule conflict. It's going to be tough to find a replacement this late in the game, if you'll pardon the pun," he added with a slight but tired grin. "I've tried calling in favors, but I've come up empty." He raised his hands to demonstrate.

"Well, have you heard of Cat Carson?"

"The cute country singer with the big voice?"

"Yes." She pressed her lips together while it sunk in.

"Wait." Noah suddenly leaned in closer. "Are you saying you can get her to fill in?"

"It's possible." Mia nodded and said a silent prayer. "Um, what is the date again?"

"June third."

She gave him another businesslike nod and a confident smile. "If not Cat, then perhaps someone else. I have lots of connections." When he opened his mouth as if to probe, she hurried on, "She's incredibly busy, but I'll call right now and see what I can do, if that's okay with you?"

"Really?" Noah blinked at her as if trying to size her up. "You *really* think you can pull this off?"

"I do." They had become fast friends after Mia had given a large check to Cat's favorite charity at a fundraiser several years ago. "I know her very well, in fact." She pulled out her cell phone. "Now, would you like me to make the call? It's much more likely for me to get her now versus later in the day."

"How much would she charge? Our budget here is, well, let's say, not big. The band I had coming here was doing me a personal favor."

Mia smiled. "Cat gives generously to several charities. I'm sure she would be happy to perform a short set simply for a donation to one of her charities." She gave a little wave of her hand.

"Not a problem. I'll even pitch in some personal money. Give Cat a call."

"Excellent," Mia said and then scrolled down to Cat's number and pressed the CALL button while saying a silent prayer that Cat would be available. Although Mia had other connections, Cat Carson was her best shot. While Cat loved her music, she avoided the limelight, and the two of them had often traveled via Mitch's company jet to exclusive but private beach destinations. And oh, how they gave new meaning to shop 'til you drop! But what Mia liked about traveling with Cat was that they both enjoyed local merchants more than big designer brands. While Cat's music was played on country radio, she really had a bit of a pop-music Colbie Caillat vibe that had universal appeal. And while she often sported a cowboy hat and boots, her flowing skirts, billowy blouses, and chunky jewelry added a bohemian flair that suited her often beach-oriented songs.

Mia smiled at the thought of seeing her friend. While Cat's crammed schedule prohibited her from getting away very often, and even less now that her career was starting to skyrocket, Mia knew her friend would help if it was even remotely possible. If it worked out, Mia was going to use this coup to butter up Noah rather than call it in now as leverage. She had learned from event planning, especially charity balls, that it was better to butter up than to demand. Nice, she had found out, went a long way.

When the phone rang for the third time, Mia felt a jolt

of alarm and flicked a quick glance at Noah. When his shoulders rose and fell, she knew he was thinking the same thing. Cat wasn't going to pick up. But just when her voice mail was about to chime in, Mia heard a breathless, "Hello! Mia?"

"None other," Mia said and gave Noah a thumbs-up. "Did I catch you at a bad time?"

"No, just got back from a run and it is so hot out that it kicked my butt. How are you, girl? Feeling the need for some retail therapy?" Cat asked with a laugh.

"Actually, I have a favor to ask of you."

"Sure, what is it?"

"Well . . ." Mia cleared her throat and wondered just how to explain her current situation in front of Noah, so she chose her words carefully since she wouldn't be mentioning her father. Once again, she wanted to do this on her own. "I'm in Cricket Creek, Kentucky."

"Kentucky? Really? For the Derby? Can I come? Get a big floppy hat and everything?"

Mia chuckled. "No, that's in Louisville."

"Oh. So what's in . . . ?"

"Cricket Creek? Actually, my car broke down, and, well, it's a long story that will keep until we get together."

"Okay, but you've got me intrigued! So what's the favor, sweet pea?"

"Ex–baseball pro Noah Falcon is willing to give some serious cash to the charity of your choice if you will do him a big favor and sing a set before the opening-day baseball game for the Cricket Creek Cougars. He manages the team and has, well, a situation. The band he booked bailed."

"Oh, well, that's not good. But serious cash to one of my charities is good! When is the event?"

"Saturday, June third," Mia said with a wince and held her breath.

"Wow, that's right around the corner," Cat answered slowly. "Let me pull my schedule up on my computer."

"Thanks!" Pulling her schedule up meant Cat was at

least willing. Mia heard the clicking of the keyboard and nibbled on the inside of her cheek.

"Luckily my manager just updated it so it's current or I would have to call her." *Click, click . . . click.* "Oh . . . well, wow, no way."

"Oh . . . what?" Was that a good *no way* or a bad *no way*?

"Is Cricket Creek far from Nashville?"

"Only a couple of hours, I think."

"Hmm, what time is the concert?"

"Wait a second," Mia said then looked at Noah. "What time is the concert?"

"The game is at seven in the evening but the concert is at five thirty," he answered, and she repeated the information to Cat.

"Well, I open for Toby Keith in Nashville on Friday. I'll be on his tour bus so I won't have a car, but he's staying on Saturday to do some interviews. As long as I'm available by Sunday afternoon, I'll be fine. In fact, come on in on Friday night and we'll hang out. I'll be at the Marriott right downtown. It'll be a blast. I haven't seen you in so long, girl!"

"So you can do it?"

"I'll have to clear it with my manager, but I don't see why not. And when Toby learns that I'm doing this for charity, I'm sure he will work it out with me. Just have me back after the game or Sunday morning and we're fine. I might even be able to arrange to get picked up."

"Excellent!" Mia smiled brightly at Noah. "I'll work out the details and give you a call tonight. Thanks so much, Cat!"

"Are you kidding? Mia, this obviously is important to you, and money for charity is always a plus. We have a win-win situation on our hands. Not to mention this is going to be a blast. Besides, my schedule is tight and I could use a night of good old fun. We'll eat barbecue at Jack's and hang out at Tootsies and the Stage. Maybe I'll even get up and sing a song or two."

"It does sound like a lot of fun," Mia agreed. Cat might be well on her way to becoming a superstar, but she was one of the most down-to-earth people that Mia knew, and Mia always had a great time with her. "And congrats on opening for Toby Keith! Wow!"

"Hey, it's sold out, but I might be able to score you some tickets. After all, if you have to drive me back Sunday, you might as well stay for the concert. I'll work on it."

"I would love that! Talk to you soon." Mia ended the call and then turned to Noah. "I think we're all set."

"I have to admit that I'm impressed." He lifted one eyebrow. "But I have to ask . . . who are you and how did you end up in my office?"

Mia swallowed hard. "Funny you should ask," she replied slowly while racking her brain for the right way to cash in on her favor. She leaned forward and offered her hand. "I'm Mia Money."

Noah shook her hand and then leaned back in his big leather chair. "You obviously have connections and a friendly but persuasive attitude. Wait, how would you like to be a promotions manager? Ty has been all over me to hire one. I told him I could do it all myself, but I was dead wrong."

"I . . ."

"Mia, you would be perfect! Do I already have your résumé for a position?" He glanced down at his cluttered desk with a frown. "Sorry. I promise I'm not usually this disorganized, but with opening day coming up and Ty so busy with practice and a newborn, well, I've been pulling double duty."

"Not a problem," Mia assured him.

"So do you want the job?"

"Seriously?" Mia blinked at him while her mind raced.

"We'd forgo the usual hiring process and get you started right away."

"And my duties would be?"

"To combine promotions and advertising to put fans in the seats. Plan events like the concert to keep the games fun and attract attendance with giveaways and stuff like that. Now, as I mentioned, our budget is limited, so you have to be creative."

"Not a problem. Do you have a Web site?" She had created several for charity events, so she did know a thing or two about promotions. "And a Facebook page?"

"We have a Web site but not a Facebook page."

"I could create one right away," Mia said with a businesslike nod. "We could get some publicity going with local media." She was good at this as well. "I think I could be an asset to your organization, Mr. Falcon."

He nodded slowly. "I get the impression you have some experience in event planning?"

"Lots of it. Mostly with nonprofits," Mia added, hoping he didn't want details. Noah looked at her closely, as if sizing her up, making Mia's heart pound, but he suddenly nodded as if making a decision.

"Fantastic! Look, it will be a lot of work with a not-so-big salary, but I can provide a small but nice furnished condo overlooking the river in the high-rise right next door. Most of the baseball players and some of the staff live there, so you'd have plenty of people to hang out with. There's a pool and hot tub, workout room, and so on. You can rent pontoon boats and Jet Skis over at the marina if you enjoy that sort of thing." He smiled. "And the commute to work is a short walk across the parking lot. Sound like something you could live with?"

Mia's heart hammered. This would be perfect! Right up her alley, and she actually felt so excited that it was difficult to sit still. She was floored that he would hire her without knowing her background or skills, but she wasn't about to look a gift horse in the mouth. She supposed she had caught him in a time of desperation, and not to pounce on the opportunity to earn a paycheck and respect from her father was too good to pass up. Plus this just might give her the unexpected but additional leverage to save Cam's position on the team. Well, it was time to find out. Oh, but wait . . . she already had a job! Myra had been so good to her. She just couldn't accept this offer without calling Myra first. "Would you mind if I made a phone call?"

"No, of course not. Go right ahead. You can go out into the hallway and close the door if you want some privacy."

"Thanks." Mia gave Noah a grateful smile before stepping outside the office. After closing the door, she dialed Wine and Diner and crossed her fingers that Myra was available.

"Wine and Diner."

"Myra?"

"The one and only."

Mia felt a nervous flutter in her stomach. "Hi, Myra, this is Mia Mon-ey." Oh boy, she'd almost blown her cover.

"Everything okay, sugar?"

"Well." Mia swallowed hard and then continued, "I just got a fabulous job offer from Noah Falcon. He wants me to be their promotions manager."

"You don't say! Take it!"

"Really?" Mia leaned against the wall in relief. "I hate to leave you shorthanded after all you've done for me."

"Hey, things are looking up, but jobs are still hard to come by in Cricket Creek, just like everywhere else. I'll fill the position."

"Oh, thank you, Myra. I won't need the apartment either, since Noah's offer includes accommodations too."

"Sounds like an offer you can't afford to pass up."

"I was hoping you'd see it that way, but rest assured that I will pay you back for the bail money."

"Cam already took care of that."

"Oh . . . great. Well, is there anything I can do for all the trouble I put you through?" Mia had learned from her father never to burn any bridges.

"Just send customers our way."

Mia smiled. "Oh, I certainly will! Thanks for being so understanding."

Myra chuckled. "Hey, the restaurant business is tough. I've learned to be understanding. But I appreciate that you called, Mia. It shows that my intuition about you was correct."

Mia cocked her head to the side. "And what did your intuition say?"

"That you might be in a spot of trouble but that I could trust you. You've got a nice way about you and a good heart. You should do real well at this kind of promotions thing. Now, run along and take that job."

"Thank you! I'll see you soon." Mia pushed the END button but stood there for a moment to gather her composure. It felt good to be trusted and valued. With a lift of her chin, she marched back into Noah's office filled with determination.

"Well?" Noah raised his brows in question.

"I'll take the job, but I have one little request."

"Shoot."

"I'm guessing you already know about the bit of . . . a situation Cameron Patrick got into?"

Noah frowned. "How do you know about that?"

"I was the waitress that he rescued." Mia went on to explain the chain of events that had led up to the arrest. "So I just want to make sure that he isn't cut from the team."

Noah leaned back and sighed. "Then I guess you know the stipulations with which Cam was put on the roster. He had to keep his nose clean. He failed."

"It wasn't his fault!"

"Not my problem."

Mia thought about threatening to call the Cat Carson deal off or not take the job. While she hated to go that route, it might work and she was feeing desperate. But she gave Noah a long, steady look and said, "What would you have done in his situation?"

"That's not the point. I made a hard-and-fast rule

with Cameron Patrick, and he broke it by landing in jail," he said firmly, but when his eyes flickered with regret Mia pressed forward.

"Please answer my question, Mr. Falcon," she pleaded softly.

"I would have done the same damned thing," he admitted.

"Then give him another chance. Rule or no rule, it's the right thing to do."

Noah gave her a steady look. His lips twitched. He sighed. "Okay. I will give him one last chance. But if he lands himself in jail again, it's over. Understood?"

Mia's heart sang with joy. When she stood up and offered her hand, Noah shook it firmly. "And if you don't mind, would you keep this conversation to yourself? I promised Cam I wouldn't come here on his behalf, and there's no reason to disclose this little meeting to him."

"Done," Noah said, "and you just made me realize that I made the right decision." He smiled. "Welcome to the staff of the Cricket Creek Cougars!"

12

A Time for Us . . .

"WAIT, NOAH, DID YOU JUST SAY THAT YOU HIRED MY daughter? Mia?" Mitch stopped pacing and sat down heavily on the kitchen chair in Nicolina's little breakfast nook. "Yes, I know I only have one daughter. I'm just, well, floored."

Nicolina put her coffee mug down and pushed aside the pastel paint chips she had been considering for the shop. When Mitch raised his eyebrows at her, she reached over and covered his hand with hers.

"She's going by the last name Money? How'd you know she was my daughter? Oh, that's right, you did meet her briefly. Yes, thank God for Facebook. Well, thanks. I'm glad that you think she will do a good job for you. Yes, she actually does have lots of experience planning huge events," he said with a chuckle. "No, don't let her know that you know who she is. I want her to do this on her own and find her way without me interfering. She needs to do this for herself. Wow . . . really? She did that?" Mitch glanced at Nicolina and shook his head. "I guess she's got more of me in her than I realized," he added with another chuckle. "Whatever you do, don't let her know I'm here in Cricket Creek. I'll stay holed up here with Nicolina. Yeah, come on over here later and we'll talk about some ideas for the area around the stadium I've been mulling over," he said before ending the call.

"Well, now," Nicolina prompted as she poured more steaming coffee into Mitch's mug, "tell me about the latest in the life of Mia Monroe, or should I say Mia . . . *Money*?"

"I couldn't have made this up." After a brief chuckle, Mitch leaned back in his chair and laced his fingers together.

"I'm all ears."

"Oh, I beg to differ," he said playfully, making Nicolina blush. After another bout of incredible sex that lasted most of the morning, they had finally crawled out of bed, needing food and caffeine.

"Mitch!" she scoffed, but he gave her a once-over that deepened her blush. She was wearing a pair of Mitch's boxers and a white V-neck T-shirt that played with her breasts every time she moved. Mitch declared that Victoria's Secret be damned, having her ultrafeminine body in his masculine shorts and shirt was sexier than any silk and lace teddy. "Now, go on with your story," she said, but he was looking pretty damned sexy too, in low-slung drawstring lounging pants and no shirt. It had been difficult to concentrate on paint colors with his bare chest within reaching distance. Even now her fingers itched to trail through his dark wedge of chest hair threaded with silver. That same silky hair tickled and teased her nipples during sex. For the life of her she couldn't understand the current trend to shave it off. She reached down and took a sip of her coffee to distract her train of thought so she could listen to this latest information about Mia.

"Noah Falcon just hired her as promotions manager for the team. Isn't that something?" He tilted his head and chuckled, looking more relaxed and happy than she had seen him in quite a while. "After talking to her for a while, he suspected who she was, and Facebook pictures confirmed it. He said Mia had some of my hand gestures and mannerisms, which clued him in as well."

Nicolina smiled. "Guess the apple doesn't fall far from the tree."

"Apparently," he said, and then his eyes misted over, making Nicolina's heart melt. "She's a lot tougher than I thought. And Noah thinks she will do a great job."

"Mitch, I'm sure she got a lot of her business savvy from you—both learned and, well, in her genes. And I know she planned many of your parties and events for clients and charity. I read about some of them in the society page. You might have thought that was all fluff, but it takes lots of skill to pull that sort of thing off."

Mitch sat up straighter. "Damn, Nicolina, I guess I didn't give her nearly enough credit, did I?"

"Probably not," she answered softly but truthfully.

"I should have offered her a job instead of allowing her to flit all over the globe without a care in the world."

"Well, giving her unlimited spending privileges might not have been such a good idea." Nicolina pinched off another piece of bagel. "But having her get a job on her own is a much better scenario than handing her one."

"But Noah was pretty sure she was my daughter."

"Mitch, the success of the baseball team is important to Noah Falcon. He hired Mia because he believed she could do a good job, not because of who she was." She paused but felt the need to go on. "But her cover is blown."

"She doesn't know that."

"True." With her lips pressed together, Nicolina fell silent. "Do you think it's fair to allow her to think that?"

"Maybe not, but I don't see any other way to give her this chance to prove herself."

"But Mitch, she left home under false pretenses as well. Maybe you need to set her straight. She can still work for the Cougars. You're a silent partner, so no one would know the connection anyway."

"As always, you have a good point." He tilted his head as if in consideration. "But at least for now let's keep mum and let her go. Once I leave town, I'll have my PI keep an eye on her for a while. Just to give me peace of mind."

"I don't blame you there. I was worried sick when Bella came here to live on her own." At the thought of him leaving once again, Nicolina's heart constricted, but she managed to smile. "Okay, I'll respect your wishes and keep my silence. I won't even tell Bella. That girl has a tough time keeping a secret." She tore off another piece of bagel and added it to her little pile.

"Nicolina, baby, what is it?"

She looked up in surprise. "What do you mean?"

"You've been shredding your bagel like confetti. What's bothering you?"

"Nothing," she scoffed with a very Italian wave of her hand. *Nothing, except for knowing you're leaving me tomorrow and could be gone for days—maybe even weeks—on end. Nothing, except for me breaking my hard-and-fast rule never to fall for another man with wealth and power. They tend to upgrade their women much like they do their businesses.* "Nothing at all."

"You can't fool me," he gently coaxed. "Talk to me. I'm here for you."

Spill her guts? No, thank you.

"Nicolina? What's worrying you?"

She sliced her hand through the air again. "Just that secrets have a way of coming back and biting you in the butt. I know you want to do what's best for Mia, but keep that in mind."

"Duly noted." Mitch nodded. "I won't let this go on for too long, just enough for Mia to make her mark and get settled."

"You do know that if she does, she just might settle down here for good and not move back to Chicago. How would you deal with that?" She held her breath, hoping he would say that he would move here to be near his daughter.

Mitch hesitated, and then when it appeared that he was going to disclose something important, he swallowed and picked up his coffee mug. "We'll cross that bridge when we come to it."

Nicolina nodded and did her best to keep her disappointment from showing. "I'll keep an eye on Mia too, Mitch."

He smiled warmly. "Thank you, sweetheart. That means so much to me. Hey, perhaps our daughters will become friends. Wouldn't that be wonderful?"

"Yes," Nicolina agreed, but then pulled off another piece of bagel. When he noticed, she popped it into her mouth and chewed, but when it stuck in her throat she had to wash it down with a gulp of coffee. "Okay," she said with false brightness, "let's get back to these paint chips." She held up a card full of various shades of yellow. "What do you think of buttercup?"

"Soft, cheerful," Mitch commented. He knew that there was something else eating at her, but he wasn't going to probe, even though it was killing him not to. He loved her, trusted her . . . damn well needed her and enjoyed every minute of her company. Mitch could marry her tomorrow and be happy for the rest of his life—he knew it. And he would also make it work even if he had to relocate here to Cricket Creek, Kentucky. In fact, along with a strip mall, he had started to envision building a hotel and perhaps a convention center to bring in revenue to the town during the off-season. He and Noah had discussed the possibility of winter workshops and training camps. Olivia's daughter, Madison, thought there was some potential for writers' seminars and workshops and possibly book fairs that could fill the facility as well. The marina could host boat shows. The list went on and on . . .

Mitch shook his head. If all his plans for Cricket Creek and the stadium worked out, Mia's job could go well beyond the mere promotions of the Cougars. But the development was in the preliminary stages and he didn't want to get his hopes up until he did the marketing research and started getting permits in place.

"For a color supposedly so cheerful, you have quite a frown on your face," Nicolina commented.

"I'm sorry. I guess I have a lot on my mind."

"Understandable," Nicolina replied before holding up another paint chip. "Is banana split better?" she asked with a chuckle. "Where do they come up with these names anyway? Do you suppose there's a color-naming committee?"

"I don't know, but it sure makes me want a banana split," he said. He tried to stop thinking about the future and concentrate on the beautiful woman sitting across from him. *Sometimes, it's better to simply enjoy the moment,* he reminded himself. "I just bet this little town has an amazing ice cream stand. Want to get dressed and find out?" He gave a slight shrug. "Even though I really hate to get dressed when I'm with you."

"You're forgetting that you have to be incognito."

"Right," he glumly acknowledged and then nibbled on the inside of his cheek. "Hey, maybe I could go in disguise. Get one of those baseball caps with the mullet attached to the bottom?"

Nicolina laughed. "If I get you one, will you really wear it?"

"Are you kidding?"

"Not in the least."

"Sure I will," Mitch said, even though he had never done anything so crazy-fun since he was a kid. He chuckled, thinking that being with Nicolina made him feel young and alive in more ways than one.

"Awesome! I'll get right on it. I can be very creative, you know."

"Oh, baby, I know."

"Mitch!" she scolded, but she gave him that throaty laugh of hers that made him long to hop right back into bed. "Okay, you get out your laptop and do all of that making-millions stuff that you do all day, and I'll come back with a handy-dandy disguise that makes you look like Joe Dirt. Then we'll head out to the Dairy Bar for a big banana split. Are you game?"

"Absolutely," Mitch assured her, and he knew she wasn't teasing. He couldn't remember having this much fun with a woman . . . well, ever. Mitch knew he was supposed to be back in Chicago in the morning, but he was already thinking of calling his assistant and telling her to reschedule all of his appointments for tomorrow . . . hell, for the rest of the week. Being with Nicolina was making Mitch want to do so much more than work all of the damned time. He was starting to see how much being with the right partner could make a difference in how you viewed life . . . about what was really important. And it sure as hell wasn't money. Why had it taken him so long to realize that? The thought of all of the years lost with Mia suddenly clawed at his gut.

"Hey," she said gently, "now it's my turn to ask what's wrong."

"Just worried about Mia," he answered, but he wanted to say so much more.

She smiled and squeezed his hand. "You miss her so much, don't you?"

"Yes. It's so tough not to talk to her every day. I miss my little girl."

"Oh, believe me, I understand. Just ask Bella. I am the queen of needing to know her every move."

"You love her, Nicolina. What Mia wouldn't have given to have had a mother dote on her like you do. Mia is such a sweet girl, but I spoiled her."

"Stop," she said, gently putting a fingertip to his lips. "We can't change the past, remember?"

Mitch nodded and wanted to gently remind her to heed her own advice, but hopefully she would come to that conclusion on her own. God, he had come to love her so. Leaving Nicolina Diamante wasn't just getting harder. It was becoming nearly impossible, and so was keeping his growing feelings from her. If he wasn't careful, he was going to slip up and drop the *L* word. She wasn't ready yet; he *knew* it, so he told himself to just be patient and everything would eventually fall into place.

13

Swinging for the Fences

"THROW HIM SOME HEAT," TY YELLED FROM THE DUGOUT after Cam hit another one up into the center-field stands. Cam grinned when another ball sailed over the fence but landed just left of the left-field foul pole. "Pitch another five to him!" When Cam hit a line shot over the second baseman's head, Ty took his cap off and whacked it against his leg. "Yeah! That's what I'm talking about."

The bat felt solid in Cam's hands, and for the first time in a long while a sense of calm washed over him. Noah had been surprisingly understanding about the arrest, although he did make it abundantly clear that Cam should stay the hell out of any kind of trouble if he wanted to remain on the team. "Not a problem," Cam had assured Noah; he was met with a firm handshake and a slap on the back.

Cam felt as if both Noah and Ty believed in his talent and wanted to do what was best for him and also for the team. It was the type of coaching that made a player want to give one hundred percent and then some. Their hard-nosed but positive attitude relit the dormant pilot light beneath Cam's motivation, and it was as if a huge weight had been lifted from his shoulders. Gritting his teeth, he swung and foul tipped the next curve ball but then smacked a line drive that almost took the pitcher's head off and would have been a solid double had he been running the bases.

"That's what I'm talkin' about!" Ty yelled again before slapping his baseball cap back on. Out of the corner of his eye, Cam saw Ty nodding to Max Dugan, the gruff-voiced hitting coach, and he just bet they were discussing where to place him in the lineup. Cam had mostly been leadoff batter since his on-base percentage tended to be sky-high. He was patient and drew more than his fair share of walks, and he also had the speed to steal bases, but the way he had been hitting the ball, Ty might just consider penciling him into the cleanup slot. Showing that he could also be a power hitter could rack up some runs batted in and very well make his ascent back into the minor leagues happen a whole helluva lot faster.

While digging his cleats into the dirt, another sense of satisfaction and hope gripped Cam hard. He reached up and adjusted his batting helmet, thinking that coming to Cricket Creek had been a good decision. For someone who had made a fair number of bad decisions, it felt damned sweet.

Cam popped another ball up a mile in the air and was poised in the batter's box to take another pitch when he spotted Noah and a gorgeous woman coming down the steps behind the first-base dugout. The woman was chatting and smiling, using her hands in an excited, animated way that made him grin. Sunlight glinted off her blond hair, and she was wearing a businesslike suit but somehow made it look sexy. Big black sunglasses covered her eyes, but as she and Noah came closer, there was something familiar about her that tugged at his brain.

And then the sound of her laughter drifted his way . . . Wait.

Mia?

Swing and a miss.

"One more," Ty shouted. "Cam, don't take your damn eye off of the ball this time!"

Cam nodded and stepped out of the batter's box, plucked at his shirt, and kicked dirt from his cleats as if getting his composure back, but what he really wanted was to take another glance up at the blonde. It couldn't be Mia. She was a waitress at Wine and Diner, and this should be her shift. Cam had planned on eating there later—telling himself it was for the amazing food, but in reality it was to see her. Cam squinted against the sun into the stands. What could she possibly be doing with Noah Falcon? He must be mistaken. But when he heard her sweet, husky laugh again, he knew it was the same alluring woman he had kissed senseless in the elevator. Some of his feeling of well-being faded, but a flash of anger that she had somehow duped him had him swinging for the fences and going yard. Cam felt a familiar surge of adrenaline at sending the ball over the fence, but his mind was still centered on Mia. His home run got another whistle of approval from Ty and Max as he walked over to the dugout, but he all he could think about was what Mia thought of him crushing the ball.

Cam looked up, hoping like a high school kid that Mia had seen him smack the ball deep into the center-field bleachers. She had. She actually pointed to thc stands and looked at Noah, who nodded and grinned. He could hear their voices drift his way but couldn't make out what they were saying. Of course, thrown off-kilter at this unexpected turn of events, he pretended not to notice her.

But then Noah had to go and call to him, "Hey, Cam, very nice at bat!"

Damn! Cam didn't have any choice but to look up and tip his cap to Noah Falcon. Even though he tried his damnedest not to look at Mia, his eyes would not obey, and in spite of his resolve he felt a strong tug of attraction. He tried to glance away, but his gaze remained locked on her and would not budge. He wanted to know if she felt that same spark, but her sunglasses hid her expressive eyes. When she gave him a weak little wave of her fingers, he responded with a slight tip of his hat and was finally able to look away.

"Dude, who in the world is *that* chick?"

Cam turned to Casey Martin, the shortstop, who was as quick as lightning on the base paths and would probably end up as leadoff batter. Casey stared up at Mia, slack-jawed, making Cam's blood pressure rise. Because Casey was so engrossed in gaping at Mia, he failed to see the muscle jump in Cam's jaw.

"Day-um, that girl is superfine. Does she work here or somethin'? I damn sure hope so."

"I don't have a clue," Cam said in a bored tone, when in fact his heart was thumping against his ribs. Normally in this situation he would have had a comeback . . . maybe something suggestive on what he would like to do with a hot chick like Mia, but an unwanted surge of jealousy bubbled up and caught him by surprise. To make matters worse, he looked around and saw much of the same damned reaction from the rest of the team. It didn't help that Mia's blond hair glowed like a beacon, drawing the attention of every single male within shouting distance, including the batboy. Her laugh seemed to float across the air, mesmerizing the entire team. Even happily married Ty gave her an appreciative once-over but then turned back to his notes.

When Ty started jotting things down, Cam reminded himself that he was here to impress his coach, not some chick who obviously wasn't who she had presented herself to be and then some. He had felt it from the beginning, and his instinct had been true. Cam sighed as he took his bat over and slipped it into his slot in the dugout. He tried not to feel a sense of disappointment, but it reached inside his heart and squeezed. "Women," he muttered. "Stay the hell away from them."

"What'd you say?" Casey slid a sideways glance at Cam. Apparently Casey had finally been able to tear his lovesick gaze away from Mia and come into the dugout.

"Nothing," Cam replied a bit shortly, even though he liked hometown, easygoing Casey.

"Whatever, dude." The shortstop gave Cam a curious look but then shrugged and walked over to the bench and plunked down.

In spite of Cam's resolve not to think about Mia, he leaned against the metal railing and pretended to watch the next batter up. But after a moment he couldn't help it and said to Ty, "Hey, Coach, who is that chick with Noah Falcon? She work here?"

Without looking up from his notes, Ty nodded. "I think you're the fifth or sixth person to ask me that question," Ty replied with a chuckle.

That information didn't sit well with Cam, but he pretended otherwise. "Really . . ." He lifted one shoulder and didn't go any further with his questions, but he secretly hoped Ty would elaborate.

"Noah hired her as our new promotions manager. Well, make that our first promotions manager. Evidently, she scored Cat Carson to perform before the opening-day game and it got her the job pretty much on the spot." He looked up from his notes. "Cam, you might not have recognized her all dressed up, but that's Mia Money, the waitress from Wine and Diner, you know, the one who got your ass in trouble." He leaned in closer. "Off the record, it was Noah's decision to give you another shot, and I backed him up on that, but damn, keep on the down low, okay? The way you've been hitting the ball today has me damn excited. You're getting your groove back. Don't screw it up."

"Don't worry, Coach. I'm not going to let a chick get into my head." He spit into the dirt. "Ain't gonna happen. No way . . . no how. She was in a tight spot and I helped her out. Truthfully, any guy would have come to her defense. Look how she already has the whole damned team gawking at her," he said through gritted teeth.

"And clearly that doesn't bother you one bit."

"Of course not," Cam answered firmly, but then he inhaled a deep breath and got his ass under control. He shrugged. "Why should it?"

"You tell me."

"Look, Coach, it just happened to be me that day at the diner. End of story."

Ty shook his head. "I might have believed you if you hadn't protested way too much."

"I was just getting my point across," Cam insisted. "Hey, you would have done the same thing. Those guys were assholes," Cam insisted darkly. The thought of anyone hurting Mia made his blood boil, and he spit again.

"You're right," Ty admitted in a more serious tone. "Any man who harasses or threatens a woman is a coward."

"Amen to that," Cam agreed. He tried to push away the remaining fear that Mia could be in some sort of situation that needed a male presence. Cam had seen his mother get involved with violent men and had been too young to do anything about it when she had gotten pushed around. When he had gotten older he had tried, only to be reprimanded by his mother, of all things. Cam had painfully realized that his mother often blamed his presence as the reason men left her, and so he would make himself scarce . . . and play lots of sandlot baseball. Cam realized now, as an adult, that she had been desperately searching for someone to save her from her miserable life, but unfortunately she had looked in all the wrong places.

Cam gripped the railing tightly but allowed himself a wry grin. His miserable mother and his deadbeat dad were in a weird way responsible for his success as an athlete. Smacking the baseball had released his aggression and at the same time had given him a sense of self-worth when he made the high school roster without the benefit of select teams and expensive equipment. From pedaling to practice on his bike to cleaning pools for cash, he had made it all on his own.

Cam wanted to ask Ty more questions about Mia, but to his credit he remained silent and stared out over the field. Besides, it would have totally blown his not-caring cover. When he heard her voice coming nearer, he swallowed hard and continued to stare ahead, but his ears strained to gather more information. He inhaled deeply, hoping the blissful baseball-field scent of cut grass and dusty earth would clear his head. But the slight floral scent of Mia's perfume found its way to his nose, giving him warning that she was coming closer . . . and closer.

Just be cool, he told himself as he stood up straighter and rolled the kinks out of his neck. *She's just a chick. No big deal.*

Yeah, right, his damned pesky inner voice of reason warned. Why did his voice of reason have to show up *now* rather than in the elevator yesterday? *Oh, and if you think this is the end of the story like you so bravely announced to Ty McKenna, dude, you're fooling yourself.*

14

Clueless

MIA'S BREATH CAUGHT, AND IT HAD NOTHING TO DO with her walk up and down the stadium stands. It happened the moment she spotted Cameron Patrick in his baseball uniform. When he hit the home run, she got so excited that she almost jumped up and down applauding, but then she remembered to maintain her professional attitude. Mia had known she would most likely see Cam and had even mentally prepared herself for it, but when the moment arrived, she simply couldn't control her racing heart.

"Follow me. I want you to meet Ty McKenna," Noah said, and Mia gave him a brisk, businesslike nod.

Mia followed Noah down to the dugout. Although she smiled and shook Ty's hand firmly after he walked forward, she was acutely aware of Cam standing just a few feet away. He appeared to be studying the pitcher, but she felt a pang of disappointment when he didn't come over and at least say hi. She wondered if Noah had broken his promise and had told Cam about their deal, but from the little bit that she knew of Noah Falcon, she simply couldn't believe that he would do such a thing. Mia had learned from her father to trust her instinct when it came to people, and for the most part she had been right in her assessment.

"Glad to have you on board," Ty said with a megawatt smile that could make a girl melt. He had a bit of a bad-boy twinkle in his eye, but Mia knew from Wine and Diner conversations that he doted on his son and adored Jessica. "I just hope I'm not in trouble with Jess for stealing you away from Wine and Diner."

Mia felt heat creep into her cheeks. "Um, I think it's more likely that you'll receive a big thank-you."

Ty laughed. "Well, I have to admit that in your short stay in Cricket Creek you have become something of a legend. I'm sure customers have been pouring in just to get a glimpse of you."

Mia felt the blush go from her cheeks to her neck, but she had to grin. "Kind of like bad publicity is better than no publicity?"

Noah chuckled as well. "More like a bit of excitement in a small town. If we hadn't snatched you up, I bet Olivia would have tried to cast you in this summer's play."

"Oh, I do love the theater," Mia said. She almost mentioned Chicago but caught herself just in time. "Are they doing another one of Madison's original productions? I heard about her talent from Myra."

Noah shook his head. "No, Madison's still working on writing a new play. Olivia said that between teaching creative writing and traveling occasionally with Bella to watch Logan play baseball, she is way behind in her writing."

"And she loves to babysit Ben," Ty added. "She complains to Jessica all the time that she waited way too long to have a baby brother. Evidently it was on her Christmas list every year as a child."

"She must have been on the naughty list," Mia joked, drawing a laugh from Ty.

"That's what Jess told her," Ty replied. "At any rate, it's great to have you, Mia. I know that Noah explained that this is our sophomore year and we want to keep the excitement going and the stands filled with fans. I'll do my best to win games, but I can tell you that having fun promotions also brings people to the ballpark. The fact that you've landed Cat Carson is amazing. I hope you have more tricks up your sleeve."

Mia felt a surge of excitement. "I might have been a lousy waitress, but I excel at event planning. I'm really looking forward to my job, and I will do everything in my power to put fans in the stands."

"I believe you," Ty said and then looked at Noah. "Have you shown Mia her condo?"

"No." Noah glanced at his watch. "I would do it, but I have a meeting in just a few minutes." Noah looked past Ty and said, "Hey, Cam, would you take Mia over to her condo and show her around?"

Mia's heart pounded while she waited for Cam's answer. When he hesitated, she knew something wasn't right. What had she done to push him away?

"Mr. Falcon, I'm in the middle of practice."

Ty waved a dismissive hand at him. "You've already had your at bat, and it was a damned good one. Go gather your gear and show Mia around."

Noah reached in his pocket and handed Cam a credit card. "Take Mia shopping for some basic staples she needs in her place . . . food, linens, whatever, but of course within reason. And then dinner."

"You don't have to do that," Mia protested, but Ty and Noah waved her off.

"Hey," Noah said, "think of it as a small signing bonus. We can't pay you a big salary, but your living accommodations will be nice. We want you to be comfortable. Oh, and hey, both Bella and Madison live there, so you'll have some girlfriends to hang out with by the pool."

"Well, thank you so much." She peered closely at Cam, trying to figure out what was going on with him. His expression was hooded, but he didn't really appear happy to have this duty. Her stomach did a weird little dropping thing and she swallowed hard. "I can go shopping. You don't have to do this," she offered in a rather small voice.

"You don't have a car, remember?" Cam reminded her.

"Oh . . . right," Mia replied but wished he had said something like *I'd be glad to* instead of making it sound like an obligation.

"I'm sure Cam won't mind," Ty said in a firm enough tone to let Cam know that he had better not protest.

"Not at all, Coach," Cam answered readily. "Mia, I'll meet you over at the condo office. Give me about fifteen minutes."

"Okay," Mia replied with a small smile. While his response had been polite enough, she felt his reluctance. His brush-off bothered her, but she reminded herself that this was a golden opportunity and she needed to focus on doing a good job as promotions manager. The little interlude in the elevator had been an in-the-heat-of-the-moment kind of situation, and she would do well to keep her emotional distance from Cameron Patrick. Besides, she thought as she watched him disappear down the steps into the locker room, he was a rough-around-the-edges bad boy and not her type at all. Mia was into Italian loafers, not cleats. This job was a means to an end, a great opportunity but by no means permanent. She would prove her ability and her worth and then move back to Chicago, where she would go on to do bigger and better things.

"Mia?" Noah asked, making her jump. Ty was deep in conversation with a baseball player.

"Sorry, I was lost in thought.

Noah gave her a curious look. "I need to get back up to my office. You have some material to read over tonight, but if you have any questions about anything or any concerns, for that matter, be sure to give me a call."

"Thank you, Mr. Falcon. I already have your phone number in my contacts."

"Good. Don't hesitate to call for any reason whatsoever."

Mia thanked him again before walking back to her

new office to grab her purse. For such a big, tough athlete, Noah Falcon sure had a nice way about him. Tough guys with a soft side were every girl's fantasy, Mia thought with a dreamy smile. Olivia sure was a lucky woman.

Cam is like that, popped into her head, but she quickly dismissed it. She and Cam were both in Cricket Creek as a means to an end, nothing more, nothing less. End of story.

When she arrived at the front office of the condo complex, Mia was greeted by Madison Robinson, whose mother was co-owner of Wine and Diner. "Well, hello there, Mia. You sure move up fast in this town," she said with a chuckle.

"Myra was cool about it, but I really hope Myra and your mother aren't mad at me. They were kind enough to hire me on the spot, and then I dip out on them!"

"Nah . . ." Madison shook her head. "Don't worry about it. From what I hear, you saved the day for Noah. Aunt Myra and mom will find another waitress. The economy is improving but jobs are still scarce, so you'll make someone's day by giving them a job." She handed Mia a packet followed by the keys. "Here is some basic information about the property. I'd show you around, but I have to man the phones today."

"So you work here too?"

She waved her hand in the air. "I help out part-time to offset my rent."

"Oh, wow, your ring is gorgeous." Mia leaned forward to get a closer look at Madison's engagement ring. "When are you getting married?"

Madison sighed. "Jason and I keep setting the date back because he keeps getting more and more jobs. He's doing the finish work on the strip mall across the street from the stadium. We just can't seem to fit getting married in, much to the displeasure of my mother. She says by the time Jason and I tie the knot that baby Ben can be a ring bearer," she added with a laugh followed by a shrug. "She might be right. But Jason wants to build a dream house for us up on a ridge overlooking the river. He just bought the land."

"That's so romantic," Mia said with a touch of wistfulness. She was getting used to having near strangers tell her personal things, and it was making her feel at ease and oddly at home.

"Yeah, it's been fun looking at house plans. I'd just as soon elope and save the money, but mom wants me to have a big ceremony with all of the trimmings. She's a pretty awesome mom, so I can't disappoint her."

"Oh, I understand," Mia said breezily, but she felt a pang of sadness at the distant relationship she had with her own mother. "Make her happy and truly enjoy planning it together," she added, thinking of the many bridezillas she had witnessed over the past few years.

Madison tucked a lock of curly hair behind her ear. "Yeah, I'm sure I will. My mother is actually more laid-back than me. I take after my aunt Myra."

"Nothing wrong with that," Mia stated firmly. "Your aunt is an amazing person."

Madison gave her a bright, engaging smile. "I sure think so too. I really thought I'd hate moving from Chicago back to this small town, but I've grown to love it here," she said. She shook her head. "We came back to save my aunt's diner from going under, and I thought we'd move back to the city. At first I whined about moving back. I didn't realize how much stress my mom felt working at Chicago Blue. It was brutal."

"I can imagine." Mia thought back to going to that very restaurant with a group of friends. Two of them had sent back their entreés with one trivial complaint or another and then had proceeded to only pick at their food. Mia knew from personal experience that it had nothing to do with the quality of the food.

"This was one of those blessing-in-disguise kinds of things." Madison tilted her head and smiled. "Wow, the same thing happened to you too! Your car broke down in Cricket Creek and now you're working for the Cougars. Life sure is crazy sometimes, isn't it?"

"Yes," Mia agreed.

Madison gave her level look, making Mia feel as if she could see a bit of what she was thinking. "But has a funny way of working out if you let it."

Mia nodded slowly, thinking that though Madison had to be about her age, she felt as if she were getting sage advice from someone much older.

"Oh boy . . ." Madison rolled her eyes. "Mia, if you let me, I'll never shut up."

"Believe me, I don't mind," Mia admitted. "Except for that sheriff, everybody here has been more than friendly. Fred is looking for used parts to fix my car and letting me keep it on his lot free of charge. Myra gave me a job *and* a roof over my head and didn't fire me when I caused a bit of a commotion at Wine and Diner. She lent me money! And now Noah Falcon just hired me virtually on the spot." She shook her head. "Incredible."

"I won't argue," Madison said. "This little town was going under pretty quickly last year, but everyone banded together and refused to let this way of life die."

"Good for them!"

Madison nodded her agreement but then chuckled. "Not that small-town life is perfect. Everybody seems to know your business, and gossip spreads like wildfire. You can't break wind in this town without someone knowing, as Aunt Myra would put it."

Mia tossed her head back and laughed.

"I'm just telling you the truth. We're pretty outspoken here."

"Nothing wrong with that," Mia said. "Believe me, it's better than talking behind someone's back."

"Oh, there's always some of that in a small town, but by and large we all get along." Madison grinned and then pointed to the packet. "If you have any questions, let me know."

"Thanks."

"And I hope we can hang out, Mia. There are lots of baseball players who live here, and on the upper level, more expensive condos are being bought by older, retired couples. But except for Bella, girls my age are a bit scarce. We can sit by the pool or watch movies together if you want to?"

"I'm sure I will after I get settled."

"Great! And I'm sorry I can't show you around."

"That's okay. Cameron Patrick is going to be here any minute to take me on a tour."

"Well, now!" Madison wiggled her eyebrows. "He's a hottie."

"I guess," Mia agreed with a slight shrug.

"Oh, come on, now," Madison teased.

"Okay, he's hot."

"It's nice of him to show you around," she said with a hint of suggestion in her voice.

"Noah pretty much ordered him to," Mia admitted. "He has to take me shopping and out to dinner, and I'm not too sure he was down for all of that."

"What? You guys already have history. Believe me, nothing happens by accident."

Mia looked at Madison to see if she was joking, but her blue eyes were sincere. "You think so?"

"Just listen to your gut, Mia. It works every time," she advised.

"Do you really believe that?"

"Oh yeah," Madison replied. "And by the way, your condo is right next door to Cameron Patrick's."

"Really?" Mia said in a steady voice, but she felt a surge of excitement that she couldn't suppress. "I just can't get away from the guy."

"Imagine that . . ." Madison's knowing voice held a hint of humor, but Mia also felt as if Madison had some sort of uncanny sense of destiny, prompting her to ask more, but the phone rang and Madison had to excuse herself. Mia had a weird kind of feeling, as if she had just had her cards read and didn't know exactly what to make of the prediction.

A moment later, Mia heard the whoosh of the door opening, and before she had a chance to turn around, her Cam-is-in-the-room radar went on full alert. The clean, spicy scent of his aftershave trickled her way, making her want to groan.

"Are you ready?" he asked in a rather bored tone that made her a feel a little bit disappointed.

Mia turned around slowly and shrugged. "I suppose," she answered in the same tired tone, when in fact her heart was bumping against her ribs. Why was he acting this way? But she'd be damned if she'd let him see how much he affected her. "Let's get this show on the road. I have lots of work to do."

"No problem," he said as he stepped back to open the door for her.

Mia turned and gave Madison a wave and then headed out into the bright sunshine.

"Let's go over to your condo so you can take a look around and get a feel for whatever you might need," he suggested briskly. "You can make a list, and then we'll head out to shop. Wilson's Supermarket is just down the road. That should have everything you need, from soup to nuts."

Mia frowned. "I'm fond of soup, but I can take or leave nuts."

Cam chuckled. "You're kidding, right?"

"Not really. Well, I do like pistachios—oh, and macadamia nuts and an occasional pecan if it's in a dessert, but that about covers it. Now, soups—"

"Mia, that's an old saying meaning from start to finish and everything in between."

"Oh . . . well, good, then," Mia answered, but it suddenly dawned on her that she had never stepped foot in a store like the one he'd described. She gave him a brave smile when in reality she was a bundle of nerves and felt sort of . . . ashamed. She didn't know how to do, well . . . anything remotely domestic. Everything from washing her clothes to cooking her meals had been done for her. The closest she had come was microwaving a few things while away at college. But even then she and three other rich girls shared a luxury condo and had a weekly maid. Mia tried to think back to if she had ever even made her bed. Nope. She had been spoiled rotten and was, in a word, clueless.

Thus far, Mia had been eating her meals only at Wine and Diner, but really . . . how hard could cooking and cleaning be? Everything had instructions, right?

15

Movin' on Up!

ONCE AGAIN, CAM WAS AT A LOSS. NOTHING ABOUT MIA made a bit of sense. But he told himself not to dwell on trying to figure her out and just get this whole little excursion over with. "Lots of stuff is already provided," Cam said after Mia unlocked the door to the condo. She nodded as she took a look around. He also tried not to think about the fact that she was going to be living right next door to him and that their patios shared the same brick privacy wall. "There's even a small stacked washer and dryer in here." He opened the double doors to a small laundry room to the left of the kitchen.

"Good to know," she said in a businesslike tone. She looked at the washer and dryer with wide eyes that gave her away. "Nice and handy," she said as she opened the lid to the washer and peered inside. She straightened up and looked around the kitchen, randomly opening drawers and cabinets. At one point she took her suit jacket off and hung it over the back of a chair. The silky sleeveless blouse clung to her curves, making it difficult to tear his gaze away. "The kitchen is nice. I really like the tile floor and countertops. The recessed lighting is a nice touch too."

Cam thought it was interesting that she noticed everything but the actual appliances. "Yeah, these condos are pretty sweet. I understand that they were high-end real estate by the river but the project was completed right after the drop in the economy. This whole town was in financial trouble until Noah and Ty brought the baseball complex to town. I heard there was another silent partner as well."

She gave him an odd look he couldn't read but then said, "I'm glad that things are bouncing back here. Everyone is so nice," she said but then scrunched up her nose. "Well, except for the mean old sheriff."

"Yeah, he was a jerk," Cam agreed with a chuckle. "But believe me, I've been treated worse," he admitted, but then he decided to change the subject. "Do you like to cook?" he ventured, as if trying to make small talk, when he was really trying to figure her out.

"A little," she answered vaguely, and he took that to mean a big, fat no. "Do you?"

"Yes," Cam admitted. "My mother worked a lot, so I learned how to fend for myself as a kid. I got pretty good at it over the years. If I could round up at least three things, I could find a way to make a meal out of it. My culinary skills became very creative."

"Oh, well, that's good," she said, but Cam didn't really think she even heard him, and she continued to wander around the kitchen as if she were visiting a foreign country.

"Not really. It sucked."

"Really," Mia murmured from where she had just opened a drawer full of gadgets. She frowned down at them while tapping her cheek with her index finger. She picked up a meat tenderizer and peered at it with interest.

"Yeah, my specialty was smoked rattlesnake," he said, wondering if he would finally get her attention. "Would you like some tonight? My treat?"

"Sure . . ." she mumbled, but then she dropped the tenderizer and whipped around to face him. "Wait. Did you just say *rattlesnake*?" Her voice rose an octave.

"And here I thought you weren't listening," Cam replied with a shake of his head. "Sound good, does it?"

"Are you *serious*?"

"No."

"I'm sorry," she said and actually blushed. "I'm just . . ." She trailed off, and when she suddenly appeared lost and vulnerable, Cam softened.

"Something missing? If so, jot it down and we'll pick it up."

"That's just it."

"What, Mia?" he gently prodded.

"Well." She nibbled on the inside of her lip for a second and then said, "I have a confession to make."

"Go ahead." In spite of his resolve to keep his distance, Cam's ears perked up. When her tongue darted out and she licked her bottom lip, Cam remembered how sweet she tasted, but he forced his brain not to go there. "Tell me what's bothering you."

"Although I went away to college, I had roommates. But I've never actually lived by myself before now."

"That's it?" Cam sensed there was more, but she simply shrugged. "Really?"

"Well . . . no."

"Go on . . ."

"Nuking things is the only cooking I have ever done." She gave him a small smile. "And even then I tend to make food explode. It's amazing what happens when you reheat takeout too long. Are you getting the ugly picture?" she asked wanly.

Cam had to grin. "Exploding food? Uh, yeah, pretty much."

"So, are you willing to help me in times of dire need, like showing me how to boil water? Scramble an egg?"

Say no. "Sure," he offered and wanted to kick his own ass for not keeping his mouth shut. "I've been on my own forever, so I know how to do it all. Cook. Clean. Even fix things," he felt the need to add. Whatever spell she had cast on him was sticking like Super Glue, because he couldn't shut up. "I've been washing my own clothes since I was a kid."

"I'm sorry to hear that." When she gave him a look that bordered on sympathy, Cam turned away.

"No big deal," he said as he rummaged around in a drawer for a pen and paper. When he found it, he said, "Come on, let's take a quick look around and make a list of things you need. These lower units are used to house baseball players, so they're furnished and stocked with the basics. But let's get any items you can think of while we have the company credit card." When she gave him a blank look, he said, "I'll help."

"Thank you!" Mia smiled brightly, doing funny things to his gut. The hold she had on him seemed to tighten. "You've come to my rescue once again."

Cam wanted to remind her that he was no hero, but her grateful smile had him biting back his usual curt remarks. "Do you need to get anything from the apartment above Wine and Diner?"

"I have my suitcase there, but that's about it. I feel bad about walking out on Myra without any notice."

Cam gave her a level look that made her giggle.

"Okay, maybe Myra should throw me a going-away party."

Cam laughed. He liked that she could make fun of herself. But as he walked through the condo making notes of things she would need, like toilet paper and extra towels, he slid in a question here and there. "So you think you'll like being the promotions manager?"

Mia turned around from the shower stall she was examining. "Oh, I think I will! I've had some experience in event planning and have a few connections."

Cam waited, but that's all the information she gave him. "Well, good, it's an important part of a successful baseball franchise. Fans want to have fun at the ballpark."

"I'll do my best," she said as she walked into the bedroom. Cam made the mistake of following her. "Nice," she commented with a nod. "Lots of closet space, not that I need it," she added in low, wry tone. "And the bed looks comfortable." She sat down with a bounce and a grin.

Cam swallowed hard. Seeing Mia on a bed sent his arousal into full throttle. He had to clear his throat before he could speak. Something of what he was feeling must have shown in his face, because her eyes widened and she put her feet on the floor and stood up so quickly that she stumbled forward. "Whoa, there." Cam reached out to steady her, and it was all he could do not to drag her into his arms.

"Sorry, I'm so clumsy!" she said, but she didn't move.

"We should go," he said gruffly, but he couldn't make his legs move away from her, and his hands remained circled around her upper arms.

"Yeah." She nodded firmly, but her breathless voice gave her away. If she leaned forward as much as an inch, he was going to kiss her. And with the big bed right behind her, a kiss would be venturing into some dangerous territory. "I guess we . . ."

"Yeah?" Cam's eyes dropped to her mouth, which looked so soft and so kissable that he couldn't look away. His head dipped a little bit closer and his hands on her arms tightened.

"Should . . . ," she continued just above a whisper.

Screw caution! Cam dipped his head to capture her sweet mouth, and to his delight she tilted her head up, giving him the green light, but just when he was about to make contact, his cell phone chose that very moment to chime, "Take Me out to the Ballgame." The unexpected sound had Cam dropping his hands and backing away. "I should get this." He flicked a glance at her as he reached in his pocket and pulled the phone out, not sure if he should be pissed or grateful for the interruption.

"Hello." When Cam answered and it was an automated offer for a cell-phone upgrade, he went with being pissed. "Damn telemarketing," he grumbled, but when his head cleared slightly he decided that he should be grateful. The bed felt like a white elephant in the room, and he noticed that Mia was careful not to look in that direction. He also noticed that her cheeks were flushed and her breathing seemed shallow. Yeah, kissing her would have definitely been dipping into dangerous territory. But still, damn . . . she had a vulnerable set to her mouth and appeared a little confused. Cam could relate.

"Are you ready?" he asked, glad that his voice sounded pretty much normal.

"Oh." She blinked as if coming out of a daze. "I just need to grab my kiss . . . I mean my *purse*," Mia replied and turned beet red at her slip of the tongue. She quickly pivoted away, but not before Cam caught a look of disappointment and possibly even hurt in her expressive eyes, and he didn't like it one bit. He guessed she must feel rejected and he knew firsthand how crappy that felt.

"Mia . . ." Cam had a sudden urge to try to explain that this wasn't a good time to get involved with someone. He had the feeling that they were both at some sort of crossroads and getting in each other's way would cause nothing but trouble.

"Yes?" she ventured softly, and when she turned and looked at him with longing, he dug deep and somehow found some resistance.

"I have a black SUV sitting right outside. I'll go open the windows and let the heat out for you." He tried to keep his voice matter-of-fact to break through the spell.

Her face fell, but she quickly masked it with a small smile. "Fine, I'll be there in just a minute."

"All right," Cam said in the same tone, but as he turned to go her voice stopped him.

"Cam?"

He pivoted slowly and faced her.

"Thanks. I know you were strong-armed into doing this. Maybe I can get Madison or Bella to take me later on. I won't let Noah know."

Mia was letting him off the hook, and he should have

jumped at it. The words, however, simply would not come out of his mouth. "No big deal, Mia. I need a few things from the store myself."

"Okay. Well, good, then." Her smile returned, and the force of it was enough to knock him for a loop. "I'll be right behind you."

Cam nodded, but as he headed out the door he was having second thoughts. The more time he spent with her, the more he liked her, and she had let him know that she felt the same attraction. This might not have been such a bad thing except that there were still too many unanswered questions about her that tugged at his brain and warned him that trouble could be following her around. And he sure as hell didn't need any more trouble. Cam clicked the keyless unlock button and firmly told himself to keep his damned distance. He would do this one thing that Noah requested, and then he was done hanging out with Mia Money. He simply couldn't risk it.

Cam lowered the windows and then tidied up the front seat, tossing mail, a baseball, and random items over his shoulders. After a moment he flipped down the visor and checked out his hair and then his teeth but then suddenly felt silly for worrying about the state of his vehicle and how he looked. "What the hell is coming over me?" he grumbled, flipping the visor back with more force than necessary. He slipped on his Oakleys and a baseball cap and told himself not to worry about his damned hair.

Mia kept her word and came out the front door of her condo just moments later. Cam tried his best not to watch her progress and failed miserably. He was relieved, however, that the jacket was back on, hiding the sexy blouse that drew his eyes to her breasts. He considered getting out so he could open the door for her but decided to just sit there and chill. After all, they were having dinner, but this wasn't a damned date! "Hey," he said casually after she shut the door.

"Hey yourself," she replied, and he wondered if she was feeling any of the same emotions.

"Ready?" he asked to fill the silent gap. But after the near kiss in the bedroom, Cam knew that the ride to Wilson's was going to be more than a little bit awkward. So even though he had never been very good at small talk, to fill the silence he gave it a shot. "So did you add anything to the list?"

"The list?"

"Your bucket list."

"Well, I do want to see the Grand Canyon and—"

"Mia, I meant the things you need from the store. Wait—you have a bucket list?"

"I've had a list since I was a kid." She tilted her head to the side. "Of course, I didn't think of it as a bucket list."

Cam shot a frown her way. "Well, don't start now!" He really didn't like even the idea of her dying. "For Pete's sake, you have lots of living left."

"Well, I hope so . . ."

"Mia!"

"Okay, geez, well, let's see . . ." She reached inside of her giant purse, rummaged around, and after much grumbling finally located it. "Um, toilet paper. Towels." She looked over at him.

"That was what I wrote down."

She gave him a slight shrug. "I might require a little help."

"A little help?" He wanted to sound sarcastic, make her not like being around him so much, but his question came out teasing and made her smile. Damn, where was his jackass attitude when he needed it?

"Okay, a lot of help."

"Right, domestic stuff isn't your thing." Cam flicked a quick glance at her. "I guess not having a mom around made it kind of tough.."

Mia's smile faltered. "Yeah. She divorced my father for someone who made more money."

"That sucks."

"Yeah, I've come to discover that, as they say, money can't buy happiness. The root of all evil. All that stuff."

When he stopped for a red light, he looked her way again. "So I'm guessing your mother isn't happy? Regrets her decision?"

Mia gave him a startled look. "I guess I never really thought about it all that much." She pressed her lips together and then said, "That's not really true. I *have* thought about it now and then. I especially wondered if I wasn't good enough, you know? Somehow caused the split."

"Mia, you were just a child," he reminded her gently. "Sounds to me like she was just looking for greener pastures. It happens a lot."

Mia seemed to consider that for a minute. "Well, she sure loved her new family more than me. Or at least I always felt that way."

"Maybe you should talk to her about how you feel," Cam surprised himself by saying.

"We're not close." When she offered this additional bit of information, Cam hoped for more, but she fell silent and stared out the window.

Although his question about her mother had been innocent, Cam felt like an ass for asking.

She toyed with the strap on her purse and continued to gaze out the window. "I guess I just always felt like an outsider."

"I'm sorry," Cam couldn't help but say. He wanted to keep her at arm's length, but he was doing a very poor job of it. For some reason Mia had a way of drawing him in. "That couldn't have been easy."

"Nope. I have two brothers who are both in college. I always thought they were bratty, but they were probably okay." She shrugged. "Maybe someday I'll get to know them better. I guess I should have made more of an effort instead of disliking them so much."

"Maybe you'll get the chance someday. Your life isn't over, you know."

Her smile returned. "Good point!"

"So are you close to your dad?"

"Yes," she said brightly, but then she frowned. "We're going through a rough patch right now, but . . ." She paused to clear her throat. "I do know that he loves me."

"Well, that's good." He wanted to reach over and give her leg a reassuring pat but refrained.

"Yeah," she answered softly. "What about you? Sounds to me like your childhood wasn't so easy either."

Cam swallowed hard and turned his attention to the road when a car behind him honked. He rarely mentioned his parents, much less talked about his childhood. Drawing him in was one thing . . . but drawing him out was something he wasn't willing to endure. Admitting his unhappiness felt like taking off his armor, and so he merely shrugged. "Let's just say that I totally get your feeling of being unwanted."

"I'm sorry to hear that," she said.

"It is what it is . . . ," he said with a shrug, but her admission touched him in places that he usually kept carefully guarded. When he was a kid, other parents, especially team moms, would often feel sorry for him and offer him cold sports drinks or snacks after a game because he was usually empty-handed. Although they meant well, Cam had often refused as if he wasn't thirsty or hungry. Sympathy usually made him feel unsettled, but because they had this common ground he accepted her gesture with a grateful smile. "You know?"

"Oh . . . well, we all have our baggage, I guess."

"True enough," he agreed as he pulled into the local supermarket parking lot, which was as crowded as always. Cam had to cruise around to find an open spot. "Are you ready to do some damage to Noah's credit card?"

"Oh, I love to shop! Question is . . . are you ready for this?" She rubbed her hands together with obvious glee.

"As ready as I'll ever be." He hated crowds and lines, but her enthusiasm was, as always, contagious. If Cam wasn't careful, Mia was going to have him laughing and smiling all night long.

16

If the Shoe Fits . . .

"WE HAD BETTER EACH GET A CART," CAM ADVISED when they entered through the automatic double doors. "I have a feeling we'll need it."

Mia grinned at him. "Most likely. I mean business when I get into the zone." Mia tried not to like the fact that Cam kept referring to everything in terms of *we*. It made her feel as if they were a couple, and she liked the notion way too much. But when he slid a curious look at her, she busied herself tugging a cart from the long row. It refused to budge. She pulled with more gusto. Was there a trick to this? Not wanting to appear as if she had never been in a grocery store before, she tugged really hard, but the cart remained stubborn. Cam had no such trouble, so she decided to give it one last, hard, two-handed pull.

Cam came up behind her. "Need some help?"

"Um . . ." Mia opened her mouth to answer, but his sudden nearness threw her off balance. She could feel the heat of his body, and the spicy clean scent of his aftershave made her long to lean back against him. "It's stuck," she finally managed to say in a breathless tone that she hoped didn't give her away. She was supposed to be a professional. This was strictly business, not a date, she reminded herself.

"Oh, the problem is the baby seat belt," he said so very close to her ear. "Pop it out."

If Mia had been thinking clearly, she would have figured out that the baby seat belt was those two straps connected to the little seat where she had placed her purse. The plastic buckle was caught between the metal bars. But all her brain was registering was Cam's nearness. So instead, she simply stood there staring at the cart and thinking that he smelled delicious. What was he wearing anyway? It should be outlawed.

"Mia?"

"Hmm?"

"Slide the buckle out," he instructed, and of course she remained clueless.

"Buckle?" She wondered if he would notice if she leaned against him. She could pretend it was part of the tugging process, she was thinking, and she almost purred when he reached forward, bringing his chest against her shoulder blades.

"Here." Cam reached forward and unhooked something and then took an unfortunate step backward just when Mia decided tugging and leaning was a grand idea. She slammed against his chest but somehow thought that hanging on to the cart was a necessity. The force sent them and the cart careening backward, barely missing a teenager, who jumped out of the way with a startled, "Dude!" They brushed up against the ancient greeter, who stepped sideways as if line dancing, and knocked over a poster for a Disney movie out on DVD.

"Dude!" yelled the teenager, who had to dodge the cart again. He felt the need to give it an angry shove with his foot, sending Mia and Cam tumbling into a machine with a big claw and a pile of stuffed animals and other various items. The force of their crash landing started the hook slowly moving downward while opening its jaws. Mia righted herself and watched with odd fascination when the hook snagged a domed plastic container with a toy treasure inside.

Cam noticed as well and pressed a red button that brought the captured dome over to the edge and dropped it into an opening. He reached down, came up with a prize, and handed it to Mia. "Here," he said with a lopsided grin. "I've been trying to win that game for years. My competitive nature would have me emptying all of the change in my pockets before giving up."

"But we didn't pay for it," Mia protested, but the shaken greeter waved them on, obviously fearing for what remained of his life. Mia dropped the prize in her purse, but when she reached for her cart, Cam nudged her to the side. "I thought we needed two."

"Um, I've rethought that decision. We'll make do," he said with a shake of his head, but Mia was relieved when he grinned. "And I'm pushing."

"Here you go." Mia gladly gave over the reins and then fell into step beside him.

"Okay, accomplished shopper, where to?" Cam asked.

"Um . . ." Mia nibbled on the inside of her cheek, wanting to direct him, but this type of store was a new experience for her. In fact, she looked around at, well, everything and didn't know where to begin.

Cam pulled up short and gave her a sideways look. "Are you okay? You look lost."

"Just getting my bearings," Mia replied, using one of her father's tricks of not telling a lie by stating a fact. She had been in countless department stores and boutiques, even a grocery store now and then, but never a huge store piled full of, well, everything, including some very interesting people, many of whom needed to be on *What Not to Wear*. Stacy and Clinton would have had a field day.

Cam gave her a long look as if he were going to dispute her claim but shrugged and started pushing the cart. A couple of minutes later they were in a section labeled HOUSEWARES. Mia, who had been deprived of shopping for the past few days, felt her adrenaline flow and went to work. Very soon the cart was overflowing with Martha Stewart items that were so very cute! And so cheap!

"We need another cart," she announced brightly.

Cam arched one eyebrow. "Ya think?"

"Yes!" Mia nodded, too happy to take his comment as sarcasm. "Would you get one, please?"

Cam sighed but then shot her a grin. "Okay, I'll be back, but two carts is your limit."

"Okay, I promise," she said but all of this under one roof was shopping heaven! Well, not the same kind of high-end shopping she was used to, but fun. She turned the corner and . . . Shoes! Rows and rows of shoes. Surely she could find something more comfortable than what she had brought along in her hasty departure. After spotting the size eights, Mia started trying on different styles. She slipped on a plaid canvas flat that was perfect for summer and checked out the edge of the shoebox. "Look at these prices!" she exclaimed to no one in particular, but then again she had grown up talking to herself.

"Yeah, the doggone price tags keep goin' up and up. *Roll back*, my sweet hiney."

Mia turned around, hopping on one foot to keep her balance. A tired-looking woman wearing worn tennis shoes looked up from her stooped position. Mia noticed a clearance price of six dollars and ninety-nine cents on the pair of shoes she held. The woman sighed and shoved the shoes back into the vacant slot. She sat down heavily on the stool provided for trying on shoes. Mia felt a pang of compassion. "What are you looking for? Maybe I can help."

The woman gave Mia a sideways once-over. "Well, now, sugar, why is someone like you shopping in a place like Willy World?"

Mia frowned. "Willy World?"

The woman chuckled. "That's what we fondly call Wilson's around these parts. It's family owned and refuses to bow down to the big chains. You never know what you're goin' to find here one day to the next, but you'll always find a bargain that's hard to pass up. Last week they had ground chuck for a dollar ninety-eight a pound. You can't beat that with a stick!"

"Sure can't," Mia agreed, even though she didn't have a clue what ground chuck was or why you would beat it with a stick.

"But you have *high maintenance* written all over your pretty face and fancy clothes." She glanced down and pointed to Mia's discarded Jimmy Choos. "And would you look at those shoes! Day-um, looks like something Carrie would wear on *Sex and the City*."

"Oh, I loved that show! I hated to see it end."

"Well, I only get to see the reruns that leave out all the dirty parts," the woman said with a laugh. She wiggled her finger at the shoes. "Just how does one walk in those things anyway?"

Mia grinned. "Very carefully." She leaned over and extended her hand. "I'm Mia, by the way."

"Sunny Collins." She gave Mia's hand a firm shake. "Pleased to meet ya."

"So what was it that you're looking for?" She thought that the perky name didn't suit tired-looking Sunny and felt the need to assist her.

"Well, two things. Something nice for my son's graduation and that can also be worn on job interviews." She sighed again. "I got laid off, so things are tight right now." She managed a grin. "Well, make that tight*er*."

Mia felt her gaze drift to the worn tennis shoes and her heart constricted in her chest. "So your son graduated from college?"

"Naw . . . high school, but he done me proud. Daniel is a straight-A student, and he is a member of the National Honor Society. He's got some nice scholarships for college, thank the Lord. Going to go to the University of Kentucky!" She puffed out her chest and gave Mia a firm nod. "How do you like them apples?"

"Congratulations!" Mia exclaimed, but she was secretly shocked. With her wan-looking salt-and-pepper shoulder-length hair, Sunny Collins appeared much older than someone with a teenager. "You must have been a very good mom."

"Done my best," she said with a shrug. "I just want to look nice at the ceremony," she said, but then she rubbed the heel of her hand over her eyes. "I'm so proud of my boy."

The gesture had Mia swallowing hard, and she was hit with sudden inspiration. "Hey, does Daniel know how to sell things on eBay or Craigslist?"

"I imagine so."

Mia pointed to her shoes. "Those things hurt my feet but are practically brand-new."

"I expect they do. Purty, though . . ."

Mia cleared her throat. "I want you to have them."

"What?" Sunny looked at the shoes and then back at Mia.

Mia scooped them up and handed them to her. "Tell Daniel that they go for over six hundred dollars new and are hard to find, so I'm thinking he should get several hundred for them, but he can do the research."

Sunny's eyes widened. "Get outta town . . ." She took the shoes from Mia but then shook her head and shoved them back. "I can't take them from you!"

"They hurt my feet."

"Then you sell them."

Mia waved her hands at the shoes. "I started a new job and don't have time."

Sunny swallowed, clearly torn. "I—"

"Take them, Sunny. Please." She wiggled her toes at Sunny. "My feet already thank you."

At that comment Sunny grinned, but then her cornflower blue eyes filled with tears. "Nobody's ever done something like this for me." She glanced around and sniffed. "Am I on TV or something? Are you that girl from *Ellen* that goes around and gives people stuff?"

"No," Mia replied with a laugh, but then another thought hit her. "Hey, have you ever waited tables?"

"Yeah, I've done everything under the sun."

"Do you know where Wine and Diner is back in town?"

"Sure do. Good food even though they've gotten kinda fancy-pants."

"Well, I happen to know they're looking for a waitress. Head over there and ask for Myra. Tell her I sent you. Do it right away before they have a chance to advertise."

Sunny nodded and quickly stood up. The clunky shoes dangled from her fingertips. "I surely don't know how to express my thanks."

"No need."

"Give me a hug," Sunny requested and opened her arms. The husky emotion in her voice had Mia tearing up as well. Mia thought she felt frail and bony, and she hoped that Jessica's cooking would put some meat on Sunny's bones.

Mia pulled back and gave her a smile. "Oh, and hey, if Daniel needs a summer job, tell him to come over to the Cougars' baseball stadium. I work there. I'll put in a good word for him."

"Why, thank you, Mia. I will surely do that." Her eyes filled with tears again, but she smiled. "Okay, I'm on my way! Wish me luck!"

"Good luck, Sunny!"

"Thanks, Mia. Apparently Lady Luck is finally shining down upon me, but I have to admit that I'm thinking this is a dream and I might just wake up!" Her bright smile made her suddenly appear years younger. "I'd surely be really pissed if I do."

Mia laughed. "Sunny, this isn't a dream, just a stroke of luck that you deserve. Embrace it."

"Well, I guess every dog has its day. All I can say is that it's about damned time."

"I agree," Mia said, even though she wasn't sure just what it meant. She really needed to brush up on the local lingo. She watched Sunny walk away and then sat down on one of the stools with a thump and a sigh. The price of the Jimmy Choos had never, ever fazed her but suddenly seemed obscene. In fact, she had never really thought about money or considered the cost of anything. "Wow." Mia had to shake her head at the irony of the last name she had chosen for herself. "Really . . ." She snorted. She wondered for a second where Cam had wandered off to and then thought perhaps he had gotten distracted by shopping as well. After another thoughtful moment, she lost herself in trying on shoes.

After waiting a good ten minutes for a vacant cart, Cam finally found a discarded one near the checkout line. While maneuvering his way past the long lines, he found himself stuck next to a display of magazines and pulled up short. On the cover of one of those rich-and-famous gossip publications was a picture of several women sunbathing on the deck of a yacht. "No way . . . ," Cam whispered. He picked up the magazine and peered at the picture. One of the blond-haired, bikini-clad women looked like Mia. The picture was just grainy enough to not be certain, so he gave it a closer look. The picture was actually of Cat Carson, and the other three women weren't named. He stared at the photograph but then shrugged. Surely he was wrong. Then again, there was something about the smile that felt familiar. Could it be? *Nah . . . ,* he thought, and put the magazine back on the rack.

Thinking Mia would be wondering where he had wandered off to, Cam hurried back to the bedding aisle, but she was nowhere to be found. He started going up and down aisles and finally spotted her bright blond head bent over some shoes. Boxes were scattered all around her, and to her left was a small stack that must have been the keeper pile. Cam didn't really think that Noah meant for shoes to be on Mia's list of condo essentials, but she seemed to be having such a great time trying them on that he decided that he would use his own credit card to pay for them. She would never know the difference.

"Well, there you are," he announced, startling her so

much that she nearly toppled from the small stool. He told himself to steel himself against his growing attraction, but when she giggled as she righted herself he found himself smiling back. "Find anything?" he asked, even though the answer was obvious.

"Yes! Dozens of cute little flats and summer sandals!" She pointed to the ones on her feet. "Aren't they just darling? I know it's corny, but I just love the floppy red flower on top. And only thirteen dollars. Isn't it just amazing?"

Not really, he thought, but he didn't want to dampen her spirit so he nodded his agreement. She pointed to the rows of shoes—well, the ones left on the rack—and said, "The boxes with the green dot are buy one, get one free."

"Good to know." He eyed the array and shook his head.

"I know we need to move on. I'll narrow it down to just a few. Maybe you can help?" She gave him a hopeful look.

He seriously doubted it. "Sure."

"Okay." She held up a pair of canvas shoes. "I'm torn between the plain blue and the plaid. What do you think?"

Cam tilted his head. "The plaid."

"But the plain blue will go with more outfits."

"True," he conceded, but when she frowned he heard himself say, "but at that price, why don't you get both?"

"Well, because I don't know if Noah meant for me to get shoes or clothes," she said in a near whisper, as if Noah might be listening. "But I have to have them to work in. My own shoes just won't do."

Cam looked around. "Um, Mia, where are your shoes?"

She caught her bottom lip between her teeth. "I . . . uh, gave them away."

"Gave them away?" he repeated slowly. "Why?"

Mia hesitated. "They sort of pinched my toes," she replied, as if that explained everything.

"And so you just . . . gave them away?" Cam looked at her expectantly, but when she offered no other explanation, he dropped the subject, even though something in her soft expression led him to believe there was much more to the story, and he didn't just mean shoes. "Okay, well, you need to wrap it up here because we need to head over to the groceries so you can stock up on some basic staples." When she gave him a blank look, he said, "You know, like sugar, milk, coffee . . . that kind of thing."

"Oh, right. I'll be done here in a few minutes."

"Of course you will." Cam didn't believe her for a minute and sat down on one of the stools. The few minutes stretched into almost thirty, until she narrowed her selection down to six pairs, all of which for some reason needed his approval before she added them to the cart.

"Okay, let's go." Mia dusted her hands together as if finishing a hard day's work and stood up. After leaving on a pair of new shoes that best matched her outfit, she finally said, "Are you ready?"

"Yep, right after I try on those red heels . . ."

"Ha, very funny."

"I try," he said with a grin. Cam had a sneaking suspicion that grocery shopping was going to take a lot longer than needed.

Can was right. Mia found a reason to stop in just about every section of the store on the way to the grocery side. The exception was sporting goods and toys, but even then, she paused. "Mia, are you in the market for a Barbie doll?"

"No . . . but it's all so much fun to look at," she admitted. At his fake scowl she laughed. "Oh . . . okay!" When she pushed her cart in front of him, Cam tried very hard not to look at her cute ass.

She wasn't nearly as interested in groceries, and Cam had to fill the cart with things he knew she would need, including laundry detergent. "You're lucky that the units are equipped with a washer and dryer."

"Oh, I know, and the little stacked thing is so cute."

Having never heard a washer and dryer referred to as cute, Cam had to laugh. He had a sneaking suspicion that Mia Money had never washed her own clothes.

"I'm wearing the shoes," Mia announced to the cashier and then reached into the cart for the empty shoebox. She glanced at Cam. "I'll pay Noah back for the clothes and shoes," Mia promised. "So give me the receipt when we're done."

"Okay," Cam said, even though he was already prepared to pay for her extras himself. "I'll let him know when I return the credit card."

"Good. I wouldn't want him to think I was taking advantage."

"I understand," he agreed with a smile.

When they finally arrived back at her condo, it took a long time to drag all of her bags inside. After tucking away all of the perishables, she turned to him. "Well, I don't know about you, but I've worked up quite an appetite. I *might* even splurge and eat dessert! Jessica's bread pudding is supposed to be out of this world. Do you want to go over to Wine and Diner and grab a bite to eat and get the rest of my luggage?"

Cam smiled. "Sure," he said, telling himself that it was only because Noah had told him to take Mia out to dinner that he was willing to do this. Really, that was the *only* reason; otherwise, he'd head over to his place, throw something on the grill, and grab an ice-cold beer. Maybe watch some major-league baseball or an action movie.

"I'll just put on one of the new shorts and tops I bought and get out of this hot suit."

"Okay." Cam nodded. "I'll just grab a beer over at my place and check my mail. I'll meet you by my SUV in about fifteen minutes or so?"

"Sounds like a plan." She smiled, but just when he had his hand on the door to leave she said, "Cam?"

He turned around. "Yeah?"

"Thanks for taking me. Shopping was really a lot of fun."

"You're welcome," he said, and he had to admit to himself that it had been entertaining . . . even the trying-on-shoes part. Cam also knew it had nothing to do with actual shopping, a chore he usually detested, but rather spending time with Mia. He also thought it was refreshing that something as simple as shopping at Wilson's made her happy. In his recent experience, most of the women he dated wouldn't have been caught dead shopping in a discount store, much less admitted to having fun doing it. Reminding himself that he needed to keep his distance, he didn't add that he agreed but nodded briskly. "I'll see you outside."

Her smile faltered a little bit, as if she knew he was pulling back. "Okay," she said softly, lowering her gaze, making him feel like a bit of an ass. "Hey, listen, you don't have to do this," she suddenly said, catching him off guard. He wanted to reassure her somehow, and for what he wasn't even sure . . . Damn, this was venturing into dangerous territory. After an uncomfortable moment of silence, she added, "You've done enough already."

Go. This is your chance, his voice of reason demanded. "I thought you were hungry." His voice of reason could take a flying leap.

"There's plenty of food here. I'll be fine." She waved that hand again.

"But what about your luggage?"

"I'll ask Bella to bring it to me. Really, I'm sure you have better things to do."

Cam thought about arguing, but this really was his out. He didn't need the complication of a woman in his life. He was struggling to get back on track, and she could definitely be trouble in so many ways. He stood there for a moment while good reason warred with his libido. In the end he compromised. "Hey, what about this? I'll get your luggage and bring you some takeout from Wine and Diner."

"Thanks, but that's okay."

"No, there really isn't any decent dinner in the basic stuff we bought," he insisted, giving her another small smile. "And I'll even bring the dessert you so deserve."

"Yeah, but—" When it appeared as if she was going to argue, he opened the door and left without giving her a chance to protest. He would do this one last thing and then stay out of her life. It was thc best for them both.

But as Cam headed for his SUV, he spotted a man in a black sedan sitting across the parking lot. He wouldn't have thought anything of it, but he could have sworn he'd spotted the same car earlier. The hair on the back of his neck stood up, warning him that something wasn't right. He was about to march over there and confront the dude, but he must have felt Cam's stare because the car suddenly pulled away. That, in and of itself, was unsettling.

On the way to his car, Cam tried to reason the weird incident away, telling himself that the guy could have been there for any number of reasons that had nothing to do with Mia. And if the dude did have some connection to her, it was all the more reason to stay the hell away. Still, he wondered if she was being followed. Stalked? Running away from something? None of the answers to those questions were good.

"Not your problem," he mumbled as he slid behind the wheel. He told himself to bring the promised dinner and luggage to her and stay as far away as he could, but then he ran a worried hand down his face. It wasn't going to be an easy task, since she lived right next door to him! Once again Cam came up with a compromise. He would keep his distance but also keep a discreet eye on her. Nothing more, nothing less. End of story.

17

A Blessing in Disguise

"OH DEAR GOD!" NICOLINA LOOKED AT MITCH AND laughed so hard that her sides actually hurt.

"This will never work." Mitch adjusted the baseball bill and fluffed the fake hair attached to the cap.

"Yes, it will," Nicolina assured him. She tried to put on a serious face but took another look at him and burst into another fit of giggles.

"Right, that's why you can't stop laughing."

"Because I know it's you. The people at the Dairy Bar don't have a clue that you're Mitch Monroe. And not that many people actually know me here yet. It's perfect. We're going on a date in Cricket Creek."

"What if we run into Noah or Ty?"

"Even if they figure it out, they won't blow your cover, Mitch. Besides, in the worn T-shirt and those jorts you're wearing, I doubt if they will even get the joke."

"Jorts?"

"Jeans shorts . . . jorts."

He looked down. "Oh . . . jorts . . . right." He grinned. "I guess you had fun shopping for this getup, didn't you?"

"Guilty."

"Okay, but I refuse to wear the white socks with the sandals."

She gave him a fake pout.

"I just can't and keep a straight face."

"All right . . ."

"What if we happen to see Mia?"

"Believe me, she'll never recognize you. It'll be fun. Come on, don't be such a weenie." Nicolina knew Mitch couldn't stand turning down a challenge of any kind, even one as silly as this one. In the past year she had learned a lot about his personality, and lately he had been opening up to her even more. One thing she knew for certain was that he adored his daughter and that this estrangement was taking its toll on him. She wanted to get him out and have some fun. Being cooped up in her flat was romantic and productive, but they really needed to get out or go stir-crazy. "Hey, do you really think that the Dairy Bar is someplace Mia would likely be hanging out?"

"A week ago, no, but I never thought in a million years that she'd end up working as promotions manager for the Cougars." He shook his head slowly but then smiled.

"You're proud of her, aren't you?"

"Yes." Mitch inhaled deeply as if warding off emotion. "And it's killing me not to be sharing this experience with her."

Nicolina brushed the fake hair back and placed her hands on his shoulders. "But maybe you were right and it's better for her to do this solely on her own."

"You're right, but I still want to keep an eye on her for a while."

"Remember that she is an adult."

"I know." Mitch tilted his head to the side, making the hair look even more comical, but his expression turned serious. "But Mia hasn't lived a normal life. She is an odd combination of sophistication and naïveté in so many ways." He shoved his hands in his jorts pockets. "It's my own damned fault that she's . . . Well, I've called her spoiled, but then again she's done so much for charity without asking for anything in return. And I have to admit that after thinking about it, she has done a bang-up job at organizing parties and events for my clients. I guess I took her for granted as much as she took me for granted. Ah . . . Nicolina, there is so much I want to talk to her about."

"The old saying that you don't know what you've got 'til it's gone."

"Exactly." He slipped his arms around her waist. "That's how I feel when I'm away from you too, you know. You've added an element to my life that I've never had before. Someone to talk to. I really value your opinion. I hope you realize that."

"I feel the same way," Nicolina assured him. They were dancing around a declaration of love, but she couldn't get the words past her lips. It was if she was afraid that if she went that last mile she would jinx herself. It was silly and yet so very true, and so she held back. When he looked as if he was going to head in that direction, Nicolina quickly changed the subject. "Perhaps you should call Mia and just come clean with everything."

"I'm not so sure I want to do that just yet."

"Mitch, I don't want this to blow up in your face. I know that your heart is in the right place, but she may not see it that way."

He seemed to consider that for a moment. "But I still want her to find her way on her own. I'm going to let it ride, at least for the time being." He pulled her closer and ran a fingertip over her bottom lip. "Thank you so much."

"For what?"

"For everything. Listening, caring . . . and for just being in my life." He removed the silly hat and then gently tilted her chin up and gazed into her eyes. "You really have become very important to me in so many ways."

Nicolina felt emotion well up in her throat. Her feelings were growing stronger for Mitch each and every day. He was smart enough to know that she kept steering the conversation away from a declaration of full commitment, and she was probably insane for doing so. Mitch Monroe was everything a woman could want in a man . . . smart, sensitive, and sexy. Most women would add *filthy rich* to that list, but it was the one thing that she wished he wasn't.

"I hope you feel the same way," he prompted.

"Of course I do." She admitted that much and closed her eyes, hoping for a kiss. And she got it. Heaven help her, but the man could simply sweep her off her feet at the drop of a hat. His lips were soft but firm, and when his tongue tangled with hers, a thrill of excitement slid down her spine. Even in her youth Nicolina couldn't recall feeling the kind of smoldering passion that she had with Mitch, and she knew why. Even though Mitch was a very handsome, sexy man, what she felt for him went much deeper than the surface. He kissed her with depth, with meaning, and the combination made her weak in the knees.

A delicious moment later, he slowly pulled his mouth from hers. After a low chuckle, he leaned his forehead against hers and said, "Are you sure you want to go out for ice cream?"

"You know just how to get to me."

Mitch raised his head and grinned. "You mean that in a good way, I hope."

"Oh yes." Nicolina reached up and tweaked his nose. "That was a devious plan, but you're not going to get out of going out."

He widened his eyes in mock innocence. "Whatever do you mean?"

"Right . . ." Nicolina put the hat back on his head and did her best not to laugh. "Come on, let's go."

Mitch flicked a glance at his reflection in the dresser mirror and adjusted the bill of the cap. "You do realize that you are the only one who could get me to do something as nuts as this."

"No, I didn't, but I like that notion."

"I'm a pretty conservative guy when it comes to how I look in public."

"But no one is going to know it's you." She tapped his chest and then crooked a finger at him. "It's going to be dark in a little while, so let's hightail it out of here. I need a break from all of this business-related stuff anyway."

"I can relate."

"Oh, don't get me wrong. I really can't wait for my shop to actually open! I love that the whole strip is going to have wedding-related themes. Lots of my jewelry has been for wedding parties. I can tap into that market right away. I met the woman who is going to open the bridal boutique, and Mabel Grammar from Grammar's Bakery stopped by yesterday. Her shop specializing in nothing but wedding cakes is going to be such fun too! All we need is a florist and a wedding planner and we will have Wedding Row." When he gave her a funny look, she shook her head. "What? Did I say something wrong?"

"No, on the contrary! Nicolina, Wedding Row . . . I like that concept. I'll work on adding a florist. There's a cute one called Flower Power on Main Street. Maybe they would be interested in moving their business down here. The shop owners could all promote each other."

"A salon would be great as well."

"You, my dear, are a genius."

"Pfft." Nicolina waved him off, but in truth she was pleased that he liked her idea.

"Hey, don't sell yourself short. You're smart and talented. And whatever you do, don't ever be shy about suggesting or saying anything to me. Okay? The last person in the world I ever want to intimidate is you."

Nicolina nodded. "I've learned a lot from you, Mitch."

"Listen, I've made plenty of mistakes over the years. Made money but lost it too. I've taken a lot of chances, and not all of them have panned out. And in the end I was trying to prove a point to someone who didn't deserve my effort. I can't get back lost years with Mia, but believe me I understand the value of relationships, and they mean a helluva lot more than the almighty dollar. I just wish I had figured that out a long time ago."

Nicolina knew he was referring to his ex-wife. He rarely spoke of her, and even though they had been divorced for a long time, Nicolina still felt an odd pang of something akin to jealousy. She wanted to ask him if he still loved her but couldn't find the courage.

"What's troubling you?" Mitch asked.

"Nothing," Nicolina scoffed, but she was a bit blown away that he could read her so easily.

"You can't fool me," he gently prodded.

"It's hard to take you seriously in that cap," she tried to joke, but he wasn't having it and pulled her close once more. Nicolina chose her words carefully, wanting to get her answer in a roundabout way. "Okay, since you brought it up, do you think she ever regrets what she did?"

"Clarisse?

Nicolina nodded.

"You mean cheating? Leaving me for more money?" A muscle jumped in his jaw, making her suddenly wish she had left the subject alone. And yet she had to be sure that even after all of these years he didn't still carry a torch for his ex-wife.

"Yes, all of it."

Mitch lifted one shoulder. "I admit that there was a time when that's all I thought about. Making her regret what she did," he replied with a twist of his lips. "I made piles of money and I made sure she knew it." He laughed without humor. "I always had a woman younger and prettier than her on my arm whenever we were attending the same event. I showered Mia with expensive gifts, thinking that it would make her love me more than her mother." He shook his head, and there was sadness in his eyes. "Stupid pride."

"Did you gain full custody of Mia to get back at her as well?"

Mitch sighed. "Maybe a little, but in truth I thought that a woman who could do something so ruthless and wrong shouldn't be raising and influencing my child."

"I understand." Nicolina didn't really get all of the answers to her questions, but she couldn't bear to see the hurt lurking in his eyes, so she put her hands on his cheeks and said, "You were right to do so. And I need to stop grilling you about the painful past."

"Nicolina, you can ask me anything. Don't ever hesitate."

"Thank you," she said and smiled at his offer. "Now, we really do need to get going or the Dairy Bar will close. I don't know about you, but I could really go for a soft-serve ice cream cone. I might have it dipped in chocolate jimmies." But then she patted her butt and frowned. "Then again . . ."

"Hey, stop that! You're a gorgeous woman. And I love every beautiful inch of you."

Nicolina knew he was referring to her body, but the expression of love sent her heart racing in spite of her intention to steer clear of that subject. "Good, because there's lots of me to love." She was trying for dry humor, but her voice betrayed her by coming out breathy.

"You're perfect. Don't change a thing."

Nicolina was touched by his comment, but she hid her emotion with another soft laugh. She believed him, trusted him, and yet she couldn't put her heart on the line just yet. *Maybe someday,* she thought with an inward sigh. Reaching up, she tugged on a fake curl. "Don't you go changing anything either. I love this mullet, hot stuff. So very *sexy*," she cooed and then fanned her face.

"You silly thing." Mitch laughed and slipped his hand in hers. "Okay, let's go before I lose my nerve."

"It will be fun, I promise."

"You've brought fun back into my life, Nicolina. I've been way too serious for much too long. It feels great to laugh again. You make me happy doing the simplest of things."

"I'm glad," she said, and she meant it. "Bringing happiness to someone is one of life's greatest gifts."

"I can only hope I do the same for you."

"You do, Mitch," she said, and she was floored by how such a successful man could also be so humble.

"Good," he said, giving her a firm kiss on the mouth before tugging her toward the door. "Dairy Bar, here we come."

Not wanting to draw too much attention to themselves, they avoided Main Street and walked along the river before cutting up to the street where the popular ice cream stand was located. From the solid crack of a bat smacking a baseball to the gentle swish of water lapping against the bank of the river, the sounds of summer were everywhere in Cricket Creek. The smoky scent of a charcoal grill wafted their way, and fireflies were just beginning to flit around in the waning light. Music and laughter seemed to drift toward them, bringing the perfect blend of a lazy summer evening their way. A car passed them here and there, but for the most part people were strolling around on foot.

"It's peaceful here," Mitch commented.

"Not like the city; that's for sure," Nicolina commented, wondering if he could ever live in a small town.

As if reading her mind, he said, "I could get used to this."

I could get used to having you here, ran through her mind, but she smiled and nodded. "I already have," she said, letting him know that this was her home now and moving back to Chicago wasn't in her plans.

"I can understand why."

Nicolina watched him look around with a keen eye as if wondering if he could live here without going stir-crazy. But when they reached the Dairy Bar she pushed those thoughts from her mind and decided to simply enjoy the evening. A few people looked their way, but for the most part the crowd had died down, and so Mitch being recognized wasn't an issue. After ordering two vanilla cones—one with sprinkles for her—they opted to sit down at one of the picnic tables along the side of the building and enjoy their dessert.

"This is such a treat." Nicolina chuckled when she had to quickly lick a glob of sprinkle-laden ice cream before it escaped the edge of the cone.

"And so is the ice cream," Mitch said with a grin.

"You are such a flirt."

"You bring it out in me." When he tilted his head for a melting lick from his cone, his fake hair got in the way, making him laugh. "You're right—this is fun."

Nicolina nodded. "And no one here will even begin to recognize you," she added, but then she almost squeezed the ice cream from her cone. She leaned toward Mitch very slowly and said in a low tone, "Ah, strike that last comment."

Mitch swallowed a bite of his cone. "Who?" he mouthed.

"Whatever you do, don't turn around."

Of course he immediately whipped around so fast that his fake hair fanned out over his shoulders. He quickly turned back to face Nicolina. "It's Ty and Jessica pushing baby Ben in a stroller," he said in a stage whisper. "I don't think they recognized me."

"I told you not to turn around," Nicolina whispered back and then had to lick a big drip of melting ice cream from her cone.

"Sorry." Mitch grinned. "I don't mind very well, do I?"

Nicolina arched one eyebrow. "Naughty can be very nice." She chuckled when Mitch laughed in midlick of his soft serve, making the whole thing tip like the Leaning Tower of Pisa. He had to quickly adjust by licking the other side, making her laugh even harder. At her age, she'd never thought that sexy flirting was still possible, but they played and teased so much that by the time they finally fell into bed, it was always amazing.

Mitch wiped his mouth with the small paper napkin. "That was a close call."

"Yes, you almost lost your ice cream."

"No, I mean seeing Ty and Jessica. They could have blown my Joe Dirt cover."

Nicolina laughed. "You do look like Joe Dirt."

Mitch gave the fake hair a flip. "Turn you on, does it?"

"You bet," she replied in a suggestive tone that had him grinning.

Mitch put his hand over hers and his grin faded into something more serious. "I enjoy every minute with you. I hope you know that."

Nicolina nodded. "I do."

"Good." He squeezed her hand gently and then licked away a drip from his cone. "We'd better get going soon."

"So you don't get recognized?"

"No, so I can make love to you," he said and had her melting quicker than her ice cream.

"We could eat as we walk," she suggested and was already standing up, making Mitch chuckle.

"Now, why didn't I think of that?" He stood up with her and smiled. "Let's go."

They had just polished off their cones when Nicolina's eyes widened. She tugged on Mitch's hand. "Quick, duck behind this tree!"

"This isn't going to hide us," Mitch said. "Who is it?"

"Bella and Madison walking right this way! Do something!"

"Okay." Mitch pressed her up against the trunk of the big oak tree, bent his mullet head, and kissed her.

18

Hot Summer Nights

WHILE EATING THE AMAZING MEAT LOAF, MASHED POTAtoes, and green beans that Cam had brought to her, Mia read over the promotional material that Noah had encouraged her to review. She really missed having a laptop and hoped that Noah would have a company one that she could bring home from work in the evenings, because it was apparent that her social life wasn't going to be thriving. Besides, she really wanted to excel at this job.

Munching on a soft, yeasty dinner roll that she'd sworn she wasn't going to eat, Mia made several notes in the margin while she studied her job description. Her mind already raced with ideas. If there was one thing she knew how to do, it was to get corporate contributions. Coming up with items to give away at games was going to be a fun challenge.

After a while she became restless and unpacked her clothes. "Wow," she mumbled, shaking her head at the outfits she had hastily tossed into her suitcase. Other than the suit and a few pairs of capri pants, most of what she had brought was going to be useless. She thought about Violet's Vintage Clothing store on Main Street and hoped that she could set aside enough of her salary to purchase a few blouses and one of the wide belts that Violet had suggested to mix and match the separates to create more outfits.

Mia rolled her eyes when she thought of the jam-packed walk-in closet back home in Chicago. So much of what she owned wouldn't be well suited for her lifestyle here in Cricket Creek. She also thought about the fact that the cost of just one designer dress was more money than she needed to outfit herself with the basic necessities of everyday small-town living. A hot flash of guilt hit her when she thought about all of the purses, shoes, and clothes that just hung in her closet, never even having been worn.

Mia's mind drifted to Sunny, and she hoped that she would be able to sell the shoes and pocket enough cash to get what she needed. Her eyes suddenly filled with moisture and she swallowed hard. "I'm just a spoiled brat," she muttered under her breath. No wonder she felt as if no one took her seriously. Up until now she hadn't taken *life* seriously.

With a long sigh, she sat down on the bed so hard that she bounced. The solitude reminded her of her many lonely nights as a kid, and she took her mind off of it and started flipping through the television channels but soon became bored. "Who needs a reality show? I am a reality show," she muttered, flopping onto her back. "What I need is some chocolate." She stared up at the ceiling, wishing she had bought a candy bar or ice cream at the grocery store. As much as she tried to watch her weight, she had a sweet tooth that drove her crazy if denied. She indulged once in a while, even when her friends did not. Most of them obsessed way too much over their appearance, and unfortunately much of the obsession was brought on their mothers, who encouraged Botox and plastic surgery at an early age.

Mia tried to think of just one of her friends who hadn't had some kind of work done, and she couldn't come up with even one name except for Cat. "Of course,

I didn't have a mother to push me in any direction," she thought darkly. Funny, she rarely thought of her mother, but being in this small town had her longing for a sense of family that seemed to be everywhere.

"Oh . . . I need chocolate!" Crossing her fingers, she sat up. "Please . . . ," she said as she opened her purse, hoping that there was just a little square of chocolate or at the very least maybe an after-dinner mint hidden in the deep depths, but her search in every little zipper area turned up empty. She did have to smile when she pulled the hula dancer out of the bottom of her purse. "Well, hello there, little chickie." Mia jiggled her a little bit so that her hips danced back and forth. "Welcome to your new home until my car is fixed," she announced, putting the tiny dancer on the dresser. "Are you as bored as I am?" She glanced at her silent cell phone and sighed again, thinking that except for her conversation with Cat Carson, no one from what she now thought of as her *old life* really seemed to care that she was gone.

That sad thought had her craving chocolate even more, and she groaned in pure frustration when she realized that dessert wasn't the only thing weighing on Mia's mind. The knowledge that sexy-as-sin Cameron Patrick was right next door had Mia feeling like a moth drawn to a light. She folded her arms across her chest and looked into the accusing eyes of the hula dancer. "Oh, don't look at me that way. I'm not going to go over there," she said, and then she realized that if she was so bored that she was talking to a doll, she had better get out of the condo and find some real people. Perhaps she would head to Wine and Diner or maybe walk over to the ice cream stand called the Dairy something or other. Yeah, a soft-serve ice cream cone suddenly sounded appealing. Dressed in her shorts and shirt, she wouldn't even feel out of place. She also decided not to lug her huge designer purse and just take some of the little bit of cash she had left. Plus, walking would burn off enough calories to justify eating the treat. Well, not really, but it was something.

Feeling better now that she had a plan, Mia smiled and headed out the front door of her condo, which led into the shared hallway. But just as she walked past the elevators, she realized that she had forgotten her cell phone and also had neglected to lock the front door. She was so used to keypads that she had completely forgotten. At first she decided that she would just leave; after all, this was Cricket Creek and getting robbed wasn't likely, and her cell phone had remained stubbornly silent, so why bother? She took another step toward the front entrance but then stopped and decided to do the mature thing and get her phone and lock the door. Besides, what if someone did try to call her?

"The key is in the purse you decided not to take," she grumbled to herself, but when she turned the knob on the front door, it was already locked. "Oh no, it's one of the kind that locks automatically!" She felt tears of frustration well up in her eyes but then told herself not to be a baby! She inhaled deeply and searched her brain for a solution. Ah . . . maybe the sliding door to the patio was still open. Had she remembered to lock it? "I sure hope not, but that would be just my luck," she prayed as she walked outside and headed around to the back of the building.

Mia pressed her lips together as she put her hand on the handle. "Please be open," she whispered and then finally took the plunge and tugged. "Damn!" she grumbled when the door refused to slide. "Damn, damn . . . *damn*!" She stomped her foot and tugged really hard again, even though she knew it wouldn't budge.

"Something wrong?"

Mia whirled around and lost her balance from the force of the tug coupled with her quick twirl. To her horror, she actually did a three-sixty and then added a little grapevine to the left, which would have been fine if she were doing one of those wedding line dances that she always got wrong. She righted herself just before slamming into the brick wall. "Must you sneak up on a person?"

His lips twitched, but he must have sensed that laughing might not be a good idea. "Sorry, didn't mean to. I heard you cursing."

Great . . .

"Is there something I can do?"

"No," she answered stiffly, too embarrassed to admit that she had locked herself out. He was in red Nike shorts and was shirtless, looking so good that it should have been outlawed. Just gazing at him made her heart pound, but he appeared calm, obviously not affected by her presence one little bit. The thought irritated her to no end.

Cam frowned. "Are you sure?"

"Positive," she claimed, but she stood there not really knowing what to do about her situation, only that she wasn't about to let him know her predicament. But feeling silly that she was being rude, she said, "Thank you again for bringing dinner. It was delightful."

He grinned, making her heart race at the sight.

"What?" she snapped and then amended in a softer tone, "are you grinning about?"

"Delightful."

She stared at him blankly, carefully keeping her eyes off his very nice chest. He was tanned and toned and . . . *stop*!

"You use words that for some reason I find funny."

"I'm so glad that I amuse you."

"I'm not easily amused, so think of it as a gift."

Mia knew he was trying to be funny but sensed that he was actually telling the truth. Something about his admission touched her, making her anger evaporate . . . well, that and the fact that he didn't do anything to deserve her wrath. Mia was usually slow to anger, but then again her emotions had been all over the map, making her feel off balance. "I tend to make people laugh without even trying," she admitted with a slight grin. "I'm always the one out of sync, you know?"

"I don't know about that. You seem to be able to dance pretty well."

"Ha . . . ah, very funny."

"I have my moments." Cam looked at her as if he was going to say something more but then thought better of it. When he looked away, Mia took the opportunity to allow her gaze to drift over his bare chest. When she felt heat creep into her cheeks, she averted her gaze, but then frowned. Wait, wasn't that the same sedan that she had seen earlier? Mia nibbled on the inside of her lip. Yeah, she was pretty sure the same car had been parked near the stadium, and she felt a little surge of alarm. "Is something wrong?" Cam asked, and this time his tone was serious.

"Nothing . . . ," Mia mumbled while she tried to think of who could be following her. Of course her father popped into her mind, but there really wasn't any way that he could have tracked her down. She was sure that he assumed she was hanging out with friends somewhere on a yacht or something similar.

"Mia?"

At his firm tone, Mia tore her attention from the car and looked up at Cam. At his inquisitive frown, she shrugged. "I'm not sure but I feel like someone . . . ," she began, but then, not wanting to blow her cover, she shook her head.

"Someone what?" he persisted, and when he followed her gaze the sedan suddenly took off. "Hey, do you think someone is following you?"

"No . . . ," she scoffed. "Who would be following little old me?" she asked, but she didn't sound convincing even to her own ears.

"You tell me." When she remained silent, he took a step closer. "Listen, you can tell me anything and it will remain private. I promise."

"Thank you," Mia replied, trying to sound matter-of-fact, but her voice trembled slightly. There had been a time a few years ago when her father had gotten some threatening letters. As a precaution he had sent her to Paris until it had all blown over. Mia always knew her father was a powerful man, and she suddenly wondered if someone really had been tailing her. After the harsh takeover of Hanover Candy, Mia wondered if her father had some enemies who might want to do her harm. She thought maybe she should actually give him a call but then remembered that her phone was in her purse along with the key to her place.

"Mia, I don't believe you. What's wrong? Is there someone after you?" His tone was low and insistent.

"I'm not sure," she admitted softly.

"Are you in some kind of trouble?"

"I told you before . . . no!" She shook her head firmly but wouldn't look at him.

"Is it an ex-boyfriend creeping on you? I'll kick his ass."

Mia looked up to see a muscle jumping in his jaw. The very last thing she wanted was for Cam to get into trouble once again on her behalf. Still, it was damned sexy that he wanted to come to her rescue. "Impossible, since I don't have an ex-boyfriend. Look, I'm just ticked because I locked myself out of the condo. All I wanted was an ice cream. I didn't realize that the front door would lock when I shut it."

"So you locked yourself out?"

"I was embarrassed to tell you. I just wanted something sweet," she said and then blushed. "Like ice cream or chocolate."

Cam gave her a measuring look, as if trying to decide whether or not to believe her. "Well, Bella and Madison both have a master key."

"Right! I'll head to the front desk." She put the heel of her hand to her forehead. "Silly me. Why didn't I think of that?"

"Madison's probably gone by now, though. I talked to her earlier when I dropped off my rent check. She said that she and Bella were going to Sully's tonight. We can probably find them over there. Grab a beer?"

We? Her heart pounded but she shook her head.

"Oh . . . I've taken up enough of your day. I'll just walk over there myself."

"No way."

"What do you mean, no way?"

"Mia, you just thought that someone could be following you. Do you really think I'll let you walk over there by yourself? It will be dark pretty soon."

"This is Cricket Creek, not Chicago," Mia scoffed but then almost put her hand over her mouth. She was really bad at this undercover stuff. "Or New York or LA," she added, as if throwing out random cities and not disclosing where she lived.

"True, but I'm coming with you all the same."

Mia thought about arguing, but she really did want him to come. Seeing the sedan had sent a shot of fear sliding down her spine. It was probably nothing at all to do with her, but her instinct was waving a red flag. Her father had always taught her to trust her gut, so having Cam come with her was a good idea.

"Come on over and I'll grab a shirt and my wallet." He shot her a grin. "I could use a cold beer anyway, but it's early for Sully's, so if you want to get an ice cream I'm down for that too."

Mia thought about the three dollars and thirty-three cents she had in her pocket.

"I still have Noah's card," he added with a wink.

"You can't use that!"

"I was supposed to take you out on the town. He's not going to quibble over an ice cream or a couple of beers. Trust me." He waved a hand for her to follow him. "Come on."

"Okay," she said, with a bit of question laced in her tone, but in fact she did trust him, and if she was being honest, she was giddy about spending the evening with him . . . for her protection, of course. Nothing more. Still, as she followed him she couldn't help but admire his very nice butt.

When Cam headed to his bedroom to change, Mia

couldn't help but notice that his place was as neat as a pin. What she didn't see was any pictures of family, and she had to wonder why. He was a visitor and not a resident, but still, one would think that he would have some personal touches here and there. But she told herself not to ask or pry. When he returned with a shirt she smiled but secretly missed the beauty of his bare chest. Odd, because she spent so much time around her pool or at the water she was often surrounded by shirtless guys, many of them in great shape. But the sight of his particular chest made her long to touch his bare skin.

"Ready?" he asked briskly, but when their eyes met, a hot shot of awareness passed between them. The heat hung in the air, making Mia wonder how she was going to fight something this strong.

"Yes." She wanted to sound chipper, but her breathless tone sounded like a response to something other than an evening stroll to an ice cream stand. If he noticed, he didn't give her any indication, politely putting his hand at the small of her back and urging her toward the door.

19

The Simple Things

CAM JUST ABOUT HAD HIMSELF UNDER CONTROL, AND then he had to go and touch her. His hand at the small of Mia's back was meant to be impersonal and merely polite, but damn, if it didn't make him want to drag her back into the condo and kiss her senseless. Not doing so took more control than not going after a high, hard fastball that was impossible to hit yet irresistible. He was acutely aware of everything about her, from the scent of her perfume to the lingering sunshine glinting off her hair. She appeared fresh and carefree in her casual shorts, making Cam smile for no real reason other than walking down the street with her.

"Oh, look!" Mia pointed across the street to the entrance to the park. Her laughter at the sight of two plump puppies rolling around in a patch of grass was infectious. A little girl chased after the puppies, followed by what must have been her father. "Aren't they adorable?"

"Sure are." He glanced at Mia and then back to the puppies. "I always wanted a dog." Why he felt the need to add that little tidbit, he'd never know.

"Yeah, me too." Her wistful tone drew his attention. "The closest I came was the dog at my mother's house, but Toby actually belonged to my two half brothers."

Ah, another nugget of information. "So, when did your mom and dad divorce?" He wanted to keep the information flowing.

Mia nodded. "When I was a toddler." When a shadow fell across her face, Cam wished he hadn't persisted. "Maybe I'll have a dog of my own someday."

"Hey, if you want a dog, you should get one. What kind would you get?"

Her expression brightened. "Oh, a mutt. Definitely a rescue dog." She nodded firmly, as if she had thought about it more than once.

"Good decision," Cam agreed and smiled. It seemed that whenever he was with her she managed to put him in a better mood. Although he reminded himself that it *wasn't*, this felt like a date, and Cam found himself longing to reach over and take her hand. Crazy, since he was never much of a touchy-feely kind of guy. He shoved his hands in his pockets and fell silent.

"It's a nice evening out," Mia commented. "I just love summertime, don't you?"

"Yeah," he replied, deciding to keep his answers short. He told himself to keep his distance both physically and emotionally, but it was becoming a losing battle that in truth he wasn't even sure that he wanted to win.

Mia glanced at him. "Silly question. Of course you love summertime. You're a baseball player!"

"True, although summer in Florida can be brutal, you're right." So much for short answers, but damn, her smile was so hard to resist. Mia had a way of opening him up and drawing him out, and his resistance was fading fast. *Why fight this* snuck into his brain once more, and he was having a hard time remembering his reasons for pushing her away. *Getting in the way of his career* filtered into his brain but no longer held much clout, and he surely was wrong about her high maintenance. His rich-chick radar must be completely on the fritz.

"Did you like school?"

Cam arched an eyebrow at her question. "Uh, not so

much. So summer vacation was always highly anticipated for more reasons than one," he added with a grin. "I always managed to get just above having to go to summer school." Cam really wasn't one for small talk, but it helped to keep his mind off wanting to kiss her . . . well, almost. "How about you? Did you like school?"

"Oh, I pretty much loved school," she said, and something in her eyes made him think that there was more to it than that.

"So you were a high achiever?"

"I always wanted to please my father, so getting good grades was important." She frowned and then added, "I guess since my mother left I always had this fear that if I wasn't good that he would leave me too."

"I'm sure that wasn't the case, Mia."

"Oh, I know that, at least on an intellectual level, but the little girl in me still feared the worst." When her eyes misted over, Cam wanted to draw her into his arms and hug her hard. She fell silent for a moment and then said, "And there were always people around at school, you know? My father was gone a lot, so the social aspect was something I looked forward to every day. About the only thing I got in trouble for consistently was talking too much."

"I would never have guessed," Cam said, drawing a slight grin from her. "My mother worked a lot, so I totally get where you're coming from. Loneliness is a bitch."

"So true," she readily agreed, but Cam noticed that she didn't mention her mother again. He wanted to know more, but she suddenly clammed up, though he sensed that she was deep in thought. He didn't let her know it, but he was also keeping his eyes peeled for the sedan or any other indication that someone was watching her.

Cam remained keenly aware of his surroundings, but to his relief he didn't really notice anything out of the ordinary. Cricket Creek was a throwback to the days when small towns were the American way of life, with the outlying area taken up by farmland and a few chain stores and restaurants on the main highway. To think that there was something evil lurking just didn't fit, and Cam wondered if he was being overprotective, but then Mia suddenly stopped short. "What's wrong?" Cam glanced at her and his senses went on high alert.

"Nothing."

"Mia!"

"I thought I saw someone watching me over by the trees," she replied but then chuckled. "For a minute I even felt like it was going to be my father. But the guy was wearing a baseball cap and had, you know, one of those silly haircuts . . ." She wiggled her fingers near her shoulders.

"Do you mean a mullet?"

Mia pointed at Cam and nodded. "Yeah, one of those. I must be crazy. My father and a mullet do not fit in the same sentence." She shook her head, but her smile faltered a bit. "That was pretty weird, but I guess I just miss him."

Cam hid his concern with a question. "Are you two close?"

"Yes, but we've had a bit of a falling-out," she admitted, and she appeared so sad that Cam couldn't resist and reached over and took her hand.

"I'm sure you'll work it out."

"I sure hope so," Mia answered, so glumly that Cam squeezed her hand. He wanted to let go but just couldn't bring himself to do so. He supposed that it didn't help that families were milling around everywhere.

"Are you sad that you aren't close to your parents?"

"No." Cam didn't want to elaborate but felt himself adding, "But I always wanted to be in a close-knit family unit." When a young couple passed pushing a stroller, Cam suddenly wondered if he would ever be a father. Wow, that sudden thought came from out of left field and shook Cam up a little bit. He knew it had something to do with walking hand in hand with Mia, but instead of letting go, he suddenly held her hand a bit more firmly. He had never felt this sense of longing before, and perhaps it was about time that he embraced something soft and good. Instead of trying to push Mia away, maybe he should do everything in his power to draw her closer. He knew one thing: It sure felt right being with her.

Cam had learned that when he was struggling at the plate, he should just relax and fall into a rhythm, allowing the ball to come to him. With that thought in mind, Cam decided to just let the evening take its course and evolve naturally.

"I haven't had one of these in a long time," Cam confessed after they'd ordered their ice cream cones.

Mia licked off the decorative top curl and then nodded. "Me neither, and it's simply scrumptious."

"Sometimes it's the simple things in life." Cam was sort of joking, but her eyes lit up.

"You know, you're absolutely right." She put a gentle hand on his forearm. "Just take a look around and you see the evidence everywhere."

"True," Cam acknowledged, but instead of looking around he gazed at her. There was just something so sweet about Mia, and Cam knew he was drawn to her gentleness because it was something that had always been lacking in his life. He had learned to be tough and independent. He had played when he had been hurt and shrugged off the pain. On days when he had come up lacking, there had been no one to pick him up with a pep talk, and there'd been no celebration at home if he had hit the winning run or made a diving catch. Report cards and achievements went unnoticed, and so Cam rarely tried to do more than the minimum in the classroom, figuring, *Why bother?* He had developed a very thick skin, but her light, simple touch made him melt as quickly as the soft-serve ice cream. "I had forgotten how good an ice cream cone tasted."

"Me too!"

Cam had gone for vanilla, but Mia had opted for a vanilla and chocolate swirl that she called a zebra. "I lived for these when I was a kid." He remembered saving his money so that he could get the occasional treat on his way home from baseball practice. It used to get to him, seeing families sharing the evening together while he consumed his ice cream alone. He often had to choose between an ice cream cone and a hot dog for his dinner. Once in a while some loser that his mother was dating would toss him a couple of bucks just to get rid of him for the evening and Cam could splurge on both. He never even asked his father for anything, since it was pointless.

Later on, when he was a teenager, getting out of the trailer meant looking for trouble instead of treats, and Cam knew that if it hadn't been for baseball he would have slid down a much darker path. Coaches became his father figures and provided a sense of stability and encouragement that his home life lacked. If Cam ever had a family of his own, he vowed that it would be a much different story.

Wait, a family of my own?

Cam had never really thought about getting married or having children, unless thoughts of never wanting to go that route were considered. But he suddenly wondered how it would feel to push the stroller of his own child or to toss ball with his son. He glanced at Mia's pretty profile and knew that she would look so cute with a baby bump. Then he shook his head and stared at his ice cream cone, thinking that it must be drugged.

"A penny for your thoughts." Mia licked the side of her ice cream swirl and tilted her head to the side in question.

"A penny is all my thoughts are worth?" There was no way he was going to disclose what had been going on in his brain, not for any amount of money.

"Well, unfortunately, I don't have much more than pocket change to my name," she replied, but her tone was cheerful.

"Well, then, I'll spring for the beer at Sully's. I won't even use Noah's credit card," he added with a grin.

"How can you think about beer when we're eating ice cream?"

"I'm a guy. Beer goes with anything."

Mia laughed and then had to quickly lick a drip of ice cream that was sliding down the side of her cone. "I had forgotten that there was an art to eating one of these," she said and then licked all around the base of the cone. Cam watched in fascination, forgetting about his own melting ice cream until she pointed it out. "Cam! You've got some serious dripping going on! What are you doing?"

Watching you. "Oh . . . damn!" He laughed at his melting mess and went to work. They walked to Sully's and fell into a companionable silence as they strolled past the city park once more. The sun was dipping low in the sky and the evening breeze was chasing away the heat of the day. Cam felt more at ease than he had in a long time and found himself smiling for no real reason. The urge to hold her hand returned, and this time instead of fighting it he reached over and did it. Mia looked at him in what seemed like surprise but then smiled. A soft blush crept into her cheeks, and she looked away, making Cam wonder what was on her mind. She was a mystery he wanted to unravel, but for now he chose to simply enjoy being with a beautiful woman on a warm summer night.

When they reached Sully's, the younger crowd was starting to filter in. Cam held the door for Mia to enter and was surprised that the bar was already hopping. The jukebox played an upbeat Jason Aldean party song, creating a festive, energetic atmosphere. Laughter mingled with the music and a few people started to dance. Ice-filled buckets with longnecks sticking out of the top were being thumped down onto high-topped tables and carried outside. Cam suddenly realized it had been a long time since he'd had a night out on the town and hoped that Mia would want to stay for a while and not leave right after finding Bella and Madison. As soon as the season was in full swing, these carefree nights would end.

Cam used the loudness of the music and laughter as an excuse to lean close to Mia's ear and ask, "What can I get you to drink?"

"Oh . . . um . . ." She glanced around as if to see what everybody else was drinking, making him wonder if a neighborhood bar was something she was used to, or perhaps something higher end would have been more familiar. But then he remembered her beater car and the fact that she was broke and shook off that notion. "A beer."

"Should I get a bucket?"

"A bucket?"

When she seemed confused, he said, "It's cheaper that way and stays cold."

"Oh . . . sure. A bucket would be great."

"Is Kentucky Ale okay? It's a popular choice around here, and I like it."

"Yes, that's great. I noticed that it's on tap at the Cougars stadium and Jessica has it at the diner. I like the idea of supporting the local businesses." She smiled. "And I plan on hitting them up for a beverage huggie giveaway."

"Smart idea," Cam said, and then signaled for a bartender. Sully noticed them and lumbered over to the end of the bar.

"Well, hello there, sugar," Sully said in his booming voice. He slapped the white towel he had in his hand over his shoulder and grinned at Mia. "You still stirring up trouble over at Wine and Diner?"

"Actually, I'm working as the promotions manager for the Cougars."

"You don't say." Sully's bushy eyebrows shot up. "Well, now."

"In fact, if you'd like, we could sit down sometime soon and discuss some ways that you could promote your bar at the ballpark," Mia suggested. "Maybe a T-shirt? If I can get enough interest from other establishments in town, you could all have your name on the back."

"I like that idea." Sully nodded. "I've done that for local softball teams, but this would be even better. Locals know about my tavern, but it would be great to get some of the out-of-towners over here before or after the games."

"Super. I don't have business cards just yet, but I'll stop in for lunch this week and we can brainstorm ideas. Think in terms of having discounts for patrons of the games if they show a ticket stub—something like stub-and-grub night?"

"Stub and grub . . ." Sully tugged on his beard and then nodded. "Hey, I like that!" He appeared duly impressed and then turned to Cam. "Word is that you've been smacking the tar out of the ball."

Cam nodded. "I've been making some contact."

"Well, I'm sure looking forward to opening day. Ty McKenna stopped in earlier and had a few wings, and your name came up." Sully leaned forward and said in a low but audible tone, "Ty sneaks in here for my special wings. I grill 'em and then bake 'em until the meat falls off the bones. Jessica begged me for the sauce recipe and the rights to use it at Wine and Diner, but it's a highly guarded secret." He puffed out his wide chest. "Pretty damned flattering to have a chef like her want a recipe from little ole me . . . well, not that I'm little, but you get the picture." He gave Mia a wink.

"I'll say," Mia agreed but then quickly added, "About the being flattered part.

Sully laughed. "Hey, little lady, seems like I remember that I owe you a martini."

Mia glanced at Cam. "We were going to order a pail of Kentucky Ale."

"A bucket," Cam corrected with a grin. "Have the martini if you prefer, Mia." He was beginning to guess that she didn't frequent neighborhood bars like Sully's Tavern.

Sully put his big hands on the gleaming wood bar and tilted his head. "I can make the perfect martini, very dry and extra cold, but I also make a mean Chocolate Dream, if you're interested."

"Oh, all you had to say was chocolate and I'm in," Mia admitted.

Sully grinned and reached for a generous-sized martini glass hanging upside down from a rack. "Jerry, get a bucket of Kentucky Ale for Cameron Patrick and give him the Cougar discount," he called to another bartender, who nodded.

"Thanks," Cam said. The players all loved it at Sully's, and with good reason. It might not be the pros, but it was nice for the players to feel like celebrities, if only on the local level. There was a lot of hometown pride in Cricket Creek, and Cam liked the feeling.

"Watch the master at work," Sully said to Mia, drawing applause from several patrons seated at the bar.

"I believe I will—and take notes too." Mia scooted onto a vacant stool. When her shoulder brushed against Cam, he snagged a beer from the bucket and took an ice-cold swig, but it did little to cool him down. He glanced around for Bella and Madison and didn't see either one of them, but that was okay with him since he didn't want to leave anytime soon.

A few minutes later Sully sat the frosty glass in front of Mia and poured the chocolate martini with a flourish. To her obvious delight, he added a decorative chocolate curl as a garnish and then stood back and waited for Mia to take a taste.

"Oh . . . pure heaven," Mia gushed. "No wonder they call it a Chocolate Dream." She took another sip and groaned. "This could be dangerous, but thank you so much. I do think this will hit the spot, even though I am full of ice cream. Good thing my car is still in the shop so I have to hoof it everywhere."

Sully gave her another wink. "Let me know if you can handle another one, there, sugar."

"Will do," Mia answered and then raised her glass to Cam. "Would you like a sip?"

Cam was surprised by her offer. "Sure." He really wasn't a chocolate martini kind of guy, but the gesture seemed so date-like that he nodded and took the glass from her. He took a taste and had to admit that the velvety chocolate flavor with a kick had a certain appeal. "Pretty good," he admitted and handed the glass back to her. "Would you like to go out on the deck or stay in here?"

"Oh, I almost always choose outdoors. Alfresco is my favorite way to drink or eat. My father and I eat outside, weather permitting, of course. I especially enjoy coffee outdoors in the morning."

"I'm guessing *alfresco* means 'outside,'" Cam said with a grin. She continued to give him conflicting hints as to her background, but he told himself not to care and to simply enjoy being with her.

"You guessed right," she replied with a wide smile, making Cam think that she was enjoying herself as well. He held her martini for her while she slid down from the barstool and then grabbed the bucket of beer by the handle. "Thanks," she said, taking her glass. When their fingers brushed, he was ready for the warm tingle and wasn't disappointed. He already knew what it was like to have her in his arms, and he longed to have her there once again. They wove their way through the thickening crowd. Cam high-fived a few of his teammates and waved to a few others. When he noticed a few lingering looks at Mia, he put his hand at the small of her back to send a subtle message. The Cougars were starting to gel as a team, and Cam really thought they were going to win some games. Like him, the players were either trying to break into the minor leagues or climb their way back after an injury or simply being released. This was either a first or final shot for them all. The success of Logan Lannigan was proof positive that it could happen. Oddly enough, instead of feeling that this was his last chance, Cam was starting to feel as if this was a new beginning.

But for once it didn't begin and end with baseball.

20

Raise Your Glass!

"THERE'S A SPOT!" MIA POINTED TO THE FAR CORNER OF the deck, where one last table remained vacant.

"I'll follow you," Cam said over the sound of Toby Keith singing "I Love This Bar."

"It is cute out here," Mia commented. Tiny white lights twinkled in the trees surrounding the sides of the deck, but there was a pretty view of the Ohio River straight back from the building. The music was audible but muted, allowing for conversation. Fat citronella candles flickered on top of picnic-style tables that were straightforward in a Sully's kind of way but somehow managed to create a romantic atmosphere.

Cam plunked the bucket down on the table and tucked his long legs beneath the bench seat. "I'm sure *cute* was the look Sully was going for," he said with a grin.

Mia laughed as she sat down across from him. "Well, the man makes a mean martini." She wasn't a big drinker, but once in a while a cocktail hit the spot.

"I know that Madison and Bella both say that Sully's rivals any martini bar in Chicago."

"I can see why . . . or should I say *taste* why. I'm just a little bit surprised, but Sully sure is proud of his achievement."

"Word has it that some rich-ass boater came in here last summer demanding a martini and then told Sully it was the worst one he'd ever had. Sully made it his mission to learn how to make the perfect martini."

"Well, good for him," Mia said, but once again Mia felt the internal sting of knowing that she had hung out with people like that . . . insulting and rude while thinking that they knew it all. She had rubbed shoulders with both the rich and famous, and while it wasn't fair to lump anyone into a category, Mia had seen her fair share of obnoxious behavior. "Speaking of Madison and Bella, we completely forgot to look for them," Mia said, but Cam didn't appear concerned.

"I'll scout around in a little while. I'm sure they're here somewhere."

"Do you know them very well?"

Cam shoved his empty bottle into the bucket and grabbed another one. "I haven't lived here long enough to know them all that well, but in a small town like this you get to know lots of people in a short period of time. Since they both live at the high-rise, I see them both on a pretty regular basis. I do know that both of them are fun to hang out with."

"I bet they are. Madison mentioned hanging out by the pool. I'd like to get to get to know Bella too."

"Yeah, I bet they would like that too Mia. I know that Bella misses Logan. She groans about it all the time. If he gets called up to the majors, I'm guessing she'll move with him."

"I'm sure that being separated for such long periods sucks," Mia said and then waited for Cam's reaction.

"I guess if you care enough about someone, you do whatever it takes," Cam said and then took a long pull from his bottle of beer. "I know I would," Cam added but then glanced away as if embarrassed or even surprised at his open admission. But a moment later he looked at Mia and asked, "Wouldn't you?"

"Of course," Mia answered without hesitation and

then raised her glass in salute. "Here's to finding that person."

Cam looked at her just long enough to get her heart rate going. He tapped his bottle to her glass, causing a delicate clink, and they both took a drink. Mia acknowledged that she was beginning to feel comfortable with Cam and simply be herself, but then that thought stopped her in midsip of her martini. She swallowed and then let the thought sink in. She felt more at ease with Cameron Patrick—and truthfully at Sully's—than she had ever felt out with her friends. There was no pretense here. Everyone was casual and having a good time, she thought, and then as if on cue a couple of Cougars players came over and sat down. One of them was apparently too close to Mia, because Cam gave him an arch of one eyebrow that had the guy scooting farther away.

"By all means, have a seat," Cam said with a shake of his head but then grinned. "Mia, meet Ryan Moore and Cory Baker."

Ryan gave her a polite nod but Cory said, "You're the new promotions manager, aren't you?"

"That would be me." She felt a sense of pride at the admission.

"If you're looking to get a sellout crowd, I think you need to have big, glossy pictures of me to give away," Cory said, pointing his thumb to his chest. "I'm just trying to help you out." He put his palms up. "No thanks needed."

"Or better yet, a really big poster," Mia replied in a mock-serious tone and extended her hands to show the size she was talking about.

"Why, thank you. A huge poster sure is an awesome idea," Cory said.

"No thanks needed, but the next round on you would be nice," Mia suggested, drawing a laugh from them all.

"It's the least I can do." Cory good-naturedly agreed to the suggestion, and then he signaled for the waitress to come over to their table. He ordered another bucket of beer along with a martini for Mia, even though the first one already had her feeling pretty mellow. For the better part of an hour they had Mia laughing until her face hurt. She couldn't remember when she'd had so much fun but turned down her third martini and opted for a bottle of water instead. She had work to do tomorrow and wanted to keep her mind sharp. After joking around, they talked seriously about some promo items that Mia thought had promise; she jotted down the suggestions on her napkin.

"Well," Cory said, "I think it's about time to show off my dance moves."

"Show off?" Cam asked. "Cory, I've seen you dance."

"I didn't say good dance moves . . . ," Cory admitted and laughed. "Mia, I bet you're a great dancer," he said, but when he extended his hand toward her, Cam shot him down with a look of warning. "Okay . . . I get it," he said but then grinned at Mia. "But if you ever want to dump him for a stud like me, let me know."

"I'll keep that in mind," Mia said and was secretly pleased that Cam was leading his teammates to believe that they were a couple.

"Dude, you're crazy," Ryan said and gave Mia a look of apology for his teammate, but she knew it was all in fun. When Ryan and Cory finally got up to hit the dance floor, Mia shifted to the side, causing her knees to bump up against Cam's beneath the table. The contact was brief and inadvertent, and yet she felt the touch all the way to her toes. Mia gripped the edge of the bench seat, thinking that she wanted to throw herself across the wooden table and kiss Cam, but she schooled her features in what she hoped was a bland that-didn't-make-me-melt expression. She glanced at him beneath her lashes to try to see if there was any indication that he felt the same reaction but couldn't get a bead on what he was thinking.

"Do you think we should head out?" Cam asked casually, and at first Mia was disappointed that he wanted to go home, but there was something just slightly suggestive in Cam's eyes that made her breath catch.

He wanted her. She was certain.

"All right." Mia narrowed her eyes in an effort to get a better look at him to make sure she was right, but he was looking down at his cell phone, so she couldn't see his eyes. Damn . . . well, okay she was *kind* of sure. Wait, you couldn't be kind of sure . . . you either were or you weren't . . . *sure. I am,* she thought with a stubborn lift of her chin. No, what if she was wrong? Her chin fell. Completely, totally wrong and about to make a complete fool of herself. With that thought in mind, Mia decided she had better play it cool. For all she knew, he could be texting another girl.

"Sorry," Cam said after looking up from his phone. "It was a message from Coach McKenna about practice starting late tomorrow."

"No problem," she said breezily. Wow, he had an amazing smile.

"So are you ready to leave?"

"Yes, I'm getting a little tired," Mia answered in what she hoped was a nonchalant tone. She tried for a yawn, but she was pretty sure it looked faked so she stretched her arms wide and managed to smack a complete stranger on the butt. "Sorry," Mia squeaked and then decided that the vibe she felt that Cam wanted her must be completely off. Who would want a dork like her?

He sure wanted you in the elevator. Yes, but those were unusual circumstances. Mia continued the internal argument as they walked down the steps at the side of the deck that led to the parking lot. "Oh my gosh!" Mia said and pulled up short.

"What is it?" Cam tilted his head and then followed Mia's gaze to an older couple walking toward the entrance to Sully's. "Do you know them?"

"Yes." Mia nodded vigorously and smiled up at Cam. "It's Nancy, the secretary from the courthouse," she answered in a stage whisper. "And she's with Tucker!"

"Should I know Tucker?"

"He's the groundskeeper at the courthouse. Nancy's into him and it was plain as day that he feels the same way. She bakes cookies for him, Cam. Isn't that the sweetest thing?"

"It's nice," he agreed hesitantly, clearly not understanding her excitement.

"I noticed it right off while I was waiting to bail you out of jail."

"I hope you never have to say that again." Cam grinned slightly and then shook his head slowly. "And you told Nancy to go for it?"

"How'd you know?" Mia caught her bottom lip between her teeth and nodded.

"An educated guess," he replied with an arch of one eyebrow. "Do you want to say hi to them?"

"No, I don't want to intrude. But don't they make a cute couple? Oh look, she just laughed at something he said!"

"That's amazing," Cam said with a mock sigh. He grabbed her hand and put it to his chest.

"You're making fun of me." She tugged at her hand, but he didn't let go.

"I'm just teasing," he said, but he gave her a hooded look that she couldn't quite read. "You know, your little nudge just might change their lives," he said in a more serious tone. He nodded in the direction of the front door, which Tucker was opening for Nancy to enter.

"Do you think so?" Mia watched Tucker put his hand at the small of Nancy's back and wondered if Nancy felt the same thrill of awareness that Mia felt when Cam touched her that way. She felt a sudden lump of emotion form in her throat. Would Nancy and Tucker end up together because of what she'd said yesterday in the courthouse? The thought made Mia feel significant.

"Are you okay?" Cam asked gently.

Mia nodded. "Yeah," she said, but her voice was husky.

Cam frowned, but she gave him a reassuring smile.

"Let's get going." He gave her hand a slight tug.

"Okay." Mia gazed up at him, but he suddenly seemed in a bit of a hurry. She swallowed hard while wondering if she had done something to change his mood. Had she read him wrong? Was the attraction all on her end?

On the way back, Cam was pretty quiet, making her internal argument even more heated, and it wasn't until they were almost back at the complex that Mia stopped short and grabbed Cam's arm. "We forgot to look for Bella or Madison! I still don't have a key to get in."

"Wow . . ." Cam put the heel of his hand to his forehead. "I completely forgot too!" he said and then smacked his leg. "What are we going to do?"

Mia blinked at him for a moment. The heel of his hand to his forehead seemed a little dramatic for Cam, but she might have bought it if he hadn't added the leg smack. He didn't want her to have the key to her place, so she would have to stay with him. She was sure of it this time.

Well, she wasn't sure . . . but this time she decided to find out. "We could go to either of their condos and see if they're home."

"Well . . ." Cam paused and tilted his head from side to side as if considering the suggestion. "I think it's pretty late, don't you? It might not be good idea to bother either of them." He raised his eyebrows slightly and then snapped his fingers. "Hey, I have an idea. Why don't you stay at my place tonight? The key situation might be easier to deal with in the light of day."

"Hmm . . ." Being with Cam until the light of the day sounded so appealing that she wanted to give him a high five and do a little jig, but she decided not to make it so easy and pretended to consider his suggestion. "But I don't have a toothbrush."

"I have an extra one. A new one. It even massages your gums."

She tapped the side of her cheek. "Nothing to sleep in . . ."

"Not a problem," he said, and when Mia raised her eyebrows he added, "You can wear one of my T-shirts."

"But what about my teddy bear?" she asked to trip him up.

"Your *teddy bear*?"

"Cam . . ." She gave him a pout. "I can't sleep without my teddy bear."

"You're onto me, aren't you?"

Mia grinned.

"And having fun with it."

"Immensely." Her grin widened.

"I've wanted to kiss you all night."

"What are you waiting for?"

"To get you inside of my place."

Mia yelped but then laughed when he grabbed her hand and quickly tugged her up to his door so fast that she practically stumbled after him. "Are you in a hurry or something?"

"Yes!" Cam fumbled for his key, dropped it, and let out an oath but then paused to apologize.

Mia laughed again when he tugged her inside. The fact that he was so nervous was so cute, and it made her heart sing to think that he wanted her as much as she wanted him. And here she was in discount shorts and shirt, very little makeup, and windblown hair. This was honest and true, she thought, but then a little alarm went off in the back of her mind at the thought. Cam didn't know she was the daughter of a multimillionaire. Maybe she should tell him, she wondered, but then decided that it was better that he didn't know. Cam thought she was a down-on-her-luck waitress who'd landed a nice job. He wasn't coming after her because she was Mia Monroe, and that was so refreshing. Not only that, but he had made it clear on several occasions that he resented wealthy people and had even been treated poorly by them. Mia needed to show him that not everyone with money was an ass. Even so . . . she decided to tell him her real name so that there weren't any lies between them.

But before she could, he pushed her up against the wall and smothered her words with a hot, sexy kiss.

Mia grabbed his shirt and kissed him back with passion that she didn't even know she possessed. A moment later her hands were in his hair and then up his shirt to feel his smooth, warm skin. He moaned . . . no, wait—that was her moaning. She suddenly felt lighter than air, and then she realized with a giggle that he had picked her up. "Cameron Patrick, you're sweeping me off my feet," she announced as he carried her into his bedroom.

"Literally," he joked, but when Mia put a gentle hand up to his cheek, he stopped in his tracks and gazed down at her.

"You've been sweeping me off my feet since the moment I met you."

"Wait, you dumped ice water on my food and in my lap," he tried to joke, but her gentle touch and sincere eyes drew him in and held him fast.

"Okay, after that," she admitted, making him laugh. "Hey, you keep coming to my rescue. Caring about me with no agenda. I'm not used to that. You make me feel good about myself." She lifted her head from his shoulder and pulled his head closer and then kissed him.

"And I will keep on doing it."

"Coming to my rescue?"

"If you need it." He grinned. "And you probably will. We haven't tackled things like washing clothes." He didn't add that he was still worried about someone following her but would be damn sure to keep an eye on her. Truthfully, he was going to suggest sleeping on her sofa if this situation hadn't presented itself.

Cam lowered her gently to his bed. He was falling in love with Mia Money. He knew it because he had never felt like this before. He was falling hard and fast, and he realized that something so good in his life would make him a stronger athlete; make him a better man. Cam remembered Jack Nicholson saying that line in a movie, and he had thought it was cheesy. Well, it wasn't. Having someone care about him would surely help his game, not get in the way.

"What are you thinking?" Mia asked softly.

Cam smiled. "Every cheesy line from every sappy movie or love song is going through my head right about now."

"Really?"

"Yeah, but mostly I'm thinking about doing this." Cam dipped his head and captured her lush mouth with his, and when she arched her back and wrapped her arms around his neck, he deepened the kiss and pressed his body against hers, loving the feel of her curves molding to his chest. Ever since the elevator, Cam had fantasized about this moment, and although passion had simmered between them, nothing could have prepared him for the sweet and tender feelings welling up inside his chest. He touched her gently, caressing her cheeks, her shoulders, before sliding his hands beneath her top. Her skin felt deliciously warm and silky soft, making him long to have her naked beneath him.

Ah, Cam wanted to take this loving slow and savor each kiss, each caress. He wanted to taste every inch of Mia's gorgeous body, but her touch excited him so much that he had to concentrate on keeping control.

And above all else, Cam wanted to please her. He wanted to see the flush of pleasure on her face and feel her body tremble beneath him. He wanted to please her in every way possible, over and over, until she all but melted.

"Take your clothes off for me," Cam said, and then watched with pure fascination when she came up to her knees and tugged her top over her head. Her bra was a peach-colored sexy thing that pushed up and made her breasts swell over the lace trim. Her bikini panties matched, and for a moment he could only stare. "God, Mia, you're amazing."

"You think so?" When she smiled shyly, it blew Cam

away that she wasn't cockier about her looks. He reached over and ran a fingertip over the swell of her breasts, and she shivered and tilted her head to the side.

"Surely you know how pretty you are."

"People I know obsess over their looks. I guess that mentality had rubbed off on me and made me worry."

"Well, baby, worry no more. You damned sure blow me away." When she shrugged, he reached over and slid the satin straps over her shoulders, exposing most of her breasts. Instead of tugging the bra down the rest of the way, he pulled his own shirt over his head, hoping she liked what she saw as well. Cam had spent many a day shirtless while cleaning pools and always knew he turned heads, but this was the first time it really mattered to him, and he knew why. This wasn't about how he looked. It was about how he felt.

When Mia reached out and ran her fingertips over his chest and down to his navel, Cam's abs tightened. He was already superaroused, and when her fingers found his zipper he sucked in a sharp breath. She looked up at the sound and smiled. "This going-slow stuff is for the birds," she said.

"I couldn't agree more."

Mia laughed, and for the next few seconds their clothes went flying off the bed, landing haphazardly all across the room. Cam loved this side of her . . . carefree and without pretense. After quickly reaching for a condom, he rolled it on and then was back in her arms.

"I wanted this to last for a long time, but damn, girl, you get me going with a simple touch." Cam was surprised that he admitted this to her, but after holding back, it felt great to be able to tell her how he felt. "I'm just being honest," he said, and when she turned her head he gently pulled her back. "I'm serious, Mia," he said, but when she opened her mouth as if to protest, he pulled her flush against his naked body and kissed her. They all but fell onto the pillows without breaking contact and continued to kiss wildly, madly. Cam ran his hands down her back and over the sweet curve of her ass. "You're driving me nuts," he whispered in her ear and then eased her onto her back. He cupped one breast with the palm of his hand and then captured the other one with his mouth. When he licked her nipple, she gasped and threaded her fingers through his hair. He licked gently and then harder, switching from one breast to the other until she was arching her back, offering him more.

"Oh!" Mia said when he sucked harder. He trailed his fingers lightly down her abdomen and then parted her thighs. She gasped while he teased her mound with a light caress, getting closer and closer to where she wanted. Finally, when she arched her hips, he sank one finger into her slick, wet heat. He caressed her clit with a light touch but stopped short of bring her to orgasm. Instead he rolled over and kissed her deeply and then entered her with one sure stroke.

Cam loved the feeling of being inside of her body but had to pause and gather his composure while buried deep. He wanted to please her and make the moment last. Sweat broke out on his forehead and trickled down his chest. He just about had himself under control, but when she slid her hands down his back to his ass and then squeezed, he just about lost it.

"You have a great butt—made for baseball pants."

Cam's laughter was strained, and he gave her a gruff, "Thanks." He moved slowly at first, easing in and out of her silky heat, but when she wrapped her legs around his waist, all bets were off. Cam thrust deeply, and although she was a little thing, she matched his rhythm and urged him on, giving as much as taking. He kissed her wildly, loving the feeling of her breasts crushed to his chest. She held on tightly with her arms and legs and he gave her a wild ride. A moment later his name was a throaty, sexy cry of pleasure, and when Cam felt her pulse and squeeze, he let go of his restraint and felt an incredible rush of pleasure that seemed to come from his toes. The intensity of his orgasm left him shaken, and when he rolled over he took Mia with him and held her in his embrace. He kissed her deeply, tenderly, and after brushing her damp hair from her face said, "That was amazing."

"I agree." Her smile trembled a bit at the corners, telling Cam that she felt the same way. "I do believe the earth moved," she admitted, making Cam chuckle. She tucked her head in the crook of his arm and for a few moments neither of them spoke.

After a while he asked, "Do you want me to look for Madison or Bella and get a master key for your place?"

"That can wait until morning," Mia replied drowsily and snuggled closer. Her soft sigh made him smile.

"I was really hoping you'd say that," Cam admitted but then wondered if he was taking this a little bit too fast. When she failed to respond, he knew she had fallen asleep, and although Cam was tired he wanted to stay awake a little bit longer in order to enjoy holding her in his arms. He kissed her on top of the head and then caressed her bare shoulder. *I could get used to this,* he thought just before he drifted off to sleep.

21

I Hope You Dance!

MITCH LOOKED AT THE SMILE OF SATISFACTION ON NICOlina's face after she placed the last ring in the display case in her jewelry store and was flooded with a warm rush of happiness. He suddenly knew without a doubt that he wanted to marry her. Just like that the thought that had been swirling around in his head for months took root and held fast. When Mitch Monroe knew that something felt right, he never hesitated to take action. Acting upon his instinct had made him millions, but this time his heart beat in his chest and he felt a flash of worry, not because he didn't adore Nicolina but . . .

What if she said *no*?

As if feeling his gaze upon her, Nicolina raised her head from where she'd started to rearrange the jewelry once more. "Oh, sweetie." Her smile faded and she set her reading glasses down on top of the glass case. "You look as if you have the weight of the world on your shoulders. What's wrong?"

"I'm fine," he assured her, but his voice sounded strained even to his own ears.

"You can't fool me. Are you worried about Mia?"

Mitch felt another warm rush of love for Nicolina.

She was so caring, and it moved him beyond all reason. Most of his life he had lived with the knowledge that all anyone ever wanted was what he could provide, but Nicolina was a giver, a nurturer, and the concern in her soulful eyes caused a lump in his throat. Except toward his daughter, Mitch was slow to show emotion, but he wanted to give himself freely to Nicolina, and so he decided it was time to be straightforward. "No, I do think my baby girl is going to be just fine. Noah thinks that she's going to do a bang-up job as promotions manager. And seeing the smile on her face last night with that young baseball player put my mind at rest." He chuckled. "When she turned and looked right at me, I thought for sure she recognized me, even in that crazy getup that you had me parading around in."

"Oh, you had fun. Admit it."

"Okay." Mitch chuckled. "I did."

"Isn't that amazing, though? Mia must have actually felt your presence. That tells me how strong your bond is with her, Mitch. And the fact that she's doing a good job says that she's learned a lot more from you than you gave her credit for."

"I know." Mitch felt another rush of emotion. "She's going to find her way, I'm sure of it," he said gruffly. "And as soon as I know she has her feet planted firmly on the ground, I'll make my presence known."

"Well, then." Nicolina cupped her hands over his cheeks in that typical Italian way that he loved so much. "If it isn't Mia's welfare, then what's on your mind?"

"I want you to design something for me."

"Oh, what fun." Nicolina smiled brightly. "What is it? Something for Mia?"

"No." Mitch cleared his throat and was hit with another attack of nerves. Being nervous was a weird feeling for him, but he embraced it and lifted his chin. "An engagement ring."

"Oh." Nicolina's eyes widened and she took a step back. "For who? A friend?"

"Yes, a very dear friend. This friend makes me laugh and feel young at heart. In fact, she means the world to me. I love her very much."

"Oh," she repeated, and then her eyes opened even wider.

"I want you to draw the design, and then I will buy the setting and stones."

"Mitch . . ." Nicolina put a hand to her chest and swallowed hard. "W-what are you saying?"

Mitch scrubbed a hand down his face. "Oh, Nicolina, I'm bungling this terribly."

"Bungling what?"

"I love you and want you to be my wife."

Relief washed over her features and she gave him a nervous little laugh. "Oh, for a terrifying moment I thought you were talking about another woman!"

"Nicolina, you are the one and only woman for me," he insisted, and when her eyes misted over, he shook his head. "I'm sorry, I didn't mean to ask you to marry me this way." He scrubbed a hand down his face. "I should have been more romantic. Taken you off to . . . to Paris! Monte Carlo. Wherever you want to go."

"No!"

"No?" He squeezed his eyes shut. "You're saying . . . no?"

Nicolina laughed. "No! Mitch, what I'm saying is that you didn't need to fly me to Paris." She shook her head and her hands returned to his cheeks. "All I want is . . . you. Not your company jet or fancy jewelry. Just . . . *you*." She looked up into his eyes. "I don't want your money. You can give it all away as far as I'm concerned, and I wouldn't care a flying fig." She waved her hands in her dramatic way that he found both amusing and delightful. "I'm dead serious."

"I believe you."

"I'll even sign something that says so." Her waving hands moved up to his shoulders and she squeezed hard.

"Mitch, I know you've been hurt and you've felt that you have to prove yourself by making millions, but all I want from you is love," she said but then glanced away. "But . . ."

"But what?" he asked gruffly, and fear snaked down his spine. "Tell me."

"I need for you to be *here*, Mitch. I love this little town and I want to be near my daughter even though she will most likely follow Logan to whatever team he ends up with." Her hands waved through the air again. "I come here to be with her and she leaves! Go figure!"

"She is in love and following her man."

"Yes, but I can't do the same thing. Mitch, this little jewelry store means so much to me. Designs by Diamante is my dream come true. I don't want to move back to Chicago." She shook her head sadly. "I love you dearly, but I don't see how this can work out."

Mitch took her hands in his. "I've been thinking about this for a while, now. Your idea of Wedding Row is golden, Nicolina. Adding additional wedding-themed shops is timely and brilliant. And there really isn't anywhere for wedding receptions except for the outdoor gazebo at Wine and Diner. I want to add a hotel and reception hall and a convention center. This is a small town, but there are larger cities close by and it's a central location for both the Midwest and the South. We could draw business from all over."

"Goodness! You really have been thinking this over?"

"You bet I have." Mitch smiled. "A convention center would bring business here in the winter months. I've already started looking for investors and I've begun the process of getting permits. It's a huge project, but that should tell you how invested I am. Nicolina, I can sell my house and make the move here without a qualm. I want to and will be with you. I promise you this. Well, if you'll let me."

She ducked her head again.

"What?" he asked gently.

"Well, it makes me feel really bad that I just said I wouldn't move for you and here you are willing to give up so much! I wouldn't give up one little store and you're willing to give up an empire!"

"Well, that should tell you how I feel," he said with a grin and then laughed. "Oh, Nicolina, this shop is more than just making money for you. You are incredibly talented. I would never ask you to give up your dream. I can make money anywhere. It sure isn't a sacrifice to be with you."

"But what are you going to do about your other business dealings? Your office in Chicago?"

He shrugged. "I won't have any trouble selling any of my assets, Nicolina, and I don't care about making money. I want to be with you. Spend the rest of my life with you. Period. I don't care what it takes." He tilted her chin up. "Listen, *you* are the first person who wants me for who I am and nothing more. And I have to tell you that it feels—*simply amazing*. It sounds trite, but you are amazing."

"And so are you."

When her eyes fluttered shut, Mitch dipped his head and captured her lips with a tender kiss. "Well, then, can I take that as a *yes*?" He pulled back and looked at her expectantly while his heart pounded like he had just run a marathon.

"What was the question again?"

"Nicolina! You're killing me."

"Yes!" She raised both hands skyward and then spun around in a circle. "Yes, I will marry you!"

"You little minx." Mitch laughed and then caught her around the waist and danced with her. "We look silly."

"Who cares?"

"Not me," Mitch said and spun her around again. He had spent so many years being intense and serious that he really did feel like dancing. "What is this dance called?"

"The Snoopy dance of happiness! Put your nose up in the air!"

Mitch followed her lead, laughing and spinning until he felt dizzy. But when they stopped, breathless and still laughing, Mitch looked at her with serious eyes. "You have made me a very happy man. Thank you."

"You're welcome." Nicolina's smile trembled at the corners, and a big, fat tear slid down her cheek.

"I love you so much." Mitch swiped the tear away with his thumb and then kissed her once more. "It is going to be hard not to call Mia and tell her the news."

"Perhaps you should."

Mitch considered her suggestion for a moment. "I'll wait until opening day. I don't want to interfere with the work she's putting into getting the season set up."

"Okay." Nicolina nodded but looked at him as if she wasn't quite convinced. But after a moment she grabbed his hand and then picked up a sketch pad. "Now I think I will design my very own engagement ring!"

Mitch looked at the happiness glowing in her eyes and smiled. He vowed to himself that he would keep that glow in her eyes forever and always.

While Nicolina sketched, Mitch's thoughts drifted to Mia and the young man she had been strolling with in the park last night. Hearing his daughter's laughter had been music to his ears, and he wondered if she too had found someone special in Cricket Creek, Kentucky, of all places. He smiled, thinking how his love of baseball had been the catalyst to becoming a partner with Noah Falcon and Ty McKenna. The decision had been more about having fun and helping his friends than making money, but it had been the best decision he had made in a long time. In a roundabout way, his love of the game had led him to the love of his life, and perhaps it would lead his daughter to hers too.

Mitch suddenly thought about Clarisse, and he wondered if she ever regretted her decision to run off with another man, leaving him and her small child for the sake of money. But as he gazed at Nicolina's bent head while she sketched her ring, Mitch no longer felt the old resentment rise and threaten to choke him. He had been healed by the love of a good woman. It was time to let go of the past and embrace the future.

22

Who's Your Daddy?

CAM TOWEL-DRIED HIS HAIR WHILE THINKING RANDOM thoughts about hitting a curveball, but as usual for the past week, his brain somehow switched over to Mia. He shook his head when the mirror showed evidence of how just thinking of her could instantly turn him on. Fighting this attraction was pointless, he reasoned with a grin when the sound of his ring tone cut into his thoughts. With a grumble of impatience he hurried into his bedroom and picked the phone up from his nightstand.

When Cam spotted Noah Falcon's name on the small screen he frowned and quickly picked up. "Hello."

"Hi, Cam, what's up?"

Cam arched an eyebrow and looked down. "Not much," he answered but wondered why he was getting this call.

"Are you with Mia right now?"

"No." Cam felt a bit of alarm and sat down on his bed. "Why? Is she okay?"

"As far as I know . . . but I have to tell you something."

"Okay." A hard knot formed in his stomach at Noah's formal tone.

"This stays between us. And I really mean it."

"Understood."

"Mia's real last name isn't Money. It's Monroe. She's Mitch Monroe's daughter."

"Mitch Monroe as in the famous rich dude?" Cam raked his fingers through his damp hair and waited.

"Yes, as in the famous rich dude," Noah replied with an edge of laughter in his tone, but Cam failed to feel the humor. "Mitch is a silent partner in the baseball complex. He's also an investor in the strip mall down by the riverfront, among other things."

"Seriously?" Cam didn't want to believe that Mia was wealthy.

"Yeah. Listen, if you've seen someone following her, it is a private detective who is keeping an eye on her for Mitch, so don't be alarmed and kick his ass."

"Oh," Cam said a bit tightly, feeling a flash of anger. To think he was worried about her welfare! "So . . . why is Mia Mon*roe* playing this little game of pretend?"

"Well . . ." Noah hesitated for a second. "I probably shouldn't tell you personal information about the situation, but you seem to really care about Mia, and I have orders from Olivia to tell you not to let this come between you or alter how you feel about her. I personally don't think it's any of my business, but Olivia and Madison seem to have this sort of intuition where it comes to matchmaking, and they'd both have my ass in a sling if I didn't tell you to give Mia a chance to explain."

Cam laughed without humor. "You mean to explain why she has been lying not only to me but to this whole town? To people who stuck their necks out, gave her jobs and money, and most of all had faith in her, and all along she was playing a little rich-girl game of pretend until she goes back to . . . whatever she does, or should I say *doesn't do*? Is this a reality show or something?"

"Calm down, Cam."

Cam shook his head up at the ceiling but then took a deep breath. "Why are you telling me this?"

"Because I want you to drive Mia to Nashville tomorrow to pick up Cat Carson. She's opening for Toby Keith and needs a ride here to Cricket Creek. If someone recognized her there, I didn't want you to be blindsided."

"You've got to be kidding."

"Mia's beat-up old Toyota is ready, but Mitch doesn't trust it. I assured him that you would take Mia in that SUV I've seen you driving."

"Okay, answer me this. Why in the hell was Mia driving that old car anyway?" Cam gripped his phone so hard he was surprised he didn't crush it. He remembered watching her scramble for loose change to pay for her lunch. It didn't make sense.

Noah sighed. "This is personal information that I shouldn't be telling you, but since you're spitting mad, I'll explain a few things."

"Okay, that would be nice." He leaned against the pillows and sighed. At least the mystery surrounding her was going to be solved.

"Mia overheard her father in a phone conversation with Hanover Candy, a Chicago-based family-run company. The owner is a family friend and Mia mistakenly thought her father was in the middle of a hostile takeover. According to Mitch, she went into orbit."

"Why didn't her father just explain?"

"Apparently he tried. When Mia stomped out he decided to let her venture out on her own to see how long she would last before coming back home."

"Okay . . ." Cam was trying to wrap his brain around all of this and was having trouble. "So is Mitch Monroe here in town?"

"Yes, he's been coming to Cricket Creek on the sly. He's a friend of Nicolina Diamante's and he's assisting her in the opening of her jewelry store."

"So, he's been staying with Nicolina?" It sounded as if they were more than friends, but Cam kept his mouth shut.

"Yes, but again this stays between us."

Cam thought about Mia thinking she had spotted her

father in the park the night they went for ice cream and sighed again. This was all too crazy.

"Cam, I'm sure that Mia wanted to keep her identity a secret so that she could make it on her own and not as Mitch Monroe's daughter."

"But you knew? That's why you hired her?"

"No, I hired her because she came to my rescue and landed Cat Carson to sing before the game on Saturday. I figured it out, though."

"And does she know this?"

"No. And I want to keep it that way until after opening day. It's her father's wish. He doesn't want to screw up all that she's worked for by upsetting her."

"Sorry . . . but this is fucked-up."

"Yeah, probably, but it's also about a father's love for his daughter. She wants to prove herself, I'm sure, and I can tell you for the past week she has worked her tail off. She's going to be good, Cam. Mia deserves this job. Actually, she did a lot for her father and he pretty much took her for granted. He admitted as much to me. I'm sure that Mia just wants to be taken seriously."

Cam thought back to some of her comments, and it all suddenly made perfect sense.

"Everything will come out in the open on Saturday. For now, all you need to do is take Mia to Nashville tomorrow after practice and the team meeting. Practice is called off on Friday so you guys can rest. Just be back in time for the parade on Saturday."

"You mean I'm supposed to spend the night in Nashville?"

"That's the plan that Mia has with Cat. Hey, I'll pay for everything. Just keep your receipts. It will be fun."

"What if Mia doesn't want me to go along?"

"I have a feeling that you can persuade her."

"What if I don't want to?"

"I'm asking this as a favor."

Cam closed his eyes and took another deep breath.

Noah Falcon was giving him the chance of a lifetime by letting him play for the team. How could he refuse?

"Look," Noah said, and all teasing was gone from his tone, "I know that you care about Mia."

"I care about Mia Money. I don't even know Mia Monroe."

"How you feel about her is pretty transparent. Is her name really all that important? Listen, Mia talks about you all the damn time. This was kind of shitty not knowing who she really was, but get over it, Cam. She's a sweet girl."

"Easier said than done," he admitted.

"Well, then, let me ask you this. Would you have gotten involved with her had you known who she really was?"

"No, probably not," Cam answered honestly. "But the question now is, do I want to be involved with the daughter of a billionaire?"

"Um, too late, you already are."

Cam shook his head. "This changes everything."

"Does it? Look, I'm not trying to be funny under the circumstances, but *money* has nothing to do with it. You fell for Mia, period. Who cares about the rest? Olivia was all hung up on the fact that I was a celebrity, and she had preconceived ideas about what I was all about. Man, I'm telling ya, it doesn't mean a thing. I'm just sayin'."

Cam had to grin. "Word has it that you're totally whipped." After he said it, Cam worried that he'd offended Noah.

When Noah chuckled, Cam was relieved. "I am," Noah said. "I fully admit it. I would do anything for Olivia. If you love someone, everything else is crap."

Cam laughed, suddenly feeling a little bit better about the situation. "Can I tweet that?"

"Hell, I don't care. Like I said, Olivia thought that because I was a pro baseball player and a soap star, I was going to be an arrogant ass. She remembered how cocky

I was back in high school when she was my English tutor."

"She tutored you?"

"Yeah, and I was intimidated by her brains. I thought she was going to think as an adult I was a still a dumb jock, but with money."

"So how did you get past it?"

"Olivia brought out the best in me, and moving back here was the right choice. I rediscovered my love for the fundamentals of baseball and small-town life. It just feels right here."

Cam sighed up at the ceiling. "I knew there was something about Mia that I just didn't know. Nothing fit."

"Listen, Cam, we're all a product of our past and carry some baggage."

"Yeah, but her baggage is designer." Cam shook his head. "Me? I'm a duffel bag. I had a deadbeat dad and a mother who resented me for living. Mia Monroe and I are on total opposite sides of the tracks. I cleaned pools for rich people like her."

"Maybe you shouldn't judge somebody for how much money they do or don't make."

"It's hard not to."

Cam heard Noah sigh. "Well, I'm running my mouth off when I probably shouldn't, but I'll tell you this much anyway. I've known Mitch Monroe for a long time, and he's a straight-up guy. But he admitted that he regrets that Mia was pretty much raised by nannies while he was off making millions."

"Mia's mother must have been some piece of work."

"She ran off with another man when Mitch's first company hit the skids."

"Yeah, Mia told me she'd left them for a guy with more money. What kind of mother does that?" Cam felt anger rise in his throat. Again he thought back to some of Mia's comments, and it all fell into place. Cam knew all too well how it felt not to be wanted, and he could relate. Pain and rejection are the same, no matter who you are. "I guess money can't buy happiness," Cam said, thinking back to some of the people he'd worked for as a kid.

"Well, if I'm right, and I think I am, you have the talent to make it to the major leagues. Let me ask you this: Are you going to change when you're making big bucks?"

Cam was surprised by the unexpected question and sat up straighter. "Hell no."

"I've seen that happen all too often," Noah said slowly. "My point is that money can make you arrogant and poverty can make you angry. But in the end we're all just people. We all bleed red."

"You're telling me to treat Mia the same way I have been all along, aren't you?"

Cam imagined Noah's crooked grin. "I shouldn't be butting my nose in where it doesn't belong, but yeah. I guess it comes from being in a small town where we make it our business to know everybody's business. Olivia and Madison are matchmakers, and they learned what they know from Myra. It's a small-town, southern thing. Meddling is their job. Or at least they think so. Sorry if I've overstepped my bounds."

"I respect your advice no matter what it's about," Cam admitted. "And you're right about the money thing. It shouldn't matter . . . but I won't lie. It will take some getting used to."

"No doubt."

"But I'll take Mia to Nashville to pick up Cat Carson. And I'll keep quiet about knowing her true identity."

"Thanks." He could hear the relief in Noah's voice. "It will all work out in the end."

"You mean it will all *come out* in the end." Cam was trying to joke, but he didn't like Mia not knowing that everyone was onto her little scheme.

"Yeah, that too. But I really think we should let father and daughter work it out."

"I guess you're right," Cam said, but he wasn't at all sure.

"Look, get a good night's rest. Tomorrow's practice is going to be a tough one. You can leave for Nashville late in the afternoon but get there in time to have some fun. I appreciate you doing this. I've already come to care for Mia like a daughter."

"Will do, Mr. Falcon. Trust me, I'll watch over her." After hanging up the phone, Cam leaned back against the pillows propped up against the headboard and crossed his ankles. He worried that Mia would be really upset when she learned not only that she had been followed but that her father had known her whereabouts all along and was actually in Cricket Creek. She would most likely think that Noah had hired her not on her own merit but because of who she was, and it was all Cam could do not to call her up and warn her. But then he told himself that Mia had gotten herself into this mess in the first place and would have to deal with the fallout of her little charade.

Cam searched for the anger he'd felt when Noah had disclosed who Mia really was, but it was gone. He had felt all along that something in her story was missing, and now he knew. She wasn't in trouble or running from an ex-husband or boyfriend, only trying to prove herself to her father . . . or maybe even more than that, to herself. Cam had always felt the satisfaction of knowing all that he had accomplished he had done on his own. It had to be a pain in the ass for Mia not to feel that sense of pride about herself. He understood what she'd done and why, making it difficult to feel anything more than empathy.

Cam knew that it wasn't going to be easy to not let on that he knew Mia's real name, but he had made a promise to Noah Falcon and fully intended to keep it. He sighed and decided to grab a quick sandwich and hit the hay early. Noah was right. He was going to need a good night's sleep. It was going to be a long, eventful weekend.

23

On the Road Again

MIA LOOKED OVER AT CAM AND TRIED NOT TO FROWN. They had traveled for several miles without exchanging more than a few words. He didn't seem angry about anything, but there was something in his demeanor that was . . . different. With an inward sigh, she leaned forward to turn on the radio but then leaned back against the leather seat instead. There had to be something on his mind, and Mia was suddenly determined to get it out of him. "So are you excited about opening day?"

"Yeah, all but the parade. Throwing candy from a float shaped like a baseball bat isn't exactly my thing."

"Oh, don't be such a party pooper."

"Don't ever say *party pooper* again."

"Well, if the shoe fits . . . ," Mia said and arched an eyebrow at him. This was more like the banter they had been exchanging lately, and she liked it a lot. "I hear that the town loves the parade and has been planning the event since the one last year. This is a small town, Cam. I think it's sweet that everyone is looking forward to it so much. Madison said the whole town shuts down for opening day like it's an actual declared holiday. Of course, she did say that so many people are in the parade this year that she thinks there will be as many townspeople in the parade as there will be watching."

"I do know that everyone is excited about Cat Carson singing before the game. How do you know her anyway?"

Mia flicked a nervous glance out the window. "We met while working on a charity event a few years ago. She might be on the fast track to being famous, but Cat is fun to be around and down-to-earth. I simply pulled in a favor and Noah is giving money to her favorite charity." She lifted one shoulder. "It was no big deal," she insisted, looking back at Cam. She couldn't see his eyes behind his mirrored aviators, but there was something strange in his tone. Perhaps he was intimated to hang out with a celebrity. "Hey, don't be nervous. You'll like Cat and we'll have a blast tonight in Nashville."

"I'm not nervous."

"Good." She smiled and was relieved to see him smile in return. She just wished she could see his eyes to try to figure out what was going on with him. There was definitely something different in his demeanor today, but she couldn't quite put her finger on it. Maybe she should just simply ask him what was up.

"So you like country music?"

Mia nodded firmly. "Oh yeah."

"You don't seem the type."

"I'm not a *type*," she told him. "I like what I like and don't pay attention to what my friends are listening to," she continued, realizing that it was true. Her friends were always into whatever trend was hot, but Mia had always stayed with what she liked. Maybe that was why she always felt more like she was on the outside looking in and why after leaving town she really wasn't missed. *I don't miss them,* she thought with a shake of her head.

"I didn't mean to sound rude," Cam said. "And you're right, I shouldn't make assumptions. I guess I just pegged you wrong from the very beginning," he said, and then gave her an expectant glance before turning his attention back to the highway.

Mia hesitated before answering. She knew that this could be her opportunity to come clean and tell him who she really was and why she had kept her identity a secret. She just wasn't quite ready. What if being the daughter of Mitch Monroe chased him away? Mia swallowed hard and realized how much he had come to mean to her in such a short time. Losing Cam would be hard to handle. She took a deep breath and decided to keep the subject on safe ground. "I love the stories in country music. I've been to lots of concerts and I especially like Rascal Flatts and Keith Urban. I also really like Zac Brown Band and Kenny Chesney since they sing about the beach. The water is my happy place. You?"

"Yeah, I like country too, but I prefer old school like Hank Junior, Charlie Daniels, and George Straight. Kid Rock is awesome to work out to."

"Well, they'll play plenty of old school in places like Tootsies and the Stage."

"So you've been to Nashville?" He slid Mia another sideways glance before turning his eyes back to the road. "You don't seem like the honky-tonk kind of girl . . . Not that you're a type," he added with a grin.

"I might surprise you by doing some line dancing at the Wildhorse Saloon. Maybe you don't know me as well as you think," she joked but then realized that there was way too much truth to her statement.

"Yeah, maybe I don't," he said, and there was that tone again that Mia couldn't put her finger on. It was almost as if he was trying to tell her something. "But if there's something you want to tell me, go right ahead."

Mia shifted in her seat and suddenly wondered once more if she should tell him her real name and get the whole charade out into the open. But she didn't want to ruin the trip or upset Cat, and so she kept silent about her secret. "Now, what could that possibly be?" she asked in a teasing way.

"You tell me."

"I'm a superhero and fight crime at night."

"Ah, thought so," Cam said but then fell silent.

Mia wondered what Noah Falcon was going to think when he knew the truth. She knew she was going to have to tell her father soon too. She missed him so much! Tears welled up in her eyes and constricted her throat at the thought that he wouldn't be at opening day to see what she had accomplished in a short period of time. Mia simply loved her job, and Noah gushed about how good she was at it. Now that her car was ready and paid for, she could leave Cricket Creek, but she no longer wanted to move away from the town that had embraced her and accepted her without blinking an eye.

"Are you okay?" Cam asked. She could hear the concern in his voice, and it chased away her tears.

"Yeah," she replied, but her voice was gruff with emotion.

"Doesn't sound like it."

"I guess the excitement of opening day has me a bit emotional," Mia replied. "I want to have big attendance with lots of fun and games all season long."

"Well, I hear that you've done a great job, Mia. Both Ty and Noah have said so."

"Really?"

"Yeah, really."

Mia twisted her hands together. "That's good to hear."

"Hey, Ty McKenna and Noah Falcon Bobble-Head Night is already sold out. Wacky Hat Wednesdays is going to be a hit, and Thirsty Thursdays is classic in the minor leagues. I also think it's pretty damned cool that you've got lots of events geared toward charity. Good causes are a great reason to come to the ballpark."

"Oh, Cam, I've had so much fun with it!"

He smiled at her warmly. "What's your favorite?"

Mia jumped all over his question. "A Taste of Cricket Creek is my favorite event so far. Grammar's Bakery is providing all of the bread. Jessica from Wine and Diner is going to make Kentucky Burgoo and several desserts. Sully has promised to make his special wings and is trying out a rib recipe. We also talked about him doing a grub-and-stub promotion discount day."

"Awesome ideas, Mia."

"I want to have something special for the Fourth of July too . . . fireworks, of course, but something even bigger. I have a few more favors to call in." She wiggled her eyebrows. "I'm going to try to get Cat Carson to come back for Labor Day and maybe get some other country stars to put on a full day of music. A mini–music fest would be great, especially since we're so close to Nashville."

"That would be cool."

"Cam, I can't sleep at night because my mind just races with ideas!"

"Good for you," Cam said, and her heart skipped a beat when he reached over and squeezed her hand.

"Thanks." She was falling so hard for Cameron Patrick that sometimes she couldn't fall asleep because she was thinking about *him* . . . but she wasn't going to let him know it just yet.

"You should be very proud of the job you've done."

"Well, now you guys need to win! Winning will fill the stands too. No pressure or anything . . ."

"Ty thinks we're going to be competitive. The better we are, the more scouts we'll get. But having cheering fans in the stands sure motivates a team. Your job is important, Mia."

"Oh, it's going to be a fun season, for sure. I might like to go to some road games to check out what goes on at other ballparks." The added attraction would be seeing more of Cam when the Cougars went on road trips. As much as she hated that she was keeping a secret from him, Mia had to admit to herself that it was so nice to have everyone know her as Mia Money and not the daughter of a billionaire.

"Good, it will be a blast to have you on some road trips." His hand remained over hers, making her fingers tingle.

"I will cheer like a crazy person."

"Thanks, babe." Cam had made it clear that his feelings for her were getting stronger, so she didn't want her wealth to come between them. Mia also acknowledged that as much as she liked to travel and shop, she found the charm of Cricket Creek to be soothing and less stressful than Chicago.

Mia smiled, thinking she just must be a small-town girl at heart and just never had known it. "How much longer?"

"About an hour. You can snooze if you want to."

"No, I'm okay." Mia was a little bit tired since she hadn't been kidding about staying up at night with her mind racing, but she wanted to talk to Cam on the way. "I prefer to keep you company," she admitted and was rewarded with a smile.

"Good, I enjoy being with you. If there's anything you want to talk about, let me know. This is a pretty boring stretch of highway." Cam looked at her expectantly, but Mia shook her head.

"No, I just want to enjoy the trip." A night in Nashville was going to be fun, and she wasn't about to mess it up. Luckily she had remembered to tell Cat not to blow her cover. Her real identity was going to come out soon enough.

24

You Wear It Well

"We have some time before Cat's finished opening the concert," Mia said as they approached Nashville. "Are you hungry?"

"I could eat." Cam looked her way. "What do you feel like?"

"Well, there's a Hard Rock Cafe, and Jimmy Buffet opened a Margaritaville in Nashville if you're in the mood for an awesome cheeseburger."

"I'm always in the mood for a cheeseburger," Cam admitted, "but have you ever been to the Loveless Cafe?" He grinned when she immediately gave him a bright smile.

"No, but I saw a show about it on the Food Network and it's supposed to be amazing. Cat's eaten there and I think her picture's on their wall of fame."

Cam nodded. "Lots of famous people eat there. It's a bit off of the beaten path, so I don't remember how to get there."

"No problem." Mia popped the GPS off the windshield. "I'll punch it in. Gee, I miss having one of these," she said with a slow shake of her head.

"So you had one in your Toyota?"

"No, in my Mer—another car."

Cam hesitated. He wanted to tell her to drop the charade because it didn't matter. Wait . . . He gripped the steering wheel tighter. It didn't matter. It didn't! He had enjoyed every minute he'd spent in her company, well, except for the first food-spill incident, but even now they both looked back on it with amusement. *It would be something to tell our grandchildren* filtered into his brain and shocked him so much that he actually swerved into the next lane.

"Are you okay?" Mia asked with a slight frown.

"I . . . I, uh, was just looking at the GPS. Sorry. I should keep my eyes on the road."

Mia reached over and patted his knee. "It's okay; I have those moments a lot. Don't worry about it. Well, worry a little because you could crash."

"Good point." Cam laughed, but then again she was always making him laugh. "You're funny."

"I get that a lot—"

"Only you're not trying to be," he finished for her, and she stuck out her tongue at him.

"Oh, look—how cool! We're on the Natchez Trace Parkway." Mia pointed to a sign after they turned off the interstate. "I think it would be fun to travel all four hundred and forty miles of it. There is so much history from here all the way to Mississippi . . . parks and points of interest. There's everything from Indian mounds to waterfalls to cypress swamps. I would love to do it someday."

Cam raised his eyebrows. "And you know this . . . how?"

"Well . . . I've watched a lot of travel and history channels on television. I know a lot of trivia."

"So you're a history buff?"

She lifted one shoulder. "No, not really, just lonely, I guess," she answered with a sigh, but then true to form she shot him a crooked smile. "I watched a lot of crazy stuff but I learned a lot."

Mia's quiet admission touched him, and he once again

felt the need to reach over and touch her. This time he reached for a lock of her hair. "Hey, I can totally relate. My mother was gone most evenings and my dad didn't care. That's why I ended up playing a lot of baseball. So you're right. Our pasts have made us who we are, and I have to admit that we're not too shabby." He dropped her silky hair and fisted his hand for a knuckle bump. She looked at his fist in confusion, but when he wiggled it she laughed and knocked her small fist against his knuckles.

"Agreed," Mia said with a grin.

"And the future isn't looking too bad either." God, but he wanted to kiss her. Maybe if he told her how he felt about her she would feel free to tell him her real name, but they pulled into the Loveless Cafe and he decided to take her advice and just enjoy the trip.

"Oh, how cute! I just love the old-school sign," Mia gushed when they turned into the parking lot. "It must have been a hotel at one time." She peered out the window and then pointed. "There's a gift shop! Oh, and I finally have some money! I can shop!" She rubbed her hands together in glee and got out of the SUV before he could even kill the engine.

When they passed a small structure, the smell of smoked meat wafted their way, making Cam's stomach rumble. "Oh, it's going to be hard to choose what to eat. The breakfast here is amazing, but so is everything else on the menu."

"It smells divine," she agreed but then tugged on his hand. "Oh, look! There's one of those things where you stick your head through and get your picture taken. Let's do it!"

Cam laughed. She would be so much fun to travel with. Good thing, he thought, because baseball players sure did travel. But the thought rocked him once again. The only future he could think about was one with Mia in it, and he hadn't even known her all that long. Crazy, but he couldn't imagine his world without her in it. He took his cell phone out of his pocket and took a picture of Mia's beautiful face pushed through a wooden painting of old-fashioned girls. She had to do all three before he laughed and pointed to the entrance to the restaurant. "Come on, we'd better get in there before it gets too crowded. I promise we can walk around after we eat."

"Okay," she said, and he had to admire her cute butt as she walked up the steps to the entrance. She was wearing hip-hugging Levi's jeans and a short-sleeved, floral shirt with pearl buttons. She said she had picked them up at a vintage clothing store in Cricket Creek, and vintage or not she sure as hell wore them well.

"Oh, it's just as cute inside," Mia said when they entered the Loveless Cafe. Because there was already a fifteen-minute or so wait they were given a buzzer and told that they could walk all over the grounds and it would still buzz. Mia shook her head, making it clear that fifteen minutes of shopping would be pointless.

As promised, the walls of fame sported hundreds of framed photos of celebrities, mostly of country singers, but there were also politicians and actors. "Oh, look, there's Cat Carson!" Mia pointed to a signed picture below Dolly Parton's. "I can't wait to hear her sing tomorrow. It's been a while."

"Yeah, I'm looking forward to it too. Is she going to be in the parade?"

"Yes, she's going to ride up front with Noah and Ty so she can get inside the stadium and get ready for the concert. She's only singing a few songs and then the national anthem . . . and that took some talking to get her to do that."

"Didn't want to pull a Christina Aguilera?"

"Hey, Christina got a hard time about that, and it's harder than it might seem."

"Wait . . . are you friends with Christina Aguilera?"

Mia's face blushed a shade of pink. "I wouldn't say that we're friends."

"But you've met."

"A time or two," she said, but then she picked up a menu from a stack offered to those waiting and quickly changed the subject. "Well, now, you're right. It's going to be difficult to choose. Says here that they are famous for the biscuits, and I saw that lots of the signed pictures mentioned the same thing. Oh, and the jams are homemade too!"

Cam nodded and let the Christina Aguilera comment go. It stood to reason that as Mitch Monroe's daughter, she must have rubbed shoulders with lots of famous people. Damn, he supposed that Mia was a celebrity in her own right, if he wanted to think about it. A part of him wished she was still little ole Mia Money, but then again, just like Noah had said, someday he might be a celebrity in his own right, and he certainly didn't plan on changing one bit.

After they were seated in the crowded dining room, they both ordered sweet tea. Cam had decided on the sampler platter, but Mia was still looking over the menu. By the time their biscuits and jam arrived, she had changed her mind several times. Cam found everything about her cute, and the reminder that they were sharing a hotel room kept sliding through his brain.

"Oh dear God, these biscuits are simply to die for!" Mia closed her eyes and moaned. "I shouldn't eat another one."

"They're small," Cam said as he buttered his second one. He had to do something to distract his gaze from her mouth.

"I think I'll try the strawberry jam instead of peach."

Cam had to shift in his seat when she slathered a bit of biscuit with butter and strawberry jam. When she moaned again, he had to laugh.

"What?"

"Reminds me of when you had your first meal at Wine and Diner."

"Oh, I have totally been bad, but I try to make up for it by doing lots of walking. And I've put on a little weight, but I try not to obsess over it." She rolled her eyes. "I've known people my age who have had lipo and Botox treatments. Crazy."

"Have you done anything like that?"

Mia shook her head. "No, my father would have had a fit."

"Well, you're beautiful. You don't need to do any of that crap."

Mia shrugged. "Hey, I don't care if someone decides to have work done to make them feel better, but it can get out of hand. And so can the whole not-eating thing." She shuddered and then said, "My butt might be bigger, but I have more energy and feel a lot better than when I would pick at my food like my friends did." She rolled her eyes. "They would make me feel guilty if I took a real bite or heaven forbid ordered dessert!"

Cam wondered if Mia realized that she was hinting at a more lavish lifestyle, but just when he would have steered the conversation in that direction, their waiter returned. Mia frowned at the menu but ended up ordering fried chicken, fried green tomatoes, and creamed corn, all house specialties. Cam ordered the sampler, which included meat loaf, chicken, and barbecue. He went for the mashed potatoes and gravy and slow-cooked green beans. When he reached for another biscuit, Mia laughed.

"I'd tell you that you'll spoil your lunch, but I know better. You can tuck it away."

"You do realize that you're starting to sound southern."

"I've certainly discovered my inner southern girl." She reached for her sweet tea and tapped her tall glass to his. "And I like it!"

"So do you think you're going to settle down in Cricket Creek?"

Mia toyed with her straw for a moment and watched the lemon wedge float in a circle. Cam watched the emotion play on her face, and he wished he hadn't promised not to tell her that Noah knew who she really was and that her father was in town. Finally, she looked over at him and said, "I miss my father, but I really don't miss much about the city. I love the sense of community and the feeling of belonging in Cricket Creek. I feel as if I matter there, if that makes any sense."

"It does." Cam nodded and reached over and took her hand. "It sucks to feel invisible," he said, once again thinking that they had more in common than he'd first thought. He would have said more, but their southern feast arrived.

"Enjoy," the waiter said with a smile. "I'll be back with drink refills in a few minutes."

"Wow," Mia said, and they both stared at the array of food for a minute and then burst out laughing. She started with her fried green tomatoes. "Oh, yum," she said, closing her eyes and chewing with appreciation.

Cam watched with a smile, and he suddenly realized that he smiled all the time when he was with her. He started thinking sappy lines from songs once again and chuckled.

"What? Do I have food on my face?" She widened her eyes and licked her bottom lip.

"No," Cam said.

"Well, then?" She tilted her head and waited.

"I just like being with you, Mia."

She smiled softly, and her cheeks turned a pretty shade of pink. "Then you won't mind sharing some of that meat loaf?"

"I'll trade a bite for a taste of your creamed corn."

"Deal," she said, and for the rest of the meal they shared bites, making Cam feel as if they had been together forever. It hit him that Noah was right. Had he known her true identity, he never would have approached her, and so it was all going to work out in the end . . . Well, he hoped so anyway.

"Okay, seriously, I can't eat another bite, and it's killing me not to be able to try one of those desserts."

"We can get something to go and eat it later."

Mia pointed a finger at him. "Smart thinking! But I'm going to have to do some dancing tonight to work this off." She put a hand to her stomach and groaned.

Cam immediately thought of several ways to work off some calories. "We could go to Coyote Ugly and you can dance on the bar."

"No, thank you."

"I was just kidding. I wouldn't like other guys staring at my girl."

Her eyes widened slightly. "So I'm your girl?" she asked softly.

"I hope so," Cam said honestly, and although the crowded restaurant buzzed with noise, it suddenly felt as if they were they only two people in the world. He reached over and took her hand. "Are you?"

"Yes," Mia replied, and damn, he wanted to take her back to the hotel and make slow, sweet love to her. When her smile faltered slightly, he knew she must be thinking that she was going to have to tell him sooner or later who she really was. It no longer mattered to Cam that she was Mia Monroe, and he wished that he could assure her that it was going to be okay, but she was going to have to own up to it on her own terms.

"Good, that means I get to buy you something in the gift shop," he said in a playful tone. He had to be careful or he was going to go and start saying some of the sappy stuff on the tip of his tongue. Funny, because Cam hadn't known he had a sappy, romantic side, but then again he had never felt this way before.

"Sweet!" Mia said, and after he paid the bill they headed over to the cute little store that had everything from country ham to jewelry. After looking at every single item in the store, she finally settled on a pretty bracelet that she immediately put on. "I love it," she said with a bright smile.

Cam remembered the diamond tennis bracelet she had worn on the day they met and shrugged. "It's not much," he said, suddenly feeling a little bit worried. What if he couldn't provide what she was used to having? Would it matter to her?

Mia pulled up short and put a hand on his arm. "The cost of something doesn't matter, Cam. Expensive things don't make me happy. I treasure gifts because of who they come from, not how much they cost."

Cam looked into her beautiful eyes and knew she was sincere. She knew firsthand that money couldn't buy happiness. "Good, because I don't make much money," he said lightly. He hoped that would change one day soon, but in a roundabout way Mia had opened his eyes to what true wealth really meant. All of the years he had resented the rich people he worked for and envied all of their wealth, but getting to Mia made him realize that there was much more to life. Sure, he hoped to make the major leagues, but being on this small-town team made him realize that he loved the game above all else. If he got to play baseball for a living, everything else was gravy.

"Are you ready to hit Nashville?" Mia asked with a big smile.

"Let's get this party started!" He grabbed her hand and hurried for his SUV.

Mia laughed as she hurried along with him. When they were in the vehicle, instead of starting the engine he reached over and pulled her closer. He threaded his fingers through her hair and then captured her mouth in a lingering kiss that left him shaken and wanting more. Mia made him happy and he was going to do everything in his power to keep her in his life. "I've wanted to do that all day," he admitted.

"I hope you want to do it all night too," she said and then clamped her hand over her mouth. "I didn't mean to say that out loud."

Cam laughed. "That's okay, because you were reading my mind. But first things first."

"Let's party!"

"Once again . . . reading my mind." Cam laughed and put the SUV in gear. "Look out, Nashville, here we come."

25

God Bless the Broken Road

AFTER VALET PARKING THE SUV, THEY WHEELED THEIR overnight bags into the hotel and checked in. While it certainly wasn't the first night they had spent together, there was just something so very sexy about a hotel room that Mia wanted to throw Cam onto the bed and have her way with him over and over again. But she knew that if they got started they would end up staying in each other's arms until the break of day, and Mia had promised Cat that they would have some fun bar hopping on Lower Broadway. Although lots of college students hung out at some of the clubs on Fourth Street, Mia preferred the old-school honky-tonks like Tootsies and the Stage and Legends Corner, where so much country music history was made.

"I think I'll freshen up a bit," Mia said, making a point of not even looking at the bed.

"Okay, I'll turn on ESPN and catch some sports," Cam agreed in a casual tone, but Mia knew that he was as jumpy as she was because he carefully avoided touching her. The room practically crackled with sexual tension. And although they joked about painting the town red, they both knew that they were going to have some fun with Cat, who would most likely call it a fairly early night with opening day tomorrow. As much as she was looking forward to seeing her friend, she couldn't wait to come back to the room with Cam.

"We're supposed to meet Cat at Tootsies around eight. She's opening for Toby but is actually the very first act, before Trace Adkins, and she told me she has permission to leave after her short set. So we have plenty of time to walk around."

"Which translates to shopping," Cam said with a laugh.

"A little." Mia wrinkled her nose and held her thumb and index finger about an inch apart. "I want to get a cowboy hat for Cat to sign so we can give it away tomorrow, or maybe I'll save it for the Fourth of July."

"I was teasing. I can handle going in some shops downtown. I could use a new pair of boots."

"Well, then, I'll hurry up so we can get out of here. Everything is within walking distance." Besides, if she looked at him lying on that bed a minute longer, she was going to join him—and not to sleep. So after a quick touch-up of her makeup and running a brush through her hair, Mia was good to go. She used to take much longer getting ready to go out, but she had lightened up and simplified her social life along with her wardrobe. She found that she preferred the more natural look instead of preening over every detail of her makeup. Physical perfection, she decided, was way overrated.

When she emerged from the bathroom, Cam looked over and seemed a bit startled. "What's wrong? Is my hair a mess or something?" She looked down. "Or is my fly open?"

"No, it just seems like you get prettier every single day since I met you."

"Thank you, Cam." Mia felt her heart turn over in her chest. She really wished he knew who she really was, but she felt a shot of fear slither down her spine. He'd made it clear on several occasions how he felt about arrogant, wealthy people, and she only hoped that he cared about her enough that it wouldn't matter. She was in love with him. She had known it for a while now, and it would tear her apart if he turned his back on her after learning that she was Mia Monroe instead of Mia Money. "Cam?" She thought it was about time that she came clean and got it over with. Face the music . . . you know, since they were in Music City and everything . . .

"Yeah?" He sat up from his lounging position and looked at her expectantly.

Mia swallowed hard and lost her nerve. "Are you hungry?"

His expression softened and he leaned back against the headboard. "Not yet, but I thought it might be fun to split a burger or an appetizer at Margaritaville. I'm a Jimmy Buffet fan and I might want to shop in the store there too."

"Oh, I won't turn down shopping anywhere," she replied and inhaled a deep breath. "I saw a T-shirt in the one in Key West that said I'M THE WOMAN TO BLAME, and I wish I would have bought it." She mustered up a smile. "Let's go!"

Cam eased his long frame from the bed and walked over to her. "Hey, are you okay?"

"Sure, just a bit nervous about opening day, I guess."

"Shouldn't I be the one nervous, since I have to hit the ball and all that stuff?"

Mia smiled. "Probably. But hey, let's go grab a drink and chase away those nerves."

"You don't have to ask twice."

Mia grabbed her purse and they headed out the door. They walked past Printer's Alley and down to Lower Broadway, where there were lots of shops nestled between the honky-tonk bars that Nashville was famous for. Mia posed by a statue of Elvis and then took Cam's picture as well. She missed sending pictures to Facebook, but that would have blown her cover long ago.

Even though the sun was still shining, the music never stopped in Music City. Country music hopefuls could be heard from inside each and every bar. Mia had to laugh when she spotted a guy sitting on a stool singing in an ice cream parlor. She turned to Cam. “Really?”

Cam shrugged. “I guess you have to do whatever it takes. How did Cat get discovered?” Cam wanted to know while they waited for a light to change.

“She was discovered at a talent competition over at the Wildhorse Saloon. She didn’t even win, but it was one of those being-in-the-right-place-at-the-right-time kinds of things. A record producer liked her sound and she was signed soon afterward. I think it helped that she was a fresh, new kind of sound. She was lucky, I guess.”

“I can relate to that,” Cam admitted. “There are lots of talented baseball players that never get scouted. You have to have a thick skin if you want to make it in something as competitive as sports or entertainment.” He shook his head. “Getting a second shot is even tougher. I should have learned how to mend my wild ways.”

“Oh, really? Let me ask you this. How many of those times were you coming to someone’s defense like you did with me?”

Cam shrugged. “I’d do it again in a heartbeat if anybody messed with you.”

Mia felt a feminine flutter of appreciation at his alpha-male comment. “Well, I’ll try not to cause any commotion.”

“Baby, you’re going to turn heads in these bars. You can’t help it. Just remember that you’re with me.” He jabbed his thumb toward his chest and gave her a playful wink.

“Hey, I can kick some booty too, you know. There had better not be any chickies hitting on you,” she boasted with her fists on her hips.

“No doubt.” Cam arched one eyebrow and nodded. “I’ve seen you in action.”

Mia narrowed her eyes. “Nuf said, huh?”

Cam nodded, but she could tell he was having trouble not laughing. “Hey, how about if I just hold your hand. That should keep everybody at bay.”

Mia nodded and grabbed his hand. "Excellent idea."

They shopped for a couple of hours, and it was actually Mia who had to pry Cam away from a boots and belts store. Like a true gentleman, he offered to hoof it back to the hotel with the hat that Mia had bought, along with his boots, which looked so very sexy on him. Of course, she thought everything looked sexy on him, especially his baseball pants.

"I'll grab a table in Tootsies since it gets crowded there early. I'll have a cold beer waiting if you stop at a vendor and bring me a hot dog. After that huge lunch, that's all I need, and for some reason a hot dog sounds good. Maybe we'll make it to Jimmy Buffet's next time, if that's okay?"

"Baseball food," Cam said, placing his palm on his chest. "Ah . . . a girl after my own heart. Margaritaville will have to wait."

"Hey, put the boots on and break them in," Mia suggested lightly, when she really wanted to tell him that he had already captured *her* heart. She chuckled at his theatrics when he pretended to swoon and blew him a kiss as he walked away.

Mia entered Tootsies, and as Cam had predicted, she turned every head wearing a cowboy hat. She loved the famous Orchid Lounge, where it was said that Willie Nelson wrote "Crazy." The wall of fame was filled with music legends, and it was one of those places where she wished the walls really could talk. There was a round table open across from the bar and she grabbed it, knowing that the floor would soon be packed. This wasn't the kind of place where her friends liked to hang out, but Mia had loved it the moment she walked in a few years ago when she was with her father while he was attending a convention. She had gotten bored with shopping and had strolled into Tootsies on a whim but oddly enough felt right at home as soon as she entered. Who knew that it was just the beginning of discovering her inner . . . redneck? She grinned at the notion and held up her fingers for two longnecks. She wasn't much of a beer drinker, but it just felt right here at Tootsies.

Mia drummed her fingers to the beat of a Kenny Chesney cover sung by a cute guy in a black Stetson and worn jeans. She knew from Cat that these singers played for tips in the jar that they passed around and nothing else, not even a cut from cover charges. The percentage of the people who made it had to be small, making her heart go out to the guy up there singing his heart out. He was really good, with a whiskey-smooth, mellow voice, perfect for country songs. He tipped his hat at her when she applauded with gusto, and she smiled, hoping there was someone who discovered his talent.

Mia supposed her love of country music was partly because so many of the songs were about family. She had grown up listening to the music that many of the hired help preferred, and it had stuck with her through her teens and remained her favorite genre today. Most of her friends listened to Top 40 pop tunes and couldn't understand her preference for country music, but Mia totally got it. It was the lyrics. While she was all alone in her huge house, she would rather have been in a normal home with a loving family full of noisy siblings and a big, sloppy dog. Mia sighed and was glad when he stepped it up with a cover of Zac Brown Band's fun song "Chicken Fried." Just about everyone in the bar, including Mia, started singing along.

Just after the barmaid brought her drinks, the cute cowboy started singing "God Bless the Broken Road," one of her favorite Rascal Flatts ballads. The lyrics spoke to her in a very real way, and she felt her eyes well up as the cowboy crooned as if directly to her. It occurred to Mia that perhaps "Broken Road" was so true in that everything happened for a reason, bringing you where you were today, and all of the pain endured was just part of the journey. While Mia had dated, she had never really experienced a broken heart, but she fully understood heartache and loneliness. She had often felt lost and over the past couple of weeks had learned to look at life from a different angle and with new meaning. Somewhere she had read that happiness could be achieved only when you had purpose in life, and she understood that to be true in more ways than one.

The thought made Mia feel stronger, and she smiled in what felt like pure joy just as Cam walked back through the door. He held up two hot dogs and grinned. Mia knew it was probably partly from hearing the empowering lyrics of "Broken Road," but she really did feel as if her whole life had led her to this moment. Everything seemed to be coming together in a positive way.

"I'll trade you a hot dog for a beer," Cam said as he sat down on one of the tall stools.

"Deal." Mia took the warm bun from Cam and took a big bite. "Mmm, sometimes I just crave a hot dog," she said as she licked a bit of mustard from her bottom lip. "It's one of those things that just taste better from a street vendor."

"I know, and once you get a whiff, you have to have one," Cam agreed. "Popcorn is the same way for me," he said, tapping his boot to the beat of the music. "I can't watch a movie without it."

Mia took a swig of her tangy beer and nodded. "Me neither." She loved the way their relationship felt easy, not forced. She hoped that wouldn't change when he found out that her father was Mitch Monroe. But before she could dwell on it, her phone beeped with a text message. She looked down. "Oh, it's Cat. She's on her way. She said to save her a seat and have a cold Bud Light ready."

"Will she cause some commotion when she enters?"

Mia shrugged. "I'm sure she will. When I hung out with her in the past, she was up and coming, but after a few hits under her belt I would guess she gets recognized. It helps that she looks a lot like Shania Twain." Mia grinned. "Hey, it won't be long until you'll be asked for autographs."

"I sure hope so," Cam admitted. "I know one thing: If that day comes, I'll never turn a kid down."

"Good for you," Mia said, recalling some of the celebrities she had rubbed shoulders with who weren't always as kind to their fans.

Cam ordered another round, and their cold drinks arrived just as Cat entered Tootsies. She turned several heads, and the guy singing seemed to know her right off the bat. Mia had a feeling that she was going to get asked to sing, and she sure hoped that she would. Not only did she have an amazing voice, but Cat Carson had stage presence, that certain star quality that she would need to make it to the top in this business. Mia only hoped that her friend would stay grounded and not let the business get the best of her.

Cat waved when she spotted Mia and hurried over to the table. "Mia!" she gushed, opening her arms for a hug. "It's so good to see you!"

"It's been too long." Mia slid from the stool and hugged her friend. "And I can't thank you enough for doing this for me." She pulled back and gestured toward Cam. "Cat, I'd like you to meet my friend Cameron Patrick."

Cam stood up and shook her hand. "Nice to meet you, Cat, and I want to thank you for doing this for the Cougars too."

Cat waved them off. "Hey, it's my pleasure," she said as she sat down. "Well, as long as I get the national anthem right," she admitted with a roll of her eyes.

"So you've never sung it before a crowd?" Cam asked.

"Nope. Not only is it a tough song to sing, but there's something intimidating about it for some reason. But hey, I'm honored anyway." She grinned at Cam. "I'm a baseball fan, so I'm looking forward to taking in a game."

"I'm sure you're so busy these days that you don't get to do much of that kind of thing," Mia said.

"Yeah, I miss doing the little things, but I'm not complaining. I get to do what I love for a living. Cam, I'm sure you feel the same way."

"I sure do, and I hope I don't blow it."

"So how was the concert?" Mia asked. "Is Toby a pretty cool guy?"

Cat nodded. "I like him a lot and I've learned so much from him. That man can work a crowd."

They chatted about Toby Keith and country music for a few minutes, but then Cam's phone rang. He looked down and said, "Oh, it's Noah. I need to take this. Excuse me," he said and headed to the sidewalk outside, where he could hear.

Cat wiggled her eyebrows and leaned closer. "Wow, he's hot, Mia. And a baseball player . . . Damn, I'm jealous! So have you told him who you really are yet?"

"No." Mia shook her head slowly. "I've wanted to, but the time never seems right." She sighed. "I guess I'm scared at how he'll react."

Cat reached over and covered her hand and squeezed. "You've got to fess up soon."

"I know." Mia toyed with the neck of her beer bottle and nibbled on her inner lip.

"Hey, it's not like you have a criminal record or you're married or something. Your daddy is rich . . . so what?"

Mia frowned. "I know that it seems silly, but, Cat, he's mentioned several times how he detests arrogant, wealthy people. He grew up poor and cleaned pools."

"And, let me guess, wasn't always treated kindly."

Mia pressed her lips together and nodded.

"But you're not like that, and neither is your dad."

"Oh, I think I can be pretty shallow at times."

Cat leaned forward. "What are you talking about? I've seen you work tirelessly putting charity events together."

"Thanks, Cat. You're such a good friend, and I've missed you."

"Hey, I'm not feeding you a line to make you feel better. Lots of people have benefited from your hard work. You were very good at it, Mia. Look, I know that with a full-time job it will be more difficult, but I hope you find the time to do more good works."

"I will," Mia responded, but Cat's comment had Mia's head spinning. While it was true that she had always thrown herself into planning the events, Mia hadn't really thought so much about where the funds actually went afterward. Of course, she knew the money went to good causes, but only in an abstract way. She was suddenly reminded of Sunny and how a single pair of shoes made such a big difference in her life. Seeing someone benefit firsthand had been a moving experience. Mia sat up straighter. "I'll never be too busy to help people."

"I guess the apple doesn't fall far from the tree."

"What do you mean?"

"I just read that your dad saved some company called Hanover Candy from going under."

"What?" Mia sat up straighter, and her stomach did a little flip. "Are you sure?"

"Yeah, there was an article in the *Chicago Tribune*. I don't usually read the business section, but I saw a picture of your dad and read the whole article.

Mia felt her heart pick up speed. "Oh my gosh."

"Why do you look so stricken?"

Mia put her hand to her chest. "I thought he bought the company out from under them! I was so angry!"

"Why would you think that? I know firsthand that your father gives a lot to charity. I never thought him to be the cutthroat type."

Mia shook her head. "It's a long story. I have to admit that I'm confused but terribly relieved. Wow . . . ," she murmured as she soaked in this information, but she had to wonder why her father would want for her to think such a terrible thing in the first place. She recalled how she had accused him and felt a little bit ashamed about how she had stormed out. Of course he had goaded her into it by his comments, but still it had been childish of her and a bit arrogant.

"Are you okay?"

"Yes, I'm just . . . Wow, I don't know. Relieved but confused."

Cat tilted her head. "He must have had a reason."

"Yeah . . ." It was amazing how differently she looked at things after just a few weeks on her own, and she had a lightbulb moment. She would just bet that her father had let her believe the worst so that she would finally venture out on her own. She would have to call him as soon as she got the chance and let him know that his plan had worked like a charm. She hoped he would be proud of her accomplishments, and hopefully he would be thrilled that she'd landed a job with the Cricket Creek Cougars, of all things! What an amazing coincidence! "I'm just so relieved that I was wrong. I should have known better."

Cat nodded and then gave her long hair a flip over her shoulders. "Yeah, your dad is a straight-up guy. But enough about him. Tell me about cutie-pie Cam before he gets back in here."

"Hi, Mr. Falcon, what's up?" Cam walked a little bit away from the front door so that the music was muted in the background.

"I just wanted to make sure that everything is going smoothly. Mitch wanted me to call and check in."

"I wish we could let Mia know that her father is in town," Cam confessed. "It doesn't seem right that we know she isn't Mia Money."

"Olivia said the same thing, but like I explained, this is between them, and I have to respect his wishes. It will all be out in the open soon enough."

"That's what I'm afraid of."

"Well, just get her back here early tomorrow and it will all fall into place. Things like this have a way of working themselves out."

"I hope you're right." Cam sighed after he ended the call. He stared down Broadway at the neon lights, which blinked with silent invitation. The sun was setting and honky-tonk row was coming to life. He was surprised that Mia Monroe loved Nashville, but then again she continued to surprise him. He knew one thing . . . He was in love with the girl and didn't want to see her get hurt. He would have to respect Noah Falcon's orders, but it was killing him.

When he walked back into Tootsies, Cat was up on the small stage singing her latest hit. Mia was singing along, and when their eyes met he felt as bright and alive as the blinking neon lights. He was having fun, but more than anything else, he wanted to get back to the hotel room and have Mia in his arms.

Luckily, after Cat sang another song and then a duet, she came back to the table and announced that she was a little bit tired and hoped that they didn't mind if she headed back soon.

"No problem," Cam replied, hoping he didn't sound too eager. "We'll walk you back."

"Oh, I'm a big girl, so don't cut your night short. I had wanted to stay out, but I'm fading fast and want to get a good night's rest."

"We don't mind," Mia chimed in. "Tomorrow is a big day for us all."

Luckily the walk was a short one, and as soon as Cam was in the room he pulled Mia into his arms and kissed her. "I like your friend, but I was so glad that she wanted to call it a night."

"Are you tired too?" Mia asked, but he could tell that she knew exactly what was on his mind.

"Not one bit."

"Then do you want to watch some television?"

"Nope, all I want is you . . ."

Mia laughed softly and pulled him over to the bed. "And you shall have me . . . over and over and . . ."

He cut her off with a kiss that left him shaken and hungry to have her beneath him. He wanted to go slow, but clothes went flying and after pausing for protection he was kissing her wildly. Everything about her, from the smell of her hair to the taste of her skin, was pure pleasure. She was sweet and pliant in his arms, but when she wrapped her legs around his waist, Cam was lost in the feel of her body beneath him. This was passion, but so much more than sex. He wanted to hold her, to protect her and love her, not just tonight but forever.

26

Lost and Found

MIA WAS FEELING PRETTY GOOD ABOUT HERSELF. THE opening-day parade had gone off without a hitch, and the sound check for Cat Carson was moving along smoothly. From where she was standing in the bleachers listening, Mia could see the Cougars dugout, and she had to grin when she noticed the entire team watching intently. Cat didn't have a band with her but was doing an unplugged set with just a stool and her guitar. The national anthem, which she was still terrified about singing, would be performed a cappella. Mia actually liked the idea since it showcased Cat's voice and made the transition to the baseball game seamless and easy. A slight disappointment was that instead of staying for the game, Mia had learned that morning that Cat would be whisked away quickly on Toby's tour bus. They had vowed, however, to keep in touch, and Mia had promised to keep her abreast of the details surrounding her transition back to being Mia Monroe.

While Mia wanted her old name back, she knew that in just a few weeks she had changed and evolved in ways that made her feel good about herself and hopeful for a bright future, both in her personal life and in her job. And although she hadn't spoken to her father yet, she planned on calling him as soon as she could catch more than a ten-minute break. Mia smiled as she looked around the stadium, which was bustling with activity, but then she realized that all of her work was actually done and this would be a great time to call her father. Perhaps he'd even fly into town and take in a game or two and they could patch up this misunderstanding.

Mia smiled, already feeling much better about the situation. He father would probably even have some sage advice about how to handle telling Cam her real last name. Surely after their lovemaking last night it wouldn't matter . . .

After waving down to Cat, Mia turned and headed inside to her office. Because the day was going to be a warm one, she had opted to wear a simple yellow sundress and a Cougars baseball cap. The weather was perfect baseball weather and was supposed to stay that way for the rest of the home stand. While humming one of Cat's songs, she opened the glass door and was met with a blast of cool air. After the last few frantic days of getting everything together, the offices were quiet and vacant. Mia wasn't surprised. Everyone in the front office had headed out to watch the parade and would soon be returning for the baseball game.

Mia walked down the short hallway to her office and had to shake her head when she saw Mia Money on her nameplate. "That will soon change," she said with a slight grin. She had to wonder how surprised Noah was going to be when he found out that she was Mitch's daughter! "What were the odds?"

Mia opened her big desk drawer and pulled out her pretty white straw purse, which she had bought at Violet's Vintage Clothing. It was perfect for the summer and matched her cute wedge sandals, which she had found on the clearance rack. But when Mia reached for her cell phone, she felt a sudden attack of nerves. She hesitated while she rehearsed what she was going to say to her father, and then, after taking a deep breath, decided it was time to make the call. But before she pressed the green DIAL button, she could have sworn she heard her father's voice! Wait . . . how could that be true? She frowned at the phone and then realized that it was her father's voice talking to Noah Falcon and they were standing close to her office door. She held her breath and listened.

"So where is Mia?" she heard her father ask.

"I saw her outside listening to Cat Carson rehearse," Noah answered. "Do you want me to have her paged?"

Mitch sighed. "I was hoping she might call me. She still doesn't know that I'm here, does she?"

"No, I made it clear to Cam not to spill the beans. I'm sure that he respected my request," Noah replied, making Mia put a hand over her mouth. She silently backed away from her desk and flattened against the wall so that they wouldn't see her if they walked by. Her heart pounded like a jackhammer. They knew?

Cam knew!

"I can tell you that Cam was relieved to know that you were having Mia followed," Noah replied. "He was about to kick some serious ass."

Mitch chuckled. "Good for him. Nicolina's kept me filled in on what's been going on. She thinks he's a good kid."

Nicolina? Mia swallowed hard. Did everybody in the whole town know who she really was? Her hands started to shake.

"Olivia said that you two are serious," Noah commented.

"Yes," her father answered softly. "Nicolina Diamante is a wonderful woman. I'm lucky to have found her."

What? Mia had to press her hand tightly over her mouth.

"Yes," Mitch continued, "she has some amazing ideas for the strip mall. She wants it to be called Wedding Row and have the stores all have something to do with weddings."

"I think it's a great idea," Noah replied. "Have you

gotten any further with the hotel and convention center plans? Adding that to the stadium down by the riverfront would really keep this town on its feet. You know that I'm all in, and I know that Ty is receptive to being an investor as well."

Mia's eyes widened and her hand remained clamped over her mouth. This was all too much!

"Thanks, Noah. Yeah, I'm going full steam ahead. We'll talk more after the game. I think I'll go back out and try to locate Mia."

"You sure you don't want me to have her paged?"

"No, I'll find her. And I can't thank you enough for looking after her. I was scared to death when she drove away in that old car. I'm just glad that she landed here, of all places."

"Hey, she's done an amazing job. I'm lucky to have her on the staff."

Well, that's something anyway, Mia thought glumly. She remained flattened against the wall until their footsteps faded. For a few more minutes her feet remained rooted to the spot. After inhaling a shaky breath, she knew she needed to get out of there. How could she face anybody? They all knew? It was like a practical joke had been played on her. Her face felt hot and her hands shook. She felt like crumbling into a ball in the corner of the office and having a good cry, but she didn't want anyone to find her. So after another deep breath she headed down the hallway and took the steps that led out of the side entrance, where she wasn't likely to be spotted.

Mia didn't even know where to go. Back to her condo? No, there were memories of Cam everywhere, but she knew that she needed to keep moving or collapse into a puddle, and so she started walking down the sidewalk alongside the riverbank. The sun glinted off the water and the boats looked so pretty and peaceful, but the scene did little to calm Mia down. Because her legs were feeling weak, she plopped down on a bench overlooking the bridge. For a moment she simply sat there, and when a tear escaped she reached inside her purse for a tissue. As she was pulling the tissue from the little plastic container, she spotted the little hula dancer. The sticky stuff had worn off the bottom, so she had put the dancing doll back in her purse until she bought the glue to attach her to the dash of her car.

Mia pulled the hula dancer out and shook her head at the doll. "Here I was worried about coming clean, and everyone already knows! Isn't that some shit?"

The hula dancer looked at her with a solemn expression.

"Oh, don't stare at me like that. I know I started this whole ball rolling. It's just that I was feeling so good about my accomplishments, and . . ." She paused to swallow hot emotion. "The joke was on me! I feel as if I've been this reality show for everyone's entertainment, but they didn't even have to suffer through commercials. What will Mia do next? Stay tuned!"

When Mia shifted on the bench, the doll's hips shook.

"How can you dance at a time like this?" Mia smiled slightly and then carefully put the doll back into her purse. Cars were starting to pull into the parking lot for the concert, but Mia got up and started walking. Eventually she would be missed, but for now she needed to get away and try to gather her scattered thoughts. Tears threatened to slide down her cheeks, but she sniffed hard and was determined to keep them at bay.

After walking for a while, she made the turn up into town, knowing full well that Main Street would be deserted. Although not official, it truly was like a holiday, and for the most part the stores were closed for the rest of the day. When she passed Wine and Diner, there was a CLOSED sign on the front door, as there was everywhere else in the heart of town. It sucked because Mia had the sudden urge to shop. Retail therapy had always calmed her down, and although she still didn't have much money, she could at least shop for a little something to boost her spirits.

Mia sighed as she strolled down the street, but no luck. Everything was shut down. She was thinking that she would go back to her condo and try to make sense of things when she pulled up short in front of Violet's Vintage Clothing store. In the front display window were Jimmy Choos that looked like the ones she had given to Sunny. Although there was a CLOSED sign on the door, Mia took a chance and tugged on the handle. It opened with a little tinkle, telling Violet that she had a customer.

"Oh, sorry, we're closed," Violet said from where she was arranging dresses on a rack, but as she turned around she smiled. "Oh, Mia! Wait, shouldn't you be at the game?" Violet walked closer and put her hand to her chest. "Oh, my dear, have you been crying?"

Mia swallowed hard and nodded.

"Oh, sweet pea, come on over to the sofa here and tell me what's got you so upset."

Mia followed Violet to the red velvet sofa and sat down. "My real name is Mia Monroe," she began, and then she poured out her story. "Can you believe that everyone *knew*? I'm so humiliated! Here I thought I had done everything on my own merit, and Noah knew from the very beginning."

"Oh, sweetie, all I can see is that you have a whole lot of people who love you to pieces." She patted Mia's hand. "I am a true believer that things happen for a reason."

Mia sniffed hard but gave Violet her full attention. "What do you mean?"

"Sweetie, your daddy had you followed because he was worried sick. And you know he was trying to let you go out on your own. He just forced the issue."

Mia thought back to the conversation and shook her head. "I realize now what he was doing, but still . . ."

"And you ended up here in this little town for a reason." She pointed to the shoes in the window.

"Did Sunny bring them to you?"

Violet nodded. "I've sold her clothes before, and she

thought I'd know what the shoes were worth. I didn't want to see her get ripped off, so I simply bought them. Mia, she was so grateful. And it wasn't just about the money. You gave her hope when she needed it most."

Mia put her hand over her mouth, and tears started streaming down her cheeks. She removed her hand and said, "My God, I've done so many events for charity, but I was out of touch with what I was really doing. I didn't really think about the people who needed help or where the money was going. It was about the party, the event, and the pictures on the society page. I was simply clueless."

"And now you have a clue."

Mia's laughter gurgled through the tears. "Yes, I do."

Violet pointed to the doorway. "Um, might that be your daddy?"

Mia turned around and nodded. She gave Violet a hug. "Thanks for everything. Will you be at the game?"

"Wouldn't miss it. Now, go to your daddy."

"Dad!" She jumped up and ran over to him, nearly knocking over a display of hats. She hugged him. "Oh, I've missed you!" she gushed, but then she pulled back and put her hands on her hips once they were outside. "Wait, I should be mad at you!" She blinked at him, trying to ward off more tears. "But I'm not. Well, maybe a little bit. How did you find me?"

"Jessica saw you walk past Wine and Diner and called Noah."

"Oh . . ."

"You're needed back at the baseball park."

"My job is pretty much taken care of for the day. I won't be missed."

"Really, because there's a certain ballplayer who I do believe will be devastated if you don't show up and cheer for him."

"Cam knew the whole time too, didn't he?"

"No, Mia, Cam didn't. He only found out when I wanted him to take you to Nashville to pick up Cat."

Mia absorbed that information for a moment and then whispered, "So he knows who I am and doesn't care."

"He's in love with you and not your money," Mitch said and then chuckled. "Mia Money . . . really?"

Mia laughed. "I was on the spot."

Mitch laughed with her but then put his hands on her shoulders and his eyes turned serious. "It's taken me a long time to realize what life is all about." Mitch took her hand in his. "I wish I'd had your little hand in mine a lot more while you were growing up."

"We can't change the past, Dad."

He sighed. "I know that."

"But every step we've taken has led us to here and now. And I'm in a pretty good place. How about you?"

"Are you quoting country music to me again?"

"Sort of."

"What about that fine-arts degree? Shouldn't you be quoting Shakespeare?" he teased.

" 'A rose by any other name would smell as sweet,' " she said with a grin. "*Romeo and Juliet*."

"Meaning that the name doesn't matter, only what things truly are . . . No truer words were ever spoken." He leaned down and kissed her on the cheek. "We have a ballgame to catch. Are you ready?"

Mia nodded and slipped her hand back into his grasp. As they walked down Main Street toward the riverfront, Mia said, "You've got big plans for Cricket Creek, don't you?"

Mitch nodded but stopped in his tracks and pointed to the buildings. "Noah was right to breathe life back into this town. But it's not really about saving shops and restaurants. It's about people, tradition, and community. It's about a way of life."

Mia looked up at her father and smiled. "We're home, aren't we?"

"Yes, Mia, coming home is all about love and happiness, and we are here to stay."

Epilogue

Cheers!

When Sunny walked toward the table with a pot of coffee in one hand, Mia raised her mug. "Refill, sweetie?" Sunny asked with a smile.

"Please!" It was after hours at Wine and Diner, but Sunny had offered to stay late to help out at the first committee meeting for Heels for Meals, the charity Mia was spearheading. "Thanks!" Mia said after Sunny handed her the two creamers that she always requested.

"My pleasure. Anybody else need some heat? It's a fresh pot." She looked around the table for takers. Myra had informed Mia that Sunny was an excellent waitress and had a great rapport with the customers.

"Decaf for me, when you get the chance," Jessica replied with a yawn. "I could use the caffeine but I'm still breastfeeding and I don't want any stimulants getting into Ben's milk. He has a hard enough time sleeping as it is." She looked across the table at Madison. "I don't remember you having so much energy."

Madison held up her mug for Sunny to top off. "Um, Mom, I think it was probably you that had more energy. You weren't over the hill when you had me."

Jessica wrinkled her nose but then gave Madison a lift of her chin."Hey, forty is the new thirty."

"I agree," Olivia said with a firm nod. "Besides, Jess, you sure don't look it!"

"Age is just a number," Violet scoffed with a wave of her hand but then shook her white head no at Sunny's offer for coffee. She pointed to the pitcher in the center of the table. "I'll stick with the water. Coffee keeps me up, and I need my beauty sleep." She gave her cap of curls a delicate pat.

"Me too," Myra said, accepting the pitcher from Violet.

"What are y'all thinking?" Bella announced as she entered the dining room with her mother. "Water? Coffee? What's up with that?" She held up a bottle of wine in one hand and angled her head toward another bottle clutched in Nicolina's grasp. "Red or white, ladies?"

"Now you're talking!" Violet raised a fist in the air, making them all laugh.

"I'll get the glasses," Sunny offered.

"Bring one for yourself and have a seat with us," Myra told her. "You've been on your feet long enough."

Mia watched with a warm heart when Bella and Nicolina uncorked the bottles with flair and began pouring. She was so happy that her father had found such a vibrant, wonderful woman to marry, and Bella was going to be such a fun stepsister! Once they were all seated, Mia raised her glass. "I have a toast!" She cleared the emotion from her throat and looked at the smiling faces of strong-willed, beautiful women seated at the round table. "I've only been living in Cricket Creek for a short time, but this lovely town already feels like home. When I was down on my luck, I was welcomed with open arms. And I am fully aware that you are all busy, hardworking women with mouths of your own to feed, but not one of you hesitated when I asked you to be a part of Heels for Meals. I know that we can raise lots of money gathering donations of designer shoes," she said, but she had to clear her throat once more. "But tonight is also about friendship."

"And an excuse to drink wine," Bella added, raising her glass higher and getting a huge cheer from them all.

"To fund-raising and friendship!" Mia shouted over the laughter. They tapped their glasses together, took a collective sip, and then started brainstorming. After a while, Olivia, the organized schoolteacher, was selected to take notes, as Mia was unable to keep up with the fast-flowing ideas, which included everything from events at the baseball park to fund-raisers at Wine and Diner. Violet and Nicolina both volunteered to sell donated shoes at their shops, with the proceeds benefitting local shut-ins. Olivia offered to get a list of students on the free-lunch program to ensure they would get hot meals at home as well.

"I'll write up a kick-ass press release when you're ready," Madison offered.

"Thanks! You guys are amazing! I'll get donations rolling in," Mia promised. "Sunny's son Daniel is my assistant at the ballpark. And doing a very fine job," she added with a wink at Sunny, who blushed with pride. "We'll start a database of shoes and go from there!" she said brightly and was met with applause just as Cam walked through the door.

"For me?" Cam raised his hands and grinned.

"You wish," Mia chided, but as always her heart skipped a beat at the mere sight of him.

"Personally, I sure think he deserves a standing ovation," Violet announced, rising to her feet. "You don't have an older brother, do you?" she asked, batting her eyes at Cam. Her question drew another round of laughter, and Mia couldn't remember when she had enjoyed herself more. She may have lived life in the lap of luxury before coming to Cricket Creek, but nothing could compare to this moment. Mia looked up at Cam, and when their eyes met she felt a warm rush of happiness. She would be forever grateful that her car had chugged to a stop in this wonderful town.

Read on for a sneak peek
at the next book in LuAnn McLane's
Cricket Creek series,
available soon from Signet Eclipse.

"WILLIE! NO! DON'T JUMP!" THE LOUD, DESPERATE PLEA frightened social director Savannah Perry into sprinting toward the pool at Whisper's Edge. Willie's dangerous plunge attempts had been happening all too often. "Oh, baby, please don't! It isn't worth it!" Although the tearful wail had Savannah picking up her already swift pace, she did manage to notice a sleek sports car parked in front of the main office. The sun glinting off the silver hood piqued Savannah's curious nature, but a splash followed by another wail of distress kept her placing one flowered flip-flop in front of the other. The shoes with daisies adorning the rubber thongs—the result of last Wednesday's craft workshop—were not very good for running.

"Doggone it!" Savannah nearly tripped as she hopped over the curb, but she refused to slow down. Willie was not a strong swimmer. In fact, acting as a lifeguard was another hat Savannah wore at the retirement community.

Breathing hard, Savannah pushed open the gate that should have been latched and looked past umbrella tables and lounge chairs. "On no!" She spotted eighty-year-old Patty Parsons teetering precariously close to the edge of the water at the deep end of the pool. "Please back up," Savannah warned but hard-of-hearing Miss Patty was further hampered by the pink bathing cap covering her ears.

"I'll rescue Willie!" Savannah tried again but Miss Patty's attention remained focused on her sinking dog.

"Oh, Willie, swim harder!" Miss Patty wrung her hands together as she watched her beloved basset hound trying to capture a yellow tennis ball that bobbed just past his nose. Willie's ears fanned out over the surface of the water and although he doggie paddled at a furious pace, his short legs and rotund body were no match for gravity. He sunk a little lower.

"Baby, forget about the danged ball! I'll buy you a dozen!" Miss Patty wailed, but Willie was on a mission and paid his master no heed. Then, to Savannah's horror, the spry little lady pointed her hands over her capped head and bent her body toward the glistening water. "I'm coming for ya!" she promised. Although Miss Patty was in great shape for her advanced age, Savannah knew from experience that without her flotation noodle she'd sink like a stone.

Savannah was about to have quite a situation on her hands. She cupped her fingers at the corners of her mouth and shouted at the top of her lungs, "For the love of God, don't dive in, Miss Patty! I'll save Willie!"

God must have been listening because Miss Patty suddenly straightened up and looked at Savannah across the width of the pool. Her eyes were opened wide as she put a hand to her chest. "Oh, praise the lord! Child, puh-lease save my Willie!"

Savannah kicked off her flip-flops, losing a hot-glued daisy in the process. "I will," she promised, and, holding her nose, she jumped fully dressed into the pool. Although she'd cranked up the heat for afternoon water aerobics, the sudden plunge still felt shockingly cold. Ignoring the discomfort, Savannah bobbed to the surface. She lunged for Willie and managed to wrap her arm around his midsection.

"You got him," Miss Patty shouted, but her glee was short-lived. Although Savannah kicked with all her might, she and her canine buddy sank beneath the water. Willie, apparently sensing doggie death by drowning, wiggled away. With a gurgled protest Savannah followed in swift pursuit but Willie swam like a manatee while underwater. He did not, however, manage to paddle his way back up to the surface and started sinking closer to the bottom of the pool.

Although her lungs protested, Savannah knew her only hope was to get beneath Willie and push him upward. She lunged forward and gave his furry rump a huge heave-ho, repeating the action while using her legs as a spring board off the bottom. The old Olympic-sized pool was deep and Savannah was short, so by the time she and Willie reached the side of the pool Savannah started struggling. Her lungs burned but she somehow managed to give Willie one last hard shove closer to where Miss Patty was bent over paddling her hands in the water, as if that would somehow help.

The effort sent Savannah sinking backward, but she pushed off the bottom one last time and stroked as quickly as her tired arms would allow. Savannah broke the surface and took a huge gasp of much-needed air. Wet hair obscuring her vision, she dipped under the water once more to slick the long auburn tresses back from her forehead. Just as she raised her head above water another splash had her cringing. Not again! Savannah was flailing around in a circle trying to get a bead on where Willie landed when—to her surprise—a strong arm snaked around her waist and pulled her against a hard body.

"Don't worry. I've got you," a man said next to her ear. Savannah tried to twist to see his face but his firm grip prevented her from budging. "Stay calm and put your arms around my neck. I'll get you over to the edge."

Savannah obeyed but then felt silly. The words *I'm not drowning* formed in her head, but the exertion coupled with the lack of oxygen scrambled Savannah's brain. She attempted to talk once more but unfortunately only a breathy "drowning" got past her lips.

"Don't worry. I won't let you," her knight in soggy clothing promised in a whiskey-smooth voice laced with a touch of the South. Savannah loved accents because they represented a sense of home and roots, something she never had until landing the job at Whisper's Edge. "Hang on and you'll be just fine."

"Okay," Savannah managed. She tightened her hold, forgetting that she didn't really need assistance.

"We're almost there." His warm breath near her ear sent a delicious tingle down her spine and when he tilted his head back Savannah was able to see his tanned face. "Don't worry." He flashed Savannah a reassuring smile that was utterly gorgeous. In that brief moment when their eyes met Savannah felt an unexpected flash of longing she couldn't quite explain. He must have felt something similar because his gaze dropped to her mouth and lingered. Time felt suspended and slowly unfolded like one of those slow-motion movie moments that needed a Maroon 5 song in the background. Savannah tilted her face slightly closer, but before she could do something incredibly insane like lean in and kiss a perfect stranger, he turned his head and started swimming toward the ladder.

"Thank God . . ." *Damn . . . didn't mean to utter that out loud.*

"Almost there," he assured her in a soothing tone of voice.

Savannah could see the hot pink silk zinnias adorning the top of Miss Patty's flip-flops. Several of the ladies had squabbled over favorite flowers during craft time; Savannah had to make them draw straws.

"Here you go." With firms hands circling her waist he gently guided Savannah to the rungs of the ladder. She could feel the heat of his body pressing against her back and the urge to lean against him was almost too strong to resist. Luckily, Willie's deep bark startled some sense back into Savannah's befuddled brain. With a quick intake of breath she gripped the metal handrails and hoisted herself up, hoping that the wet sweatpants clinging to her body didn't make her butt look big. Belatedly, Savannah realized she'd worn a swimsuit beneath her clothing and wished she had taken the time to shed her clothes before rescuing Willie. Too late now . . .

Trying not to think about her butt, Savannah sloshed her way up the ladder. To her acute embarrassment, when she tried to stand her shaky legs gave her trouble, and she stumbled sideways like a drunken sailor.

"Whoa there." Her handsome hero placed a steadying arm about her waist. "Are you okay?"

"Yes." Her voice, which had a low timbre to begin with, came out sounding like a croak. Could this possibly get any worse? It wasn't until she pushed her wet hair from her eyes that Savannah realized they had quickly drawn a small crowd of elderly lady onlookers, most of whom were dressed in swimsuits and clutching colorful foam noodles for water aerobics.

Apparently, her day could indeed get worse.

"She's fine," her rescuer assured them, earning a collective sigh of relief. But then turned to her. "Aren't you?"

Savannah, who didn't trust her voice, opted for a smile at him and an awkward little wave at the class. During an uncomfortable moment of silence Savannah searched for what to say. *Thanks, but I wasn't really drowning. Sorry that you're sopping wet. Who are you, anyway?* None of those thoughts seemed appropriate for the current situation. She was about to go with a simple thank-you when Willie sat back on his haunches and barked.

"Just hush! You've caused enough trouble now, don't ya know?" Miss Patty wagged a finger at him, and Willie had the decency to hang his head.

Savannah wanted to be angry with Willie, but his sad basset hound face melted her heart every time he landed his rump in trouble. When his big brown eyes rounded upward and gazed sorrowfully at Savannah, she barely refrained from reaching down and patting his head.

"Thank you both so much," Miss Patty tearfully told them. She started clapping and then glanced back at the aerobic water class who stood behind her in a neat row. Most of them had color coordinated their bathing caps, foam noodles and flowered flip-flops. "Ladies?" At Miss Patty's nod they joined her applause by clapping their hands against their noodles, causing a low thumping sound that Savannah found funny. She snuck a sideways glance at her hero, but her smile faded when she noticed that he wore a watch and most likely had a wallet and cell phone in the pocket of his khaki pants. A dark blue polo shirt molded to a very nice chest and clung to wide shoulders and impressive biceps. The only thing he managed to shed before his plunge was expensive-looking leather loafers, now lying sideways near the grass. Savannah swallowed hard. Oh boy . . .

"It was no big deal," he said smoothly. When he glanced at Savannah she looked down at her toes. She wondered if his demeanor would change if he knew that his heroic efforts weren't actually needed and decided that there was no real reason to clue him in on that particular detail. "I'm just glad that I was here to help."

Before she could come up with a reply, all the bathing-capped heads turned in the direction of Clyde and Clovis Camden entering the area. The seventy-eight-year-old identical twin brothers—who resembled George Hamilton in both looks and demeanor—were the resident hotties. The brothers were blessed with full heads of salt-and-pepper hair, a rare sight at Whisper's Edge, and their arrival sent an audible feminine flutter through the row of bathing beauties.

The dapper duo had donned old-school white tennis shorts and matching polo shirts. Orange headbands and wristbands added a shot of color, and gold rope chain necklaces glinted against tanned skin. Savannah wondered if dressing the same ever got old, but they seemed to enjoy fooling people with typical twin gags. Miss Patty, however, didn't seem at all happy to see them. She pointed to a yellow tennis ball that Clovis clutched in his hand. The only way Savannah knew it was Clovis was that he had a slightly crooked nose that must have once been broken. Miss Parry narrowed her eyes. "Once again, y'all almost caused the demise of my dear Willie."

"Now, Miss Patty, we can't help that the tennis courts are next to the pool," Clyde countered smoothly. "My wicked backhand sometimes sends balls sailing over the fence."

Miss Patty pursed her lips and then raised her chin. "I fully understand the close proximity to the pool, but it's the fact that after you sashay over here to retrieve your balls you fail to close the gate after your departure, putting my dear Willie in danger! To him an open gate is an open invitation. Willie simply cannot resist jumping into the pool when an enticing tennis ball comes sailing over the fence! It happened yet again!"

Clovis arched one eyebrow. "Perhaps you should have Willie on a leash. I do believe it's in the rules."

"He has a point, Patty," Joy Potter piped up and was rewarded with a slight smile from Clovis. Joy returned the gesture with a coy eye flutter.

Miss Patty silenced Joy with an I-can't-believe-you're-siding-with-them glare and then turned her attention back to the twins. "A leash chokes Willie. Per my request he has been exempted from the resident leash law." She looked at Savannah, who quickly nodded her agreement. Although Willie's leash exemption slid through the Whisper's Edge council by a narrow margin, free Willie was indeed legal. "Under normal circumstances Willie remains obediently by my side."

"Then may I suggest taking a different route?" Clyde asked.

"You may not!" Miss Patty clearly did not like Clyde's suggestion. She narrowed her eyes. "Closing and latching the gate would solve the problem. It's clearly stated in the pool rules." Miss Patty pointed to the sign posted on the far wall and then looked to her lady friends for support, but they all dipped their colorful capped heads downward as if in a synchronized swim move. At Miss Patty's audible intake of breath most of the ladies remained staring at the flowers on their flip-flips, clearly not willing to rant against the Camden brothers. "Well, I'll be . . ."

If Savannah hadn't been in her soggy state of embarrassment with the handsome stranger dripping at her side, she would have jumped in with some sort of compromise.

Miss Patty finally sighed at the continued silence and then rolled her eyes. "And if that's not bad enough, Savannah had to rescue Willie again. Not to mention that her water aerobics class is going to start late, running into lunch!" She waved her hand in an arc in front of the twins. "See what your negligence has caused?"

Savannah felt her silent hero nudge her arm. "Wait—you can swim?"

Oh no . . . busted.

Also available in the Cricket Creek series

LuAnn McLane

Catch of a Lifetime

Top Chicago chef Jessica Robinson is back in Cricket Creek—and making her aunt's diner the go-to place for comfy gourmet fare. Former major leaguer Ty McKenna is no stranger to Jessica's cooking. At the Chicago hotspot where she worked, he was a regular—with a different girl on his arm every night. Now he's the manager for the Cricket Creek Cougars. And convincing the mouthwatering chef that he's a one-woman man may be harder than getting his team ready for opening day.

Also available in the Cricket Creek series

LuAnn McLane

Playing for Keeps

Olivia Lawson is peeved when ex-ace pitcher turned soap opera star Noah Falcon roars back into Cricket Creek, Kentucky, after all these years, to take the lead opposite her in the community theater's summer play. Noah's beloved hometown is having major financial woes and needs his status to turn this small-town play into a big-time hit. But Noah has bigger plans for this small town. And this time he's determined to show Olivia he's not just playing around—he's playing for keeps.